Feelings . . .

Isobel should have joined the others by the river instead of lingering alone with the mysterious guest from America, Adrian Renville—especially after the shocking liberty he had once taken with her. But she could not resist trying to find out the elusive truth about this man who masked his real feelings and self so well.

"You can confide in me," she told him. "You can trust me."

Adrian's lips parted in a brief, wry smile. "Did I say it was you I didn't trust?"

"I don't understand," Isobel said. "Who then do you distrust?"

"Myself." He bent his head closer so that their lips touched.

Now there was no mistaking his intention or her response as their arms intertwined and lips met in delicious intimacy. . . .

ANNOUNCING THE

TOPAZ FREQUENT READERS CLUB
COMMEMORATING TOPAZ'S
1 YEAR ANNIVERSARY!

THE MORE YOU BUY, THE MORE YOU GET

Redeem coupons found here and in the back of all new Topaz titles for FREE Topaz gifts:

Send in:

 2 coupons for a free TOPAZ novel (choose from the list below);

☐ **THE KISSING BANDIT**, Margaret Brownley
☐ **BY LOVE UNVEILED**, Deborah Martin
☐ **TOUCH THE DAWN**, Chelley Kitzmiller
☐ **WILD EMBRACE**, Cassie Edwards

 4 coupons for an "I Love the Topaz Man" on-board sign

 6 coupons for a TOPAZ compact mirror

 8 coupons for a Topaz Man T-shirt

Just fill out this certificate and send with original sales receipts to:

TOPAZ FREQUENT READERS CLUB-1ST ANNIVERSARY
Penguin USA • Mass Market Promotion; Dept. H.U.G.
375 Hudson St., NY, NY 10014

Name_____

Address_____

City_____State_____Zip_____

Offer expires 5/31/1995

This certificate must accompany your request. No duplicates accepted. Void where prohibited, taxed or restricted. Allow 4-6 weeks for receipt of merchandise. Offer good only in U.S., its territories, and Canada.

DIAMOND IN DISGUISE

by

Elizabeth Hewitt

A TOPAZ BOOK

TOPAZ
Published by the Penguin Group
Penguin Books USA Inc., 375 Hudson Street,
New York, New York 10014, U.S.A.
Penguin Books Ltd, 27 Wrights Lane,
London W8 5TZ, England
Penguin Books Australia Ltd, Ringwood,
Victoria, Australia
Penguin Books Canada Ltd, 10 Alcorn Avenue,
Toronto, Ontario, Canada M4V 3B2
Penguin Books (N.Z.) Ltd, 182–190 Wairau Road,
Auckland 10, New Zealand

Penguin Books Ltd, Registered Offices:
Harmondsworth, Middlesex, England

First published by Topaz, an imprint of Dutton Signet,
a division of Penguin Books USA Inc.

First Printing, January, 1995
10 9 8 7 6 5 4 3 2

 Topaz is a trademark of Dutton Signet,
a division of Penguin Books USA Inc.

Printed in Canada

Chapter 1

Adrian Renville cheated death three times in the year 1813. The first time was the result of a calculated risk, and his deliverance was pure chance, the smile of good fortune.

Early in that same year, in response to a few notable victories by the fledgling United States of America over the British ships of the line with whom they engaged in battle, England placed a tight blockade along the eastern coastline of America. It was a very effective maneuver, and only the occasional swift privateer managed to slip through the close-held line. For those that tried without success, death was often the result.

Renville was aware of this when in early May of that year, he arranged to make passage to the Madeiras in one of those daring privateers. His intended destination was England, but direct travel to that country from his was impossible. From the Madeiras he hoped to find his way to Portugal and from there to England. It would not have been a comfortable journey even without the threat of the blockade.

Although the captain of the *Sea Hawk* had an unequaled reputation for slipping past English ships unnoticed, this time his luck was out and the *Sea Hawk* was fired upon. She took two hits, the second of which struck the exact spot where Adrian Renville had stood only a moment before, coming so near to him that the ball actually tore and seared the sleeve of his coat and caused him discomfort in his left arm for nearly a fortnight.

Renville had chosen the *Sea Hawk* for his voyage not only because of the reputation of its captain, but also because of the name of the ship. While at school in Virginia, his friends had given him the name "Hawk" for his obsession with reconnoitering any potentially difficult or hostile situation before swooping in to attack it head-on. He had had the presentiment that a ship so named might bring him luck, and by the time the *Sea Hawk* arrived at its destination, having survived both attack by the English and two severe storms at sea, Adrian was satisfied that he had made his choice wisely.

He arrived in Bournemouth by way of Lisbon at the end of July. When he had disembarked from the ship in the waning evening light and gathered up his belongings, he made a casual tour of the docks and the area surrounding it to get his bearings before he sought out an inn known as the Three Bells.

Weariness and hunger overrode his curiosity eventually, and he strode into the courtyard of the Three Bells a little before dusk. As he approached the inn, a carriage bearing a crest on its panels swept into the yard, forcing Adrian to step aside smartly to avoid being grazed by a passing wheel. During the commotion that followed, as the ostlers rushed to the heads of the horses, he entered the inn.

Adrian Renville was not a man to stand out in a crowd unless he made it his business to do so. He was tall, though not exceptionally so, and his features, which had a faint patrician cast, were attractive rather than striking. His hair was a dark shade of gold that in poor light might be mistaken for brown, and his eyes were gray with an inclination to shade more to green than to blue. He was lean and well made, with the strength and structure of an athlete, but his physique was disguised by the caped greatcoat that hung loosely from his shoulders against the unseasonable chill of the night sea air.

The common room of the inn was as bustling as the courtyard. Three ships had docked that afternoon, all carrying passengers, and the custom of all waterfront inns that evening was lively. There was a steady din of voices and the scraping of cutlery against china. Waiters moved with purpose from the kitchen to the tables to the tap, and from the taproom came the occasional burst of semi-drunken laughter and good-natured shouts. Renville set down his burden to the side of the doorway and tagged the elbow of a passing servant, requesting a word with the landlord. The tableman nodded absently and vanished into the tap, leaving Adrian to wonder if his message would be delivered.

He was longing for a comfortable chair, a warm fire, a sustaining dinner, and a tankard of home-brewed, but for the moment he resigned himself to the wait and used the time to look about him. He saw a well-dressed man come into the inn, and surmised that he was the occupant of the carriage that had nearly struck him. The man looked about him with an impatient air and, after a minute or so of receiving no attention, thrust out a walking stick that he carried and nearly tripped a waiter with a full tray. The action appeared to be deliberate and more effective than Adrian's mild request. The waiter immediately returned to the area behind the tap and was followed out again in only a few moments by another man who by his air of proprietorship and the spotless white apron he wore proclaimed him the landlord.

The man from the carriage rather importantly put forth his name as Sir Anthony Belswick, and informed the landlord that he would require a bedchamber for the night and a private parlor for taking meals. The response of the landlord was respectful but in no way obsequious as he informed Sir Anthony that his inn was booked full for the night and only those who had rooms already bespoken for them could be accommodated.

"This is not to be borne," said Sir Anthony in a voice with a pronounced, fashionable drawl. "You will find the room, man, or I shall have your license, damme if I don't. I have friends in very high places, as you will find to your dismay."

The landlord looked more exasperated than dismayed. "Be that as it may, Sir Anthony, I've no room to spare you. Nor there's an inn near the docks with room to spare. You might try the Green Man, sir. It's more than a mile inland and may have rooms not spoken for yet. They don't get much of the carriage trade at the Green Man, but it's clean and respectable."

But Sir Anthony chose to take this sensible advice as a personal affront to his dignity and rebuked the landlord for his stupidity and insolence and demanded that he be given accommodation at once even if it meant casting others with less claim to importance out of their rooms.

Adrian ceased to listen to this tirade almost as soon as it had begun. He reflected that it was not likely that the room reserved for his expected arrival a month ago remained unoccupied, and he supposed he would find himself trudging the additional mile to the Green Man before he finally saw to his comforts. The altercation at hand was none of his affair.

Adrian had come to England determined to have no preconceived prejudices, particularly concerning members of the nobility and landed gentry. His father had left England angry and bitter toward the society into which he had been born, but he had raised his children to form their own opinions. Adrian numbered among his friends a titled Englishman whose family

owned estates in Virginia, and he had found Sir James
Stokes neither arrogant nor close-minded, as he had
often heard his father declare all his former country-
men to be. But this, his first observation in natural
habitat of a member of the class that his father had
denounced and disowned, was not propitious.

The landlord listened to this tongue-lashing in silence, but with a rising color and fists that clenched
at his sides. When the baronet paused for breath, the
landlord said in a taut, abrupt tone, "I've nothing for
you, sir. You'd best get on to another inn, or you'll
find nowhere to put up for the night." He then turned
away without waiting for a reply.

Adrian also was about to turn away to take up his
portmanteau and carpetbag again, but from the corner
of his eye he saw the baronet raise his walking stick
in a striking posture and take a step toward the retreating landlord. Adrian moved swiftly and wrenched
the walking stick from Sir Anthony's hand just as the
blow was about to fall against the shoulders of the
unsuspecting man. The landlord turned back toward
them and was just in time to see Adrian crack the
walking stick into two pieces.

Vivid color rose in the baronet's countenance.
"What the devil do you think you're doing?" he said
furiously, and then demanded of the landlord, "Who
is this damned interfering commoner?"

"A right good fellow, whatever his name," said the
landlord. "And I'll stand him to a pint of my finest."

The scene the obnoxious baronet had created had
finally attracted the attention of two or three of the
landlord's minions, and these men hovered nearby,
awaiting some signal from their employer. The landlord turned toward one of these and ordered him to
have Sir Anthony's carriage brought around.

"I have no intention of leaving," said the baronet,
almost dancing with rage. "In fact, I intend to call for

the magistrate to have this fellow taken into charge for assault."

Adrian's response to this was an unconcerned shrug. He closed his fists and took a step toward Sir Anthony, saying, "Then I might as well be hung for a sheep as a lamb."

Sir Anthony blanched visibly. He was a slight man and several inches shorter than Adrian. Without a weapon or the power to intimidate, he shrank from the confrontation. He took several steps backward and, curling his lip in a not quite successful sneer, said with disgust, "An American! Damned barbarian. I can see this place isn't fit for decent people." With this he turned on his heel and followed the servant, who had just left the common room, out into the courtyard.

The landlord's anger dissipated immediately. He turned to Adrian with a huge smile. "Better a barbarian than that bastard. Thank you kindly, sir. I'll stand you that pint now, if you will, sir."

Adrian returned his smile, his easy nature and good humor showing plainly in his expression. "Your home-brewed then, and thank you. I am not yet familiar with the customs of your country, but I hope that wretched fellow was not an example of what I may expect."

The landlord's smile tightened into a grimace. "Not always, by any means, but all too often for that. There are those of the gentry that think they own the rest of us body and soul, just for the fact of being born on the right blanket. But there, sir, I don't want to go giving you the wrong impression. Most folk you'll meet are as good-hearted as I'll wager you are yourself."

As he spoke his eyes fell on Adrian's baggage near his feet. His face fell a little. "Do you be needing a room, sir? I spoke truly to his high and mighty lordship, I've no room available, but I might be able to make you some accommodation if you're not too particular."

Adrian laughed and shook his head. "One learns not to be after more than a month at sea and a fortnight in a Portuguese inn that kept chickens and goats in the same rooms as their guests. I had hoped it was possible that you might have a room reserved for me, but I am well beyond my expected time and I can see by the size of your custom that it was a vain hope. My name is Renville. My grandfather, Lord Audwin, wrote that he would have a room reserved here for me, but I know it's not likely that provisions were made to hold it for such a length of time."

The landlord looked disconcerted for the first time. "His lordship made such provisions to keep your room waiting for you, Mr. Renville, it being understood that travel across an ocean in times such as these isn't any too certain." He heaved an unhappy sigh. "But who was to know you'd choose tonight to come and ask for it? I had in mind asking you to share a bed with another single traveler I've in one of my rooms, but that won't do for you now I know who you are. I might be able to persuade Mr. Jenkins to give up his room, though, and put a cot in another room for him."

"I wish you would not put yourself or the unsuspecting Mr. Jenkins to such trouble," Adrian said hastily. "I shall do well enough at the Green Man if you will direct me there."

The landlord did not insult Adrian's intelligence by insisting that it was no trouble, but he shook his head regretfully and said, "I have my instructions from his lordship, sir. I was to see you made comfortable and to send off a messenger at once to let his lordship know you had come so that he might send his carriage for you as soon as may be."

"Then he may send his carriage to the Green Man,"

Adrian said in the firm, patient tone of a man who intends to have his way.

The landlord looked dubious and not at all pleased by this turn of events. "Begging your pardon, sir, but his lordship wishes—"

"I shall, of course, recompense you for any return of the funds my grandfather has doubtlessly deposited with you to hold rooms for me," Adrian said swiftly and smoothly, cutting off, he hoped, further discussion. He was becoming aware of how weary he was, and if he had a mile walk ahead of him, he wanted to get on with it.

"It's naught to do with money, sir," the man said with a dour smile. It wasn't likely that this pleasant young gentleman, fresh from the United States of America, where things were much different, he had heard, would understand that a wise man didn't go against the wishes of the quality, not the real quality, which Sir Anthony Belswick certainly was not. When they were as rich and powerful as old Lord Audwin, whose name was well-known to all classes in even the farthest reaches of the realm, it was pure foolhardiness. "Lord Audwin will be most put out that you did not do as he wished, sir."

Adrian successfully disguised his growing annoyance and said with a brief smile, "I am sure I shall be able to explain my actions to Lord Audwin's satisfaction, and I shall assure him that I insisted on having my way and that you are in no way to blame for not following the instructions he gave you."

The landlord's expression showed that he was not convinced, but he was shrewd enough to recognize that Adrian meant to have his way. "As you like, sir. There's no need for you to walk to the Green Man; I'll have the gig made ready for you. Just sit yourself any place you can find, if you would, and I'll see to it and bring you that home-brewed."

Adrian far preferred riding to driving, but his baggage made this impossible, and driving a gig was preferable to walking in his present tired state. He had no argument with these suggestions and sat down at the nearest table with an empty chair. The table was occupied by two men discussing both their dinner and politics and who paused in their conversation only to nod at Adrian as he sat down at the table.

The landlord soon returned to the common room carrying the brimming tankard himself. He withdrew a sheet of sealed parchment from the pocket of his apron and handed it to Adrian. "I was to give you this as soon as you arrived, Mr. Renville." He bowed and left Adrian to his ale.

Adrian broke the seal and unfolded the letter, which he supposed was some sort of welcome or instructions from his grandfather. The message was brief and written in a bold hand. He read it twice before folding it again and placing it in an inner pocket of his coat. By the time an ostler came to inform him that the gig was ready, Adrian's features had taken on a set, grim cast that made him appear quite other than a pleasant young gentleman.

A low fire was lit in the grate in the small, cozy parlor of the Green Man, providing a comfortable warmth for an evening that was cool and damp in spite of the season. Sir James Stokes sat at his ease at the table from which the covers had just been cleared. "Unfortunately, we do number among our ranks several arrogant, nasty little beggars," he said ruefully, responding to the story Adrian Renville had just told him. "Belswick, did you say? Can't say I've ever heard of the fellow. Probably a country squire. That sort is sometimes full of self-importance. But we aren't all like that, Adrian. Be fair."

Twenty-four hours and a good meal accompanied

by an excellent claret had abated Adrian's annoyance with the rude and insufferable baronet, making the encounter an amusing dinner story. "Oh, quite. You, for example, aren't a bad sort for an Englishman," he said with a quizzing smile. "Not, I fear, an encomium I shall be able to apply to my grandfather."

He removed the letter he had received from his grandfather from his coat pocket. It still disturbed him, even though his ready sense of humor and delight for absurdities had returned to him. Adrian held out the letter, and Sir James took it and read it through, letting it fall to the table when he had finished.

Sir James grinned at his friend and said, "So you're to be locked up in the attics until you're brought up to snuff. The old tartar must be expecting you to arrive wrapped in bearskins and a loincloth."

"At the least of it," said Adrian dryly. The message from his grandfather commanded him to keep to his rooms until he was fetched from the Three Bells and to communicate his identity to no one. Even with an economy of words, Lord Audwin made it plain that he expected his American grandson to be, if not precisely savage, at the least of it unmannered, unlettered, and completely lacking in any sort of social grace; an embarrassment to the name of Renville that must be rectified before Adrian could be acknowledged to the world at large.

A servant entered the room bearing a tray with a decanter of brandy and two glasses, which Adrian directed him to place on the table between two chairs drawn up to the fire. Days such as this in July were unheard of in the warmer, drier climate of southern Pennsylvania, and he felt the unexpected chill through to his bones. "I must confess," he said, resuming their interrupted conversation as soon as they were settled in the comfortable chairs, "I owe my dear late father an apology. I always thought that the horrifying tales he told me of his father's domineering ways were fabricated to make me grateful for having a more lenient parent. Or to excuse himself for having abandoned his birthright—and consequently mine—to satisfy his adventurous spirit in the New World. It would appear I have done him an injustice."

Sir James, who had followed him, stretched out his long legs to the fire. "Lord, yes. Old Audwin doesn't get about as much as he used to, but the stories of his autocratic ways are still told. His wrath is legendary, you know. He's not the sort of man who rants and raves and becomes nearly apoplectic, but one who can fell strong men with a cold, steely glare. They say even Old Q was nothing to him. As high in the instep as they come, dear boy." He paused to enjoy a sip of the rich amber liquid in his glass. He held the glass up to the firelight, examining it with knit brows. "French, damme if it isn't," he said, momentarily distracted. "I wonder if the landlord has enough put by to sell me a cask or two."

"Ah," said Adrian in the manner of one who has solved a puzzle. "Then my own father's terrifying scowl was inherited. He rarely needed to use the birch on me or my brothers; one of his black looks was enough to make us tremble and quake and resolve to err no more. I have never known the details of the quarrel between my father and grandfather that caused my father to chuck away everything and emigrate to America," he continued after a pause for reflection, "but if they were both cut from the same cloth, I cannot wonder at it."

Francis Renville, Adrian's father, had used that strong will and determination to good advantage when he emigrated to the United States. He had taken with him a small legacy from a great aunt and parlayed it into a considerable fortune through clever land dealing. He then had added to this by marrying the heiress of a shipping magnate, a hard-nosed, obdurate man who had obligingly turned up his toes a little more than a year later, making Mr. Renville one of the richest men in the growing nation.

Though his principal holdings were in Pennsylvania, he also owned considerable property in Virginia and had sent his eldest son there to be educated at the College of William and Mary, and it was while Adrian was in his final year there that he had met Sir James, who had been sent by his own father to look after property that gentleman owned not far from the plantation of the Renvilles. Though Sir James was senior to Adrian by several years, he was apt to forget this, for Adrian, even when he had been only two-and-twenty, had been mature beyond his years. Sir James did not hesitate to attribute this to the fact that Adrian shared the strong will and determination of his father and grandfather.

Sir James regarded Adrian over the rim of his glass. It had been nearly eight years since that first meeting, and he saw in Adrian's features an even greater strength than he had recalled. Whatever the reputation of Lord Audwin, Sir James would have readily placed his money on his friend. This was clearly a man to be reckoned with.

Adrian, as if aware of this scrutiny, turned to him and smiled in the deceptively unassuming way that he had, and dispelled these somber thoughts. "I must be as great a fool as my brother Teddy informed me I was for coming here to meet the Renvilles. I didn't expect open arms precisely, but I admit I wasn't prepared to find that I would be regarded as an embarrassment." He sipped thoughtfully at his brandy for several moments and then said, "Are you acquainted with any of the others in my family, Jamie? May I expect them to regard me in a similar fashion?"

"Acquainted, yes, but not much more than that, so I really couldn't say."

Adrian regarded him through lazily narrowed eyes. "Try, my good fellow. You wouldn't wish me to be unsuspecting game in their sights, would you?"

Sir James grinned. "Every good sportsman knows it's devilish hard to bring down a hawk. Up to your usual tricks, are you, Adrian? Is that why you sent word to me before the Renvilles?"

Adrian's smile acknowledged the hit. "That and, of course, a strong desire to see you again as soon as I might. I wish you would tell me what you know of my family, Jamie. You know I dislike walking into any situation blind."

Sir James acquiesced with a sigh. "It isn't much, I warn you, mostly *on dit* and conjecture. You come from pretty exalted stock. A bit above my touch, I fear. No Renville has ever been prime minister, it is true, and the title is only an earldom, but it is said that this is because the Renvilles have been shrewd enough to know that the real power is often behind the throne, not on it. But prime ministers and even kings take note when a Renville speaks. That about describes your grandfather, and also your uncle Julian, who died three years ago. Following in their footsteps is Carlton, Julian Renville's younger son. He's not yet thirty, but he has already held important positions in government, and it is expected that he will enjoy a cabinet post before he's a great deal older."

Adrian's brows rose slightly in acknowledgment of this information. "And the elder son?"

"Ah, Quentin," said Sir James evenly. "He has made a name for himself in quite another way. He is a top-of-the-trees Corinthian, a sportsman without equal and a leader of fashion. One of the neck-or-nothing boys who spars with the Gentleman himself and drives four-in-hand wearing a Belcher necktie. Men also lis-

ten when he speaks but for quite different reasons.
He has no obvious interest in politics or anything else
useful that I've ever heard, and yet he is unquestionably old Audwin's favorite. The *on dit* is that it is
Audwin himself who made him what he is; that the
old man secretly wanted to cut a dash in the world of
fashion in his youth and that he is living that longing
vicariously through Quentin. Carlton, who is so much
more in the old man's mold, is scarcely an also-ran in
his affections. Even the Leylands, I have heard, are
better regarded."

Adrian had caught the carefully expressionless tone
used to describe Quentin Renville. Sir James did not
like the man, and his words betrayed what his tone
sought to guard. Adrian let this pass for the moment.
"Who are the Leylands?"

"Lord and Lady Leyland," Sir James responded.
"He's with the foreign office and posted in Brazil,
probably for the duration of the war now that travel
from one continent to the other is so damned treacherous. Lady Leyland is your aunt Caroline, the baby
of the family and probably still in leading strings when
your father left England."

"Any Leyland cousins?"

"One by blood and one by marriage. Leyland was
a widower with a daughter when Lady Caroline married him, and they have a son of their own, Simon. He
is something of a scholar, I've heard. Only eighteen or
thereabouts and already in his second year at Oxford.
Though there was some talk of a riding accident going
about in the spring that makes me think he had to
come down for a term or two. Don't know much else
about him, really, since he isn't out on the town yet."

"And the stepdaughter?" Adrian prompted after Sir
James trailed off and seemed more inclined to discuss
his brandy again than Adrian's connections.

He did not answer at once. "It is not easy to define

Isobel Leyland. She is quite lovely to behold. Eyes so blue the sky on the fairest day is nothing to them; hair the color of fresh minted guineas; a figure that any man with warm blood in his veins would ache to possess; the smile of an angel. And as bright as she is beautiful. She has charm, wit, spirit, and an uncommon measure of intelligence. Toast of the town in her first Season. Had every silly clunch on the town writing sonnets to her fine eyes. She might have had her pick of a title in spite of the fact that her dowry is said to be no more than respectable."

Adrian's brows shot up at this catalogue of virtues. "I would be astonished to hear what you would say of someone you thought you could define. I presume she is a duchess now. Such an incomparable could do no less than to marry a duke."

"You would imagine so, but this is why she defies understanding," said Sir James. "With titles and fortunes cast at her dainty feet, she scorned all and had eyes for no one except a man who has no title or hope of one and no fortune at all beyond a small independence left him by his father and the allowance made to him by his grandfather. Nor is he an eager lover. The fair Isobel was presented four years ago, but her betrothal to Quentin Renville was announced just this past May, with no indication of when a wedding might take place."

Adrian digested this for a few moments. "One presumes, then, that it is a love match, at least on her side," he said in a musing tone as he worked out the possibilities. "But why, if she is a woman of spirit as you say, would she countenance such a delay? Was her regard unrequited or was Audwin against the match? If cousin Isobel has only a respectable dowry and Quentin only a competence, it would make keeping up his fashionable way of life difficult if the old man cut him loose from his purse strings."

Sir James rewarded him with a smile for his quick understanding. "It is safe to presume the latter. The *on dit* is that they're waiting for the old man to turn up his toes so that Quentin may inherit; Audwin must be seventy-five if he's a day, and he has been in poor health for years. They won't marry without his express consent for fear that Audwin would disinherit Quentin just to prove he's the one who keeps them on puppet strings. From all I've ever heard of Audwin, it's the sort of thing that keeps him fit and ticking."

Adrian expressed surprise. "But Quentin is the son of a second son. I know my father made certain the family was apprised of my birth and that of my brothers, so Quentin could never have expected to inherit the earldom or the entail."

"Perhaps your father, having cut his ties, never told you the whole of it," Sir James suggested. "Audwin is said to be an exceptionally warm man. Rich as Croesus, in fact. Bound to be a tidy sum of it that don't come under the entail. Or perhaps Quentin hoped that living in a savage place like Pennsylvania, you and your brothers would get eaten up by wolves or scalped by the natives. There's one, I'll wager, who won't be pleased to make your acquaintance."

"I'm not certain I'll care to know him either," Adrian remarked. "What manner of man would deny himself the immediate joys of wedded bliss with the exquisite Isobel for the sake of a mere fortune, if it is indeed a love match? Surely happiness and an independence is better than unhappiness and a great fortune."

Sir James gave a bark of cynical laughter. "Quentin at least has not lacked consolation. A little ladybird of some renown on the stage has been in his keeping for the past twelvemonth. Audwin's generosity keeps Quentin in both high steppers and high flyers."

Adrian was silent for some time after this exchange,

and Sir James was content to enjoy the warmth of the fire and the delights of the excellent brandy and left him to his thoughts.

Finally Adrian said, "Is the offer to spend a few days with you at Stokes Hall still open, Jamie?"

"Of course it is! Spend a few weeks if you like. Stay with me until I go up to town in mid-September, and I'll sponsor you for my clubs. But what about your grandfather? He'll be expecting you, won't he?"

Adrian shrugged, unconcerned. "I am already a month later than the time I gave for my expected arrival. A few more weeks won't matter. When I'm finally ready to make the acquaintance of my family, I'll write to let my grandfather know I've arrived in England."

"They may think you've gone down with your ship," Sir James suggested.

Adrian grinned. "They may be hoping that that is already the case. I don't imagine I should be deeply mourned by the Renvilles."

"Old Audwin won't like it much if he finds out that you didn't go to him directly," Sir James said, his tone cautionary but his eyes laughing. "He's not the sort whose instructions are lightly disregarded."

Adrian's lips turned up in a half smile, and he sipped his brandy again. "Yes, I can see that he is not." His smile became fuller. "But I want something more from you, Jamie, than sponsorship to your clubs. I want to become acquainted with my family before I formally visit Audswyck Chase."

His friend's expression was puzzled. "But you can accomplish that better if you did go there at once. I've told you I don't know any of them well."

Adrian shook his head. "I didn't say I wished to *meet* my family, Jamie. It is to my advantage that you are not well-known to them, and I not at all. It is observation that I wish, not introduction."

Sir James's features spread into a slow, quizzing smile. "I see," he said. "The Hawk begins to circle."

Miss Isobel Leyland scanned another paragraph or so of the book she held and decided that it was not, after all, quite what she was looking for. She turned to place it back on the shelf and accidentally brushed against a young man standing fairly close to her, perusing titles on the shelf opposite. She cast him a quick smile, begged his pardon, and moved farther along the shelves.

Miss Katherine West, whose taste in literature was only for lurid romances and poets of a mawkishly sentimental bent, had exhausted her interest in the bookseller's shelves long since and followed behind Isobel. "Have you found anything you like, Bel?" she asked, not for the first time.

The answer to this question was self-evident, as it had been the three other times it had been asked in the past quarter hour. Isobel did not possess any exceptional store of patience, but she had had ample practice improving this virtue since Kitty, her mother's ward, had come to live with the Leylands earlier in the year. "No, alas," she said ruefully. "It is the curse of being a voracious reader that neither authors nor publishers ever seem in pace with my demands."

"It is getting rather late, Bel. We had best leave now anyway," Kitty suggested, her tone hopeful. "Carlton and Quentin will be at Grillon's by now and wondering where we have gotten to."

Isobel thought it extremely unlikely that Mr. Quentin Renville, who was notoriously unpunctual, was already awaiting them for their engagement for luncheon. But having Kitty as a constant shadow was unnerving, and she would have a far better chance of finding a new book to take with her on her visit to the country next week if she returned another day alone. Isobel agreed that it was time they went to the hotel.

Kitty, pleased that the dreary wait for Isobel to find a book that pleased her was over, was inclined to chatter as they left the shop. Neither young lady noticed, as they stepped into the warm September sunshine, the two gentlemen who followed them into the street and hailed a passing hack as soon as the crested Leyland carriage had pulled away. The drive was a short one, and the ladies were soon being shown into Grillon's elegantly appointed dining room. It was past the usual hour for luncheon, and only a few scattered tables were occupied. As Isobel had expected, they found only Mr. Carlton Renville awaiting them as promised.

It was just as well, Isobel reflected shortly after they had taken their seats, that Quentin was late. Carlton was bent on nurturing a grievance that would have made conversation uncomfortable had Quentin been present. Though only seven-and-twenty, Carlton had engaged in the difficult art of politics since his days at Oxford and knew well how to hold his tongue in when it mattered. It seemed to make him all the more free with his opinions when it did not.

"I suppose you're going to Audswyck Chase for the birthday celebration," Carlton said as soon as they were settled at their table. "Cursed nuisance if you ask me—as if the old man ever wanted his family gathered about him before." His inflection was peevish, and a frown marred his otherwise attractive features. He possessed the coloring of the Renvilles, but in a somewhat washed-out version, his hair being an indiscriminate shade between dark blond and brown and his eyes an uncompromising light gray. "I don't know why it should matter that *I* am there," he went on. "I have a thousand and one things to occupy me in town at the moment, but the old man never considers anyone's convenience but his own, selfish old tartar. One would think it would be enough for him that he has Quentin dancing on the ends of his puppet strings and that he'd leave me in peace."

Isobel cast him a warning glance. Kitty, at sixteen, was still inclined to repeat the utterances of her elders at moments most likely to be embarrassing to them. Since the girl was to accompany Isobel and her mother to Audswyck next week, it would be best to avoid any possibility of this happening in the presence of Lord Audwin. "It is *Grand-père's* seventy-fifth birthday, Carl," she said lightly. "Perhaps he is confronting his own mortality and wishes to bring us all together as a family while he still may do so."

Carlton gave her a long, incredulous stare. "You must have crows in your attic if you believe that, though I don't think you really do," he added handsomely. He raised his hand to catch the notice of a passing waiter. "God knows when Quentin will put in an appearance. He was at Cribb's last night drinking Blue Ruin with Freddy Haverwell and Miles Chutley, and I heard from there they went on to Mrs. Coltrane's gaming hell. I'm dashed peckish myself and don't mean to wait on his convenience."

When the waiter approached, he indicated that they were ready to order their luncheon, and though Isobel would have preferred to wait for Quentin, she knew, having heard the catalogue of his previous evening's entertainments, that Carlton was right in implying that Quentin had very likely only just arisen from his bed at this hour.

The two gentlemen who had left Hatchard's just after the ladies had entered the dining room while Isobel was speaking and were shown to the table next to the one that she and Kitty and Carlton occupied. One of the young men slightly jostled Isobel's arm as he passed, but she paid scant heed to him or his murmured apology. "I suppose the birthday celebration is just a convenient excuse to ensure that we will not cry off," she conceded. "Certainly neither Quentin nor I look forward to meeting our cousin from America, but as much as we all must wish him at the devil, we have to meet Mr. Adrian Renville sometime, and I would as lief have it over with so that we may take his measure and know where we stand."

"What measure is there to take?" Carlton said, a sneer curling his lips. "We all know why the fellow was willing to brave military blockades and an ocean crossing in time of war to bring himself to Grandfather's notice. It's the same reason Quentin dances attendance on the old man and that you are still on the shelf at three-and-twenty when you might have had a nursery full of bawling brats by now."

Kitty was watching them with unconcealed interest, and Isobel had to bite back a sharp retort. She had no intention of coming to cuffs with Carlton in the young girl's presence. Carlton was generally equable in temperament when he spoke his mind to her as if he were an older brother. But his good nature often deserted him when he discussed his grandfather, and Isobel reminded herself that Carlton's blunt words were more a reflection of his own feelings toward his older brother, of whom he was, not without justification, jealous, rather than implying any insult to her or her judgment. Another reason for holding her tongue was that her own thoughts more and more of late mirrored the unpalatable truth in the comment he had just made.

"I have no intention of rising to such obvious bait," she said, outwardly unruffled, "simply because you are in a foul humor and casting about for a quarrel. If the prospect of spending a fortnight with your family at Audswyck makes you so liverish, by all means you should tell *Grand-père* that you have other plans. I daresay," she added with a sweet air of innocence, "that he is no longer cross with you for having had the effrontery to praise the bill Lord Harbrook set before the House, when he himself made the journey to town solely to condemn it, and will quite understand your feelings. Even if he does not, you have not, as you have often claimed, *any* expectations from that quarter."

This was not entirely true, as they both knew, and Carlton acknowledged the hit with a grunt. Isobel was always worthy of his steel, which was one of the reasons he particularly liked her, though in the normal way he was a confirmed misogynist. After a pause to regather his recruits, he returned to the fray. "Don't tell me Quentin would go if it wasn't all but impossible for him to refuse."

It is always impossible for Quentin to refuse *Grand-père*, Isobel thought with growing exasperation, though whether for the thought itself or for the fact that Quentin was now all of a half hour late, she could not have said. The waiter arrived at that moment with their first course of clear soup and saved her the need of replying. Quentin's response to the summons to Audswyck and the information that they would meet there Mr. Adrian Renville, the son of Francis Renville, had been, for him, unusually explosive. He had always known of the existence of his American cousins and that he had no hope of inheriting the title or entail, but it was quite another thing to have the son of the profligate uncle come to England to take his place in the family. Quentin had said to Isobel that he would be damned if he would go out of his way to meet an uncultivated colonial who *might* be related to him, but she recognized this as angry bluster and had not been at all surprised when a few days later Quentin had acknowledged that he might as well go to Audswyck to "have a look at the savage."

Carlton was momentarily diverted by his soup, but when he put down his spoon, he resumed his complaint. "The worst of it is that I am obliged to overset all my plans just to meet that—that interloper because he's taken it in his head to come to England to see if he can turn up Grandfather sweet. Much luck he'll have at it too, I'd wager."

Isobel recognized two fallacies in Carlton's remarks. She was in her mother's confidence and knew it was the other way about, that it was Lord Audwin who had finally relinquished his determination to have nothing to do with the son who had defied him and resisted his control by setting off to seek his own fortune, or his son's progeny, and had written to Mr. Adrian Renville to invite him to England. It seemed that the old viscount *was* finally prepared to acknowledge that he was not immortal, and since he could not prevent the son of his eldest son from inheriting the title, he had taken it into his head to salvage what he could of what he regarded as an impossible situation. Carlton's second error was to term Adrian an interloper. Unless he was an imposter, and Isobel supposed that Lord Audwin's solicitors would do their utmost to assure this was not the case, he was unquestionably the rightful heir to the earldom, and the considerable entail of property and priceless family heirlooms that went with it through the legal means of primogeniture. But Isobel made no effort to correct these errors.

"Lord Audwin can't cut Adrian Renville out of the title or the entail, can he?" asked Kitty. It was the first she had spoken other than to murmur agreement at the dishes Carlton had chosen for their luncheon. She was always unnaturally quiet in the company of both Mr. Renvilles, being in awe of the elegant Mr. Carlton Renville and having a schoolgirl's hopeless crush on the magnificent Mr. Quentin Renville. Both Carlton and Isobel turned to look at her in some surprise, and she blushed rosily to the roots of her hair. "I am certain he would leave everything to Quentin if he could," she said in a small voice. "When we visited Audswyck last winter, I heard him say that Quentin had no equal in all of England."

It was plain from her voice that she thought so too, and Carlton stifled an absurd envy that his brother could charm even schoolgirls without effort. "Thank God for that," he said with some feeling and added, not unkindly, "Hopefully, not quite everything, urchin. There may be a few crumbs left over for the rest of his grandchildren."

"Even Simon?" she asked incredulously. Simon Leyland, who was not quite two years her senior, did not inspire her in the least with awe. The thought of him being on a similar footing with Quentin or even Carlton seemed preposterous to her.

"Even Simon," Carlton affirmed with a crooked grin. "Though Lord knows, he don't need it," he added, addressing Isobel, a return of bitterness in his tone. As Lord Leyland's only male heir, Simon would inherit not only the barony but also a very comfortable fortune, while Carlton subsisted on an even smaller legacy from his father's estate than Quentin enjoyed and his salary from the Home Office, where he was currently employed as an undersecretary. Instead of rewarding Carlton's enterprise, Lord Audwin had declared that he had no need of both a salary and an allowance and had ceased the latter.

"Simon is very likely the only one of us whose curiosity is disinterested," remarked Isobel. "It would be vastly diverting to meet cousin Adrian were there not so much at stake. At least Quentin seems to think there is a great deal at stake; I think he may be tilting at shadows."

"Trust Quentin to know his own best interest," Carlton said acidly. "You know that the old man is for doing whatever it is you least expect of him. He may dote on Quentin now, but if this American rustic takes his fancy, he may take it in his head that the ready should by rights go with the title and the estates, and we shall all go whistling for our inheritances."

"That is extremely unlikely," Isobel said with more assurance than she felt. "Quentin is the only one who ever finds favor with *Grand-père,* and I cannot imagine that a stranger, even if he is *Grand-père's* heir, could supplant him, particularly not a colonial who cannot possibly match Quentin in accomplishments or sophistication."

Quentin arrived with the last course and as usual offered only a general apology for his tardiness. "I hope the food here hasn't given you indigestion," he said with mock alarm as he took his seat beside Carlton. "You look rather more bilious than usual, Carl."

"No more than you yourself," his brother retorted. "Too much Blue Ruin and you'll end up looking like those poor devils in the stews."

Quentin's brows snapped together, and Isobel did not waste her breath chiding Quentin, but gave her energy to changing the topic. Though she was severely displeased with him herself, she had learned from experience that recriminations and pleadings alike did little to prevent him from pursuing his pleasures. "Carl is upset because he has to give up his plans to go to Audswyck Chase to meet your cousin from America," she said.

Quentin sighed theatrically. "Alas, it is a fate I suffer as well. Never mind, Carl. We shall be better entertained, I think, than we realize."

"You didn't seem to find it amusing when you received your summons from the old man, I seem to recall," Carlton said sardonically.

"That was before I had time for reflection," said Quentin, pouring himself a glass of claret. "Oh, it is a bother to be obliged to acknowledge the fellow, but all families must suffer their dirty dishes, after all. Think of what he is and whence he comes: what could he be but a source of fun? I had a letter from Mama yesterday, and she said that Grandfather said he was raised on a farm in the backwoods of Pennsylvania, wherever that may be. So he shall be not only colonial and provincial but rustic into the bargain. One may only hope he has a nodding acquaintance with civilization."

"One might presume that," Isobel said blandly. "He wrote to *Grand-père,* or at least he knew someone who could do it for him."

"One hopes one won't have to teach him how to use a fork," Quentin suggested, with a wink for Kitty.

"We cannot hope for too much," Carlton replied with a sad shake of his head. "It will be enough if he arrives in a suit of clothes not made out of sacking. I am almost tempted to arrive early at Audswyck to greet him when he comes. By the time we get there, Grandfather may have slain him with one appalled glare."

"I for one am glad that we are summoned to Audswyck next week rather than this," said Isobel. "At least we shall still be in town for Lady Emerson's masquerade party at Vauxhall on Friday. It is such a unique idea for her to hire the whole of the gardens just for her guests, though she was able to do so only because it is still early in the Little Season. I hope I shall not have to wear a domino over my costume, which is too pretty to hide, but I fear there will be too much chill in the night air at this time of year without it."

"Should have dressed yourself up like a Tudor lady in brocades and quilted skirts instead of that sprite costume Aunt Caro told me you plan to wear," Carlton suggested, at last diverted from his complaints.

"You are a wretch, Carl," Isobel scolded. "I meant for my costume to be a surprise to Quentin, and now he will know me as soon as he sees me."

"Not if you've got it all covered up with a domino," Carlton pointed out, unrepentant.

"Actually, Bel, I have been meaning to tell you," Quentin said in a carefully offhand tone that she knew from experience usually heralded something she would find displeasing. "I may not get a chance to look in at Vauxhall on Friday."

Isobel felt herself stiffen inside, though she continued to eat the candied fruit from the bowl in front of her. "Oh? I thought it was a settled thing that you were to escort me and Georgiana Wolesley, since her husband must be out of town on Friday."

"I suppose I may have said something of the sort," Quentin allowed, "but surely you may make one of Lady Leyland's party."

Isobel kept her voice level, and as light as she could make it, determined not to display her rising anger in front of Kitty and Carlton. "My mother will not attend. She and Kitty are promised to my Aunt Elizabeth for the evening. I suppose I may go with them and make a fourth for whist," she added. "Kitty never can tell one card from the other."

If Quentin caught the sarcasm in her tone, he pointedly ignored it. "Rather a comedown from a masquerade party at Vauxhall," he said with a brief laugh. "But there will be other masquerades, sweeting. I promise I shall escort you to every one of them." He took her free hand in his and gave it an affectionate squeeze. She withdrew her hand from his as quickly as she could without calling attention to her action.

Kitty, ever adept at setting the cat among the pigeons, asked him what could possibly keep him from attending something as exciting as an al fresco masquerade party, and seemed disappointed to learn that it was nothing more than a proposed visit to one of his friends' shooting boxes in Leicestershire. "Roger is pressing for us to leave tomorrow, but there is some doubt that Freddy Haverwell and Colin McAffe can get away before Saturday morning. Freddy and Colin wish us to wait so that we may all go up to Leicestershire together, but Roger prefers to go on ahead of them and insists that I join him."

What he did not say was that the gentlemen would not travel alone but would enjoy the company of their inamoratas. Carlton guessed this and raised his brows at his brother's audacity in breaking a particular engagement with his betrothed for such a purpose. Isobel was not a fool and would at least suspect that a bit of shooting would not be sufficient lure for even a sportsman like Quentin to give up what would likely be the most talked-about fashionable entertainment of the Little Season that year.

Isobel had not finished the fruit, but her appetite had deserted her and she pushed the bowl away. She never acknowledged to Quentin and barely acknowledged to herself that she knew Quentin had a mistress among the muslin company. Yet a tight ball of anger formed inside her that was beyond what might be expected for merely a broken engagement. Her anger and disappointment were so barely contained that she could not let this pass without comment, though she had no intention of quarreling with him in public. "Then perhaps the easiest thing," she said, her expression not unpleasant but her eyes steadily and coolly holding Quentin's, "would be for you to claim your prior commitment to me and Georgiana. Then you could travel with Freddy and Colin."

Quentin, who had not ordered luncheon, poured a second glass of claret and smiled condescendingly. "But Roger is more than my host, dear one," he said with mock plaintiveness. "He is my means of transportation as well. Freddy and Colin plan to travel in Colin's phaeton, and you know I took the wheel off my curricle and lamed the leader of my best team when that dashed cart drove me off the road in my race with Craven last week. You wouldn't wish to see me drive to Leicestershire in my mother's barouche with my second-best team, would you, Belle?"

She knew he was quizzing her, but she also knew that he had already made up his mind to leave the next day and that he could be as stubborn as his grandfather when he meant to have his way. "It would damage your reputation beyond repair," she said with deceptive mildness. "I suppose it is of no consequence if you cannot escort us to Vauxhall. Sir Jonathan Avery asked if he would see me at Vauxhall only last night and he is a cousin to Georgiana, so I daresay he will be happy to escort us." Sir Jonathan had made her an offer of marriage the previous Season, and though Isobel had turned him down, he remained a steadfast admirer.

But if any spark of jealousy was kindled in Quentin's breast, he gave no sign of it. "I only hope he doesn't abandon you as soon as you've stepped foot off the boat for the card tables Lady Emerson means to set up in tents."

"I rather doubt that," Isobel said with a complacent smile that she hoped was as irritating as she intended. "I have no doubt I shall somehow manage to keep Sir Jonathan sufficiently entertained so that he will have no need of gaming."

Quentin knew what she was about and ignored the bait, saying with a smile that certainly irritated Isobel, "I only hope you and Georgie don't find yourselves fighting off the advances of every buck in town if you go wandering about without an escort."

Carlton, bored with their verbal duel, brought it to an end by asking Quentin if it was true that Lord Rooke was completely done up and planning to take his cattle to Tattersall's for auction. It was not over as far as Isobel was concerned, but she realized she could not quarrel openly with Quentin in a public place.

Quentin was a sporting man of fashion, a Corinthian and nonpareil. Isobel knew she was expected to be understanding of his sporting pursuits and not reproach him every time he preferred the company of his friends to hers. She had never questioned Quentin's love for her, but she had learned that it was just not his nature to put the wants and needs of others, even hers, before his own. She did not consider him selfish, precisely; rather, she thought of him as self-absorbed, and blamed not Quentin himself but his grandfather and his mother, Adora Renville, who had all his life spoiled him shamelessly and taught him that no one's desires were superior to his own. Isobel had on many occasions swallowed her disappointment, but it seemed to her that of late Quentin was taking her forbearance far too much for granted.

The conversation remained on general topics for a time until Isobel declared several minutes later that she and Kitty still had shopping to do before returning to Leyland House to change for dinner. "I shall see you tonight, Quentin," she said, maintaining a casual tone in her voice but casting him a significant look. "You have not also forgotten that you escort Mama and me to the Abermores' card party tonight?"

She spoke with just the hint of an edge in her voice, and he responded in an identical manner as he rose from his chair. "It is uppermost in my thoughts, beloved." He flashed her the roguish smile that nearly always succeeded in dissolving any anger or annoyance she might have for him.

Isobel gave no indication of its present success. She turned to Carlton, took leave of him, adjured Kitty not to forget any of their parcels, and left Grillon's dining room.

Chapter 2

Isobel did not so much as glance at the two men seated at the table behind her as she and Kitty left. Neither did Quentin nor Carlton Renville have the least notion that the American cousin who was the object of all their speculation was so near at hand, and they too left Grillon's without according him any notice at all.

As Carlton and Quentin passed out of the dining room, Sir James Stokes let out his breath in a long sigh. "You have the devil's own luck, Adrian. But you had better hope it holds," he admonished. "You'll be in the suds if one of them recognizes you when you are introduced at Audswyck Chase next week."

"I doubt the back of my head is all that memorable," said Adrian with a brief laugh. "It was a near thing at Hatchard's, though. When Miss Leyland backed into me, I thought for certain I was dished, but the English are too reserved to look directly at a stranger jostled in a bookseller's stacks. I admit I didn't think much of your idea of frequenting Hatchard's with the vague hope that my cousin Isobel would happen by, but it proved quite propitious."

"I'm not at all certain I would have suggested it if I had had any notion that you meant to do more than observe her as you did the others," Sir James said severely.

Though this was the first Adrian had seen Isobel,

Sir James had pointed out Carlton earlier in the week when he and Adrian had taken dinner at Brooks', and Quentin they had viewed the night before from a safe distance both at the theater and afterward at Cribb's Parlor, where Sir James had taken Adrian to introduce him to the rites that English gentlemen referred to as blowing a cloud and drinking Blue Ruin, a brand of gin that had indeed lived up to its name for many unfortunate imbibers.

"I had no notion myself that I meant to do more," Adrian said with his gentle smile. "But the opportunity to eavesdrop was irresistible."

"For once I think your passion for always testing the ground before you put a foot forward has played you false," said Sir James. "You now know for certain that your cousins have no better opinion of you than Lord Audwin does—worse, in fact," he added brutally. "They think you are a fortune hunter and a figure of fun. They have no wish to meet you and frankly wish you at Jericho. Do you really believe you will deal better with them for knowing these things?"

"Forewarned is forearmed," Adrian replied, conceding no error in his methods. "At least I have proven the truth of the maxim 'Eavesdroppers hear no good of themselves,' if nothing else. She *is* beautiful, my cousin Isobel," he added to change the subject but also because she was very much in his thoughts. "I thought your description of her generous, but instead I see that you understated her loveliness."

Isobel had stirred something inside him from the moment he had set eyes on her. The attraction was instantaneous and unexpectedly compelling. Lovely as she was, beauty alone was rarely sufficient to captivate him, and though he did feel a strong desire to possess her, he recognized that the attraction was stronger than something merely physical. The very notion of love at first sight, as it flashed through his thoughts, made him smile at the absurdity of it. He had no belief in such things.

Quentin, on the other hand, had an equally strong but quite opposite effect on him. At the theater the previous night, Quentin had been in the company of his actress paramour, a pretty creature, certainly, but undeniably common. The company of his mistress had not prevented Quentin from ogling the scantily clad opera dancers whenever his lady's attention had been diverted, making it obvious to Adrian that he was no more faithful to his actress than he was to Isobel. At Cribb's, Quentin had been a part of a boisterous group of young men, each apparently set on outdrinking the other. In the early hours of the morning, Quentin, as cast away as his companions, had left in the company of a notorious demimondaine, confirming Adrian's belief that Quentin had the sexual morals of a tomcat.

Drinking and wenching were as much a part of the rites of passage for young American gentlemen as they were for their English counterparts. Adrian rarely drank to excess, but he enjoyed the uninhibited camaraderie of imbibing with friends, and he had certainly not passed the whole of his nine-and-twenty years in the manner of a monk. But if he had found Quentin's absorption with debauchery distasteful before he had seen Isobel, afterward he disdained him more for being a fool than a libertine. He could not understand why Quentin would prefer such tawdry pleasures and so little cherish Isobel's company.

Sir James broke into his reverie, saying, "Have you had your fill now of spying, Adrian? When you arrive at Audswyck Chase, you can have the pleasure of making them eat their words by proving that you are not the barbarian they are expecting."

"Yes, I could," Adrian replied slowly. He picked up his glass and sipped the wine before going on, his tone thoughtful. "But shall I?"

Sir James stared at him in momentary puzzlement. "And what does that mean?" he asked suspiciously.

"One so hates to disappoint," Adrian murmured, a light of mischief in his expressive eyes, but with something darker lurking in the depths of them. "I confess, before I arrived I felt some anxiety to gain the approval of my father's family, for my father's sake, if not my own. But obviously I am already judged and found wanting, as I gather my father was so many years ago."

"So you intend to go to Audswyck as exactly the sort of boorish oaf they are expecting," Sir James said, his inflection making this a statement rather than a question. "I take it you mean to teach them an object lesson in the folly of predetermining the character of a man they have yet to set eyes on. And when you have tired of the game or it becomes inconvenient, and you wish to shed your rough skin and sprout fine feathers? I should think it would be deuced awkward to admit you'd been hoaxing them all along. From everything I've ever heard of him, old Audwin would never tolerate being made to look foolish. I know you don't need any of Audwin's money, but only an imbecile would whistle away his chances for a fortune for the sake of such a paltry requitement."

Adrian didn't answer him, but said, "Do you think I *could* cut my cousin Quentin out of his inheritance?"

"No, not entirely, at any rate. But you might do a sight better than just the entail if the old man does take a fancy to you, which is unlikely if you mean to make a May game of him. Do you wish to cut Quentin out?"

"Not in that respect perhaps," Adrian said obliquely. "Would you say there was any family likeness between me and Quentin?"

Stokes regarded Adrian thoughtfully for a few moments and then said, "No one would mistake you as brothers, but there is some resemblance and you have similar coloring."

"We are also much the same height and build, I think?"

"Much the same," the baronet agreed, his tone bland.

"Have you by any chance been favored with an invitation to the masquerade party to be given by, ah, Lady Emerson, I think it was?"

"I believe I may have received a card from Lady Emerson," Sir James acknowledged. His expression was stern, but he could not keep the smile from his eyes. "I collect you wish me to accept the invitation. What maggot have you in your brain now?"

Adrian's features broke into a brief grin as he rose from his chair. "I shall tell you on our way to purchase some ready-made clothes. And a domino. Black, I think. Yes, no other color would do."

Isobel hoped that she would find a few minutes alone with Quentin that evening, and her hope was rewarded. When he arrived at Leyland House to escort her and her mother to a card party, Lady Leyland discovered a tear in a seam of her gown and returned to her dressing room to change. Time alone together had once meant stolen embraces and words of love between Isobel and Quentin, but of late they were as likely to argue. Quentin did slip an arm about Isobel's waist as soon as the door closed on Lady Leyland, but before he could kiss her, Isobel deftly freed herself from his grasp.

She believed she had fallen in love with Quentin on the day they met during her first visit to Audswyck Chase with her father and new stepmother fifteen years ago. Quentin had been a handsome young stripling of fifteen who already had aspirations to fashion, a talent for all athletic pursuits, and a gift for charming females of all ages. To Isobel he was the embodiment of the handsome, brave heroes in the nursery stories she so loved.

Her dream had come true ten years later when Quentin had declared his love for her the very night of her presentation ball. There could be no objection to the match on grounds of birth or fortune being unequal, but Quentin's grandfather, on whom he depended financially to maintain his rather splendid style of living, had been heard to express both frequently and publicly his opinion that any man who married before the age of thirty was a fool. All who knew Lord Audwin knew he did not make such comments idly or suffer fools gladly. Quentin convinced Isobel that they must wait to become betrothed until he felt the time was right to approach Lord Audwin for his formal consent to the match.

To a young girl in the throes of her first love, the world was well lost for that love. Isobel would have preferred to live in a humble cottage with Quentin as her husband to a grand fortune and an indefinite wait for her happiness, but she knew that Quentin's prominence in the first circles of society, which he could not have maintained without the support of his grandfather, did matter a great deal to him, and so she resolved to be patient.

Isobel never had dreamed in those early months of elation that Quentin truly meant for them to wait until he had reached his thirtieth birthday, but the months somehow had passed into years. When Quentin had declared his love for Isobel, he had meant every word of it, but in fact, he also agreed with his grandfather's philosophy that a man ought not to marry too young. Even a fashionable marriage, which decreed that husband and wife enjoy separate lives of their own as well as the life they shared, would place certain restrictions on his behavior that he was not yet ready to concede. Five or even six years, in his mind, was not such a long wait, and it was for him the best of both worlds. While he possessed complete freedom to pursue his interests and indulge his whims and penchants, he also enjoyed the devotion of a beautiful and clever woman who would make him an ideal wife and a fitting mother for his children.

The only drawback had been that Isobel had insisted that they be formally betrothed before they became lovers, hating the need to deny both Quentin and herself the consummation of their love, but fearing that if she gave her body to him as freely as she had given her heart, she would be relinquishing the only control she had in their relationship. But once their betrothal finally had been formally approved by Lord Audwin and announced to the world, Isobel at last gave way to Quentin's impatience, abandoning virtue in the name of love.

Isobel at three-and-twenty was not the starry-eyed girl fresh from the schoolroom that she had been when she had pledged herself to Quentin, but a sophisticated young woman, neither missish nor naive. She was not a prude, nor was she entirely ignorant of what to expect the first time she made love with a man. But Quentin, his lovemaking colored by impatience and a large quantity of after-dinner brandy, had not been the gentle lover of her fantasies. Their coupling had been for her violent, painful, and abrupt. Isobel was left shaken, disappointed, and a little disgusted by the experience, emotions she had never imagined she would feel in the arms of the man she loved.

She certainly knew enough to know that Quentin had acquitted himself poorly, and she evaded him when he again made advances toward her as much out of hurt and anger that their first time together had meant so little to him that he had come to her cast away and heedless of her feelings or his own performance, as out of an unwillingness to repeat the experience.

This had a far from happy effect on their already strained relationship. Quentin was not generally as insensitive a lover as his performance with Isobel suggested, and he might have applied himself to the task of mending the misstep he had made with her—if he had realized he had made it. The truth was that his recollection of that night was hazy at best, and it was more palatable to believe that Isobel was reacting missishly than to wonder if the fault was his own. Resentful of her continued rejection of his advances, he made up his mind to delay the wedding to punish her a little. He did not seem to notice that Isobel herself seemed in no haste to set a definite date for their nuptials.

The result of their shared but uncommunicated resentment was disaffection and a constant falling-out over small things. The breaking of his promise to escort her to Lady Emerson's masquerade party might be a trifling thing to Quentin, but it mattered to Isobel. It seemed to her that of late he found the company of his friends and sporting activities preferable to being with her, and she was increasingly inclined to nurture feelings of neglect and ill-use that were not usually any part of her true nature.

Quentin, piqued, gave vent to an exaggerated sigh when Isobel eluded his embrace. "Tell me in what unfathomable fashion I have offended you this time, Isobel," he said, a bored and weary note in his voice. "Then I may beg your pardon and you can spare me your sulks for the remainder of the evening."

His words were consciously provoking, and Isobel's eyes momentarily flashed in anger. But she would not give him the satisfaction of seeing that he could so easily control her response. "It is not so very unfathomable," she said in a voice of deliberate coolness.

"I simply wish that when you pledge yourself to an engagement with me, you would have the courtesy to honor it."

"I thought I had," he said sardonically, "though it would seem there are a great many terms and conditions of which I was unaware at the time. Or is it that these are made up as we go along?"

She understood that what he referred to was their betrothal, not the masquerade party on Friday. It was not the first time he had done so in a similar manner. "You know that I mean Lady Emerson's party at Vauxhall," she said, refusing to be deflected. "We discussed it on more than one occasion, so you cannot have forgotten it."

"Well, I did," he insisted. "For God's sake, Bel, we aren't going to quarrel over some stupid masquerade party, are we? If you are determined to argue tonight, we can surely find a less paltry topic."

"It is not paltry to me," she said frigidly. "I begin to think I shall have to cut off my hair, begin wearing breeches, and attend cockfights to successfully compete for your company."

"Oh, come now, Bel," he said with a smile she read as condescending. "That is complete nonsense. We are together more nights than not. I am here right now, aren't I? And we shall be the whole evening together at the Abermores'."

"We shall be in the same house together," Isobel corrected with a slightly twisted smile. "In two or three rooms filled with people, and we shall probably not exchange more than a dozen words in passing."

"I think you exaggerate, my love," he said, his tone not fitting the endearment.

"I want you to come with me to Vauxhall on Friday, Quentin."

"Do you know," he said as if greatly puzzled, "I

thought we had discussed this to a satisfactory conclusion this afternoon?"

"To your satisfaction," she said, more acrimoniously than she intended as her temper finally began to slip from her rigid control. "There is no need for you to drive with Roger to his hunting box tomorrow. You know you could easily persuade Freddy Haverwell to take his curricle as well on Saturday, or you could even rent one if need be. It makes me wonder what the real reason is that you must leave tomorrow instead of Saturday," she added, though she had not meant to. Giving voice to her darker suspicions was dangerous ground she was frightened to tread.

Quentin was leaning negligently against a high-backed wing chair. He stirred uneasily and straightened. Though there were times, through pique, that he would not have been averse to Isobel knowing that there were other women who welcomed him into their arms and beds, he recognized, if unconsciously, that their relationship was at a crossroads and might as likely lead to estrangement as it might to marriage.

He walked over to her and took her hands in his, a faint, placating smile on his face. His tone of voice, when he spoke, was no longer sardonic. "Nothing more than an extra day's sport," he assured her, smiling a little to himself for the double entendre. He took her into a light embrace, and this time she did not resist him, though her eyes never wavered from his. "It is Roger who is keen on going tomorrow and he insists that I go with him, and I said that I would. I did forget Lady Emerson's wretched party. I promise I shall make it up to you, Bel, as soon as I return to town."

It was his intention to officially end their quarrel by a kiss to seal this promise, but Isobel spoke and forestalled him. "You would rather offend me than Roger Cavelle?"

"Of course not," he said, forcing himself to smile ingratiatingly. "But it is not as if you need be deprived of your pleasure without me. You said yourself that you shall be with Georgie and Sir John Avery, and shan't even miss me. You know all the world is invited, and it is likely we should not spend any more time together there than we shall tonight."

Isobel's growing anger was cold rather than hot, and it was only as a point of pride that it still mattered to her that he honored his promise to her. She wanted to know that just this once he would acquiesce to her wishes rather than expect her to understand his. "I want you to come with me to Vauxhall on Friday, Quentin," she repeated, neither anger nor command in her voice. "I need to know that you will do this for me."

He suppressed another sigh. His plans were already made and he had no intention of changing them, but he said to appease her, "I expect to see Roger later tonight, and I'll speak with him. If his plans for us to leave tomorrow afternoon are not already too advanced, I'll make my excuses."

"Now, that is a handsome promise," Isobel said tartly.

But Quentin was done with arguing, and he only laughed and at last succeeded in bestowing on her a light, quick kiss. "Tell me you will stroll with me along the lovers' paths on Friday, my beautiful Bel, and I shall gladly send Roger to the devil," he said in a rallying tone and kissed her again.

Isobel responded to him but without eagerness. She wondered if his words were idle or if he expected a concession from her for his acquiescence. "Moonlight can be very romantic," she said, her promise no more definite than his. She too recognized that further discussion was pointless. At the beginning of their relationship Isobel would have taken his words to mean that he would do all that he could to change his plans to please her; experience had taught her that her simple faith was misplaced. Friday night would tell its own tale.

When Lady Leyland joined them several minutes later, Quentin and Isobel were seated on the sofa, a decorous distance between them, no hint in their demeanor that any argument had taken place. At the Abermores' later that evening, a number of people remarked on what a charming couple they made and how devoted they seemed to each other. After years of deceiving the world about her true feelings for Quentin, Isobel found it quite as easy to hide her annoyance with him as she had once concealed her love.

On Friday evening, Isobel donned the white silk gown with the silver spiderweb gauze overdress in preparation for Lady Emerson's party at Vauxhall. Carlton was right that her choice of gown was inappropriate for the time of year; it would have better saved for some masquerade party to be given in late spring. But there was no denying that it was vastly becoming. The dress was very sheer, and naturally clinging to every contour and curve of her body. The bodice was cut as low as fashion and decency permitted. It was a rather fast gown for an unmarried woman to wear, even one who was formally betrothed. Its saving grace, of course, was that it was a costume. There were fairy wings of silver-shot gauze stretched over wire that were to be attached to the back of the gown, a matching headdress, a fairy wand, and a silver half mask with a short veil.

The gown very much suited Isobel's delicate coloring, and as she twirled in front of the cheval glass in her bedchamber, she quite enjoyed the way the gossamer material caressed her breasts, her hips, and her long, shapely legs with every movement. But there was no doubt that she would have to cover it with her satin domino if she was not to spend the night shivering. The most sensible thing to do would be to wear some other dress, but Isobel could not bring herself to change. The dress made her feel sensual and a little excited, and it gave her the self-confidence of knowing she looked her best. In the end she compromised. She would leave behind wings, headdress, and wand and cover the gown with the midnight blue satin domino, but she would leave it untied and open so that tantalizing glimpses of her exquisite dress could be seen.

She had not spoken to or heard from Quentin since he had escorted her and her mother home from Abermore House. This neither surprised nor concerned Isobel. It did not necessarily mean that he had left town with Roger Cavelle. Men, she had observed on more than one occasion, could be quite childish at times, and Quentin was not above wishing to punish her a little for attempting to bend his will to hers.

Isobel was not even upset when Quentin had not appeared by the time that Georgiana Wolesley's carriage arrived to take her to Vauxhall. Very likely Quentin would appear at some point in the evening after he had decided that she had had sufficient time to believe that he had left for Leicestershire after all. Mrs. Wolesley was surprised to hear Isobel make excuses for Quentin's absence; Sir Jonathan Avery was delighted.

Once at Vauxhall, she refused to give her thoughts any direction beyond enjoyment of the entertainments at hand. Lady Emerson's daring party seemed to be attended by the better part of the Upper Ten Thousand and was everything she had promised it would be. Musical entertainment was provided for the whole of the evening, tents were set up for impromptu card rooms, dancing was available in the main pavilion for those who wished it, and champagne punch and light refreshments were served to guests in private boxes throughout the night. At midnight there were to be fireworks and a lavish supper to follow.

Though a good many of the people present were known to Isobel, the masks, costumes, and dominoes created an air of anonymity that made outrageous flirtation possible. Isobel hugely enjoyed herself, dancing a good part of the night away, playing piquet with Sir Jonathan in one of the tents, flirting with him almost to the point of indiscretion and drinking a bit more of the champagne punch than she knew was prudent. It may have been the punch, it may have been the risqué feeling wearing her daring gown gave her, it may have been the caressing autumn breezes, but the slight feelings of excitement that Isobel had felt in her bedchamber when preening before the mirror intensified into something almost physical. If Quentin did come to the party, as she now optimistically had all but convinced herself he would, she thought that she might respond quite differently than she had of late if he tried to make love to her.

It was not until nearly midnight, when the guests began to make their way to the various vantage points to view the fireworks, that Isobel's confidence that Quentin would come began to wane. She felt at first a sort of hollowness that she recognized as hurt and disappointment, but this quickly turned to anger at the realization that he had never meant to come but had only seemed to capitulate to her wishes to end their argument. This emotion in turn faded into a feeling of recklessness stronger than any such feeling she had ever had before.

Isobel regarded Sir Jonathan, who was walking slightly ahead of her with Georgiana and her escort, Mr. Rattaby. The wild thought came to her that if she gave Sir Jonathan sufficient encouragement, he could easily be persuaded to forget that she was betrothed to someone else and make love to her, perhaps here and now, tonight. The idea both appalled her and sent a shiver of excited anticipation through her. Sir Jonathan was an acknowledged rake, with a string of *affaires* with some of the most beautiful women of the *ton* to his credit; she was certain he would not use her as unfeelingly as Quentin had done. She savored her mental infidelity for a few minutes, but in her heart she acknowledged that she felt no real desire for Sir Jonathan as a person; he would be to her only a means of revenge against the man who was supposed to love her best in the world, but who behaved as if her feelings were of no consequence to him at all. Isobel felt oddly deflated at these reflections. She suddenly lost all desire to see the pyrotechnics and wished she might just leave at once.

Mrs. Wolesley's party, which consisted of about a half dozen of her dearest friends, gathered together on a small rise just beyond the main pavilion. Everyone was at least mildly foxed and laughing and talking with considerable animation. Only Isobel remained a little apart from them. Someone brushed lightly against her, but she paid no heed other than to move a bit closer to the others. Again she felt a presence very close to her, and she glanced behind her to observe a man in a black domino, his eyes smiling into hers through the slits in his half mask. Light from one of the hanging lanterns strung along the lane beside them caught the golden highlights in his brown hair.

Isobel gave a silent sigh of relief and linked her arm in his. "Quentin, you are a horrid, horrid man," she scolded. "You waited until you knew I would be certain you did not mean to come after all."

He gave her an indolent smile, but otherwise offered neither defense nor comment. Isobel's wide-ranging moods of the evening shifted once again, and her brief unhappiness was replaced by a sudden swelling of elation and pleasure. It didn't matter at all to her at the moment that he had arrived so late. It was enough that he had acceded to her wishes and put off Roger Cavelle in her favor.

She felt a rush of triumph that seemed to act as a boost to the champagne punch she had drunk and made her feel more light-headed and reckless than even before. She decided to keep her half promise to walk with him along the moonlit paths after all.

"Do you mind if we stroll for a bit instead of watching the fireworks?" she asked, brushing her lips lightly against his ear in a provocative manner as she spoke. She turned toward the lane and the paths leading deeper into the gardens, assuming his answer before he could make it. He did not even attempt to do so, but she thought nothing of this. The fireworks had begun, and the booming of these combined with the cries of the people watching them would have made any attempt at conversation difficult.

It was much darker under the canopy of trees, not all of which had yet lost their leaves. Cut into the shrubbery here and there were small grottos and arbors with inviting stone or iron benches or seats offering lovers at least some degree of privacy. They did not stroll, as Isobel had suggested, but instead she led the way into the undergrowth with purpose. She did not pause until she happened upon a more secluded area, and then she drew him into it with her. She had not consciously made a decision that tonight she and Quentin would be lovers again, but the odd humors that had beset her all evening, combined with her delight that he had chosen to please her, caused her to persuade herself that perhaps this time would be different from the last. Maybe it had been her fault too in some part. Maybe she had been too tense, too expecting.

She sat on the wrought iron seat and nearly pulled him into her arms as she sought his lips. For a moment he seemed almost to draw back as if with surprise, and then he responded to her bold advances enthusiastically. The kiss began almost chastely and gradually and deliciously deepened. His kiss was gentler than usual, yet somehow more intense and erotic.

Isobel could not have said what subconscious factor was the cause of it, but she had the sudden alarming conviction that this man, for all his similarity in height, build, and coloring to Quentin was not Quentin at all. She drew away from him abruptly. "Who are you?" she demanded in a furious whisper.

He bent his head toward her and softly kissed the rise of her cheekbone before saying in a husky whisper, "Not Quentin."

He kissed her again before she could react to this admission. She knew she should be terrified that she had put herself in the power of a stranger, that she could find herself ravished, but she did not draw away from him in fear as she knew she should.

His tongue was gently insinuated between her teeth, teasing and tantalizing; his hand beneath her domino traced the delicious curve of her hip. A wonderful throbbing in her thighs followed his touch. Her heart was beating furiously, but still she neither called out nor attempted to escape him. Instead she responded to his lips, his touch, knowing that what she was doing was madness but feeling more aroused than she ever had been before. She knew her inhibitions were being lulled by a combination of champagne and the anonymity of the encounter. Incredibly, she knew she wanted to make love with this man even more than she had when she had thought him to be Quentin. After her first experience she had wondered if sex was designed to be a pleasure for men and an endurance for women after all, but now she knew this wasn't so.

Her mind recoiled at such wantonness even as her body ached with desire. She had to bring an end to this and quickly, before passion overcame the last shards of her sense. With a long, soft moan of reluctance she pulled away from him. "Please," she said, surprised by the thick, hoarse sound of her voice. "I can't do this."

She had been a little frightened that he would not heed her—even if she screamed, she might not be heard over the noise of the fireworks and the crowd of people—but he rose from the seat with alacrity, perhaps not trusting himself either. "I know," he said. His voice too had an odd raspy quality and inflection. "I'm sorry." He held out his hand to her, and she took it and permitted him to lead her back to the rise in the clearing.

It seemed to Isobel a considerable time since they had gone into the moonlit wood, but it could not have been more than a quarter hour, for the fireworks continued and no one had seemed to even notice that she had been gone. He released her and stood a little behind her when they reached the others. She hoped that he would leave her before the unmasking after the fireworks. She had a faint curiosity to know who he was, but the last thing she wanted was for him to know her identity if he had not guessed it already.

There was a grand finale of explosions, creating a brief, artificial daylight. She dared a glance behind her and felt a curious mixture of relief and disappointment to find that he was gone. She turned back to see Georgiana staring at her curiously.

"Who are you looking for, Bel?" she asked. "Did I see Quentin here with you just now?"

Unaccountably Isobel felt her color rise as hotly as if she had been discovered in the arms of her unknown lover. After the brightness of the finale it seemed much darker with only the light of the moon and the lanterns, and Isobel was grateful for it. "No," she said as evenly as she could. "I suppose Quentin must have gone to Leicestershire with Roger Cavelle after all."

Georgiana's pretty features furrowed in puzzlement. "But there was a man behind you just a moment ago. I thought—"

Isobel interrupted her quickly. "So did I, for a moment. But I was mistaken, he was not Quentin," she said, aware of the irony of the truth within her lie. "I have no idea who he was." She turned and asked Sir Jonathan if he would fetch her another glass of champagne punch. She no longer had any fear of intoxication. She was as sober now as if she had drunk only water all evening, and she hoped the punch would steady her pulse, which seemed to her to be racing nearly as much now as when the stranger in the half mask had first kissed her.

Chapter 3

Isobel found it impossible to put the night at Vauxhall completely from her thoughts, nor at first did she try. She relived her encounter with the man in the black domino many times over, sometimes mortified at her behavior and at others allowing a remembered excitement to creep over her.

For a day or two she could afford the indulgence, but duplicity did not come easily to her, and she feared if she did not banish the memory, she would risk betraying herself to Quentin when they met at Audswyck Chase. She did not feel as guilty for her brief infidelity as she should, but supposed she would when she saw Quentin again.

Isobel, in company with her stepmother, brother, and her stepmother's ward, set off for Audswyck Chase on Monday morning, traveling by easy stages and spending the night at an inn so that they would arrive in good time on the following day. Lord Audwin was notorious for keeping country hours and had been known to give guests a severe dressing-down rather than dinner if they arrived too late. It was mid-afternoon when they reached the village of Ryde Audswyck, and though they had only a few more miles to Audswyck Chase, they were forced to stop at the local inn to repair a wheel that had been damaged when their carriage had been jolted into a deep rut a mile or so before the village.

The inn was not a posting inn, though the stage-coach stopped there to take on and let off passengers, but it was respectable, and even though it did not boast a private parlor, the common room was quiet and nearly empty at that time of day. They took a table in a corner near the hearth, and Lady Leyland sent Simon to seek out refreshment for them.

Their quiet was ended a half hour later by the arrival of the afternoon stage. Moments after the crammed, ungainly vehicle lurched into the courtyard, the passengers came pouring into the common room, raucously demanding immediate service so that they could enjoy a bit of refreshment before the stage was again on its way. They were an odd-sorted group: a farmer, his wife and daughter, a clergyman and his spouse, a rather prunish-looking woman, and another woman whose extreme obesity must have made for rather cramped quarters inside the stage. There were also three young men whose rather tousled appearance proclaimed that they had ridden outside on the roof of the carriage. Two of these young men were obviously friends and traveling companions; the third came into the common room last and alone. He stood just inside the doorway and surveyed the room rather than rushing to the tap to add his demands to those of the others.

Isobel noticed him for no particular reason, and as he came into the room it seemed to her that he was in some way familiar to her, though she was certain she did not know him. He was dressed in an ill-fitting dark brown coat and fawn-colored breeches that looked a size too large. His neckcloth was of a hideous spotted pattern and was tied in a careless knot at his throat. He carried a carpetbag that looked considerably the worse for the wear.

There was something plainly alert and intelligent about him that surprised Isobel, for she had taken him at first sight to be a poor, downtrodden clerk or a laborer dressed in his best for travel, for not even the servants in houses like Audswyck Chase or Leyland Priory were so poorly outfitted. She wondered that a clever man might not have bettered himself, and it occurred to her then that he might be dishonest, a Captain Sharp preying on the lower orders. It was at this point that she realized that his survey had reached their table and his eyes were now on her, returning stare for stare. Isobel blushed and quickly looked away.

But to her surprise and discomfort he approached them. At the table he bowed and addressed Lady Leyland. "Begging your pardon, ma'am," he said, his accent plainly foreign. "Could you point me the way to the big house about here? 'Odd-something' it's called."

Lady Leyland was obviously a little taken back by his approach, but her breeding was impeccable. In a cool but not unfriendly nor condescending voice, she said, "If you mean Audswyck Chase, you must continue on the main road for another five or six miles until you come to a turnoff by a stand of oaks. A mile or so beyond that is the gatehouse, and it is about two miles farther before you reach the house itself."

The man's expression became rueful. "A bit of a walk, then," he said with a sigh. "Well, I've walked pigs to market over longer roads than that, though not in flimsy shoes fit only for a parlor." He raised one foot as if for their inspection. On it was a man's dress shoe of dubious quality. "I didn't think my boots would be fittin' for the occasion."

Simon and Isobel exchanged glances, his dancing eyes clearly inviting her to laugh with him at this absurd stranger. Isobel quickly looked away and bit her lip to keep a betraying smile at bay. Lady Leyland said politely, "Perhaps you could find stouter shoes in the village, or the landlord may have some sort of conveyance for hire to take you there."

Distance had crept into her voice, but the young man seemed impervious to the impending snub. He shook his head sadly and sighed. "Didn't think ahead. Reckon I'll pay for it now. I've a letter from home to get me some money from a banker in the city, but I didn't think I'd be needin' much visitin' my grandpa. If anything ever be needin' on the farm at home, a chicken or some eggs do well enough in a trade."

Simon, who could be irrepressible at times, said, "Well, then, there you are. If you've got a chicken or some eggs in that carpetbag of yours, you can trade them for a pair of boots or a ride in the gig. You didn't happen to bring along one of those pigs you spoke of, did you? You could rent the landlord's gig for a fortnight in trade for that."

Kitty gave vent to a choked giggle, but the man smiled, either unaware that he was being made fun of or not minding it. "Reckon I wish I did. Grandpa might lend me one of his for a trade, though I don't think I should promise it without asking him first."

Isobel had watched the stranger throughout this exchange and could not quite shake the feeling that he was in some way familiar to her. His accent, which was definitely not English, also intrigued her. This man was a colonial, she decided, possibly American, though his inflections were quite unlike the well-bred and cultured accents of the two or three Americans she had met before. She supposed he was the grandson of one of Lord Audwin's tenant farmers or laborers, the offspring of a son who had journeyed to the New World to seek his fortune or been transported there for some crime.

Once or twice his gray-green eyes flicked toward her, and she saw there something that struck her as a teasing gleam. It reminded her of the way Quentin would look at her sometimes when he was roasting her, and the man's smile, which seemed to turn up on a corner of his mouth ever so slightly higher than the other, put her in mind of Carlton.

Such thoughts should have been absurd, but Isobel was struck by a sudden inspiration. All these things— his familiarness, his American accent, his comments about visiting his grandfather—suddenly came together in her mind and were made obvious. By an odd quirk of fate, a rut in the road, a broken wheel, the arrival of the stage, they had come face to face with Mr. Adrian Renville.

She regarded him with renewed interest and also with dismay. She had made disparaging suppositions about him, as had Quentin and Carlton, but she realized now that she had not really expected him to be anything other than what he was by birth: the grandson of an earl. Yet he was as dreadfully rustic and colonial in his speech, dress, and manner as any of the worst of their predictions about him.

Francis Renville had fled to America before she was born, but she could not imagine that the eldest son of a man like the Earl of Audwin could have been anything other than educated and well bred. How could it be that his son was neither? She knew from books she had read and reports of visitors to North America that it could be a wild, savage place, most of it scarcely charted; a place where people carved out homesteads and survived rather than lived. Breeding and education would have little value in such a place, and Francis Renville might have decided not to burden his children with useless refinements.

She was not quite sure what to do with her knowledge. If she said nothing, it would be awkward for them all when they met him again at Audswyck Chase. But if this proved to be mere fancy on her part, the embarrassment would be even worse. She glanced at her stepmother and her brother and saw no light of recognition in their countenances. But she did see that her stepmother's expression was becoming increasingly set and knew she was about to deliver a setdown to the presumptuous stranger, and Simon, as was his way, might say something outrageous at any moment.

She knew what she had to do and swallowed the small fear that she would make a complete cake of herself if she was mistaken after all. She held out her hand to him and said, "Mr. Adrian Renville? I am Isobel Leyland. This is my stepmother, your aunt, Lady Leyland, this is Miss West, her ward, and this is your cousin Simon."

Lady Leyland was far too well bred to gape, but her eyes on her stepdaughter were round with astonishment. Simon and Kitty both regarded Isobel in open-mouthed wonder. The man also registered a momentary incredulity. In the space of that moment Isobel felt the first flush of mortification. She had been wrong. But then a slow smile spread over his features, and the light in his eyes that had first intrigued her was intensified.

He took Isobel's proffered hand, but instead of bowing over it in the usual manner, he pressed it in a firm grip and shook it vigorously. "Well, if this don't beat all. A pleasure it is, ma'am. You too, Aunt Leyland," he added, dropping Isobel's hand and seizing Lady Leyland's. Simon and Kitty were separated from him by the width of the table, and he had to curtail his greetings to them to smiles and vigorous nods of his head. "I was thinking this was a right happenstance, but given the neighborhood, I should've reckoned it." Without waiting to be asked, he pulled out the chair next to Isobel and sat down. He called loudly to the landlord and demanded that he bring his best ale for them all.

"I thank you, no. We must be leaving in a few minutes," said Caroline Leyland in a faint voice. "Are you indeed Mr. Adrian Renville?"

Her tone implied that there must be some mistake, but once again Adrian appeared either not to mind or to notice. "That I am, and it looks like my problem is solved. I can hitch a ride with you to my grandad's, if you be goin' there."

"Oh, we be goin' there," Simon said, his words mocking but his tone one of amused amiability. "Reckon Grandad's going to be even more surprised than we are at such a, ah, happenstance."

"He shall probably have one of his turns," Kitty said with more truth than tact.

Lady Leyland glared them both into silence and then turned with a tentative smile toward Adrian. "Of course you may ride with us to Audswyck."

"We are going there, you know," Isobel said, "for the express purpose of meeting you. But we thought you would be there before us."

"I was a mite delayed," he admitted. "Grandpa wanted to send his own coach for me, but I wanted to see a bit of the country and not from the inside of a closed box."

"Then we have stolen a march on the others," Isobel said, adding with private emphasis, "They shall certainly be surprised."

"But you knew me right off," he said with wonder. "Must have more a look of the family than I know."

Being so invited to study him further, Isobel did not hesitate to do so. Now that it was acknowledged, she could see even more clearly that he had the coloring common to many of the Renvilles, though Quentin, Carlton, and Simon were all a bit fairer than this man. There were similarities in facial structure as well, though Adrian's nose was perhaps a bit straighter and his cheekbones higher. There was no doubt he was of

Renville blood, but was it really so marked that she felt she had seen him so clearly before? She tried to remember the portrait of Francis Renville in the long gallery at Audswyck. Perhaps he was very like his father, and that was why she felt such a strong sense of familiarity.

"Yes, you are rather like Francis," Lady Leyland said, giving a voice to her stepdaughter's thoughts. "But not so much that I should have remarked on it at once." She cast her stepdaughter a quizzical glance.

"Bel probably recognized Cousin Adrian because he looks exactly as she expected him to," Simon suggested, his dark gray eyes wide and innocent.

"Is that so?" Adrian said with a show of surprised gratification.

"Oh, yes," interpolated Kitty, always brave when following Simon's lead. "Bel and Quentin were discussing what you would be like only the other day, and you are exactly as they expected you to be."

Isobel felt her cheeks grow a little warm and was grateful that the landlord came up to them at that moment to inform them that their carriage had been repaired and was awaiting them in the courtyard.

Simon's hack was also saddled and being held by an ostler. Simon disliked closed carriages and had ridden for much of the journey. He started toward the horse and then turned on impulse and said to Adrian, "Perhaps you'd prefer to ride the distance, cousin? Bred on a farm, you've probably not done much traveling in one of these wretched closed chaises. Plays the devil with a fellow's stomach if he's not used to it."

"Is that so?" Adrian said, his eyes wide and the expression in them dubious as he looked at the waiting chaise.

"You do ride, cousin?" Simon said as if struck by the realization that he might have made a false assumption.

"Oh, aye," said Adrian. "We've horses enough on the farm. I've thrown a leg over one or two in my time."

"Then by all means let me offer you my horse," Simon said.

Adrian did not appear much pleased at this prospect, but he took the reins from Simon. "I've ridden bareback much of the time on the farm," he said as he put his foot in the stirrup.

Lady Leyland and Kitty had been handed into the carriage, but Isobel hung back, observing this exchange. She saw that Adrian had put the wrong foot in the stirrup, which would have put him facing the rear of the horse. Simon, standing behind Adrian, was biting his lower lip to keep from laughing, and Isobel could hardly blame him. Much store was set by horsemanship by both the Renvilles and the Leylands, and Adrian Renville would suffer yet further ridicule from his cousins and grandfather for his lack of this skill.

"No, the other foot," Simon said when he could trust his voice not to quaver. "Then lift yourself over the saddle."

But as Simon spoke he poked the horse's hind quarters surreptitiously with the end of his crop, causing it to sidle and Adrian, one foot in the stirrup, to hop after it. The ostler grabbed the reins just under the bit and steadied the horse once again, but as Adrian again made the attempt to lift himself from the ground, Simon again foiled his efforts.

Adrian did present a ridiculous picture, but Isobel's amusement turned to sympathy for him. As Adrian was about to make the effort to mount yet again, Isobel could see that Simon had not yet tired of his game and was about to repeat his prank. She intended to call out to her brother to distract him from his purpose, but the words died on her lips. Adrian, with a determined grasp on both pommel and rein, moved backward and upward in one smooth, swift motion, finally catapulting himself into the saddle. Simon, standing closely behind Adrian, was taken unaware and was pushed backward by Adrian's efforts. Simon's boots slid out from under him on cobbles made slick with mud from an earlier rain. At the moment that Adrian lowered himself into the saddle, Simon was tossed into an ignominious heap at his feet.

As unlikely as it seemed, Isobel could not be certain that Simon's fall was purely accident, though the expression of horrified dismay in Adrian's eyes suggested that there had been no intent on his part. But she recalled her first impression of Adrian when he had entered the inn, the shrewdness she had observed in him that had made her suspect him of being a Captain Sharp. It was easy to dismiss him as a bumptious oaf, but because others thought a man a fool did not make him one. Rather, it disarmed those who thought it.

Uttering a few muted curses, Simon picked himself up from the cobbles. He waved aside Adrian's stumbling apology, and, brushing the mud off his breeches as best he could, he followed Isobel into the carriage.

"What a complete ass," he said as the carriage started off.

"That will do, Simon," his mother admonished. "He is your cousin and your grandfather's heir, which will make him head of the family one day. I know you think his speech and manners ridiculous, but you must regard them as merely different. He has clearly lacked your advantages in life, in spite of being the son of a viscount and the grandson of an earl. Poor Francis hoped to make his fortune in America, I have been told, but it is obvious he did not prosper, and it is very wrong of us to judge his son from our vantage point. You know better than to ridicule those who have been less fortunate than you."

"Less fortunate!" exclaimed Simon incredulously.

"He'll be the earl of Audwin one day and inherit Aud-swyck Chase and the rest of the entail. Imagine how Quentin shall feel, giving place to this oaf who can't even get himself into a saddle without making a mull of it." For all his bookishness, Simon judged a man by his ability to sit a horse in good form as much as by his intellect. "God knows if he'll manage to stay in the saddle until we reach Audswyck."

But Simon's opinion of his newly met cousin might have changed considerably if he could have observed Adrian now that they were on their way to Audswyck. Adrian had been on the back of a horse since he had been old enough to sit upright and hold onto the reins. He was a natural rider, his seat so perfect that man and horse appeared to move as one.

Adrian did not need to disguise his horsemanship. His absurd display in the courtyard had earned him the contempt of the servants as well as that of Simon, and he was completely ignored as he trailed behind the carriage. He had taken his role as a bumptious colonial a bit further than he had intended, once again allowing himself to be goaded. He did not regret this for its own sake; it was no more than they deserved. But he found he disliked playing the fool in front of Isobel. It was masculine pride, he supposed. What did it matter that she thought him a fool when he pos-sessed a knowledge of her that was a thousand times more shaming than his own ridiculous behavior?

He put aside these thoughts and put his observant powers to good use as soon as they had passed the gates of Audswyck. They traveled along the drive, passing elegant stands of trees, and finally emerged into a wide and deep park. As they came over the top of a rise before descending into the valley in which the house was situated, the home farm and many scattered tenant farms came into view, covering hundreds of acres to the end of the horizon. A narrow tributary river threaded the land like a carelessly tossed ribbon.

He could not help comparing Audswyck to Black Oaks, the estate his father had built in Bucks County. This was a vast tract of land, as were most of the sprawling estates of the landed gentry of Pennsylvania. It boasted forests that stretched for miles, the park surrounding the house might have encompassed a minor city, the acres of farmland numbered in the many thousands, and the house, built not in a valley but on a rise, overlooked the magnificent Delaware River.

Gradually the house came into view. It was a sprawling structure in the shape of a truncated H set in extensive gardens. It was principally Jacobean but later influences were also present. It was not at all like the neat symmetrical mansion in which he had been raised, but Adrian felt something stir inside him at the sight of it. The mellowed old brick glowed and mullioned windows sparkled like jewels in the afternoon sun and gave the house a beauty it might not have possessed on an overcast day. But whether Adrian was struck by the beauty of the house or if it was something deeper in his blood that sent a thrill through his veins, a covetous pride he had not expected to feel came upon him.

The coachman eased his team to a walk and then stopped on the broad gravel sweep in front of the house. The wide double doors swung open soundlessly, and footmen sprang from the house as if poised for their arrival.

Adrian waited until his audience had descended from the carriage before dismounting. He did so with a clumsiness to equal his mounting, catching his foot in the stirrup and grasping for mane to keep from being wrenched off his feet. He managed to right himself and smiled wanly in response to the disdain in Simon's expression.

"Enjoy your ride, cousin?" Simon asked sardonically.

"Well enough," Adrian said as if oblivious to Simon's inflection. "A sweet goer."

The horse was a job horse whose gait, Simon well knew, was anything but smooth. He turned away in disgust to follow his mother and Kitty into the house. The footmen had carried their baggage into the house, and the chaise clattered on its way to the stables. Adrian was left standing on the gravel alone.

Isobel had not welcomed his coming and her opinion of him was scarcely higher than her brother's, but she could not help feeling some compassion for him. It would be a shabby thing, she thought, to have him trail into the house behind them like a forgotten servant. She paused at the entrance of the house and turned to wait for him. But a moment later, as her attention was diverted by the sound of another carriage approaching the house at a spanking pace, she had completely forgotten him.

Simon, hearing it also, emerged from the doorway behind her. "It must be Quentin," he said, admiration plain in his tone. "Who else would spring 'em along the drive?"

This assumption proved correct a few moments later when a smart racing curricle became visible, bursting upon the drive in its full glory. It was an exquisite vehicle. Even at a distance its black sides glowed with a high polish, the wheels and trim, picked out in gleaming yellow, flashed like gold in the afternoon sunlight. It was pulled by a team of four high-stepping, perfectly matched bays, which were quite plainly not job horses. They swept along the drive much faster than was necessary or safe, but their beautiful, fluid motion demanded praise, not criticism.

Adrian would not have required Simon's comment to guess the identity of the driver. As the curricle came nearer the house, it was obvious that it was being driven by a first-rate whip, whose attire, as well as his skill, proclaimed him a top of the trees Corinthian.

Carlton Renville came out of the house. His expression betrayed neither admiration nor envy. "Ah, the nonesuch approaches," he said, his voice level.

A moment later Quentin drew up his sweating horses in front of the house in a spray of gravel. Once again servants rushed from the house. One footman ran to the leaders' heads, another began at once to unload the baggage strapped to the rear of the vehicle. There was an obvious extra degree of deference in their manners, as if dealing with the master of the house or the heir. Quentin carelessly tossed the reins to yet another footman and leaped to the ground with fine dash.

Simon trotted down the stairs to greet him first. "I've never seen these beasts before, Quen," he said, going to the nearside leader and running his hand down the horse's muscular neck and shoulder. "They must be new. Where the devil did you find such beauties? You must have had them sent ahead for the last change, for they never carried you so far looking so fresh."

"They are Lord Rooke's breakdowns," Carlton said, descending to the drive. "Foolish me for supposing I had a chance to purchase them once you had wind of the sale, dear brother."

"Well, I could hardly let such magnificent creatures be wasted on a mere whipster, now could I?" Quentin replied, his manner quizzing.

Carlton stroked the near wheeler's velvet nose and laughed good-naturedly, but Adrian, attending to their exchange, saw that there was a steeliness in the younger man's eyes. Carlton said in the same tone he had used before, "You are wise, Quentin, to stock your stable with the best cattle now. You may not have the luxury soon if the old man decides the bounty is to be shared."

These words made no particular sense to Adrian, but it was plain that Quentin and Simon understood him. Something unpleasant flashed in Quentin's eyes, and Simon looked dismayed. As if it were a part of this response, Simon turned to look at Adrian, who stood at the base of the steps.

Isobel followed the direction of Simon's regard and felt another stab of pity for Adrian. Simon's caustic utterances were mere pinpricks compared to the rapier cuts likely to be made by the sharper skills of both Quentin and Carlton. Whatever native cleverness their American cousin might possess, it was not likely that he would be able to match steel for their steel. She could scarcely protect Adrian from this, and was not even certain that she wished to, but she could at least spare him one small degree of humiliation by making him known at once to Quentin and Carlton.

She descended to the drive again, calling a greeting to the brothers and then adding, "The most remarkable thing occurred when we stopped at the Duck and Drake to repair a wheel. We met up with Mr. Adrian Renville quite by accident. Quentin, Carlton, this is your cousin from the United States, Mr. Renville." As she finished speaking, she moved to stand beside Adrian.

Adrian took a step toward Quentin and Carlton, hand outstretched, and was made to look foolish when neither man moved to greet him. Quentin's expression was plainly incredulous, proving to Isobel that he had not expected his cousin to match his dire predictions any more than she had. Carlton, with his Whitehall training, did not give his thoughts away but looked merely blank.

It was he who recovered his manners and stepped forward to take Adrian's hand. "Well, cousin," he said with a false-sounding hardiness, "you are come a long way to be made known to us. I trust your journey was not taxing."

"No more than a gale or two and a bit of cannon fire," Adrian responded, clasping Carlton's hand with both of his and pumping it even more vigorously than he had Isobel's. "Likely I'll have more to tax me ahead, that being the way of most things."

Carlton managed to free his hand, and he took a hasty step backward as if he expected Adrian to clutch at him again. Quentin ignored Adrian's hand, which was now extended toward him, and, taking up his quizzing glass, surveyed him through it. A faint shudder was seen to pass through Quentin, and he let the glass fall the length of its ribband. "So here you are, cousin," he said in a bored drawl and then brushed past Adrian and mounted the steps to enter the house.

Isobel felt her cheeks grow warm, embarrassed for Quentin's rudeness and Adrian's humiliation. Carlton, after a moment's pause, followed Quentin into the house. Simon looked from Isobel to Adrian and felt uncomfortable. He could see that his sister was distressed by the little scene that had just played out, and though he was not inclined to be critical of his cousin Quentin, he realized that the older man had behaved in a manner unworthy of one who was renowned for his usual address. His mother's rebuke was also recalled, and he acknowledged that he had behaved no better. He walked over to them and said, in a tone that was both kind and a little shamefaced, "Grandfather must know by now that you have arrived, Cousin Adrian, and wonder why you have not come in to be made known to him. He may seem a bit standoffish, but you mustn't mind. He is that way with most everyone, even Quentin at times. It is just his way."

It was not to be expected that Lord Audwin, who suffered from gout and had not the mobility he had once possessed, would be in the hall to greet them. Mr. Beal, Lord Audwin's butler, stood as proxy for him. He bowed to precisely the correct depth for greeting the heir to an earldom for the first time, and when he straightened he showed that he had better command of his features and his manners than his betters. He did not betray by the smallest flick of an eye or any nuance of tone that he found in Adrian anything out of the ordinary. "May I say, sir, on behalf of the staff and myself," he intoned correctly, "that we are most pleased to welcome you to Audswyck Chase. His lordship had expected you to arrive yesterday and has been most anxious. I am instructed to bring you at once to the green saloon, where his lordship will join you as soon as I have apprised him of your arrival."

"He must be deaf if he don't know of it by now, Beal," Simon said. "His rooms are at the front of the house, after all."

The butler put this remark down to the youth of the young gentleman, and without the slightest tarnish to his dignity he ushered Isobel and the gentlemen up the stairs and into the green saloon. All of the others who had gone into the house before them were already in the room. Isobel went immediately to the sofa to sit beside her mother and Kitty, and Simon took the chair adjacent to the one in which Carlton sat. The chairs and sofa were in a grouping facing the hearth, against which Quentin stood in a negligent pose, one exquisitely polished top boot crossed slightly over the other. Though he and Adrian were of similar build, Quentin's coat was padded to add even greater breadth to his broad shoulders, and his buckskin breeches molded like a second skin to his long legs, giving the illusion of considerable height. He was an imposing figure, and the confidence of his manner seemed to proclaim him master of his surroundings.

Adrian bit back a smile at the tableau presented to him. Intentional or not, it was exclusionary. A straight-backed chair was set aside at one end of the hearth, and he crossed the room and sat in it gingerly, as if unsure of his acceptance at this gathering. There was actually not the least doubt in his mind. They all wished him at Hades.

Footmen arrived carrying trays of tea, biscuits, and cakes, and dry sherry and Madeira for the gentlemen. The former were placed before the ladies, the latter on the table between Carlton and Simon. Carlton poured out wine for the gentlemen while Lady Leyland took command of the teapot. The ensuing activity of refreshments being passed about precluded any need for normal conversation. It was a short-lived respite. No one was quite certain what to say to Adrian, and the alternative, the desire of every one of them, to discuss him among themselves, could scarcely be done while he was present in the room. Quentin could have contributed nothing in either case. He was so appalled to find that the man who would succeed to the dignities of the earldom and the entail was, in his opinion, just a step above the savage in breechclout and animal hides he had sardonically predicted, that he could not yet trust himself to speak without a degree of venom that would surely offend his aunt.

Isobel used the cover of activity to study Adrian once again. She could not have said why she took such interest in him. He was an attractive man and would be more so, she thought, if he were dressed decently and his hair was not cut so dreadfully. She deplored his appearance and manners as much as the others, but she could not help feeling some empathy toward him. She could still remember the day her father and new stepmother first had brought her to Audswyck Chase, and the flutters in her stomach at the prospect of meeting the Renvilles. She had felt alone, an outsider, until Quentin had extended her his notice and kindness. Adrian must have felt the same, only this time Quentin was likely to foster his cousin's discomfort, not alleviate it.

To the relief of all, the unmistakable sound of Lord Audwin's Bath chair being wheeled down the hall toward the room was heard at this point. Except during the most severe attacks of gout, Lord Audwin had no real need of a Bath chair and made do very nicely with a cane, but it was well-known to his family that he was want to play up his infirmities for their benefit when it suited him, usually when he meant to be at his most demanding. Those who recognized this for what it was exchanged rueful glances.

When Beal pushed the Bath chair through the doorway, Simon and Carlton rose. Lord Audwin looked every day of his seventy-five years. He had been a tall, muscular man in his youth, but increasingly poor health had emaciated him. He looked small and fragile in the large chair, thin flesh covering brittle bones and in turn covered by yellowing parchment skin. His hands clutching a stout cane across his lap were gnarled and age-spotted, and his left foot was heavily bound in bandages and stretched out before him on a brace at the bottom of the chair. His eyes, though, could they have been taken alone, would have proclaimed him a much younger man. They were neither red, nor rheumy, nor faded as was often seen in the old, but bright and clear and sparkling with some interior vigor that he no longer possessed physically.

This bright gaze turned almost fierce for a moment as he scanned the room. "Well, where is the fellow,

Beal? I hope you've not dragged me through the halls in this damned contraption merely to look at this lot."

Before Beal could point him out, Adrian, his manner diffident and hesitant, rose from his chair near the hearth. In sitting he had somehow pushed up the sleeves of his coat so that an extra measure of cuff was exposed, emphasizing both the ill fit of his coat and the unfashionable cut of his breeches. He looked around unsuccessfully for a place to put his glass and, placing it on the floor, managed to tip the contents onto the rug. He looked up ruefully and met Lord Audwin's astonished expression. "You must be my grandpa," he said with a tentative smile.

The earl made no immediate reply to this. A lifetime spent in government and politics had taught him to betray none of his thoughts, but apparently the sorry sight of his heir robbed him of this gift. Astonishment was perhaps too mild a word to describe his expression. Shock and horror passed over his withered features and then gave way to a cold anger. "Beal," the old man shouted as if the butler were half the house away from him rather than standing behind his chair. He gave a vicious tug at the wheels of his chair to turn himself and was half propelled out of the room before the surprised servitor caught up with him to take him back to his sitting room.

An awkward silence covered the room like a pall for several moments after Lord Audwin had left them. Adrian thought they all looked rather green, with the exception of Quentin, who wore what Adrian classified as his usual sardonic smirk, but to Adrian it was better than a play. He said doubtfully, "Grandpa must suffer powerful from the gout to be taken with a turn so sudden."

"Not gout, cousin," Quentin said quite definitely. "I see I must salute you. You have accomplished in the space of two minutes what the lords, various cabinet members, and several prime ministers could not manage in four or five decades. You have deprived the great Earl of Audwin of speech. It might, of course, be that Grandfather was taken by your remarkable likeness to your father like a ghost come to haunt him, but if I were to place a safe wager on the matter, I should bet that it is your own rather unique appearance that has so amazed the old man."

Adrian did not look offended but rather puzzled. He glanced down at himself and shot his cuffs. "I collect you're roasting me, Cousin Quentin."

"*I* collect," Quentin returned, mocking Adrian's accent, "I may ask you the name of the shop where you bought that remarkable coat rather than the name of your tailor. Dare I guess? Claghorne Street?"

Far from being chagrined, Adrian's features lit with delight. "You've a good eye, Cousin Quentin. As soon as I set foot in London, I saw the rig I had brought with me wouldn't do, and I had the innkeeper at the Golden Cross direct me to the best place to get a set of togs in the flash of a pig's wink." He stood before them regarding them with a somewhat fatuous smile, as if he fully expected to be admired for his choice.

"No doubt the very establishment the innkeeper patronizes himself," Carlton suggested.

Adrian nodded. "That it was, and right grateful I am to the man."

Lady Leyland was a beautiful, decorative woman who excelled in the social niceties and was a hostess whose invitations were much in demand. Like Isobel she felt the awkwardness of Adrian's situation, but was more concerned for the discomfort and unease it brought to their company. She did not feel equal to rebuking Quentin and Carlton as she had Simon, yet to let the bloodletting continue was a breech of the breeding that was so instilled in her. She did the thing her training and temperament best suited to her. She hastily drank off the remains of her tea and rose to declare the hostilities suspended. "If *Beau-père* is not to join us, I think it is time we went to our rooms to refresh ourselves from our travel," she said. "Quentin, be so kind as to ring the bell for Beal; you are the nearest." She then said to Adrian, "We all know our way, but you shall need guidance, Mr. Renville. Come, Kitty, Isobel."

Kitty rose obediently, but Isobel remained seated. "I think I shall stay to finish my tea, Mama. I shan't be long."

Aware that Isobel had not seen Quentin in several days, Lady Leyland did not press her. "Simon, I insist that you go up to your room and lie down on your bed for a while before dinner," she said instead, dealing next with her son. "I know you think you are all healed from your accident, but we have been traveling for two days and you are looking rather pulled."

Simon, who was at an age when he did not like having his infirmities taken note of, flushed and rose as well, knowing that if he argued with his mother, she was likely to make more of the matter than not. Beal reentered the room at that moment and said, "Mr. Quentin, Miss Isobel, his lordship would like you to join him in his sitting room at your soonest convenience." Quentin and Isobel exchanged glances, and Quentin nodded, saying they would do so in a moment.

When the others had left, Carlton set aside his sherry and went to a japanned cabinet on the far wall and extracted a decanter of cognac. He poured himself a liberal dose and did the same for Quentin, who took the spirits and tossed them off in one rapid motion. He held out his glass for another without speaking. "What's to be done, Carl?" he said when this too had been drunk.

Carlton, sipping the strong amber liquid with greater respect, shrugged. "What can be done? Even if you planned to murder him, it would serve you nothing; he has two brothers, very likely each one more dreadful than the next."

"Flippancy will also serve nothing," Quentin said, glowering at his brother. He held out his glass again to be refilled.

Isobel rose at this and took the glass from him and put it on the cabinet. "Nor will that," she said coolly. "It is a great shock, but we cannot murder him or wish him away. Is he any worse than what we all said he would be? Perhaps we are well served for our unkind expectations."

"Don't talk nonsense, Bel," Quentin said crossly, retrieving his glass. He handed it to Carlton, who, giving Isobel an apologetic shrug, filled it. "That damned oaf cannot become the earl of Audwin. It is unthinkable."

Though Carlton shared this view in theory, he said in a flat voice, "It is inevitable. If you do intend to drown our deplorable cousin in the river, you may manage on your own."

"Of course he is not thinking murder," Isobel said quickly, though this was as much to reassure herself as Carlton.

"Am I not?" demanded Quentin and then with a bitter laugh, added, "You may both close your mouths and take breath again. I may be thinking it, but as Carlton points out, the act would be fruitless. Perhaps an asylum would answer. I should actually prefer the world to think the next earl of Audwin a madman rather than an unmannered, unlettered savage." More prudent this time, he downed only half his glass and set it on the cabinet again. "The old man must be reeling. No point in making it worse." He held out his arm for Isobel to take and she did so.

Chapter 4

The events of the afternoon had put from Isobel's mind all thought of Vauxhall; both guilt for her actions and anger with Quentin for his defection temporarily were banished. She listened with half an ear to Quentin's continuing animadversions on the injustice of a fate that would permit a clodpole to wear an earl's coronet, while denying it to an accomplished man like himself, as they traversed the long gallery to reach the wing where Lord Audwin had his apartments. Her own thoughts were preoccupied with speculation on why the earl would wish to see her as well as Quentin.

Quentin paused before a mirror on the wall between the doors to the earl's sitting and dressing rooms. He made an infinitesimal adjustment to his neckcloth, dusted imaginary specks from the sleeves of his coat, and then nodded to Isobel, who waited outside the sitting room door in some impatience. It was her opinion that he would have done better to have disguised the strong odor of alcohol on his breath, for though Lord Audwin had in his younger days a reputation as a hardheaded drinker, he had become abstemious in old age and was vocally opposed to the imbibing of hard spirits before dinner.

Quentin gave her an encouraging smile, seized a brief kiss, and opened the door. The earl was staring broodingly out of the window when they entered. He turned his chair to face them and wheeled himself to a small sofa that he indicated to them with a nod of his head. Isobel seated herself on it and Quentin placed himself beside her.

"It's the devil of a coil, is it not, sir?" Quentin said at once. "I suppose, from what I know of my uncle Francis, I should not be surprised that he rejected his own upbringing to the extent that he would raise his own sons as little more than savages."

Audwin's eyes on them both were hard and cold. Dark gray in color, Isobel likened them to granite. "Nothing that hell-born brat of mine did would surprise me," he said, his level voice more chilling than anger or bitterness would have been. "I'd deny siring him if he hadn't been in the image of me. God knows that mother of his was a slut. But that is history. The boy is Francis's son, no doubt of that by the look of him. It won't be an easy task to make him fit to be the fifth earl."

"Permit me to say, Grandsire," said Quentin, "nothing will do that."

"I'll permit no such thing," responded Audwin with unexpected force. "I know perfectly well that your nose is out of joint over this entire matter, Quentin, but I expect you to behave toward your cousin like the gentleman you were bred to be." This was a rare rebuke for his favorite. "Do you think I wish someone like him to succeed me? It cannot be helped, so it must be salvaged. I would have had him in hand in a month's time, but the task is beyond me now, little as I care to admit it. You shall both have to be my instruments to shape and mold this—this . . ."

"Savage," Quentin supplied helpfully.

". . . pathetic creature into something at least presentable. His full education will take years, of course, but we shall have to introduce him to the world in a matter of weeks. There is already gossip that my heir has come to England, perhaps the result of a tongue loosened by wine." He paused for a moment to glare at Quentin, who returned his stare unperturbed. "There is a need therefore to apply at least a veneer to the rough surfaces. I dislike having my hand forced, but I will not have either myself or anyone of my blood be the subject of conjecture and innuendo."

Isobel knew the earl's suspicions were justified. But she had a long habit of defending Quentin and said, "The gossip would begin almost at once in any case, *Grand-père*. No matter how well paid, well treated, and reasonably loyal servants are, they will always talk to family and connections in the village. It is not possible to keep the knowledge that your heir has come to Audswyck from leaking into the neighborhood and transmitted to the rest of the world from there."

"And what the servants must think of your heir arriving at Audswyck looking like a butcher dressed up in his Sunday best, I should not even wish to imagine," said Quentin acidly. "We could chain him in the attic and hire a discreet keeper."

Audwin ignored his grandson's inappropriate levity. "Dressing him properly is as good a place to start as any."

"I suppose I might introduce him to my tailor," Quentin suggested, "but clothes don't make the man whatever the saying may be. Dress him up fine as a fivepence and it still won't make him a gentleman born, for all he has Renville blood in him. He admits—with pride, mind you—that he had his clothes from Claghorne Street on the advice of an innkeeper."

"Then it is up to you to show him how to go on," Audwin said grimly. "He won't be the first sow's ear turned at least to the semblance of a silk purse. My birthday celebration is to be held a week from Saturday. I thought we would have some time to work with him before then, but he impudently ignored my instructions to come here at once when he arrived over a month ago, and it is too late to cancel the party without an unexceptionable excuse. If we keep him shut away, speculation will be worse than the reality."

"No! How could it be," Quentin wondered with a show of astonishment. "Surely, Grandsire, you would not contemplate introducing this barbarian to even the most inconsequential of our neighbors in so short a time. I suppose some sort of improvement could be made just by getting him a decent suit of clothes, but that won't prevent him from disgracing himself and us all."

"That is why no time must be wasted beginning his education," said the earl, unperturbed. "You, Quentin, are to be his model. You will instruct him in dress, behavior, and the fine points of conduct befitting a gentleman. I wish the lessons to continue until I judge he is fit enough to make a bow to society, and then you will take him to town and see that he is established in the world as befits my heir."

"You mean me to remain here until that is accomplished," said Quentin with mock horror. "Good God, sir! You condemn me to a life sentence."

The earl's lips moved into what might have been taken as a wry smile. "At least you shall not lack company or consolation. From you, Isobel," he said, turning his head to address her, "I expect him to be schooled in the proprieties and how to go on in polite society. Caroline, for all her frivolity, has trained you well. You have an uncommon social grace. You might also see what you can do about his speech. His accent did not seem to me to be much worse than other colonial accents I have heard."

Quentin gave a bark of laughter. "If that was only the worst of it. His speech has all the appropriateness of a bootblack's at the Queen's drawing room."

"But surely, *Grand-père*," Isobel said, alarmed at

the prospect of an indefinite stay at Audswyck under the watchful eye of the earl, "such a task would be better accomplished by my stepmother or Aunt Adora, and what you wish Quentin to teach him would be better learned from yourself. We have the benefit of the instruction of our elders, but scarcely the experience to make such tutoring practical, or perhaps even palatable to Mr. Renville."

The earl's smile became more evident. "You've a very pretty way with you, girl, and spirit. You'll bring him to heel. Caroline pines like a maiden wearing the willow if she is out of society for more than a fortnight, and I wouldn't set Adora the task of training the kitchen maids in deportment. She is grown so indolent and takes pleasure in so little beyond seeing to her own health and comfort that she has become as silly and absurd as her name. I've set my mind to give the task to you."

"And have I a pretty way with me too?" said Quentin.

He spoke in the deceptively dulcet accents that Isobel knew were the harbinger of rapier slashes from his sharp tongue. She cast him a surprised glance, and had she been able to do so without catching the earl's notice, she might have kicked or nudged him discreetly. A display of temper was a foolish indulgence and a dangerous one. For all that Quentin was Lord Audwin's favorite, the earl would not hesitate to give swift retribution to any open defiance of his will. She feared it was the hastily drunk cognac that betrayed Quentin into foolhardiness.

"You have a damned impudent tongue," Audwin said, his tone cool and level as always, but the warning clear in his words. "And expensive habits. Those are two facets of your personality that you will not pass on to your cousin, I trust."

The warning went unheeded. "And if I refuse the

role of bear leader?" Quentin asked, matching his tone to his grandfather's.

Lord Audwin regarded them silently for a moment or so as Quentin's question hung in the air. "I've no illusions that the lot of you dance attendance on me out of affection or duty," he said, a harsh note coming into his voice. "It's my purse you've an eye to. I've called your tune since the day you were breeched, but you've had fair trade for it, boy. You might have sent me to the devil rather than dance, but you like the rewards of obedience. That is a new curricle and team you arrived with today, isn't it? Did you bring along the bill or have it sent to my man of business?"

The implications of these words sent a swift shiver of alarm through Isobel. She turned her head to see if she could catch Quentin's eye and will him to silence. But he was looking into the distance, as if fascinated by something on the mantel at the far end of the room, though it was unlikely that he saw anything his eyes rested on. His jaw was clenched, his lips firmly compressed. It was obvious that though he seethed with anger at the veiled threats made by his grandfather, he was aware that he dared take his defiance no further.

Lord Audwin turned his chair and wheeled it over to his writing desk. He opened the center drawer and took out a folded sheet of parchment. "But let us say rather what I shall do if you are obedient to my requests," he said, returning to his usual cool accents. He regarded them for a moment and then gave a brief laugh deep in his throat. "You make a fine-looking couple," he remarked, "I will say that, though I can't say I much care for the match. I'd an idea it was a boy-girl attachment and hoped you'd outgrow it; I think you are damned ill suited, and I know well what it is to find that out after the wedding. My unlamented first wife once described sharing my bed as congress with the devil." He laughed again. "But she thought she loved me once, and I her. Her early death was a release for us both."

This was the first time, as far as Isobel knew, that the earl had acknowledged their betrothal, and what he said sent another frisson of alarm through her. She glanced again at Quentin and saw that he had not moved or altered his expression, and yet she was aware that he was listening intently to what his grandfather said.

When she looked back toward Audwin, she saw that he was staring now at her. She would not let him intimidate her. Her pin money, all of her expenses, and her dowry were supplied by her father. What power had Lord Audwin over her other than through Quentin? This thought made her brave, and she raised her chin a little and said, "I think you are mistaken, *Grand-père.* Quentin and I have long enough acquaintance that we need fear no unpleasant surprises after we are wed."

The earl gave her a brief, sad little smile, as if in pity for her naivete. "You are betrothed now; you do mean to be wed soon, I imagine."

Isobel would have preferred it if Quentin had answered the earl, but he continued to sit as if made of stone, so she said, a trace defiantly, "Of course we do."

"What date have you set upon?"

Isobel cursed her fair complexion as she felt a warm glow spread through her cheeks. "We have not decided as yet," she said, even more openly bellicose. She would not readily give ground. His cold, condescending laugh in response made Isobel wish she could strike him.

"It took him five years to come to the point," the earl said, just a hint of contempt in his voice. "Perhaps it'll take another five to draw him to the altar. Not so mad in love you think the world well lost for it, eh?"

Isobel saw that he had once again turned his unsettling gaze on Quentin. Perhaps this was only punishment for his daring to challenge the earl, but intuition told her it was something more, as if Quentin had lost some of his favor with his grandfather by his sullen refusal to do as the old man had asked.

Since Quentin would not answer the earl's taunts, Isobel felt she must, and that it was time for plain speaking. "What did you expect of us, my lord, in our circumstances?" she said, her voice steady, but her agitation given away as she unconsciously pleated folds of her skirt through her fingers. "If you knew we wished to wed, you might have made it possible with a single word of approval."

"But I didn't and I don't approve," said Audwin. "Though I would not oppose the match either. But you want something more of me, don't you? Or Quentin does. Isn't that right, boy?"

Quentin finally focused his gaze on his grandfather. "What has any of this to do with the savage?"

Instead of replying, the old man addressed Isobel again. "You've a dowry of thirty thousand pounds, Isobel, and Quentin has nearly five thousand a year from his father. A man could live in some comfort on that. But Quentin isn't like most men, is he? A prime goer, a top o' the trees Corinthian in the forefront of fashion. An expensive rather than comfortable way of life."

"And what you have always encouraged, even rewarded me for being," Quentin said baldly.

"And so I mean to continue," replied Audwin, suddenly equable. "I shall bestow on you that blessing you believe I've denied you. As soon as you have turned out your cousin in such a manner that he does not disgrace us when he makes his bow to the world, you may marry and have the funds to live in style in the first circles. A settlement, not an allowance."

The earl's offer met with silence long enough for Isobel to become aware of the ticking of the mantel clock. This time she did not step into the breech, but sat staring unseeingly at her hands in her lap. What Lord Audwin was offering to them was the means of marrying at once. It was not so long ago that his words would have filled her with joy. Now she acknowledged no feeling at all as she waited for some response from Quentin, whose silence underscored a want of eagerness, which also once would have evoked emotion in her.

"It is impossible to do what you ask," said Quentin finally. "A month or more wouldn't make him fit to meet anyone outside the family. Cancel the celebration and let the world say what it will."

"No," said the earl simply and unequivocally. "Monkhouse is coming up from town and staying with his daughter at Turvey Hall for the occasion," he said, naming a member of the cabinet with whom he had during his own glory years enjoyed a close personal friendship and an intense professional rivalry. "You shall have to manage the best you can."

The muscles of Quentin's face were tense with unexpressed anger. "And if I refuse?" he asked again.

This time it was Audwin who let the silence go on until it became palpable. He wheeled himself over to the hearth and pulled the bell. He turned his chair toward them and said again with quiet but unmistakable menace, "You shall have to manage the best you can."

Isobel felt her heartbeat quicken at these words, and looked up. The earl's steely expression and cold smile nearly made her shiver. She looked at Quentin and saw that mutiny still raged in his eyes, but the scarcely veiled threat was not lost on him either. Fearing for what he might say, she spoke first. "Then I suppose there is really no choice at all."

As Beal entered the room in obedience to his master's summons, the earl turned his cold smile on Isobel. "You were always the cleverest of my kith, Bel, and also the least responsive to the bit. You have a choice, the pair of you, it is simply a matter of what you want." On these last cryptic words he nodded to Beal, and the servitor wheeled him through the connecting door into his bedchamber.

The moment the door had closed on them, Quentin rose abruptly and went quickly out of the room. Isobel, startled by his sudden action, stood also and realized how deeply the conversation had disturbed her by the rubbery feeling in her legs. But she had no intention of letting Quentin go without speaking to him, and she stumbled out of the room after him. He was gone from the hall by the time she came out of the room, and she ran along the gallery to the wing where their rooms were, reaching it just in time to see the door of his bedchamber close with a snap. Isobel did not hesitate; she opened his door without knocking and went into the room.

Quentin turned at the sound of her entrance, took one look at her stormy countenance, and said, "For God's sake, Isobel, not now. Can't you see I'm in a temper?"

"So am I," she said, raising her voice in an angry inflection. "If you have no wish to be married to me, Quentin, why don't you say so and let us have done with this farce?"

She had never used such a tone to him before, and he was startled enough to give her his attention. "What ridiculous megrim is this, Isobel?"

"*Grand-père* has finally given his unqualified approval for us to be married, but you have made it plain that it is no incentive for you to do as he asks set against your own vanity," she said, still not bothering to lower her voice, though the door had been left half open and it was likely they could be heard in the hall. "What is so dreadful in being asked to tutor your cousin so that he does not put us all to the blush for his rustic manners?"

"What is so dreadful?" he said, mocking her. "It sickens me to be in the same room with my oafish cousin. That is what is so dreadful. And I am, if you please, to turn him into a proper gentleman for the old man to show off as his heir. It is intolerable. He might as well hand me a shovel and ask me to dig my own grave. If I accomplish the impossible and succeed, I am as good as handing over my inheritance to a savage; if I refuse or fail, I suppose I shall spend the rest of my days until the old devil dies living on an allowance like a schoolboy begging for pin money."

"What inheritance, Quentin?" she asked, scorn in her tone. "The title and entail never were yours, and you have never had any guarantee that you would inherit any more than would have been your father's portion. If you do as *Grand-père* asks, you shall have the settlement you've always wanted and we may finally be married."

He crossed the room to his dressing case, placed on a low chest. "Marriage is the last thing on my mind at the moment," he said irritably over his shoulder as he opened the case.

"Apparently so am I," Isobel said in a tight voice as she felt her throat begin to close and had to fight back tears. "You never intended for a moment to come to Vauxhall on Friday, did you?"

"Vauxhall?" Quentin said, puzzled. He turned toward her, and he held a gold-plated flask in his hand.

Isobel saw that his attention was on opening the flask and pouring brandy into his tooth glass. He had probably never given another thought to Lady Emerson's party again after he had made her his false promise. Any trace of guilt she might have felt for letting the stranger kiss her had vanished, and for a wild moment she wished with all her heart that she had let him take her in the moonlit garden.

Quentin proved that his thoughts were far from her with his next words, which completely ignored all that she had said. "The old man probably wants me to put the fellow up at White's and Watier's as well. I'm damned if I will. I'd as soon ask them to take on my valet as a member."

The heat of Isobel's anger dissipated at the realization of the futility of argument with him in his present humor. Once again she buried her emotions, to be kept simmering for another day. "I am not so certain that our cousin is as dreadful as he seems," she said, merely to contradict him.

"Very likely he is worse," Quentin responded with a snort of cynical laughter. "He was probably on his best behavior today to meet his, ah, kinfolk. As if anything could disguise his stupidity."

"Actually, I think he is quite intelligent," she responded impulsively, remembering her first impression and the brief flashes of amusement in Adrian's eyes.

Quentin gaped at her in astonishment for a moment. "That is the most complete piece of nonsense I have ever heard you utter."

Isobel's anger flared briefly again at his derision. She had not meant to say anything to anyone of her suspicions of Adrian, but she was piqued by his denial of her perception. "He was amused, Quentin," she said. "I saw it in his eyes."

"Blackguards and fools frequently have a way of cozening naive women."

There was no mistaking the full extent of his meaning. Isobel's delicate control on her temper vanished again. "By which I suppose I may take it that I am a fool to think that there is more to the character of our cousin than you have perceived. Perhaps you are the fool if you underestimate him."

"If the savage cuts me out, it will be because of the caprice of an old man, not by my cousin's design. He hasn't the wit for it."

Isobel had always been a little thrilled by Quentin's cool, sophisticated arrogance and cutting tongue, and a little in awe of the latter as well. At the moment she felt only disgust. "Perhaps it is you who lack wit, Quentin," she said waspishly, and turned away from him to leave the room.

She was almost at the door when Quentin said, "Well, well. The savage has gained himself a champion. Perhaps it is not only my inheritance that is in jeopardy."

Isobel opened the door and turned to meet his angry glare with one of her own. "Perhaps," she said coolly and left the room.

Her room was on the opposite side of the corridor, farther along the wing. She passed the door of Adrian's bedchamber, which was directly across from Quentin's, without seeing that his door was ajar or, for that matter, even knowing that the room was his.

Adrian closed his door as soon as she had reached her room and he had heard her door close. He sighed and reflected that his recently acquired habit of eavesdropping, while informative, was far from pleasant. He was fast becoming in danger of as strong a prejudice against Quentin as Quentin had against him.

Adrian had supposed that appearing oafish and vulgar would be something of a strain, and it was rather lowering to him to realize that he was enjoying himself. He felt not the smallest twinge of conscience for his deception.

The barbs of his cousins glanced off him to no effect. He neither cared for nor courted their good opinion. Adrian supposed that it was just as well, for he doubted that he would have found favor with any of them even if he had presented himself in his true form. His grandfather's stunned reaction had so amused him that he had had all he could do to keep from laughing aloud.

The only one of them that interested him was Isobel. He knew from what he had overheard at Grillon's that she too had prejudged him, but in spite of this she had made some small effort to mitigate the venom of the others. At the least, she had a good heart as well as beauty and spirit.

It was perhaps for this reason that he had risked letting Isobel glimpse a little of his inner amusement. He could not deny feeling strongly attracted to her, but he knew the danger of letting this cloud his judgment. If he meant to go through with his hoax, it would not do to make her too suspicious, but on the other hand, his vanity was piqued that she should think him such a poor creature.

Adrian wondered at himself for even thinking in this fashion. He was attracted to Isobel, but he had no serious intentions; no more so than he had had when he sought her out at Vauxhall. He thought it was a damned shame that she should be wasted on a man like Quentin, who plainly did not value her as she deserved, but there was no thought in Adrian to play Lochinvar. The truth was that he wanted to make love to her, and it would be added spice to him to give Quentin his horns. That it might be something more he did not choose to consider. He had no wish at all to fall in love and certainly not with an Englishwoman.

Contrary to what was believed of him by his cousins, he had no interest in Lord Audwin's fortune and no intention of remaining in England. He had come to with no definite plan other than to meet his father's family and to see how matters stood with his inheritance, prepared to make an indefinite stay if necessary. But now that he had made their acquaintance, he meant to return to America as soon as he could arrange passage, no easy task at the moment. He would come again, perhaps, to see that his estates were properly managed after his grandfather died, but as far as he was concerned, the title would pass on to his own son, should he sire one, before it would be in use again. It was only thoughts of Isobel that made him reluctant to follow this very sensible decision.

Shortly after Beal had shown him to his room, he had returned, bringing with him another, small-statured man, whom he introduced as Ludkin, valet to Mr. Quentin, who had come on ahead of his master in charge of his trunks containing the wardrobe indispensable to a gentleman making at least a fortnight's visit to the country. Ludkin had insisted, over Adrian's protests, on removing his clothes from the carpetbag and putting them away in the adjoining dressing room. This superior servant was obviously very well trained or better bred than the Renvilles, for not by so much of a flicker in his eyes did he give hint of his opinion of Adrian's choice of attire.

Beal made it plain that the earl wished Ludkin to see to his needs as well as Quentin's, and the valet promised—or warned, as Adrian saw it—that he would come back to dress him for dinner after he had seen to his own master. Adrian had no intention of availing himself of these services, and he changed from one ill-fitting set of garments into another. The picture he presented when he stood before the cheval glass made him grin—the suit of clothes that the shopkeeper had assured him was perfect for evening wear made him look rather like a footman. If he did not sit at table at once in the dining room, someone would probably ask him to serve the consommé.

A Quaker friend in Pennsylvania had once informed

Adrian that his most serious flaw was an excess of levity, and Adrian acknowledged this to himself as he tied his neckcloth with a lack of expertise that would have astonished all of his friends, who knew that his style and taste in dress were always impeccable. His well-developed sense of the absurd had led him to embark on this charade in the first place, and whatever else might be the outcome of it, it would provide him with a good deal of amusement.

Adrian had just completed his toilet, such as it was, when there was a discreet scratching at his door, followed by the entrance of Ludkin. Over the valet's arm were a carefully draped suit of evening clothes and appropriate linen. Of the two of them, the valet was unquestionably the better dressed, Adrian reflected with a wry inner grin.

"I have come, sir," he said in the inflectionless tone of the perfect servant, "to assist you to dress for dinner this evening. Mr. Quentin also hopes you will accept the loan of evening clothes, since he knows you are but newly arrived in this country and have not yet had the opportunity to have yourself outfitted by a tailor in town." The was a nicely turned falsehood, for in fact it was Beal who had informed Quentin that the earl wished him to lend clothes to Adrian at once and had brooked no argument.

Adrian let a grin spread slowly over his features. "That's mighty nice of Cousin Quentin, but I stopped in town for a day or so before coming here and I've got all I need. In fact, I'm all ready and set to go to dinner, so, though I thank you and Cousin Quentin kindly, I won't need to put you to the trouble."

The valet did not display shock or chagrin at this statement except for a possible slight widening of his eyes. "Very good, sir. But perhaps it might be best if you accepted Mr. Quentin's offer. His lordship is most particular about the style of dress he expects at his dinner table, and these clothes are more in that mode."

Though this was so very gently put, Adrian refused to be tempted. "Thank you again, Mr. Ludkin, but I'll do well enough in this rig. I paid upward of a pound for this coat and twenty shillings for the breeches. Might as well get my use of them."

Recognizing the finality in Adrian's tone, the servitor bowed, though his bland expression had taken on a grimmer cast. "As you wish, Mr. Renville," he said, and left the room.

Adrian had barely time to stick a glass pin, cut into facets to resemble a diamond, into his cravat when his door was opened again and Quentin marched unceremoniously into the room. "What the devil are you about sending Ludkin away? If you go into dinner dressed like that, the old man will give us all indigestion by ringing a peal over you for the first three courses." He had no desire to lend Adrian so much as a handkerchief, but he had no wish to face his grandfather's fury if he thought that he had refused his command to outfit Adrian.

Adrian walked up to Quentin and looked him over for a moment. Quentin was still in his shirtsleeves, the high points of his collar sloping to his shoulders. "Looks to me, cousin, that it's you as needs to dress. I'll do well enough as I am."

He walked past Quentin to the door. Kitty, who was always the first dressed and first down for dinner, was just coming out of her room at the opposite side of the hall. "Just what I need," said Adrian when he spied her. "I'd been thinking I'd lose myself in this great place trying to find the dining room, but if you'll show me the way, Miss West, I'd be right grateful."

Kitty was a little startled to be addressed by Adrian, whom she regarded in some awe as an oddity. "Oh, but we do not go directly to the dining room," she said lamely, seeing a half-dressed Quentin, his features lowering, standing in the doorway behind Adrian. "We assemble in the long gallery first."

"Do you, now?" Adrian said, as if astonished. "Then, it is a good thing I came upon you, for I should have taken a place at table and wondered where you had all gotten to."

Quentin came out of the room behind Adrian, his expression scowling. "It is considered gauche for guests to go down to dinner before their hosts, cousin," he said.

"But I'm not a guest, I'm kin, cousin," Adrian said, frustrating this attempt to instruct him.

"Your relation to Miss West is negligible, however," Quentin said, almost through his teeth, "and you are virtually unknown to her. It is not proper for you to be alone with her. I am certain my aunt or mother will soon be ready to go down. You may do so then if you will not wait for my grandfather."

"Oh, Miss West will come to no harm at my hands," Adrian said, forever unabashed. "Come on, girl. I'm right peckish and I'd rather be moving about than sitting in my room listening to my stomach grumble."

Kitty wished she could go back in her room and shut the door. While she was too well bred and lacked the self-confidence to refuse Adrian's request, she certainly had no wish to defy Quentin. "I am not certain. . . . That is, perhaps it is a bit early to go down to dinner. I think I shall read in my room for a bit, if you do not mind, Mr. Renville."

"Adrian," he corrected. "I don't hold with formality among kin. I was hoping you'd help me out before the others come by showing me those pictures on the wall and telling me who's who. Never saw so many in one place before in my life." He tossed Quentin a grin and a nod over his shoulder and led the reluctant girl inexorably down the long hall toward the gallery.

Chapter 5

Hearing voices in the hall, Isobel went to her door and listened to the discussion at hand for a minute or two. She hurried back to her dressing table, applied the last touches to her toilet, and then quickly made her way to the gallery. She did so, she told herself, to rescue Kitty from an awkward situation, but Adrian was the true reason for her haste. She was still annoyed that Quentin had dismissed her reading of Adrian's character, and she was determined, through further study of him, to prove herself right.

When Adrian saw Isobel enter the gallery, he found it took considerable effort to hide his frank admiration of her. Her hair, glowing like new minted gold, was drawn up into a riot of curls at the crown, and delicate tendrils framed her lovely, oval face. She was dressed in a pearl-colored silk gown that shimmered in the light cast by the candles in the wall sconces and made her delicate coloring bloom. The effect on him was considerable, but his features showed nothing at all except perhaps a somewhat bovine placidity.

Kitty did look relieved to see her. Isobel cast Kitty a brief, reassuring smile as she let her gaze travel over Adrian's unprepossessing appearance without comment. She had no doubt the earl would say all that was necessary on that subject at dinner. "You are dressed early, Kitty, even for you," she said, smiling. "I was certain I should be the first in the gallery tonight. Good evening, Cousin Adrian," she said, turning to him. "I see you have learned our custom of assembling in the gallery for dinner."

"Kitty set me straight before I made a right fool of myself by going to the dining room and setting myself down," Adrian said with a grateful nod toward the girl. "She's just been telling me that this rum-looking crew hanging on the walls are my ancestors."

Isobel bit back a smile at this description of generations of proud Renvilles, and conjectured that the earl would turn dyspeptic if Adrian made such a remark in his presence. She looked at him closely to see if she could discover a quizzing light in his eyes again, but there was nothing there but unremarkable blandness.

"Adrian asked me about them, but I don't know a great deal," Kitty said. "You could tell him much more than I, Bel." She then murmured something about fetching a book and fled back to her room.

They watched her retreating form for a moment or so, and then Isobel turned to Adrian and said brightly, "Well, then, let us get on with sorting out this 'rum-looking crew' before the others join us." Her words were rewarded with an appreciative glint and the hint of a smile, and she felt vindicated. He might be vulgar and rustic, but his apparent thickheadedness was undoubtedly assumed.

Isobel led Adrian along the gallery, stopping to introduce Adrian to each of his forebears. He regarded each portrait dutifully and made few comments that were not directly solicited by her. When they reached the portrait of his own father as a young man, he paused and stared at it silently and intently.

Isobel watched him with a steadiness that would have been rude if his study of his father's likeness had not been so complete that he seemed oblivious to her presence. They stood fairly close together, and she found herself very conscious of him as a man. There had been nothing further in his expression, manner, or words in the quarter hour they had spent alone together to reinforce her belief that he was more than what he appeared, and she began to wonder if she was imagining qualities in him other than he possessed because she found him attractive. It was a lowering thought that she might be physically attracted to him if he was just an uncouth rustic after all.

Isobel looked from the portrait of Francis Renville to Adrian and saw that the resemblance between father and son was stronger than she had been led to believe. Although he was not much like Quentin except in general build and coloring, it occurred to her that there might just be something about Renville men that appealed to her, but then she had never felt the smallest interest in Carlton, whom some declared more handsome than his older brother.

Adrian took a step backward from the portrait and stepped into Isobel, nearly throwing her off balance. He turned quickly and grasped her arms to keep her from falling. He held her for only a moment to reassure himself that she had steadied herself, but it was enough to send a small shiver deep within her. He sensed that the physical contact had some effect on her and smiled inwardly. The attraction was plainly mutual. He wanted very much at that moment to bend his head and kiss her, but he knew better than to rush his fences.

"I beg your pardon, cousin. It's the first time I've seen my pa as a young man, and I forgot you were behind me," Adrian said a little sheepishly. "I favor him, I think."

"Very much so," Isobel agreed, retaining her composure admirably. "I was just thinking that myself. I never met your father, of course; he left England before I was born. I confess that when I was in the schoolroom, I thought him a very romantic figure. It seemed very dashing of him to go off and seek his fortune in America after he had quarreled with *Grand-père*."

Adrian smiled. "My mother thought so too. That's how he was able to persuade her to leave Philadelphia and move out to the farm. Or so she claimed."

"Abandoning civilization for true love?" Isobel quizzed him.

"That's the way of it," he said, grinning in pleasure at her quick understanding. His gaze flicked to a point beyond her, and before her eyes his features transformed, slackening visibly, his eyes taking on a dullness that made him look stupid and cloddish again.

Isobel's astonishment had no opportunity to evolve into suspicion before she heard voices and other sounds indicative of the fact that their tête-à-tête was about to end. Moments later, her stepmother and Lady Adora Renville turned the corner from the east wing into the gallery.

Isobel performed the office of introducing Adrian to his aunt. Lady Adora's manner as she gave Adrian two reluctant fingers to clasp was one of obvious distress. She had been no more inclined than her sons to look favorably upon Lord Audwin's heir, and it was plain she was appalled by the reality of him. "*You* are Francis's son?" she said faintly.

"That I am, ma'am," Adrian said with no sign that he noted her dismay.

Carlton and Simon, with Kitty returning in their wake, had come into the gallery as well, and Lady Adora turned to her son and said in failing accents, "I am feeling rather weak tonight, Carl dearest. If you would just help me to sit down for a moment. Perhaps I should have taken a tray in my room after all."

Lady Adora's response to anything she found unpleasant was to take to her room indefinitely. She was the daughter of an impecunious earl who had been foolish enough to fall in love with a handsome face instead of the fortune her parents had hoped she would bring through marriage to restore the family coffers. She and Julian Renville had learned the same lesson as the earl and his unfortunate first countess: marry in haste, repent at leisure. But if Lady Adora had lived to regret her choice of a younger son with his own way to make in the world and a father who held a tight grasp on his purse strings, she had long since found a means of some control in her life. She had perfected the art of emotional manipulation, and it answered well enough. Her husband had left her in peace for his horses and mistresses once she had done her duty and produced two sons, and her father-in-law, after Julian's death, had let her make her home at Audswyck Chase, declaring that he supposed the house big enough that he need not be subjected to her sighs and flutterings every day. She was nominally his hostess, but in fact she had no duties other than pleasing herself, which consisted principally of cosseting herself for imaginary illnesses and boring her friends in the neighborhood with tales of these and the exploits of her sons.

Carlton did as she asked, and Lady Leyland went over to sit beside her while they waited for the earl to arrive so that they could go in to dinner. Once again Adrian was left to himself and ignored, and the only one this seemed to concern was Isobel. "I have been showing Adrian his ancestors and recounting their exploits," she said, raising her voice a little and addressing no one in particular. "If Adrian was to don a short tunic and tight hose, I think he would be mistaken for Sir Lucien de Renville."

Adrian glanced over at that fifteenth-century portrait, and his expression was doubtful. "But I don't think I could have switched horses in midstream the way he did without ending up mighty wet," he said, referring to the story that Isobel had told him about that gentleman's penchant for changing allegiance several times from York to Lancaster and back again, and thus saving not only his own skin but his property from being confiscated as well.

"He may not have been a loyal man, but he was a clever one," said Audwin, who had just entered the gallery. He had abandoned his Bath chair, and he leaned heavily on Quentin's arm with only a walking stick to further support him. "Any Renville with Sir Lucien's blood flowing in his veins will do well enough for himself."

Isobel was mildly surprised to see Quentin with his grandfather. To get to the west wing in the normal way, he would have had to have passed through the gallery. Quentin had to have used the service stairs to the next floor and down again to go to his grandfather's apartments, and Isobel could only wonder why he would do so. From his solicitous manner toward the earl it was plain, though, that he was mending the fences he had heedlessly crashed through that afternoon. Isobel was not at all sure whether she was pleased or inclined to regard it with uncharacteristic cynicism.

The earl coolly took in Adrian's appearance. He lowered himself painfully into a wide sixteenth-century chair and fixed his piercing gaze on Quentin. "I thought I told you to lend him some decent clothes. If I wanted to break bread with the footmen, I'd take my dinner below stairs."

"No need to be cross with Quentin, sir," Adrian assured him. "I purchased all that was needful when I was in London, and I sent his man away with my thanks for the offer."

It was not in Lord Audwin's nature to give vent to verbal explosions, but his color darkened alarmingly, and they were all more than half expecting some outburst. But Audwin's voice was merely goaded when he said, "Dear God! This must be the payment for my sins. My heir indeed!"

Dinner was not a comfortable affair, but at least it appeared that the earl did not mean to treat Adrian to the full scope of his displeasure as Quentin had predicted when Adrian had sent Ludkin away. For the first three courses there was very little conversation. Lady Adora, as usual, did not exert herself in the role of hostess, and everyone felt it was just as well that the earl kept his peace. Quentin, when he spoke at all, was at his most acid, and Carlton maintained a stony silence, his countenance becoming grimmer whenever he chanced to look at Adrian. Even Kitty and Simon, whose youthful exuberance was usually irrepressible, apparently felt it wisest not to call attention to themselves.

Adrian alone seemed to find nothing unnatural in such taciturn company. He ate his dinner enthusiastically, and at least his table manners could not be faulted. Only Isobel and her stepmother made the least effort to behave naturally. Caroline Leyland made several efforts to initiate unexceptional topics for conversation, but her efforts met with most monosyllabic replies and did not prosper. In desperation she abandoned the niceties and spoke diagonally across the table directly to Adrian, hoping that at least she might succeed in drawing him out a little.

"I hope your crossing from America was not too difficult, Adrian," she said. "Papa said you arrived later than we expected because you were delayed by storms at sea."

He seemed surprised to be addressed by her, but answered readily enough. "There was a storm or two to be weathered along the way, but they weren't so bad. T'was the shooting I disliked the most."

"Shooting?" said Simon, his interest piqued.

"The blockade," he responded. "The ship I was on, the *Sea Hawk*, was hit, but remained underway, and we outran the man-of-war that tried to scuttle her. But even that wasn't as bad as the pirates."

"Pirates?" Kitty parroted, emboldened by astonishment.

"Yes, ma'am," he replied. "Just off the Barbary Coast. We stopped to pick up a bit of cargo in the Indies. We thought it was just another merchantman at first, but she changed her colors a mile or two out to sea, and we saw they were the skull and crossbones. Scared us silly, that did, for everyone knows that a Barbary pirate will slit your throat without so much as a how-do-ye-do, so we took on sail and outran them as well. But they fired shot right across our deck, they did, though not so accurate as His Majesty's sailors. One round from the English ship came so near, it rent a long hole in my sleeve. Never would have had the chance to come here and make the acquaintance of my pa's kinfolk if I'd been standing just a bit to the left."

Isobel thought there was an ironic inflection in his last words. There was nothing in his expression to suggest it, but she was certain that he was trying to see how much he could make them swallow of his wild tales. Certainly he had the attention of Simon and Kitty, the former being particularly interested since he hoped to write exciting adventures like the lurid romance *The Mysteries of Udolpho* one day. But it was not only the youngest members of the family who seemed to accept what he said. Both Lady Adora and Caroline Leyland looked startled and amazed and, in Lady Leyland's case, a little dismayed. This was hardly appropriate fare for dinner conversation.

"Indeed! How dreadful for you," said Lady Leyland uncertainly. "We have friends with property in Jamaica and the West Indies, but I had understood that the lawlessness of the early days of settlement was a thing of the past."

"For them that live in fine houses, no doubt," he agreed. "They've an army of servants to keep the cutthroats at bay."

"Surely if it was as barbaric as all that, trade would never prosper," Isobel said dryly, "and I know that is not the case."

"Trade always prospers where there are men willing to take risks for the sake of it, I reckon. There was a trading post set up not twenty miles from the farm, and the first four traders were scalped before the natives tired of it and the fifth one prospered. It's easier on the womenfolk now that the raids aren't as frequent. Used to be, once upon a time, a settler's woman was something of a trophy to the natives," he added, so matter-of-factly that Kitty, sitting to his left, shivered visibly.

"But I understood that Francis lived in Philadelphia or near to it," Lady Leyland said, her brow knit. "I have heard from others who have been there that it is a delightful, civilized city."

"Oh, it's a grand place on market day," Adrian said, a reminiscent smile touching his lips. "My pa would let me and my brother drive the pigs to market from time to time if we didn't misbehave ourselves."

Isobel decided to call his bluff. She met his gaze squarely and said one word: "Fustian."

She had no doubt that he had understood her. There was a faint twitching of his lips, just barely visible to her across the table. "Ma'am?" he said, letting his brow crease into puzzled lines.

"I said fustian, cousin," she repeated, ignoring the frown cast her by her stepmother. "It may be true that you were fired on by English ships in the blockade, and even survived an attack by pirates, but I take leave to doubt that my uncle, who was bred as a gentleman and the heir to an earldom, would set his sons to driving pigs to market. Barefoot, no doubt."

"Oh, aye," Adrian admitted blandly. "Shoes were for the churchgoin'. We did have our best breeches tied about our waists, though."

"To take pigs to market?"

"Market day was a great occasion, and mud washes better from cloth than from leather," he said, nodding.

"Very practical," Isobel commented, a slight curl to her lips.

"That was my pa all over," Adrian agreed.

"I should have said rather that my uncle was a fool," Quentin said unexpectedly.

A surprised silence followed his words, broken after several moments by Lady Adora, who attempted to admonish her son, though such action was foreign to her. "Quentin, dear, really I don't think you should—"

"What would you, Mother, call a man who gave up a fortune and an earldom to found a pig farm?" His voice was harsh. "It is not surprising, then, is it, that a fool is what he has sired."

Kitty gasped audibly and Simon gaped. Even Carlton forgot for a moment to school his features. Lady Adora said nothing this time. Seated at the foot of the table across from the earl, she could see by the sudden setting of his features that he would deal with Quentin himself.

"That will do, Quentin," Audwin said frigidly. "Your task is to raise him to your level of breeding, not sink to his."

Thus adjured, Quentin relapsed into silence, but an unpleasant little smile hovered on his lips that proclaimed that he considered the rebuke a fair price to pay for venting his opinion of his American cousin.

"No offense taken," Adrian said amiably. "I can see how Quentin might think that from his point of view. And I've had worse names heaped on my head, from time to time."

"Really?" said Simon with an air of innocence. "Such as?"

Adrian looked uncomfortable and stammered, "I-I don't rightly think I should say in the present company."

"No?" said Simon with a show of surprise. "You disappoint me, cousin."

"That is quite enough, Simon," Lady Leyland said, blushing for her son's rudeness. She knew he thought of Quentin as a sort of ideal, but she had no intention of letting him pick up his older cousin's more obnoxious habits.

"You, young man," the earl said to Simon, "would do well to ponder your own foolishness, for there is no excuse for you. You were taught to ride almost before you could walk, and you should know better than to put a green horse at a hedge of that height with a ditch at the other side of it. You should consider yourself fortunate that you broke only your arm and your collarbone and not your neck."

Simon, who detested harsh words and quarrels, had learned from long experience that the easiest way to get through a raking-down from his grandfather was to bear it in silence. But Quentin took up his defense. "That's doing it rather brown, Grandfather. You're forever saying that none of us have any bottom. I'd expect you to think more of the boy for it."

"Unlikely that I ever said such a thing about you, Quentin," Audwin said caustically. "Bottom is all very well, but the boy has a way to go to fill your shoes, and I would as soon prefer that he didn't break his neck trying to imitate your follies in sport."

Carlton, who had scarcely spoken a word since entering the gallery before dinner, unwisely chose to enter the fray at this point. "Surely the exploits of a nonesuch like Quentin could never be described by such a term," he said in a voice so bland that there was no doubt of the mockery behind it.

"Nonesuch! A title given to every whipster with sufficient ready to rig himself up as a whip. It was not so in my day. But I'll give you this, Quentin, you're not cow-handed—like some I could name," he added with an icy glare cast toward Carlton.

Having thus demolished the pretensions of his male grandchildren, he nodded almost imperceptibly to Lady Adora, who rose at once to suggest to the ladies that they retire to the drawing room.

Isobel was more convinced than ever that Adrian was not as loutish as he wished to appear. What puzzled her was why he would wish to appear that way at all. The only thing that occurred to her was her first suspicion that he was a Captain Sharp, but that didn't make a great deal of sense to her either. There could be no doubt that he was Francis's son. He already stood to inherit the title and the entail, and behaving in such a way was hardly likely to gain him a further portion of Lord Audwin's fortune. If he was playing some deep game that she could not yet fathom, it was indeed stupid of him to let her see that he was doing so, and if she was certain of nothing else, she knew he was not stupid. She had every intention of getting at the truth of the matter, if there was any such truth to be found.

Isobel abandoned the puzzle of Adrian Renville and turned her attention to the conversation taking place between her mother and aunt. But this too concerned Adrian.

"I knew, of course," Lady Adora was saying, "that he would not be at all the thing, but I didn't think we should be put to the blush simply in acknowledging him. Francis must have come to a very bad end when he left England for his son to have been raised in such a vulgar manner."

"Francis was not an exacting correspondent," Lady Leyland said musingly, "but I did not receive the impression that he had fallen on ill luck in America. I understood from his letters that he had married a girl from a very respectable family in Philadelphia and purchased a small estate on the Delaware River not far from the city."

"Well, what would you expect him to write, Caroline?" Lady Adora said with a sniff. "That he had married a tavern wench and had purchased a pig farm? It must be so. Nothing else would account for the way his son has turned out."

"He is very bucolic," Isobel said, entering their conversation. "So much so that one wonders if he can possibly be as he seems."

"We have the evidence of our eyes, unfortunately," Lady Leyland said sadly.

"And our ears," put in Lady Adora with a shudder of distaste. "It is not only his odd accent but the dreadful things that he says. I thought I should have one of my spasms at dinner when he began talking of cutthroats and pigs. It is obvious that Francis was very remiss in his upbringing of his sons."

Isobel had not really meant to discuss her suspicions with anyone else after the way that Quentin had dismissed them, but she was curious to know if she was the only one who had noticed anything to cast doubt on Adrian's behavior. "Perhaps that is what he wishes us to believe."

Her stepmother, sharper than her sister-in-law, understood Isobel at once. "Do you mean you think he is only pretending to be vulgar? Why on earth would he, or anyone, do such a thing? Meeting the family from which one's father was estranged would not be a comfortable thing in the best of circumstances.

Surely he would not wish to incur our censure deliberately."

"I don't know why he would do such a thing," Isobel was forced to admit. "But I know he is not as stupid as he would have us believe, and sometimes I can see in his eyes that he is amused by our reactions to him."

The sisters-in-law exchanged glances. "Really, Isobel," Lady Adora said. "That is absurd. Either you are imagining things, or it is you who are hoaxing us trying to make us believe such nonsense."

It was plain that neither her mother nor her aunt were prepared to believe in her perceptions any more than Quentin had. "But it was on more than one occasion," Isobel insisted. "I could not have imagined it every time."

"Good heavens, Bel," exclaimed her stepmother. "Is that why you said what you did to him at dinner? I thought you were only quizzing him when you accused him of talking fustian. What a very odd idea you will give him of us, to be sure, if you continue with these ridiculous notions."

Isobel bit back the rejoinder that it was nothing to the odd idea they had of Adrian, which some of them did not hesitate to make plain to him. It was pointless to continue the conversation in the face of their disbelief, so she let the subject drop and after a few minutes went over to sit by Kitty, who was idly turning the pages of the latest issue of the *Ladies Magazine*, and engaged her in a conversation about some of the fashion plates in the magazine.

Beal brought in the tea tray, and as he was leaving the room, the gentlemen entered to join the ladies. The earl was once again relying on Quentin for support. They were laughing at some jest as they passed through the door, and Isobel reflected that Quentin had managed to weather his venomous attack on

Adrian once again. She wondered if he meant to, or for that matter could, given his loathing of Adrian, do as his grandfather wished and tutor Adrian in the role of a gentleman.

Carlton, pleading weariness, had retired to his room when the ladies withdrew, and Adrian, in the company of Simon, followed the earl and Quentin into the drawing room. They seemed to be engaged in an amiable enough discussion, but Isobel noted that Simon cast occasional glances toward Quentin as if afraid that his older cousin might censure him for any kindness he showed to Adrian.

In spite of occasional bouts of boyish mischief, such as the one that had made him behave so reprehensibly in the courtyard of the Duck and Drake, Simon Leyland was a good-hearted young man, not yet spoiled by the cold cynicism that was so fashionable among men of the town. Isobel knew that Simon was a little embarrassed at times for his scholarship and his interest in intellectual pursuits, and felt obliged to prove to Quentin, who was his ideal of a man of fashion, that he was cast in the same mold. There was no doubt in his sister's mind that left to himself, he would have shown understanding to Adrian for his uncomfortable position, but if he believed that Quentin's approval was contingent upon his disdaining their American cousin, she was uncertain that Simon's better nature would win out.

Quentin, who had seated himself in the chair adjacent to his grandfather's, tapped a stool beside it invitingly and asked Simon if he planned to do some fishing while he was at Audswyck. Fishing was Simon's favorite pastime away from his books, even slightly edging out riding and hunting, and the chance to discuss his favorite topic, combined with the flattering interest expressed by Quentin, was an irresistible lure.

Lady Adora and Lady Leyland continued their conversation over tea while the gentlemen were engaged in an animated discussion on fishing, and Kitty was still chatting to Isobel about the latest fashions as depicted in the magazine. Adrian was effectively shut out of the family groupings and left to stand uncertainly just inside the door. Isobel glanced up from the magazine and saw him turn away and walk to the pianoforte to look through the music.

She could understand why Quentin and Carlton would resent Adrian, why the earl, her stepmother, and aunt deplored his lack of breeding, and even why Simon and Kitty felt the need to parrot the opinions of their elders. She might have been glad enough herself if he decided he did not belong here and went away again. But she could not sit quiet and allow him to be ostracized for no greater crime than being the son of the black sheep of the family and bred to a different way of life than the one that they knew.

Isobel murmured an excuse to Kitty and walked over to the pianoforte. "Do you like music, cousin?" she asked Adrian.

He turned to her, and the smile in his expressive eyes was not disguised this time, but was mirrored in the gentle upturning of his lips. Isobel recognized it as appreciation for her act of kindness and, absurdly, felt herself blush. She quickly dropped her eyes and pulled out the bench. "Shall I play something for you?"

Still silent, he handed her a Bach invention, not an easy piece but within her ability to play. She was a little surprised at his choice, but she made no demur. It was one of Bach's longer inventions, and Adrian turned pages for her. To her astonishment, he plainly followed the music as she played.

As the last chord died away, she looked up at him and said, "You read music, Cousin Adrian."

He looked away from her as if embarrassed to

admit his skill and acknowledged that he did. "My ma's sister was a music teacher, and she had a liking for me. When we went into Philadelphia to visit my ma's family, she'd teach me my notes."

"No doubt that was the reason you brought along your best breeches when you drove the pigs to market," Isobel suggested dryly.

Adrian nodded enthusiastically. "That it was. Aunt Rebecca is a kindly soul, but she would have shown me the door if I'd come for a lesson still covered in mud from swilling the pigs."

"It is my belief you are making game of me, cousin," Isobel said severely, not entirely certain if she was amused or annoyed with him.

"No, how could I?" he said, his hooded eyes opening wider in a display of innocence that she did not believe in the least. "I'm a simple man and all."

"Not as simple as we had believed, I think."

"But then I don't know what you believed, do I?"

There was something in his tone she could not quite define, some sort of edge to it. "Let us see if you practiced well on market days, cousin," she said, pulling a simple Mozart duet from the stack of music. She moved to the opposite edge of the bench and looked up at him challengingly.

After a moment's hesitation, Adrian sat beside her. The opening measures were hers, and she launched into the piece without giving him any time for study. Adrian did not disappoint her, though. He came in on the correct measure and played with a skill equaling her own, and she suspected that he could have bettered her if he wished. Not only was his technique refined, but, knowing the piece well, she dared to look away from the music when he played a solo passage, and she saw that he played with the sort of intense concentration that obliterated all else about him, a characteristic she had noted in most of the finest musicians of her acquaintance.

When the piece was finished, she turned and stared at him until she compelled him to meet her gaze. "You *have* been making game of us, cousin," she said without any doubt in her voice.

Adrian made a swift judgment and said, "A little."

"The acknowledgment of a small deception can be designed to deny a larger one."

If she hoped to discompose him, she was disappointed. He smiled. "More often it's a matter of self-deception, I've found. We all of us see what we wish to see," he added cryptically.

"That is a process that can be assisted," she parried.

"Oh, aye," he said, letting his accent deteriorate and his features slacken, "that be true enough."

As she had earlier when she had witnessed a similar transformation, she looked up to see that they were no longer alone. Her stepmother was standing behind them, and Adrian rose politely from the bench. "You play very well, Adrian," Lady Leyland said, sounding both astonished and a little confused. "Did your mother teach you?"

Adrian launched into his story about his aunt again, only this time he managed to imply that she subsidized a paltry income from teaching music by playing in low taverns, if not worse. While he spoke, Isobel regarded the others in the room and saw some degree of surprise in the expressions of them all. But, to her private amazement, she saw not a hint of suspicion, though she could not credit that anyone would believe that a bucolic clod-pole, such as Adrian presented himself to be, would be able to perform in the way that he just had.

If what Adrian had said to her was an admission that he was shamming them, apparently he meant to make it to no one but her. It occurred to her that she could put an end to whatever it was he was about if she choose. If she confronted Adrian now, in front of Lord Audwin and all of the others, and forced him to admit the things he had just said to her, it was likely that the earl would be so infuriated at Adrian's impudence that he would cast him off as he had once done Adrian's father more than thirty years ago. As if Adrian read her thoughts, when their eyes met again, his were watchful even while his expression remained guileless.

Lady Leyland obviously decided that her nephew was not quite as hopeless as she had feared, and her manner toward him was perceptibly warmer as she folded her arm in his. "I wish you would tell me something about America and what manner of life my brother Francis enjoyed there, Adrian," she said as she guided him over to a chair next to the sofa on which she sat with Lady Adora.

Isobel, with much to reflect upon, turned back to the pianoforte and began to play a medley of popular airs that she knew so well her fingers moved mechanically over the keys without any need for thought or concentration. She had no wish to hear further Banbury tales from Adrian, for she was now completely convinced that that was what they were. She wondered what was the truth about him, and the question persisted of why he would pretend to be a rustic oaf when he was not.

As her fingers pressed keys as if of their own volition, she turned over in her mind the things he had just said to her, particularly about people seeing what they wished to. Quentin had said earlier that clothes wouldn't make Adrian into a gentleman, but the dreadful clothes that he wore, she suspected, had made his deception easy for them to accept. The more she pondered this, the more their unquestioning acceptance of Adrian as uneducated and ill bred was an absurd as his pretence seemed to be. Lord Audwin, her stepmother and aunt, and even

Quentin had all wondered that Francis Renville should have so forgotten all his breeding and raised his son to be a mannerless oaf, but they had taken Adrian at face value all the same.

When Isobel had turned over everything in her head at least a dozen times, she wearied of the exercise and closed the instrument. Using the excuse of being weary from traveling, she bade them good night and went up to her room. She had been in her room only a few minutes, and had not yet even rung for her maid, when she heard a scratching at the door. She opened it without hesitation, thinking it was Kitty, who sometimes liked to talk about events of the day before she went to bed. She was surprised to see Adrian standing there, but she made no protest when he came into the room and quietly closed the door.

"I thought I'd take your lead, Cousin Isobel," he said. "It's been a wearing day for me as well."

It was exceedingly improper for him to be in her bedchamber, but Isobel gave no thought to this at the moment. "Have you come to ask me to keep your confidence?" she asked boldly.

He smiled and shook his head. "There are no secrets to betray, Cousin Isobel."

Isobel gave him a slight, ironic smile. "You can't virtually admit that you are hoaxing us one moment and then deny it the next, you know. I suspected it from almost the moment we met, and now I know you are deliberately deceiving us, but I don't understand why yet."

"Why haven't you told the others if that's what you think?" he countered.

"I tried to tell Quentin and my stepmother and aunt," she admitted. "They all think I am imagining it."

His smile grew. "That's as may be," he said at his most bucolic.

She regarded him with a darkling gaze. "What you most definitely are is infuriating."

"That's one judgment that's true enough. I've been told so before." To her astonishment, he brought the back of his hand against her face in a gentle caress, and then lightly kissed her lips. "Good night, Isobel, *ma belle*," he said in a softer tone and turned and went out of the room.

Isobel stood looking at the door he had disappeared behind for several moments, her heartbeat hammering in her ears. She could scarcely credit that he would dare to do such a thing, but then she herself had made no effort to prevent it. One thing she was resolved upon: she had every intention of getting to the bottom of the mystery that was Adrian Renville.

Adrian was quite glad that he did not have to deal with the ministrations of a valet. He undressed himself slowly and thoughtfully, examining his behavior of the evening and his motives as well. Why, indeed, had he embarked on this charade, and having done so, why was he stepping out of his role with Isobel when he had cautioned himself only that afternoon that he must not let her be a distraction from his purpose? He had thought his reasons for all that he did well defined then, but everything now seemed murky and uncertain. His attraction to Isobel was strong, stronger than he liked to admit. He had toyed with the fantasy of seducing her, but now he knew it was what he fully intended. He had felt compelled to follow her to her room, as if he could not quite let her go, and this time he had not been able to resist kissing her, though certainly he had not done so in the manner that he wished.

The sensible thing to do would be to find an acceptable reason to leave this house as soon as possible and put an end to this masquerade. But as he lay in bed, wakeful in the darkness, he knew it was not what he was going to do.

Chapter 6

Over the next several days, such instruction as Quentin gave to his American cousin was in the form of biting criticism, but there was a noticeable improvement in Adrian's speech and manner nevertheless. Since Lord Audwin had no suspicion that Adrian could improve by willing rather than learning to do so, he was well pleased with Quentin's presumed efforts. And since Quentin did apply himself to dancing attendance on his grandfather at every given opportunity, he appeared to recover nicely any ground he had presumably lost to his earlier defiance.

Isobel felt bound by her word to Lord Audwin and was determined to make a sincere effort to impart her knowledge of the social graces to Adrian, though she was all but convinced that he had no need at all for such lessons. When she met him at breakfast the following day, she felt considerable constraint in his company at first, in part because of her suspicions, but more so because he had kissed her the night before, and even if it had not been a lover's kiss in the physical sense, she knew what it betokened, for the rapid beating of her heart betrayed her own desires. She put such thoughts firmly from her, but even in the most mundane circumstance she could not quite forget that he was a man to whom she felt attracted.

The awkwardness she felt, though, had dissipated by the end of the day following Adrian's arrival at

Audswyck. This was due entirely to Adrian's efforts to put her at ease, though these were sufficiently subtle that she was scarcely aware of them. In the first place, he had himself well in hand by the following morning and made no attempt at all to flirt with her and gave no hint that he intended any further advances. In the second, he was an attentive pupil. Though he still teased her a little with the uncertainty of his true character, the fact was that he felt he had things to learn about the customs and behavior acceptable in English society, which he had already discovered were subtly different from those prevalent in his own country.

Quentin showed uncommon interest in Simon and his pursuits during this time, and spent more time than usual with the young man, even taking him out twice to teach him the fine points of driving a team. Carlton, who regularly received dispatch boxes from London, spent virtually all of his time in the library, frequently in the company of Lord Audwin. Lady Leyland, deprived even of making country visits until Adrian should be made known to a few select neighbors at her father's birthday celebration, contented herself with disseminating all the town gossip at her command to her sister-in-law, and Kitty, though it was normally her habit to tag along after Isobel whenever she had no activity of her own to occupy her, avoided censuring comments from Simon by avoiding Isobel and Adrian and spent most of her time either in the company of her godmother or reading in the sitting room she shared with Isobel.

The result of this was that Isobel and Adrian spent considerable time alone together, on long walks about the estate, playing together on the pianoforte, or simply engaged in conversation. This proved to be dangerous in a way that Isobel had never suspected; she discovered that she liked Adrian very much for his own sake, no matter what his purpose was in masquerading as something he was not. He was as quick-witted and intelligent as she had first detected when he walked into the Duck and Drake, with needle-sharp perceptions that could by turns be stimulating and unsettling. He had a dry, sometimes quirky sense of humor and an unholy enjoyment of all things absurd. Without realizing that it was happening, she began to look forward to each time they would be together.

Sometimes Adrian would stay in character, rustic in speech and manner, and at others his breeding and education were openly displayed. She knew that he betrayed himself to no one but her, and she could not help feeling subtly flattered by this.

Isobel scarcely noticed that Quentin, busy with his own pursuits, gave her perfunctory attendance at best. When she was in Quentin's company, she could not help the irritation she felt with him for his constant venomous jibes at Adrian, whom he now addressed solely by the sobriquet "Savage," and his easy assumption that she would keep for both of them the promise made to his grandfather and silently let him take the credit that the earl assumed was his.

The morning of the earl's birthday celebration gave Isobel further cause to be vexed with Quentin. The night before, becoming sensible at last of her displeasure with him, Quentin had suggested that they ride before breakfast, a custom they had once adhered to religiously when visiting Audswyck for the precious privacy it gave them. When his manner was conciliatory, Quentin could be quite charming and persuasive, and Isobel felt just a sufficient amount of guilt that Adrian occupied so much not only of her time, but her thoughts that she allowed him to make love to her a little and to convince herself that it might be the beginning of reclaiming their former joy in each other's company which seemed to have eluded them of late.

She made her morning toilet in happy expectation, but when she entered the breakfast room she discovered that Quentin had already left the house in the company of Simon. "Beal mentioned that they had taken fishing poles and tackle," Lady Adora informed her, "so one may assume that they have gone to the river for the day."

The fact that he had left her no message and made no excuse proved to her that he had forgotten his engagement with her, perhaps in the wake of Simon's enthusiasm for his favorite activity. It was not the first time he had done so in the past, difficult year, but it still caused her a brief thrust of pain that quickly gelled into anger. Isobel swallowed the sharp words against Quentin which stung at her lips, keeping her pride as well as her temper. She took a chair and accepted coffee from Lady Adora and an offer of toast from her stepmother.

There was no sign of Adrian either, but for once Isobel had no thought for him. The earl invariably took breakfast in his own chambers, and the party at table was entirely female with the exception of Carlton. He sat staring unseeingly at the windows facing the garden, taking his coffee in frequent, almost unconscious sips.

Carlton's manner had been preoccupied almost from the moment of his arrival at Audswyck, and it was plain that he chafed to return to London. Isobel knew that another dispatch box had arrived the previous afternoon from town and that Carlton had spent the remainder of the day until dinner attending to its contents. Thinking to divert him from his impatience to be back at his government office, she suggested that he might care to ride with her.

Lady Leyland quickly seconded her stepdaughter.

"By all means, you must go out in the fresh air and get some exercise, Carl," she said, her expression concerned. "You have been most conscientious of your duties and deserve a bit of fun. You mustn't expend all of your energy doing what others expect of you."

Caroline Leyland had in mind nothing more than Carlton's well-being and pleasure, but Lady Adora, who lived vicariously through her sons' accomplishments, took exception to her sister-in-law's words as heedless interference with Carlton's responsibilities. "Do you think you should, Carl dear?" she said, reaching across the breakfast table to touch his hand. "Caroline is quite right that the exercise would be good for you, but you know how it upsets you when you fall behind in your work. I know this was not a good time for you to leave town, and I am sure we all quite understand your neglect."

Lady Adora doted on both of her sons, who to her were paragons of every manly virtue and quality. Quentin had removed himself as much as possible from her influence from virtually the time he was breeched, but Carlton, whose character was less forceful, was still in some ways constrained by the fine but durable bond of his mother's cloying affection. Deprived of any control of her elder son, Lady Adora cosseted Carlton whenever he came into her compass and to the full extent that his patience would allow. Isobel had thought on more than one occasion that this was the real reason that Carlton was always so reluctant to leave his duties in town to visit Audswyck and why he seemed to immerse himself in work even while there.

"I suppose I might spare an hour or so," Carlton admitted with a slight, wry smile for Isobel. "I sent word to Billington yesterday in response to his dispatch, and I expect an answer today, but it isn't likely to arrive before luncheon, though Lord knows I've work enough to occupy me until then."

"And if word arrives from London before you expect, you shall probably fret that you didn't have that work done to send back to town," his mother pointed out with her sad, gentle smile.

"Then you shall have to take it with you when you return to town on Monday," Isobel said to Carlton, her answering smile one of understanding.

"And Carlton shall undoubtedly be bilious for the remainder of the time until then," Lady Adora said in the tone of one pronouncing the clincher to an argument. "When his own exacting standards are not met, his digestion becomes quite fragile."

Color seeped into Carlton's cheeks. There were times when his digestion was affected by the pressures of his position, but it embarrassed him to have this weakness discussed before his aunt and cousin. "My appetite is excellent, Mother," he said. "I may just as easily finish my work when Isobel and I return. Perhaps we could ride down to the river, Bel. I have not yet seen Quentin's new boat that Grandfather gave him for winning that race to Cheltenham."

Lady Adora visibly paled. "I wish you would not mention that wretched race in my presence, Carl. I shall never forget the palpitations I suffered when Audwin told me that the other young man involved smashed his curricle to bits and nearly broke his foolish neck. It might just as easily have been Quentin, and I think it was very wrong of Audwin to reward him for such reckless behavior."

"But it is exactly what Grandfather always has done," Carlton said dryly. "Never fear, Mother, I give you my word that Isobel and I shall ride most sedately and engage in no races."

"I wish you would also not take out the boat," she said pleadingly. "It has been very wet since the end of the summer, and the river is much higher and swifter than usual. It is enough, surely, that I must suffer all manner of vapors worrying about Quentin without fearing for your safety as well."

Carlton's high color deepened. Only his good breeding prevented him from escaping the room at once. "I wish to see it, not sail it, Mother," he said almost through his teeth, but he knew well enough that he had erred in mentioning the boat. Once an anxiety had taken root in Lady Adora's mind, nothing would persuade her that all the dire consequences she feared were certain to come to pass.

Isobel was also aware of this and said helpfully, "We might ride into the village instead."

Lady Adora sighed deeply. "I wish you might, but, alas, I know what you children are when there is no one about to check you."

"Oh, for heaven's sake, Adora," Lady Leyland said with amused exasperation. "They are neither of them children."

But Isobel could see from Carlton's expression that he had had enough, and as usual, his way of dealing with contention was to retreat from it. He shook his head and, giving Isobel a wan smile as he rose from his chair, said, "I suppose Mother is in the right of it as usual. I would be better employed today seeing to my work. Perhaps tomorrow, Isobel, if you still wish it. Even I must take a day of rest from time to time."

"If you like, Bel, I shall ride with you," Kitty suggested eagerly. "Lydia Channing made the most charming picture entirely out of painted smooth pebbles, and I want to see if I can make one too. I might be able to collect just the sort of pebble I wish by the edge of the water."

Isobel hoped her chagrin did not show in her expression. She was in no humor for Kitty's prattling conversation, but as soon as she had the thought, she felt a wave of remorse; she had spent very little of her time with the girl since coming to Audswyck. "I wish to leave almost at once, Kitty," she said, half hoping to discourage the girl, who was a notorious dawdler, "so you would have to be ready as quickly as possible. I have some correspondence to attend to when I return so that Beal may have it sent to the village for the mail coach to pick up this afternoon."

But Kitty was not to be deterred. She stood up so quickly she nearly knocked over her chair. "It will take me only a few minutes to change, and I shall be down by the time the horses are brought around." She was out of the breakfast room and hurrying to her bedchamber almost before she had completed the sentence.

Carlton offered to send a footman with word to the stables as he left the room. Lady Adora, her ends achieved, smiled in what Isobel regarded as a smug fashion and directed a question about a mutual acquaintance to her sister-in-law. Isobel had once regarded Lady Adora's attempts to cosset her sons as infuriating. Time had turned this to mere irritation that was as much directed toward Carlton for permitting it, or for Quentin, on the rare occasions that he gave in to his mother's manipulations.

Carlton was quieter and more even-tempered than his elder brother and was thus more susceptible to his mother's control, but Isobel recalled a time when there was a greater resemblance in his and Quentin's natures. When Quentin had escaped those smothering bonds, he had gone about cutting a dash with a vengeance, indulging in every dangerous sporting activity that had been forbidden him while under his mother's control and thus had gained for himself his reputation as an out-and-outer. Isobel could remember how those early exploits, similar in nature to the dangerous moonlit race to Cheltenham, had once excited her and made her proud that his name was on everyone's lips. Time had taught her that there were as many calling him foolhardy as declaring that he had excellent bottom.

Just as Isobel returned to the front hall, Kitty, true to her promise, came running down the stairs, holding her skirts a little raised to avoid tripping. "I am ready, Bel," she said a little breathlessly.

But as they were handed onto their horses, Kitty discovered that she had neglected to bring the small pouch she meant to use to collect the pebbles. A footman was sent to retrieve this while Isobel contained her impatience, and finally the young ladies, without the accompaniment of a groom for such a short ride within the bounds of the estate, headed their horses down the drive.

In addition to being a chatterbox, Kitty also had no great gift for horsemanship. Her mount was a placid mare that regarded attempts to persuade her to move at any gait faster than a trot as an indignity. The distance from the house to the banks of the river was not great, but that morning it seemed to Isobel twice what she recalled.

The place where they dismounted and tethered their horses was not likely to be one where Simon and Quentin would be found, which was what Isobel intended. The river was not particularly wide or deep at this point, and several bends reduced the current to little more than that of a swift brook until it widened and straightened once again as it flowed into Turvey property. It was the site of many childhood romps for generations of Renvilles, and there were a number of things present to excite the young, adventurous mind. There was a stone folly where Isobel had served tea to her favorite dolls, and a tree ladder led to a footbridge with a treehouse nestled in the branches of a huge oak at the opposite side, where Quentin and Carlton had played their raucous games.

It had once been an almost magical place for Isobel, but it looked a little sad to her now. The folly was in disuse and covered by insidious vines, the footbridge was missing a number of planks and was clearly unsafe, and even across the width of the water, Isobel could see that the treehouse had fallen into similar disrepair. The last time she had visited this site had been some time ago, and she had been in Quentin's company. They had laughed at the memory of childish games, and talked of the pleasure of introducing their own children to their former haunts one day.

Kitty slid from her horse and ran toward the pebble-strewn bank at once while Isobel followed at a more sedate pace. As Isobel passed the folly she could just make out, through the yellowing leaves of the vine, the figure of a man seated on its steps facing the river. She was not alarmed, at first assuming it to be Simon or Quentin, but as she came to the front of the folly she realized it was Adrian. Her pulse quickened slightly, but she attributed it to nothing more than pleasure at meeting him unexpectedly.

"Good morning, cousin," she said as he caught sight of her and rose. "When I did not see you at breakfast this morning, I thought you had decided to sleep until noon to practice being a man of fashion."

Adrian's smile in answer to her quizzing was warm and welcoming. "I was up betimes this morning and thought it a perfect day for a bit of exercise."

Isobel gathered her trailing skirts and mounted the steps of the folly. "This is the most glorious autumn I can recall," she agreed. "If it were not for the turning of the leaves, one might be persuaded that summer had never ended. Except that most English summers are not even this nice." She sat on the top step, where Adrian had been seated when she spied him through the foliage. "I see the river draws you. Are you home-sick for the Delaware you speak of so often?"

"Not a great deal," he responded cheerfully, "but I've a liking for water. The farm is hard by the river at home, and my brothers and I spent every moment we could away from our chores down at the water's edge and even in it when Pa wasn't around to tell us we were damn fools to risk a drowning."

"After the storms you encountered during your crossing," Isobel reminded him, "I should think you'd have had quite enough of water for now."

"Oh, aye. But the sea's a different sort of thing, isn't it? A beautiful mistress but dangerous, like a high-flyer who enslaves a man and leads him to his doom. A river's a more comfortable old girl that gives a man pleasure with less of a risk." There was a light of mischief in his eyes, daring her to take him to task for his improper metaphor.

Isobel, knowing his purpose, could not be so easily drawn, but Kitty, realizing that Isobel was no longer with her, approached the folly, and was shocked by his words. She saw that Isobel did not seem to take offense and was a little surprised by this as well. There was even the beginning of a smile touching Isobel's lips and laughter in her eyes. Though not especially perceptive at most times, Kitty realized with yet another shock that this was some sort of odd flirtation between them. They were not even aware of her presence.

This was more than shocking to the girl, it was deeply disturbing. Kitty had a schoolgirl's adoration for Quentin, not unlike the one that Isobel had conceived for him years before. She thought him the ideal of every manly virtue, thoroughly dashing and exquisitely handsome. If Isobel had not been beautiful, graceful, witty, and stylish, Kitty might have been quite jealous of her, but instead she thought her the ideal consort for her hero.

That Isobel could be attracted to any other man, especially an uncouth, ignorant colonial who, in Kitty's mind, had cheated Quentin of what was rightfully his, was unthinkable. If Isobel was drawn to him in some way, it had to be because Adrian was using some sort of clever, seductive artifice to lure her away from Quentin if he could. That such diabolical cleverness did not fit with her low opinion of Adrian's mental abilities did not particularly trouble Kitty, who was addicted to the sort of romance in which villains cast wicked spells over heroines as a matter of routine.

She gave a little cough to alert them to her presence and said, "I think we should be leaving, Bel, if you are to do your correspondence in time for it to go to the village to catch the mail."

Isobel looked up in surprise, not just to find the girl there, but at her suggestion. "But we only just arrived. I thought you wished to find pebbles to paint for your picture," she said, wondering at Kitty's sudden haste. "There is certainly time for you to look for your pebbles, Kitty, and this is a likely spot for it."

But Kitty had not shot her bolt at preventing a tête-à-tete between Adrian and Isobel. Ignoring Adrian's greeting to her, she pleaded, "Will you help me, Bel? You can point out the best ones to me."

Isobel curbed her exasperation and said, "Just gather all you think pretty, and then we will sort them together. I wish to speak to Adrian for a few minutes."

There was really nothing else for Kitty to do but gather her skirts and go down to the water's edge, though she cast Isobel a speaking glance of disapproval before she did so. Isobel was faintly puzzled by this, but Adrian enlightened her.

"She's thinking you're not safe at the hands of the

savage, I expect," Adrian commented as they watched Kitty's retreating back. It was rare that he acknowledged Quentin's derisive name for him. "There are a great many rocks and bushes about where I might lure you to an evil purpose."

"To scalp me?" Isobel said sardonically.

"Worse than that," Adrian said, the wickedly lascivious gleam in his eyes leaving no doubt of his meaning.

Isobel had been on the town far too long to be missish about suggestive comments, but she felt her color rise at the idea that Adrian might wish to make love to her. She had successfully kept all thought of the attraction between them at bay since he had kissed her that first night, but a delicious tickling excitement rose in her to prove that it simmered just below the surface of her consciousness. "No, that won't do, Adrian," she admonished with a deliberately light laugh. "You have all but admitted to me that you are not the rough creature you pretend to be. You cannot expect me to believe you still when you flit back and forth in that role."

Adrian was watching Kitty bending at the water's edge to select those small flat stones that captured her fancy. A breeze coming off the water whipped his hair about his face, and Isobel could not help noting how boyishly attractive this made him look.

"I am as I am. Nothing more," he said, making another of those cryptic statements that she found quite maddening.

"I wonder why it is only me that you let glimpse the truth?" she said musingly. "I am beginning to feel as if I see a ghost which haunts only me."

Adrian laughed at this analogy, and said with a slight ironic inflection, "Oh, I'm flesh and blood right enough. And not so much a mystery as you make me out to be."

Isobel looked up at him and said with sudden earnestness, "Then tell me why you are doing this."

Adrian sat down beside her. As he had before, he ran his fingers caressingly down her cheek. "I wish I could, my lovely," he said in a tone that mirrored the caress.

Isobel glanced hastily toward the river, but could glimpse only a bit of Kitty's back as she continued to stoop to examine pebbles. The sensible thing for Isobel to do would be to join her, but she remained where she was, held in place by the dually seductive lure of Adrian's physical presence and the hope that he would tell her what she so much wished to know. "You've trusted me so far," she said, matching the softness of his tone. "You may safely confide the whole in me."

Adrian's lips parted in a brief, wry smile. "Did I say it was you I didn't trust?"

He spoke so quietly that Isobel leaned toward him to catch his words. "I don't understand," she said with mild complaint. "Who then do you distrust?"

"Myself." He bent his head a little closer to hers so that their lips were alarmingly, tantalizingly near. "I may not be as uncivilized as Quentin wishes to believe, but neither am I as civilized as you imagine."

Isobel gave an uncertain laugh. He was going to kiss her again, there was not the least doubt of it, and she would do nothing to prevent it. "Half savage?" she said on a breath.

"Just now, entirely," he replied, and his mouth covered hers.

This was nothing at all like the first time he had kissed her. There could not be the slightest misconstruing of his intention or of her response. Their tongues entwined, teasing, exploring, substituting for the ultimate intimacy that was in both of their thoughts and desires. Isobel's mind cried out against what she was doing, but her senses ruled and greedily savored every moment of their physical contact. They separated for a moment, and he cupped her face in his hands while he showered a dozen gentle kisses on her cheekbones and forehead, her eyes, and the tip of her nose before finding her lips again.

Isobel's pulse raced and she realized that it had been some time since Quentin's kisses had had the power to so affect her. The fleeting thought sobered her and made her recall that she was not free to receive such advances from any man other than her betrothed, no matter how powerful the temptation. She drew away from Adrian reluctantly, and pushed him gently when he tried to draw her to him again.

"Please, I can't," she said, almost breathless. She tried to muster reproach into her voice but failed signally. "You shouldn't have done that, Adrian."

"Then you shouldn't have kissed me back," he said, quite unrepentant. This time he had fully meant to kiss her. He had restrained himself during all the time they had spent alone together at a considerable cost. But the bond between them had grown and strengthened during those days, and he believed she would not reject his advances out of hand. His desire for her had grown as well in this time and could not be held in check much longer. He would have her or he would have to leave her, which would mean leaving Audswyck and perhaps even England.

Isobel realized the foolishness of expecting that he would not have realized how fully she had responded to him, but clinging to the last shreds of her pride she said, "A gentlemen would not say such a thing."

"Which everyone knows I am not," he said affably, "and I daresay I shall never learn to be one no matter how prettily you teach me to make my bows and ask for permission to put my name on a lady's dance card. It's my base and vulgar nature, I expect."

Though Isobel tried to maintain her dignity, one recalcitrant dimple betrayed her. She knew that even to fantasize about making love with this man, let alone permitting it in reality, was madness, but the fact that she liked him as well as wanted him made the lure all but irresistible. What this would lead to she could not think, and for the moment she wished only to put some distance between them before she lost herself again in his beautiful, enticing eyes.

Isobel quite deliberately broke contact with them and looked toward the river. For the first time since Adrian's lips had touched hers, she remembered Kitty. She rose and looked quickly to the spot where they had last seen Kitty. Mercifully, the girl's back was still to them. As if aware of this sudden scrutiny, Kitty turned toward them, and seeing Isobel, she waved and called to her.

"Kitty is calling to me," Isobel said unnecessarily, and she left Adrian alone on the folly steps. When she reached the bank, she informed Kitty it was time for them to return to the house, and then she went to the horses and drew her gelding over to a large rock to help her remount, not wishing for Adrian's assistance and the physical contact it would bring.

Kitty scrambled up the bank and made her way toward the horses still holding up the wide skirts of her habit, which she had gathered to keep them from trailing in the water, and clutching her pouch full of pebbles, which was overfilled from her endeavors. She was more concerned with her skirts and keeping the pebbles from tumbling out of the pouch than with paying attention to where she placed her feet as she made her way back to Isobel and the horses.

Isobel watched Kitty's approach absently, and almost didn't believe the evidence of her eyes when she saw Kitty catch her foot in the raised roots of a large bush and begin to fall headlong. Kitty dropped her skirts, which immediately became entangled in her legs, making the fall inevitable. The pouch she carried went flying from her slackened grip, and untied, the wide mouth of it opened to spew small stones in a wide arc at Isobel and the horses. The rocks were too small and the distance too short to do any damage and those that struck Isobel merely stung her, but her horse, far more spirited a mount than Kitty's, took instant fright and shied violently.

Isobel was an excellent horsewoman and might have kept her seat if the gelding had not followed this action by suddenly rearing while she was still off balance. She felt her foot slip free of the stirrup, and she began to slide toward the boulder she had just used to mount. She knew if she fell between the rock and the frightened horse's hooves she risked serious injury, and she grasped frantically for the pommel of the saddle, her fingers brushing the leather but finding no grip.

Then strong arms suddenly grasped Isobel from behind and pulled her away from the horse. Kitty began screaming and startled the gelding even more. It flattened its ears as it became earthbound again and gathered itself to bolt. As abruptly as Isobel had been seized, she was released safely on her feet, and before her startled gaze she saw Adrian streak after the horse before it could gather speed, grab the reins to slow it, and then swing himself expertly into the saddle, where in a matter of moments he had the terrified creature under control. He walked the gelding in slow circles, murmuring soothing noises until it had settled into relative calmness, merely snorting its indignation and gnawing at a bit that was now in the firm control of its rider.

"Well done, cousin," a voice shouted behind them. In another moment Simon came trotting up to them. The admiration in his voice was genuine, and it was clear he had not yet remembered the occasion less than a fortnight earlier when Adrian had not seemed able to properly mount a horse in a far more conventional fashion. But Isobel remembered and she wondered what else was still false about Adrian. It disconcerted her to realize she had let a man make love to her when she knew that he deceived with such ease and with such ability to convince.

Adrian walked the now docile horse up to her and dismounted, patting its neck as he handed her the reins.

"You never learned that on a plow horse, coz," Simon said, memory returning and with it the suspicion that he had been duped in some fashion.

There was the sound of a sob behind them, and they turned to see Kitty, who had been quite forgotten in the excitement, still sitting on the ground and clutching her leg. Tears were streaming from her eyes, mottling the delicate porcelain of her complexion. "I think I have broken my ankle," she said piteously when she saw she had their attention.

Adrian knelt beside her and felt her leg gently through her boot and declared that though he was no expert, it was more likely only a bad sprain. "But we'd best get her back to the house at once and get that boot off before her ankle swells any more." He scooped Kitty up in his arms and started to carry her to her mare, but she buried her head in his shoulder and said, "No, please. I couldn't ride. I should be so afraid I would fall off and hurt myself again."

Adrian looked rather nonplussed at this, but Isobel said, "Take her up in front of you on Jimbo, Adrian. I'll ride Lucy back to the stables."

Adrian once again swung himself into the saddle with a grace that could only be envied. He and Simon settled Kitty as comfortably as possible on the saddle in front of Adrian. Adrian looked down and saw Simon's eyes on him, the look in them puzzled and a little accusatory. He sighed inwardly. There were decided pitfalls to the business of deception.

Simon gave Isobel a leg up onto the placid mare. "Are you coming back to the house with us?" she asked her brother as she gathered up her reins.

Simon shook his head. "I thought I might find a bit more sport first. Sometimes when the water is as high as it is now, the fishing is very good just before the last bend."

Isobel suddenly realized that Simon was alone. "But where is Quentin?"

Simon shrugged. "Back at the house, I suppose." His tone was so carefully casual that it revealed the disappointment that it was meant to conceal. "He had the headache and thought he'd best go back to bed for a few hours if he is to be in good form for the party tonight."

More likely, Isobel thought, Quentin was feeling the effects of the previous night's brandy combined with a severe dose of boredom. Quentin would gladly ride neck or nothing after the hounds for the whole of a day or spend hours in chill weather patiently stalking deer in Scotland, but angling bored him, and an hour of sitting tamely on a stream or riverbank was more than he could be expected to endure. Apparently she was not the only one to whom he made promises he did not put himself out to keep.

These reflections were interrupted by Adrian, who asked Simon a question about the type of fish found in the river and the sort of bait he used.

Simon responded warily, as if he were not quite certain what to make of Adrian, who had expressed no interest in angling before. "Do you fish, cousin?" he asked.

"Occasionally. I'm not the keen angler that you are," Adrian admitted, "but I grew up on the banks of a river, you know, and had my first fishing pole when I was still in leading strings."

"I suppose that means you could fish with Sir Henry Alford and not disgrace yourself," Simon said dryly, naming the baronet whose published works on the subject of angling were considered the ultimate source of technique by most devotees. "That is, if you picked up the skill by fishing occasionally as well as you did riding by throwing a leg over a plow horse or two."

Adrian did not try to evade the challenge in Simon's eyes but smiled ruefully in return. "We might come back here again one day next week, and you can judge for yourself."

Simon would have accepted such an invitation from the bootboy if it had been made, and he readily agreed.

Adrian had an arm about Kitty's waist to hold her in place, and he controlled the skittish gelding with reins in one hand and the pressure of his legs. As if knowing he had met his master, Jimbo moved out alongside the mare Lucy as if his nature were as docile as hers.

As they started off, Isobel's and Adrian's eyes met, and she gave him the smile of a contented cat. "You are dished, cousin," she said sweetly. Simon would not be fobbed off with some simple excuse to explain why Adrian had pretended he couldn't ride the day they had met him at the Duck and Drake. There was no reconciling the skill they had observed today with that clumsy performance.

Adrian smiled in return. "I think it shall prove not," he said and turned the subject, since they could not properly speak in Kitty's presence.

The ride home was even slower and more tedious than Isobel's and Kitty's journey to the river. Kitty, her ankle paining her, moaned piteously for most of the way, making conversation impossible. Isobel, with thoughts enough to occupy her, was glad that she had no opportunity for close conversation with Adrian until those thoughts were sorted.

It was a very long time since Isobel naively had believed that Quentin was faithful to her during their interminable wait to be married, but she could not stoop to petty revenge. For the first year and more, she had truly had eyes for no man other than Quentin, but as time went by, she would admit to herself an occasional attraction to another man. This was the first time, if she did not count the masked man at Vauxhall, that she had ever seriously contemplated infidelity herself, and that she could do so was very upsetting to her.

It was true that her feelings for Quentin had undergone change, but this was because she no longer idealized him as she once had. He was a man with weaknesses and faults like any other, and given what she knew of the character of many men of fashion, these were few and, in contrast, not terribly significant. She too had matured and changed, and it was only natural that they should both view each other in a different light. Whatever their quarrels and occasional disillusionments, there was no doubt that one day they would be married. She loved Quentin and he loved her.

Such was her logic as thoughts and snippets of memories raced through her head during the ride back to Audswyck Chase. But as much as she wished to believe it, her innate honesty made her not at all certain that she did. What she was certain of was that Adrian Renville, whoever, whatever he was, had cut up her peace, and she doubted if it would ever be whole again.

It would clearly be a mistake for her to continue to seek out Adrian's company. She had no doubt at all that he would try to make love to her again, and very little doubt that she would permit him to do so, in spite of all reason. Perhaps she would even leave Audswyck on Monday with her mother and Carlton. The earl would be less than pleased, since he expected the tutoring of Adrian to continue until he judged Adrian acceptable, but at the moment incurring his displeasure seemed the lesser evil. Adrian needed no instruction of any sort, she was now convinced, and the earl with his keen perception would find that out for himself soon enough. What did any of this matter to the imminent loss of her virtue and perhaps even the destruction of a future she had dreamed of for two-thirds of her life?

There was only tonight and Sunday to get through, and Isobel was determined to avoid Adrian as much as possible and keep him at a safe distance when it was not. With this resolve in mind, she favored Adrian with only a cool nod of thanks when he handed her from her horse at the doors of Audswyck Chase.

Chapter 7

Lady Leyland made a great fuss over her ward when Kitty was carried into the house by a footman, insisting that the doctor be fetched at once. Lady Adora was also in a taking over Kitty's injury, sending her dresser to fetch hartshorn, laudanum, bacillim powder, sticking plaster, and any other remedy she could think of to treat the injured girl until the doctor arrived.

"Quite as if," Adrian said in a whispered aside to Isobel, "Kitty had been thrown from her horse, set upon by bravos, and cast down with the influenza all at one and the same time."

All the fuss turned out to be a tempest in a teacup, however, for Dr. Rhodes, when he arrived to see the patient, pronounced that nothing ailed Kitty other than a few slight abrasions, a badly sprained ankle, and the shock of her fall. He predicted that a quiet evening and a few days of staying off her feet would see her once again right as rain.

It was not often that Kitty, whose presence among them was generally taken for granted, was the recipient of so much attention, and perhaps she could scarcely be blamed for the die-away airs she assumed that kept the ladies hovering over her and the servants exerting themselves to see to her comfort. Even Carlton and Simon, when he returned to the house, came to the sitting room Kitty shared with Isobel to engage her in light conversation for her amusement.

Finally, though, her godmother left her to see to some last-minute details for the evening's entertainment, Lady Adora returned to her room to regather her strength for the ordeal of having a half-dozen guests in the house, and the servants were recalled to their various duties. Only Simon and Carlton remained, and since they were giving more attention to a discussion on the conformation of Quentin's new team than to the invalid, Kitty was feeling rather let down and ignored after having been the center of all attention for the better part of the morning.

She listened to their conversation in growing dudgeon and found the means of regaining their attention when Simon mentioned Adrian and his offer to fish with him the following week. Simon did so only as a means of bringing Adrian into the conversation. What he wished to discuss with Carlton was the odd circumstance that Adrian should pretend to be a poor rider when he was in fact an excellent horseman. He had indeed quite forgotten Kitty and was not pleased when she interrupted him.

"You must not encourage that wretched man, Simon," she said loftily. "It is the greatest misfortune that he came here at all, and if you make a friend of him he shall probably never leave."

Simon regarded her with some surprise. "I don't suppose he shall leave in any case," he said baldly. "That's why he's come, isn't it? To take his place in the family as my grandfather's heir?"

"I wouldn't worry about it, Puss," Carlton said, mildly condescending.

"Someone should," Kitty said with unexpected boldness. "He'll ruin everything if he stays."

Simon and Carlton exchanged a puzzled glance. "Whether he stays or leaves, it is much the same, Kitty," the latter explained patiently. "He shall be the next earl and inherit the entail, and if he did not, it would go to one of his brothers."

"I know all of that," Kitty said with a note of impatience. "Quentin could lose a great deal more than that if we do not find a way to make Adrian leave us."

There was no doubt she had their full attention now. Neither Simon nor Carlton had the slightest notion what she meant by this, but Kitty spoke so positively that she had sparked the curiosity of both of them. "If you mean that Adrian might cut Quentin out of the remainder of grandfather's fortune—"

"No, I don't mean that," Kitty said grandly. "Quentin could lose something far more important to him than money."

Carlton grinned sardonically. "Now I know this is all a hum, Kitty. There isn't anything more important to my brother."

Kitty ignored this slander of her idol. "It has nothing whatever to do with money," she said, lowering her voice a little and glancing melodramatically about the room, as if she expected a spying servant to be hiding in the draperies. "I am afraid it is Isobel that he will lose."

"If you fear this because my dear brother is intent on revealing the worst of his nature by his constant cuts at Adrian," said Carlton aridly, "I shouldn't be concerned, Kit. If after fifteen years' acquaintance Bel ain't aware that Quentin can have a damned sharp tongue in his head, she hasn't the gray matter I give her credit for."

"If Quentin had seen Adrian kissing Isobel in the folly today, he would probably have challenged him to a duel," Kitty avowed, and received for her indiscretion as much sensation as she could have wished for.

"The devil you say!" exclaimed Carlton.

"What a bouncer, Kitty," put in Simon. "What would Bel be doing kissing him?"

"Well, she was," Kitty averred. She shifted a little uncomfortably on the chaise longue. She had been deeply shocked when she had turned from her task of gathering stones to call to Isobel and had seen her and Adrian entwined on the steps of the folly. She had certainly never meant to tell anyone else what she had seen, but now, having used her knowledge to regain center stage, she could not take it back without making a fool of herself.

"I don't believe it," Carlton said flatly.

"I *saw* them," Kitty insisted. "I was looking for little flat stones to make a picture, and they thought I wouldn't see them, but I did."

"Perhaps you saw him taking a speck of dust out of her eye," Carlton suggested, rising from his chair. He leaned forward and tweaked Kitty's cheek in a teasing fashion. "You'd best not go about saying such things, or it'll be you who feels the sharp edge of Quentin's tongue, and Isobel's as well, which is no mean weapon either. I'd best go back to my work. The messenger from town should be here any time now."

The door had barely closed behind Carlton when Simon turned to Kitty and said, "Exactly what did you see today, Kit?"

"Precisely what I said I saw," Kitty said with slight indignation. "Adrian kissed Isobel."

"How did he kiss her? On her cheek? Her forehead?"

"No. On the mouth. He was making love to her."

Simon looked as if he would have probed this further, but reflecting that he should not even be discussing such a thing with a girl of Kitty's tender years, he merely said, "What happened then?"

Kitty shrugged. "I don't know. I was afraid they would catch me staring at them, so I began to look for stones again. I suppose you don't believe me either, but it did happen."

Simon mused on this for a moment. "I can understand why Adrian might wish to kiss Isobel, but why would she let him? She wasn't struggling, was she?" he demanded as an unpleasant idea occurred to him.

"No, not at all, though I cannot understand why she would let him kiss her either," Kitty confessed and then launched into her pet theory. "I think he is jealous of Quentin and wants to seduce Isobel away."

Simon had even more to disturb him concerning Adrian's odd behavior, but he had no intention of discussing this with Kitty. Showing an irritating lack of sympathy for her theory, he laughed. "Much luck to him. Isobel is no green girl. The most polished libertine—which my cousin from America most certainly is not—would be likely to catch cold trying to trick her into seduction."

"I know what I saw," Kitty said stubbornly.

Simon got up from his chair and bent over Kitty, saying in her ear, "And if anyone walked in on us at this moment, they might think I was kissing you." And then to Kitty's astonishment, he did so, though in an entirely brotherly manner. "Don't refine too much upon it, Puss. All will be well, you know. Bel will marry Quentin, Grandfather will settle an absurd amount of money on them, and we'll all live happily ever after." He gave her upturned chin a brief squeeze and left her.

Kitty was very vexed, though whether she was more so with Simon and Carlton for not believing her or herself for telling what she had seen, she would have been hard put to say. Her concern for the happiness of Isobel and Quentin was quite genuine, and beyond the desire to make herself important, she had hoped that Carlton, or even Simon, who was very good at ideas, might find some way of putting a spoke in Adrian's wheel.

This justification quite appealed to Kitty, for it absolved her of guilt and made her feel quite virtuous. She wondered if perhaps she might find a way of hinting to Quentin that his future happiness might be in jeopardy, but she recalled what Carlton had said about courting the sharp edge of Quentin's tongue and decided she had been quite indiscreet enough for one day. Instead Kitty whiled away the remainder of the afternoon indulging in several satisfying fantasies that all ended with Quentin and Isobel being eternally grateful to her for exposing the wicked American interloper and saving their relationship.

But her words bore more fruit than she guessed. Carlton had taken greater note of what Kitty had said than he permitted her to realize. It might be difficult to imagine Isobel permitting a clodpole like his American cousin to kiss her, but then it had been his experience that there was often no accounting for the taste of women when it came to choosing a lover. Unknowingly, he shared Adrian's opinion that Quentin was undeserving of Isobel's devotion, and it gave him secret satisfaction to think that a man whom Quentin held in undisguised contempt might possibly hand his brother his horns.

Simon entered the library while Carlton was enjoying this pleasant reflection. Carlton sighed and pulled the papers that had been lying idly in his hand closer to him. He glanced up at Simon. "I hope you have come for a book," he said. "The messenger will be here any moment, and I haven't time for anything else just now."

Simon was not deterred by these words, but pulled a studded leather chair closer to the desk and said conspiratorially, "If I were you, I would send the whole lot of those papers back to town with him so that they are not hanging about when you are not attending to them."

Carlton's brow creased and he sighed again. "I suppose you mean to tell me the chambermaid took an extra two minutes to dust my room this morning and you suspect she is a French spy. I really haven't time for your stories, Simon."

"It is no such thing," Simon said, affronted. "And I thought you mentioned that it is the war with the United States, not the one with France, that has been occupying you lately."

Carlton had not reached his high position at such a young age without possessing quick wit as well as superb connections. "I suppose you are in some way suggesting that our cousin Adrian might be a spy," he said acerbicly. "I should sooner believe in your dawdling chambermaid."

Simon did not respond to this directly but said, "Did you believe Kitty about Isobel letting Adrian kiss her?"

"What has that to say to anything?"

Once again Simon's reply was circumspect. "Did you know that Adrian is a first-rate horseman? Isobel was riding Jimbo this morning, and you know what a skittish beast he is. Adrian saved Bel from being thrown, and then, when Jimbo tried to bolt after she came off, Adrian caught the saddle like a dashed rider from Astley's Circus and swung himself onto Jimbo's back. I saw him do it myself. Jimbo was as placid as old Lucy in a matter of moments."

For all his cleverness, Carlton could not piece together the connection of these things at first, but he was determined to do so before Simon could enlighten him. "Didn't you tell me the day we all arrived," he said slowly, "that Adrian could barely stay in the saddle with a fist full of mane?"

Simon nodded. "He didn't even know which foot to put in the stirrup."

Carlton understood. He had been trained to be suspicious of anything extraordinary, contrary, or unexpected. But he did not possess the degree of distrust common to many of his colleagues in the foreign office.

His smile for Simon was a bit patronizing, not unlike the one he had favored Kitty with a short while earlier. "Very likely it is no more than that he was awkward and unsure of himself on the day you met him, and his heroics today might have been nothing more than a cool head and luck."

Simon shook his head vigorously. "Adrian pretended he couldn't ride at all. And he may very well be trying to seduce Isobel in the hope that she will be able to help him gain access to your papers."

Though Carlton did not mean to laugh outright at his young, eager cousin, Simon's avid earnestness was too much for his gravity. "Good Lord, Simon," he said when he had regained his composure a few moments later, "you can't be serious. I know you are rather bored here, as are we all, but that is no cause to begin looking for spies in every corner. And cousin Adrian of all men! If every man who told lies and tried to seduce beautiful women was to be suspected of espionage, half of the men in government would distrust the other half and vice versa."

Simon's color was high. Whatever Carlton might say, he would not forget that England was at war with the United States of America and that Adrian was American. His gaze fixed firmly on the Turkey carpet, he mumbled, "He lied for some reason."

"Ask him."

Simon's eyes flashed upward. "I shall." With these words he catapulted himself from his chair and out of the room.

It was not out of the question that Carlton himself, supplied with these oddities in Adrian's behavior, might have harbored some doubts about him if Simon had not put forth his suspicions in such a lurid manner. As it was, Carlton laughed softly to himself once again, and then continued with his work without giving it another thought.

It might have been supposed by the more reasonable members of his family that Lord Audwin, having no notion what to expect in the character of his American grandson, would have planned his birthday celebration to include no one outside of the immediate family. But Audwin was a man who set his own rules to define reasonableness and then blithely expected everyone else to conform. Once again this blind arrogance was rewarded. There was undoubtedly considerable improvement to be seen in Adrian each day that passed. If he did not yet meet his grandfather's exacting standards for the conduct of a gentlemen, at least the earl was satisfied that he would not be disgraced in front of his old friend Lord Monkhouse and their other guests.

Adrian even had agreed to the loan of proper attire from Quentin for the occasion. He came to where they were gathered in the long gallery dressed in the correct black silk coat and breeches, his linen snowy white and of obvious quality, and his neckcloth expertly tied.

Isobel saw that her conjecture that Adrian would look very well properly dressed was quite true. Quentin might have been a slight bit taller than Adrian, but his clothes fit Adrian well enough. For the first time she realized that Adrian's ill-fitting garb had disguised a lean, muscular frame, broad shoulders, narrow hips, and well-turned legs that would never require padding. She saw that even his hair was dressed with a subtle difference, fashionably emphasizing its natural curl.

Isobel almost wished that Adrian did not look so elegant and handsome. She felt an unexpected thrill of pleasure when she beheld him and a rush of possessive pride, as if it were Adrian rather than Quentin to whom she was betrothed. She was further disconcerted by the warmth in Adrian's eyes when they met hers. He smiled at her, an intimate smile that seemed to unite them in some way, as if it acknowledged something shared by them alone. It was the smile of a lover to his beloved, for her alone. Isobel felt a tingling warmth spread through her and quickly turned away, hoping that her fair countenance did not betray her with a blush.

She reminded herself of her resolve to keep Adrian at a distance and went at once to Quentin's side. He gave her a brief smile of acknowledgment that did not touch his eyes, so very different from the way that Adrian had looked at her. Isobel was struck by the difference, and felt both sadness and anger that they seemed to have lost, or at least forgotten, the loving intimacy they had once shared.

Lady Leyland followed her stepdaughter into the long gallery, and she went directly to Adrian, intent on complimenting him on his appearance. Adrian took her hand when she came up to him and bowed over it in a manner that would not have done discredit to a Pink of the Ton.

"Well," drawled Quentin at his most sardonic, "who said you can't teach an old dog new tricks? You did that exactly right, my good savage. Now, just mind you do the same with every lady presented to you, and we might just pull this thing off tonight without irreparable damage to the family name."

Adrian grinned, the insult bouncing off him without effect as usual. "Grandpa bade me to mind my manners and threatened to send me packing if I did anything to disgrace him tonight. I'd best buckle down to this gentleman business if I'm to find myself with a whole hide by morning."

"Then mind your tongue as well, cousin," said Quentin acerbicly. "Speak as little as possible and only when spoken to. It may be possible to teach you to execute a passable bow to a lady in the space of a fortnight, but I fear your deplorable manner of speech will require a rather longer tutoring to correct."

Lord Audwin came into the gallery accompanied by Lady Adora. It was obvious that his lordship, casting a critical eye over his heir, was indeed pleased by this change in Adrian's appearance, and he said so, though the compliment was for Quentin rather than Adrian. "Well done, my boy. I trust it wasn't necessary for Ludkin to tie him down to see him dressed properly. Whatever you pay your man, it is insufficient. He has wrought a considerable wonder."

Quentin bowed acknowledgment for this accomplishment, though in fact it was Ludkin who had somewhat diffidently, and quite on his own, approached Adrian again with offerings from his master's wardrobe. To the valet's astonishment, Adrian had this time accepted without argument.

"It took considerable effort on both Ludkin's part and mine," said Quentin, misstating the truth without a blush, "to penetrate my cousin's understanding that his present mode of dress was not acceptable, let alone à la mode despite the assurances of the innkeeper of the Golden Cross. I bade Ludkin to take those repulsive garments and have them torn up for rags, so unless Cousin Adrian wishes to revert to the loincloth of his native land, he will have little choice but to make himself presentable for the future. I also had my man send a groom to town to fetch a few more things and to purchase some linen as well. I came scarcely prepared to supply dress for two."

His grandfather beamed on him. "That was wise of you. A country party with old friends is one thing, but it'll be a time yet before we dare loose him on the town to have his own things made. You won't suffer for the loss to your wardrobe, Quentin, I promise you that."

A few minutes later, the first guests, Sir George and Lady Cahill, were announced, and hard on their heels arrived the Turveys and Lord Monkhouse and finally General Simmonds and his wife entered the gallery to complete their numbers. All of the earl's guests were introduced to Adrian, and to his credit, he neither said nor did anything to put his grandfather to the blush. He seemed to take Quentin's advice, for he said no more than was necessary to each person presented to him.

After greetings had been exchanged, all the company were engaged with one another in conversation with the exception of Isobel and Adrian. She had not meant to have any direct conversation with him again until her departure on Monday, and she looked about almost in a panic as he approached her, but unless she wished to be insufferably rude to him, she had no choice but to speak with him.

"I look fine as a fivepence, don't I, Cousin Bel," he said, at his most bucolic. "Maybe Quentin can't make a purse out of me, but he can dress me up in silk right fine. Though," he added confidentially, "I'm bound to have a rash on my jaw in the morning from all the starch in these danged shirt points. I tried to hold the line at keeping my own shirts, but Ludkin told me no one would mistake me for a gentleman if I could turn my head freely in either direction."

Paradoxically, his rustic manner, though she knew it was false, set her at her ease with him again. "No one will mistake you for a gentleman if you go about confiding such things to them, cousin," she said, keeping her twitching lips as firm as she could.

"Oh, no," Adrian replied, his eyes softening. "Only to you."

Isobel felt her pulse increase and said quickly, "Do you mean to disgrace us tonight by discussing something unmentionable at the dinner table before our guests, or will you risk discovery of your duplicity by behaving with complete decorum?"

He shook his head, and Isobel noted how much more green his eyes seemed than gray when the light of laughter was in them. "I'm on my best behavior tonight," he assured her. "Though," he added thoughtfully, "I doubt I am doing you good by making it possible for you to marry Quentin with Grandpa's blessing."

Isobel's lips parted in surprise. His words had a double-edged meaning, and both took her in astonishment. But her surprise at the implication that he did not think she should marry Quentin was subordinate at the moment to other inference she made. Adrian obviously knew of the bargain his grandfather had struck with her and Quentin and their reward if successful. Isobel felt strangely embarrassed by it. "Quentin told you?" she demanded incredulously.

Adrian shook his head, his expression unchanging but a searching look in his eyes as they rested on her. "No, Simon. I beg pardon if I've been casting a rub in your way," he said, his voice suspiciously bland, "so I mean to mind my lessons herein."

Isobel wanted to assure him that this was not the reason she had spent so much time in his company, but held her tongue. It might be better if he thought that. Better for her. "You cannot blame Grandfather for wishing to prepare you for your inheritance," she said as coolly as she could manage.

"Nor you for taking an interest in me when it was all to your good to do so."

But with Adrian's eyes steady on hers, she found the lie almost impossible to continue. "You know perfectly well you have no need of any lessons," she said crisply, looking away from him.

"You're fair and far out there," Adrian said. "Cousin Quentin claims he never set eyes on such a gape-seed and gave me up as hopeless before he began."

Isobel understood very well what was implied, that Quentin was making no effort to do their grandfather's bidding in spite of the promised reward for doing so. "I have noted that you are at your most gratingly bucolic in his company," she said defensively.

"Ah, but then Quentin doesn't inspire me to my best as you do, Cousin Bel."

Isobel felt compelled to look at Adrian again and then wished she had not. She did not want to be affected by this man, but she could not prevent her response to him. She knew he wanted her to reassure him that the time they had spent together had been her choice, not expediency and, God help her, she wanted to. How could this have happened? There was an attraction between them, but it was nothing more. It couldn't be more. She forced herself to ignore the question in his eyes and said briskly, "How did Simon come to tell you that *Grand-père* wishes us to tutor you? I had no idea he knew of it."

Adrian appeared to be willing to let his question remain unanswered, for now at least. He lowered his voice before replying in his normal accents, "He tracked me down to demand to know how it was I had learned to ride so expertly in less than a fortnight. When we had that all worked out, we talked of other things. He made rather a point of telling me that you were bound to teach me my manners. To keep me in my place, I expect."

Isobel, believing herself in hand again, forced herself to smile. "He should know by now that you are not so easily snubbed," she said, determined to keep their discussion light and impersonal. "And how did you explain your unexpected skill at horsemanship, cousin?"

Adrian sighed. "I told him the truth."

Isobel nearly gasped. "The truth! I wish you would tell it to me."

"A sliver of it, all and all," he replied soothingly. "I said that I was just having a little fun at his expense at the Duck and Drake because I could see that he assumed I would be unable to ride decently. I was all but born on the back of horse, I've been told, for my mother began her travail while out for a morning ride."

"Did you also admit that you deliberately knocked him into the mud?" Isobel said, curious to see if he would confirm her suspicion.

Adrian shook his head, his ready smile returning. He did not deny it. "No. But he's a clever lad and will work it out himself if he hasn't already."

Isobel began to relax. It was obvious that he was taking her lead, or perhaps she had imagined his earlier searching intensity. She laughed softly. "Your ice is becoming thinner and thinner, cousin. Now there are two of us who know that you are a charlatan."

Adrian's expression sobered. "Now, that is a word that implies fraud, and that is not at all my intent. I'm a harmless fellow, all in all."

Isobel recalled that he had said something similar to her once before, but she now knew how dangerous he could be, at least to her. She was very glad when their tête-à-tête was brought to an end by Lord Audwin, who brought his friend Lord Monkhouse to speak with Adrian.

Dinner passed so smoothly that even Lady Adora all but forgot her early anxiety that it would somehow prove a disaster with Adrian as its cause. There was nothing in the least in his behavior to suggest other than that he was a well brought-up young man. Not only did he do and say all the right things when addressed, but even his accent showed a marked improvement. Isobel wondered how the others could not possibly see the anomaly in this, but she saw no surprised or bemused expressions on any of their faces.

Adrian and Isobel were at opposite sides of the table, and her eyes met his frequently during dinner. His were quizzing and fairly dancing with inner amusement that he clearly invited her to share. In this humor he looked to her quite beautiful, and for the first time she had the shockingly treacherous thought that she wished she was free to respond to Adrian, for she could not deny she wished to do. She was appalled that she could have such feelings, and for the remainder of dinner she steadfastly refused to even glance in Adrian's direction.

As soon as the last covers were removed, the ladies retired and were quickly followed by the gentlemen, Lord Audwin caring less for drinking port than enjoying a game of whist with Monkhouse and the Simmonds, who were all keen players. He was soon happily seated at the table set up for the game in the drawing room, with the general as his partner and Monkhouse and the general's wife opposing them.

Isobel went upstairs for a short while to visit Kitty, who had been forbidden by her godmother to join the party so that she might rest to let her sprained ankle and other bruises heal. When Isobel returned, she saw that Adrian was in conversation with Lord Turvey, who had been a friend of Adrian's father in their salad days. Lord Turvey exhibited no signs of consternation, so she safely assumed that Adrian had not reverted to the role of rustic provincial.

Everyone else appeared comfortably engaged with the exception of Quentin. He was standing by the hearth, poking the fire occasionally with a fire iron while Simon regaled him with some animated tale. Though Isobel saw him turn and make some unheard reply to her brother, it was obvious from his expression and restless movements that Quentin was bored. It was Isobel's natural reaction to go to Quentin, both to rescue him from Simon's often tiresome boyish enthusiasms and to set himself the task of amusing him. She actually took steps in that direction, but stopped and stood irresolute for a few moments. The truth was that she did not wish for Quentin's company at that moment. This thought disturbed her, but still she turned away and walked over to the pianoforte.

She did not really wish to play, but the instrument was a prop to excuse her from joining any of the small groups in conversation. She did not consciously wish for Adrian to join her, as he often did when she sat down at the pianoforte, but she heard footsteps approaching her and turned, expecting it to be him. It was Quentin who came to stand beside the instrument.

"Unless our cousin forgets himself," he said, his voice a bored drawl, "it appears as if we shall get through this evening without a major scandal occurring."

Isobel looked up at him from the perusal of a score and smiled. "I think we may count on it. He has not made a single blunder, has he?" she said leadingly.

"It is a miracle," Quentin conceded sardonically, "but I admit he has not. There has not been even one mention of bodily functions or farm animals tonight."

Isobel wanted to shake him for his deliberate obtuseness. Quentin was far too clever not to realize that it would indeed be a miracle if Adrian had improved so greatly in so short a time. "It is not a miracle in the least," Isobel insisted as she selected a piece of music at random and set it on the stand above the keyboard. "I told you the day he arrived that I thought him quite capable of behaving as he ought should he choose, but you would not believe me."

Quentin laughed. "And I don't now. The old man combed his hair with a joint stool last night, threatening him with dire consequences if he did not at least try to act the gentleman, and the veneer you perceive is the result of our cousin being severely chastened. I assure you, though, it will peel away again as easily as the borrowed clothes he is wearing tonight."

Isobel looked up at Quentin, for a moment tempted to tell him the truth about Adrian and his admissions to her, if just to convince him that he was being foolish to underestimate Adrian. She had neither asked for nor agreed to keep Adrian's confidences, but she felt that she would in some way betray him if she spoke. The truth was actually before them this very night for anyone who chose to see it. Quentin clearly did not, and she let him remain in happy ignorance. "You haven't made any effort at all, have you," she said, half as a question, half as a statement, "toward showing Adrian how to go on as *Grand-père* wishes you to do?"

Quentin clearly saw no fault in this. "I don't spend ten minutes in my cousin's company that I can help," he said flatly. Perhaps it was something in Isobel's cool, steady gaze that forced him to add, "I set him right when he blunders, of course. That in itself is full-time instruction."

"I have heard your idea of instruction," said Isobel coldly. "That is like beating a dog to make him obey. You may eventually get the desired response, but it is a defensive reaction, not learning."

Quentin's brows rose, evincing mild surprise at this unexpected attack, but his eyes were hard and angry. "I note that you have been spending a great deal of your time with the savage. What progress have you made with him, beloved?" he asked dulcetly. "Or should I say, what progress has he made with you?"

Isobel flushed darkly, feeling as if the infidelity of her thoughts had been exposed. An unexpected rage rose up in her, born partly of guilt. Quentin's taunt had scored a direct hit, but he could have no idea of her unbidden feelings for Adrian. His question was plainly just a cruel but random shaft looking for a target. At that moment she very nearly hated him.

Quentin saw that he had struck a nerve. He laughed sardonically and said, "Forgive me, my love. You would not so debase yourself, would you?"

Isobel turned away from him to the pianoforte and began to play very softly, not trusting herself to speak, hoping that Quentin would take the hint and realize that it was best to leave her until she had her own temper in hand. But he did not.

Quentin eased himself onto the bench beside her. "Your efforts with the savage are pointless, Bel. One might as well try to teach a dog dressage or a horse to fetch a ball. He will never be a fit heir to the earldom of Audwin. Grandfather will see it for himself before long and then—"

"Bother Adrian," she said, and though she kept her voice quiet to avoid being overheard, the strength of her vexation came through quite clearly. "This isn't about him. It is about us."

"Oh, for God's sake," Quentin said, more exasperated than angry. "Not again, Isobel. I don't know what the devil has gotten into you to make you so contentious of late, but this is hardly the time or place for such a discussion."

"There never is a proper time and place for us to

discuss this, is there, Quentin?" A small voice inside of her was telling her to hold her tongue, but there was a fullness to her anger, a spilling-over that compelled her to speak. "Either you are engaged with your own interests and not to be found or you are at least half foxed and scarcely in a condition to seriously discuss our future together."

Quentin's brows snapped together angrily. "That is quite enough of this, Isobel. If you are determined to provoke a quarrel between us, contain your venom until tomorrow and I promise you we shall have as thorough a battle as you could wish for."

Isobel was not moved by the implied threat. "It is always tomorrow with you," she snapped back, raising her voice slightly without realizing it. She quite forgot the presence of the others in the room. It was as if the past five years of small hurts and resentments suddenly had melded together and grown to a proportion that could no longer be contained. She had no idea why she was reacting so forcefully now over a single stupid remark when she had held her peace with far greater provocation.

To what interesting heights or depths this argument would have taken them was not to be learned. They were interrupted by Lady Leyland, who addressed her stepdaughter with a look of concern on her face. "Is something amiss, Isobel?"

"No, nothing at all," Isobel replied. The interruption was sufficient to check her runaway anger, and she grasped at the escape offered, for she knew that she was only a hair's breadth away from saying something unforgivable. She stood up and moved away from the bench. "Quentin and I were discussing the merits of Mozart and Bach and disagreed on a point of composition."

Since Quentin's interest in music was nonexistent to the point that he attended even the most fashionable musicales and the opera only on sufferance, this was a patent untruth, but Lady Leyland accepted her words as if she believed them. "Then you must lower your voices or you will have everyone thinking you are quarreling," she said with a meaningful look at Quentin.

He accepted the implication that he was at fault manfully. It was not at all the thing for a gentleman to dispute with a lady publicly. "The discussion is at an end, in any case, Aunt Caro. I bow to Isobel's superior knowledge of the subject." He made the ladies a small bow and took himself over to the sideboard, where brandy had just been put out for the gentlemen.

At that moment the tea tray arrived also, and without further comment Isobel followed her stepmother to join the other ladies at the table prepared to receive it. Isobel took her place on a small, unoccupied sofa a little apart from the others. She accepted the cup of tea that was handed to her, but made no effort to join in the conversation, still too angry to give her attention to polite discourse.

The whist game continued uninterrupted as all the players were too engrossed even to consider the sacrilege of stopping their play for refreshment. Quentin had taken his brandy over to the whist table, where he stood propped against the wall, presumably engrossed by the play. But like Isobel, his color was high, and his unfocused gaze gave testimony to the fact that he was occupied with his thoughts.

As her anger began to ebb, Isobel realized how close she had come to burning her bridges with Quentin. She had no idea why she was so angry with him or why she should have lost control of her temper, but even acknowledging to herself that she had forced their quarrel did not put her in better charity with her betrothed. Intellectually, she knew it was a good thing that her stepmother had intervened, but emotionally she felt the oppression of the words she hadn't said to him.

She was so caught up in her ruminations that she scarcely noticed when the space beside her on the sofa was taken by Adrian. "If you tilt that cup much farther," Cousin Bel," he advised, "you shall have it in your lap."

Isobel looked at him blankly for a moment and then righted her cup before the tea could spill onto her skirt. She realized with a start that she did not even remember taking the cup from Lady Adora. She smiled ruefully. "I was so deep in thought that I quite forgot I was holding it."

"You shouldn't be in a taking if you've quarreled with Quentin," he said in his direct way. "It's common enough between lovers, or so I've been told."

"Quentin and I are not lovers," she said with quiet vehemence.

"You are pledged to be his wife," Adrian said, discomforting her once again with his searching gaze.

Isobel felt warmth spread over her throat and into her cheeks. Though it was only her own inference, she felt as if he had asked her if she was sleeping with Quentin. She wanted to assure him that she was not, but she could not answer even an indirect question with a half truth. She retreated to the safety of an affronted facade. "I don't know how the term is used in Pennsylvania, but to suggest such a thing to a lady is most improper."

"Put my foot in it again, have I?" Adrian gave an exaggerated sigh. "There's no end to my ignorance, it seems. But one thing I'm certain is the same the world over. A man lucky enough to have a beautiful and intelligent woman in love with him ought not to chance his fate by setting up her back."

She gave a soft, mirthless laugh. "I wish you might

tell him so. I fear we have grown so comfortable with each other that at times we forget to be civil. Carlton says that we bicker as if we were already married for years."

"Then like as not you'll quarrel all the more when you are," Adrian said baldly.

"Goodness, I hope not," Isobel said, though she had already had the thought herself. "I think I would not wish to marry at all if I thought that."

"Marriage shouldn't be that way," Adrian said, adding provocatively, "Not if it's with the right man."

It was too absurd to suppose that he meant himself, but her heart began to beat at an alarming rate all the same. "I wish I might find such a paragon with whom I would never exchange a single cross word," she said with a small, breathy laugh. "Since I don't believe he exists, I am quite happy with my choice."

Quentin observed Isobel and Adrian from across the room. He was still nursing his feelings of ill usage from Isobel's attack, and the obvious intimacy between them caused him a fresh stab of irritation. He looked away from them again and, after a few more minutes of watching the play at the card table, made his way casually in their direction.

But his intervention proved unnecessary, for Carlton and Lord Turvey, who had been in discussion about the war with the United States, took chairs near Isobel and Adrian. Lord Turvey, happily supplied with tea surreptitiously laced with brandy, which his doctor forbade him, addressed Adrian and resumed their earlier conversation about the war and Adrian's experience running the blockade. "I think much of the government's policy in America is a great waste of time and money," he said with the assurance of one who is retired from government service himself. "Keeping able-bodied seamen afloat for months at a time in a blockade that isn't worth a damn is ridiculous."

"Actually," said Carlton, who was one of those responsible for policy in the current government, "the blockade has been most effective. Trade has been brought virtually to a standstill. I had a report only this afternoon that a tightening of the blockade off the coast of the Carolinas has resulted in the capture of no less than nine vessels in recent months."

Lord Turvey possessed a strongly cynical attitude toward all military self-congratulation. He snorted. "Your own cousin is proof that the damn thing has more leaks than a sieve. He didn't swim here, did he? And he's not alone. A number of ships have brought goods and people in and out of the United States, sailing under the noses of our precious blockade."

Quentin came to sit on the arm of the sofa beside Isobel. "Sir George mentioned just such another instance at dinner. It would seem cousin Adrian is not the only American to be found in the neighborhood," he said. "Lady Cahill's sister, who emigrated to Virginia with her husband, has sent her eldest son to the Cahills for an extended visit, and he apparently arrived safe and sound only last night. I think we must encourage Sir George to bring him to call, don't you, cousin? No doubt you would enjoy the company of a compatriot."

Quentin had little interest in the war with the United States, the blockade, or Lady Cahill's nephew, for that matter. His sole thought was that Adrian might be discomfited by the prospect of being compared to another American who had been raised as a gentleman. His words bore fruit, but not for the reason Quentin supposed.

Isobel felt Adrian tense slightly beside her. He was looking at Quentin, his expression guarded. "That I might," he agreed, but with no notable enthusiasm.

"I must say," said Lord Turvey thoughtfully, "this must be an awkward time for visiting England for both you and Lady Cahill's nephew, Mr. Renville. There is always the risk of being regarded as an hostile alien when two countries are at war."

"I suppose there are those who would fear espionage," suggested Quentin, again shooting blindly and hoping for a hit.

But his remark startled only Carlton, coming as it did so soon after Simon's imaginings. "That is a specious assumption to make for every visitor," Carlton said, casting an almost apologetic glance toward Adrian.

"Oh, I imply nothing," said Quentin. He added caustically, "Surely engaging in such a dangerous activity as spying requires cleverness, intelligence, and a talent for deception. Yes, I think we may exonerate my cousin of such base intent."

Isobel felt as if a cold hand had touched her. Quentin might imagine that he described the antithesis of Adrian's character, but she knew that he actually had characterized Adrian quite well. She felt a shiver of apprehension as the thought occurred to her that this could be the reason for Adrian's deception, but she quickly dismissed this as absurd.

Adrian didn't flinch from Quentin's deliberate enmity, but Carlton looked embarrassed and Lord Turvey's expression registered distaste.

Only Adrian seemed unperturbed by either veiled accusation or derision. "You're in the right of it, Cousin Quentin," he said in an easy voice with no trace of the tension Isobel thought she had noted earlier. "I'm too simple a fellow for any nation to put their trust in me to deliver the goods." His voice took on the rustic accent that had been little in evidence so far that night. "Most like I'd trip on the cloak and fall on the dagger. Where would I be then?"

"Indeed," murmured Quentin with a wistful quality in his tone. "Where would we all be?"

It was probable that Lord Turvey did not understand the undercurrent of deliberate insult in Quentin's words, but Isobel was mortified by this washing of their dirty linen in public. She turned to Adrian and said, "It is becoming quite warm in here. Will you walk with me on the terrace, Adrian, for a bit of air? She rose as she spoke, and Adrian followed suit with alacrity.

"I imagine you must be finding it a bit warm in here also, cousin," Quentin said to Adrian with a lazy, insolent smile, assuming he had succeeded in discomfiting Adrian.

Adrian met this with a bland smile of his own. "Yes," he said. "I do think the air has become rather hot." Executing a small bow that would have done credit to one of the King's own courtiers, he offered Isobel the support of his arm and escorted her through the open French doors onto the terrace.

Chapter 8

Isobel had not forgotten her resolution to avoid Adrian's company as much as possible, but at the moment it did not signify to her. She almost expected Quentin to come after her, or in some other way attempt to prevent her from leaving the room with Adrian, but she stepped into the warm autumn night air with the man who could send her pulses racing against all reason, and no one attempted to save her from herself.

Quentin had yet to realize the extent of the threat that Adrian posed to him, and he thought that Isobel was merely trying to punish him for their earlier quarrel. He procured more brandy and settled into a discussion of an upcoming racing meet with Sir George.

The unusually warm, dry weather continued, making even the thin lace shawl Isobel wore draped fashionably over her arms unnecessary. They walked to the edge of the terrace, and she turned and sat against the balustrade. She looked up at him and decided to treat Adrian to a dose of his own directness. "Why don't you wish to meet Lady Cahill's nephew?" she asked.

The moon was just beginning to wax again and the light was faint, but still Isobel could read his expression well enough to tell that her question had confounded him, at least momentarily. But Adrian did not deny it. He smiled slowly and said, "Because there is a possibility I may know him, of course, or rather, he may know me. I was at the College of William and Mary in Virginia, and if we are of an age, we may even have been at school together."

Isobel lost interest in Lady Cahill's nephew at this point. "You were at college," she said as if to herself. "You were raised in every way as a gentleman's son, weren't you?" she said, fixing her eyes on him as if daring him to lie to her.

"Yes," he said simply.

"And the farm?"

"Exists." He sat beside her on the balustrade, close enough to cause her to be acutely aware of his physical nearness. "It *is* rather larger than I led you to believe, though. And my brothers and I did go to market with the pigs. We thought it a rare treat when we were children, and my father trusted his herdsmen and knew we would come to no harm."

"Blackoaks is an estate, isn't it? Like Audswyck."

"Something like it."

"And it is yours now."

Adrian sighed. "A good part of it is. Primogeniture is not as inherent in my country. My brothers had their share of the estate and my sister as well."

Isobel continued to regard him steadily. "You have no need of *Grand-père*'s fortune, have you?"

Adrian shook his head. "I only came at all for my father's sake. Whatever he may have said, I know his break with the country of his birth and his family was a wound that never entirely healed. I think I had some idea that I would put old ghosts to rest if I came and took his place in the family."

Isobel was puzzled by his words, but she recognized the sincerity in them. "Then why would you pretend to be an ill-bred provincial? You would hardly redeem your father's name in such a fashion."

Adrian shrugged, and Isobel saw from his expression that his confidences were at an end. "Not to spy for the United States, in any event. I am not in the least political." He stood and held out his hand to her. "This glorious weather cannot hold, and we may not have another night like this until spring. Walk with me a little way into the garden, Bel."

Isobel hesitated, knowing full well she should not leave the relative safety of the terrace. Going into the garden with him was tantamount to encouraging him to make love to her again, which she had no doubt he would do once they were out of sight of the house. She knew what she should do, but this was at odds with what she wished to do.

He sensed her ambivalence. "I promise not to ravish you," he said, his voice quizzing. He held out his hand to her.

Isobel's fear was that he wouldn't have to resort to such a measure. But she took his hand and he led her down the stairs, placing her hand on his arm and covering it with his other hand as they turned down the graveled path toward the topiary. "I can't say I blame you for being afraid of a desperate fellow like me," he said conspiratorially. "A spy caught out at his evil trade might take a fair hostage if cornered."

His nonsense made her smile and relax a little. "You are an abominable creature, Adrian. You would be well served if I did think you had some wicked design for what you are doing."

Adrian's features altered into a look of comic dismay. "And here I was beginning to think you had come to like me a little," he said sorrowfully. "I got myself all rigged out in borrowed finery and a parcel of Sunday manners in tow and all for nothing."

"I have no doubt that you have an entire wardrobe of quite unexceptional clothes tucked away somewhere, and your manners are excellent when you choose," she said severely but with the smile still in her eyes. "I am astonished that no one thinks it at all odd that you are so different tonight."

He laughed softly. "I told you people see what they wish to see. Do you imagine Quentin wishes to see me as other than the ignorant savage of his imagining?"

"An image you have encouraged," Isobel pointed out. "I think you deliberately behave as you do in his company just to bring out the worst in him."

Adrian didn't deny this. "Ah, but if the worst was not already a part of his character, I shouldn't succeed."

Isobel felt obliged to defend Quentin, even though she deplored the way he had treated Adrian. "Quentin is renowned for his excellent address at most times. I think he has taken a dislike to you because he regards you as a threat to the inheritance he hopes to receive from *Grand-père*."

"Is that what accounts for it, then?" Adrian said blandly.

Isobel realized the futility of her defense. She sighed and abandoned the effort. "He has been horrid to you, hasn't he?"

"Thoroughly, but I'm a thick-skinned provincial, remember," Adrian replied with just a hint of dryness. "Why do you defend him at every turn? What spell has he cast over you to command your loyalty when it is so undeserved?"

Isobel was stunned by his words. "How can you ask such a thing? I am betrothed to Quentin."

Adrian halted in the shadow of a large hedge that shielded them from view of the house and turned to Isobel, clasping her arms lightly but not quite embracing her. "Do you really believe you would be happy as Quentin's wife?"

His eyes, those eyes that invited her to laughter, expressed his admiration for her beauty, and at times frightened her with the intensity of feeling they expressed, held her, mesmerized her, and shattered her will to leave him and return to the safety of the house. "You are impertinent, cousin," she said, but her indignation was feeble.

"Am I?" His voice was silky and dark. His mouth covered hers and he drew her against him. He felt the warm, soft curves of her body contour to his, and his arousal was instantaneous. He knew he needed to go slowly with her if he was not to frighten her, but his desire was hot and demanding. His tongue explored the warm, moist cavity of her mouth, his hands marveled at the soft silk of her flesh. He felt her shiver when he pushed aside her shawl and freed her breasts from the light constraint of her narrow bodice to taste their sweetness. But she did not push him away, and he heard her moan softly when he took the firm nipple of one perfectly rounded breast into his mouth.

His hands traced the sweet curve of her waist and hips, and he pulled her hard and upward against him. They moved rhythmically against each other until his longing became a persistent ache of almost unbearable desire. He knew he was very near to being out of control and cursed the autumn-scented garden. He had no intention of allowing their first time together to be a torrid grappling on the grass, but passion threatened to overwhelm judgment and he forced himself to draw away from her. But her lips, soft and a bit swollen from the pressure of his, were irresistible, and he kissed her again almost at once.

But this time her hands came up between them and pushed against his chest. Her eyes searched his insistently, though in the faint light expressions could not be accurately read. "It was you, wasn't it? That night at Vauxhall?"

Adrian was nonplussed by her question and made no reply at all. He had certainly never meant for her to know that he was her dark stranger of that night, and could not imagine what he had done to give himself away.

"Don't lie to me, Adrian. You've told nothing but lies since the day you came here. I know it was you." And she did know it, though she could not have said exactly what it was that had triggered her enlightenment either. Perhaps it was the way that he kissed her or touched her, the scent of the garden that evoked something familiar, or it even might have been a realization that in the shadows of night she might easily mistake him for Quentin, just as she had done at Vauxhall.

He came to a reluctant decision that only the truth would serve. "Yes, it was me."

She pulled abruptly away from him, breaking all physical contact. "Why?" she demanded, half furious, half baffled. "Why would you do such a thing? That means you knew who I was before you came to Audswyck, and you sought me out deliberately at Vauxhall. You meant me to think you were Quentin that night, didn't you?"

"Yes, but only at first," he admitted. "I knew it was not a pretense I could maintain for very long."

She scarcely heard his response. "I don't know who you are or even what you are. All I do know is that you have deceived me—all of us—from the very beginning. There is nothing about you that is not a lie."

"It wasn't my intention, not in the beginning," he said, still not certain whether he would tell her the whole truth. The truth was as awkward as admitting to the lie. "It was never meant to be a deception at all, just ..." He took her hand in his and said more urgently, "I have been more honest with you than with anyone else. I wouldn't do anything to hurt you in any way. Please believe that, Bel."

But Isobel was already hurt. "I can believe nothing you say," she said bitterly. She pulled away from him and turned abruptly on the path back toward the house. She heard him behind her and increased her pace until she was almost running. Even knowing his rustic demeanor was false, she had still been disarmed, foolishly allowing him to insinuate himself past her normal defenses. But he was no different from the men of the town, who spoke honeyed words to disguise their intent. Seduction.

When she reached the terrace she stopped to catch her breath and let her pulse slow, but she heard Adrian call her name softly behind her and she took a deep breath and returned to the drawing room. As soon as she reentered the brightly lit room, she realized she had been hasty to rejoin the others while her emotions were still high. Several pair of eyes, including those of Quentin, glanced toward her and stared long enough to show that she had evoked some interest by her appearance. She quickly sat again on the small sofa, which was still unoccupied, hoping to quietly efface herself. But her stepmother noted the color in her cheeks and the brightness in her eyes and inquired if she had the headache. Isobel replied without thinking that she was well, and then wished that she had used the excuse readily handed to her to retire to her room for the evening.

Though she did not once look toward the terrace, she waited anxiously for Adrian to come through the open French doors. She hoped he would have the sense not to approach her again, for she was not at all certain how she would react to him. She was still stunned by the revelation of Adrian as the stranger who had boldly made love to her in the gardens of Vauxhall.

Time passed, though, and Adrian did not return to the room. Gradually some of her tension began to drain away. But Isobel would have been hard pressed to say which of their guests she had spoken with after she had returned from the garden or what topics they had discussed.

Lady Adora was the first to rise when the last guests had taken their leave. She declared herself weary beyond measure from her efforts of the evening and requested that Carlton lend her his arm to guide her tottering steps to her bedchamber. Lady Leyland also declared that she was going to bed, but Isobel, though anxious to retire to her rooms, decided to wait a few minutes to avoid having to make conversation with her stepmother and aunt until they reached their respective chambers. They had scarcely departed the room before Isobel regretted her decision.

"What the devil became of the savage, Bel?" Quentin asked in his lazy drawl.

Isobel had hoped that Adrian's absence would not be commented on, though, of course, it had to have been noted. She had to give some sort of answer and said the first thing that came into her head. "He had the headache and went to his room."

"Did he?" said Quentin, a supercilious lift to his brows. "Did you box his ears for trying to kiss you?"

She felt a betraying flush come over her and looked away from Quentin. "No," she replied coldly and reflected that literally, at least, she was telling the truth. "We walked a little way into the garden, though, and Adrian returned to the house through the library doors to avoid making a fuss." And for all she knew, that too was the truth. She glanced up and saw that Simon, sitting on the arm of a chair a little apart from them, was watching her in a fixed way that made her uncomfortable.

The look the earl bent on her was so penetrating that Isobel was certain he must discern her prevarications. "Not make a fuss?" he repeated with a disgusted snort. "Didn't he suppose that our guests would think it odd that he just disappeared halfway through the evening? It was as much to introduce him to the neighborhood as to celebrate my birthday that they were invited."

"I shouldn't imagine such a thing even occurred to him, sir," said Quentin with a brief, sardonic laugh. "I'm not at all surprised he had the headache, though. It must have taken considerable mental exertion for him to have behaved so creditably tonight."

"On the whole, I am well pleased with Adrian's behavior tonight," the earl conceded. "Francis may have neglected his son's breeding, but there's good blood in his veins, even if it has suffered some pollution. I never doubted he'd be a quick study. By this time next month, the two of you"—he nodded toward Isobel and Quentin—"will doubtless have made him sufficiently creditable as a gentleman that he can be taken to town for the last week or so of the Little Season to introduce him about and quell any conjecture and gossip about my heir not being up to snuff."

Quentin's eyes snapped upward from idle contemplation of the amber liquid swirling in his glass. "Unfortunately, I have a commitment that forces me to return to town on Monday," he said. "I think, in any case, that what further improvement we may expect in our cousin would benefit from the sort of subtle refinement that Isobel can best impart to him."

Isobel fixed him with a darkling stare. It would suit Quentin well enough to be freed from even the semblance of responsibility for Adrian's supposed education, and he would have the further benefit of returning to town with no obligation for the remainder of the Little Season to please anyone but himself. "Surely, Quentin," she said with innocent wonder, "you would not wish to leave before you can be certain that your efforts with Adrian are firmly ingrained and that he is in no danger of regression."

"I have done my poor best," Quentin stated quellingly. "And my engagement is pressing. Perhaps I might return for a day or two to see how you go on."

The earl did not miss the import of the exchange between Isobel and Quentin. "However pressing, you shall have to cancel or postpone your engagement, Quentin. If you expect me to keep my end of our bargain, you must give me fair value for yours. You will remain at Audswyck, and Isobel with you, until I have decided that Adrian is fit to be introduced to the *ton*."

That Quentin wished he could defy his grandfather was plain to be read in his eyes. "My aunt Caroline may have something to say to that," he suggested. "It might be construed as an impropriety for Isobel and me to remain here together once she goes back to town. Aunt Adora could scarcely be called a diligent chaperone."

It was a lame excuse, since they were betrothed and at the family seat with the earl in residence. Isobel wondered that Quentin thought nothing of leaving her at Audswyck with Adrian. She had supposed from some of the remarks that he had made that he felt at least a spark of jealously toward Adrian, but in spite of this he had appeared to have no qualms about departing without her. She assumed that that meant he felt quite certain of her. For just a moment she wished she might tell him that Adrian could make her heart race with the simplest touch.

"I'll stay as well to lend you countenance," Simon said, calling attention to himself for the first time. "I can't return to school until next term, and I can study here as well as in town."

The earl's lips turned up in a dry smile. "And the fishing here is much better."

Simon grinned and ignored the annoyed gaze that Quentin bent on him. It was true enough that he would enjoy another month of fishing in the river if the fine weather held, but he had reasons of his own for wishing to remain at Audswyck. He had not seen Isobel and Adrian together in the garden, but, not possessing Quentin's self-assurance that Isobel would not be unfaithful to him, he thought the fact that Isobel had, by her own admission, gone into the garden with Adrian gave some credence to Kitty's claim that she had seen them kissing earlier that day. He intended to keep watch over his stepsister to prevent her from doing anything foolish, or Adrian anything nefarious.

Quentin began to defend his wish to leave Audswyck on Monday further, and Isobel rose and bade the gentlemen good night. At that moment she had no particular interest in the outcome of the battle of wills between Quentin and his grandfather, since it was all but a forgone conclusion. She had made up her mind that she would stay at Audswyck as the earl wished only if Quentin remained as well. She was beginning to realize how often subverted her own wishes and needs to please Quentin or to make matters more comfortable for him, and this time she was determined that she would not do so. If he could not swallow his hostility and dislike of Adrian for the sake of their future, then she had to wonder if they even had a future together.

She had just mounted the first stair when she heard a soft voice summon her. She turned and saw Adrian materialize from the shadows against the far wall.

"I must speak with you, Isobel," he said, keeping his voice low.

She made no reply but continued up the stairs a little faster than she had originally intended. He took the stairs two and three at a time until he caught up to her. When they reached the gallery he took her hand. She drew it away from him so forcibly that she nearly teetered backward toward the stairs. He caught both her hands and pulled her away from the danger.

"Bel, you wanted the truth," he said urgently as he felt her gathering herself for further resistance. "I'll tell you everything if you'll let me."

Isobel's mind was still in a state of turbulence, not knowing what she could believe about him. "If I let you, you will tell me more lies," she said, her bitter tone expressing the betrayal she felt at his duplicity.

Adrian felt a small wave of panic. He could not accept that he might never be allowed to explain himself. He said fervidly, "Isobel, I know I have given you every reason to distrust me, but at least hear me out before you judge me out of hand."

"Out of hand?" she said indignantly. "How can you—"

He placed his fingers against her lips to stop the damning words that he knew were justified. "I know. I know, Bel." He closed his eyes and bowed his head. "It is no more than I deserve." He looked up at her without raising his head, his eyes supplicating.

She knew she should trust nothing he said to her ever again, but the spell he seemed to exert over her whenever he touched her was strong even knowing the extent of his falsehoods. Against all reason she still wanted to believe him, or at least to give him the chance that he asked for. But Isobel knew that no conclusion she came to while her emotions were so tumultuous could be trusted. "Not tonight," she implored. She pulled away from him again, and this time he did not prevent her.

Adrian felt a wash of relief. "When?"

"I don't know," she said, backing away, feeling as if she wanted to turn and run the length of the gallery until she reached the peace and safety of her bedchamber.

"Ride with me tomorrow morning."

"No. Not tomorrow morning." She needed time to examine her feelings, and when he was near she could not trust her own responses to be prudent.

"After luncheon, then," he said, determined to wrest from her a promise that she would not put him off indefinitely.

She nodded reluctantly and then did flee him for the second time that night.

Isobel did not ring for her maid to help her undress when she reached her bedchamber. She sat in the window embrasure that overlooked the exact portion of the garden where she and Adrian had earlier walked. She could clearly see the topiary and the hedge where he had taken her in his arms. She felt a small involuntary thrill at the memory, and this was upsetting to her. How could she ever trust her judgment of Adrian when she reacted to him in such a fashion?

But she had more to trouble her than trying to understand Adrian and the unwanted feelings she had for him. His probing of her secret doubts about her betrothal was equally disturbing, forcing her to face emotions she wished she could deny.

Five years of her life had been directed by the assumption that she would one day be Quentin's wife. That this might never occur she found distressing; it would be as if those years had been wasted. But the question that most disturbed her was whether her present discontent with Quentin was driven by the power of her attraction to Adrian or the natural culmination of years of pent-up disappointment, hurt, and anger during the long years she had been faithful to him with a signal want of reward.

She examined her feelings as best she could as she undressed in solitude, but a definitive answer eluded her. She stripped to her chemise and petticoats, and sat at her dressing table to remove the pins from her hair.

She had been prepared to detest Adrian on sight, but almost from the moment of setting eyes on him she had felt drawn to him instead. The idea of love at first sight was absurd; the idea of love at all was ludicrous. But even at Vauxhall when she had not known his identity, she had felt then too the magnetism that existed between them.

By the time she had donned her nightdress and slipped beneath the sheets, her thoughts had succeeded in making her head ache, and she was no nearer to understanding the confused state of her emotions than when she had begun. With an effort of will, she put these aside, but when she had drifted finally into sleep, the strength of her agitation was proved, for she dreamed, absurdly, that she had married Adrian and that Quentin had gone to America to live at Blackoaks Farm.

Isobel did not ride with Adrian the following afternoon. In the early hours of the morning, Lady Adora succumbed to a severe bilious attack, and she would allow no one to attend her but her dresser and Isobel. To compound matters, Lord Audwin also suffered a setback with his gout, and commanded Isobel's time after luncheon to read to him, since he declared that her voice had a soothing quality that would take his mind from the pain in his foot. Isobel was not sorry for the delay of speaking with Adrian or the escape from her thoughts that this activity brought her. When she was idle, thoughts tumbled through her mind at a ferocious rate, as scenes she had enacted with both Adrian and Quentin played again and again but brought her no nearer to understanding how she truly felt about either man.

It would have given her scant comfort to know that Adrian suffered similarly. It was all very well for him to tell himself that it was desire for a beautiful woman that drew him to Isobel, but however skilled she might believe him to be in the art of deception, he could not lie to himself. He felt a shot of cold fear course through him when the thought struck him that Isobel might never learn to trust him again and that he had no one to blame but himself for this. He could not say exactly how and when it had happened, but he knew that she was necessary to his happiness. He had thought he had his emotions well in control, but the power of love had made a mockery of his feeble governance.

Though he gave no appearance of being aware of it, he realized that he was under close observation on Sunday. He felt certain that Isobel had not confided what had passed between them in the garden to anyone and supposed that his improved address and appearance had at last exercised suspicion. He had meant to revert back to the provincial, but with his peace cut up by the uncertainty of his fate with Isobel, the effort seemed pointless.

His deception now seemed to him to be a petty revenge, childish and ill conceived. Sir James had tried to dissuade him from the course he had been bent on carrying out at Audswyck, but Adrian had brushed his objections aside. Now he wondered at himself for having allowed his bruised vanity to get the better of his sense.

Kitty, better after her day's rest, was permitted to join the others at luncheon, and she amused Adrian by blushing and looking hastily away every time he glanced in her direction.

Simon behaved similarly, and on more than one occasion Adrian was aware that Carlton regarded him with more than his usual interest. Even Lady Leyland's eyes rested on him thoughtfully several times during dinner that evening. A man with lesser sang-froid than Adrian would undoubtedly have been discomposed.

Only Isobel seemed never to look his way during dinner, and Adrian had to keep himself in hand to avoid glancing toward her too often. With so many watchful eyes on him, discretion was necessary, but he could not console himself with the hope that that was the cause of her disregard.

He thought he might have an opportunity of speaking with her after dinner, but he found Lady Leyland and Kitty alone in the drawing room when he left Quentin and Carlton to their port. The information that Isobel had left them to attend Lady Adora dashed any chance that he might seek her out, and he finally had to accept that his fate was in limbo for yet another night.

To add to his wretchedness, the night was oppressively warm, the air was as thick and still as any night at the height of summer in Philadelphia, exacerbating his wakefulness. In the early hours of the morning, when problems always seem insoluble, he recalled that Carlton had said he was escorting his aunt's carriage back to London in the morning. Adrian feared that this meant Isobel was leaving in the morning as well, though she had not said so. If she was determined not to see him again, in London he would find it almost impossible to force a private meeting with her. This alarmed Adrian to the point that he convinced himself that he would certainly lose Isobel if he did not speak to her at once, and he got out of bed and put on his dressing gown. But sense prevailed and made him realize that he could hardly make a convincing argument that he did not intend to seduce or deceive her if he went to her bedchamber in the middle of the night and approached her in her bed clad in only a dressing gown. Once out of bed, he paced the limits of his bedchamber with his unprofitable thoughts as his companion.

All of this activity, both mental and physical, finally exhausted him, and he fell asleep with the first glimmers of dawn coming through the windows. He awoke far later than his usual hour feeling thick-headed, which made it all of ten minutes before he realized the time and felt a wash of pure panic that Isobel had gone from Audswyck and possibly from his life forever as well.

Isobel had certainly decided by the time she went to bed that she would leave Audswyck in the morning, whatever the consequences. Her busy day of attending both sickrooms had left her sufficiently tired that this time she did not share Adrian's wakefulness or emotional turmoil. When she awoke, she felt clearheaded and far less inclined to be convinced that she was doomed one way or another to a life of unhappiness.

It was not unusual, surely, that she should have doubts about entering the married state, even with a man she had loved for so many years. As much as she hated waiting to be married to him, she had become comfortable in their situation, and any change must be threatening. It was not wonderful that these doubts should lead her to anxiety, which made her discontented. In all likelihood what she felt for Adrian was nothing more than physical attraction compounded by infatuation. It was just another manifestation of her own foolish fears.

She decided that she would remain at Audswyck as Lord Audwin wished her to, and she would use the time to mend any breaches between her and Quentin. She was determined that by the time they returned to town, they would agree on a definite date for their nuptials. As for Adrian, she would hear him out, of course, for she did long to know the truth he had promised her. But she would take herself in hand and put an end to the ridiculous flutterings of her heart whenever he was near. It was nothing more than a silly schoolgirl's infatuation, and she was too old for such nonsense.

When her dresser, Dolly, came to awaken her early to be ready to leave, Isobel informed her of the change in her plans, and as soon as she had dressed, she sought out her stepmother in her dressing room, where she was directing the packing of her trunk and portmanteau. Lady Leyland glanced at Isobel in surprise when she saw her wearing a simple cotton day dress instead of dressed for traveling.

"If you don't mind, Mama," Isobel said at once, "I have changed my mind. I think I would prefer to remain here awhile longer. Simon also wishes to remain for a bit, and Aunt Adora will, I think, be glad of my company while she is indisposed."

Lady Leyland regarded her speculatively while she spoke and then said, "Yes, Simon told me yesterday that he wishes to stay on to have the quiet for study so that he is not behind when the next term starts, but I expect he wishes to do so so that he may continue his passion for angling while the fine weather holds. He also told me that Quentin will be staying on."

This statement was really in the nature of a question, and Isobel recognized this. "Yes, *Grand-père* has asked him to do so," she said, speaking the literal truth. "But since my aunt will be here and also Simon, there can be no impropriety."

Lady Leyland shrugged slightly, then turned and asked her dresser to leave them for a few minutes. She sat on a chaise lounge near the hearth and patted the seat to invite Isobel to sit beside her. "I think you know, my love, that it is not at all my way to pry into my children's affairs. But I have been troubled of late on your behalf, and I hope that it is just what your papa calls one of my megrims."

"On my behalf?" Isobel said, her voice rising slightly at the unexpectedness of her stepmother's words. "But there is nothing at all the matter with me."

Lady Leyland looked disappointed and sighed with a touch of regret. She and Isobel had always liked each other and this had grown to a genuine affection, but there was a degree of intimacy that they did not share. "I hope so, dearest," she said gently, covering Isobel's hand with her own. "But I wish you to know that if ever you find yourself in a quandary or even a scrape, I am here for you."

Isobel was puzzled and a little unsettled by this. "I hope I am past the age of getting into scrapes, Mama," she said with an uncertain laugh.

"I don't think any of us ever are past that age," said Lady Leyland, smiling. She saw that Isobel was wary and gave up her attempt to offer herself as a confidant. "If you wish to stay on at Audswyck, of course you must do so. I can't blame you for wishing to enjoy Quentin's company without the demands on your time that must separate you when you are in town. And of course Adrian will be here as well, and I know that he amuses you."

This last was said with no particular inflection, but Isobel cast a swift, suspicious glance at her stepmother. Caroline Leyland was indeed a lovely, frivolous creature, and this at times made even those nearest to her underestimate her astuteness. Isobel knew her stepmother must be aware of the estrangement between her and Quentin. Could she also suspect Isobel's infatuation for Adrian?

For a moment Isobel almost decided to confide in the older woman. Instead she gave her stepmother a brief hug and offered to assist her with what remained of her packing.

Within the hour the Leyland carriage was underway

along the drive. Kitty had made a bit of a fuss when she learned that Isobel was to remain at Audswyck and tried unsuccessfully to convince her godmother to permit her to stay as well. Carlton had merely given Isobel a long, searching look when he was told she would not be traveling with them. Isobel felt a brief wave of misgiving, but she could not retreat from her decision. A little smile touched her lips at the thought of the earl's reaction if she ordered *his* carriage made ready to take her to town in defiance of his wishes.

Only Isobel and Simon saw them off on their journey back to town. Lady Adora and the earl were still indisposed, and neither Quentin nor Adrian had come down to breakfast, though this was unusual only for the latter. Simon was a little put out by this, for he had been permitted to stay only on condition of giving his mother his word that he would not wade into the river to fish unless he was accompanied by one of his cousins. It was in vain that he pointed out that he had been doing so regularly since their arrival.

The weather continued unnaturally warm and oppressive, and though the sun shone, the air was hazy and the sky in the far distance had a yellowish brown tinge to it that hinted at storm clouds brewing. Simon scanned the sky with a furrowed brow. "It'll be pouring before the end of the day," he predicted.

"Sooner than that, I imagine," Isobel remarked.

Simon shrugged. "Enough time anyway to spend a few hours at the river. I only hope that the coming storm isn't a harbinger of any great change in the weather. I had hoped for at least another sennight of fishing before the weather turns colder."

"I would hope it is the end of this wretched heat and humidity in any case," Isobel said, turning to go into the house. She went to the morning room to write a letter to a friend in town, and she was surprised to find Simon close on her heels.

She sat at the writing desk, situated in front of a pair of windows overlooking the rose garden, where there were still some late blooms contributing small splashes of vibrant color to the white ribs of the arbors showing through the defoliating bushes. Simon cast himself into a nearby chair and sat staring without focus in the general direction of the windows.

After a few minutes of silence, he sighed heavily, an action he repeated at spaced intervals. Isobel knew he was chafing to go to the river before the storm broke, but she found him distracting and her irritation grew with each of his audible exhalations. "Since you cannot go out this morning, you might study," she advised. "You did promise Mama that you would be as diligent while you are here as you would be at Leyland House under her supervision."

Simon snorted. "You know I shall pass any examination they care to give me when I return to school," he said with the unconscious arrogance of youth. "Do you think that Quentin may be up but only not dressed yet?"

"How on earth should I know?" Isobel replied, a touch caustically. "You might knock on his door and see if he answers."

"Ho! And have my head handed to me if I awaken him. I would as soon blunder into a bear's den."

"You shall find me equally fierce, Simon," she said without looking up, quite deliberately continuing her writing, "if you don't find something to occupy you other than sitting here in a dudgeon and disturbing *my* occupation."

"I most humbly beg your pardon, dear sister," Simon said, plainly offended. He rose and fairly stomped out of the room.

Isobel gave vent to a sigh of her own. Simon might have considerable intellect and the physique of a grown man, which made it at times easy to forget that he was still little more than a boy, but his immaturity still betrayed his youth.

But his leaving gave her the peace she sought, and she finished the letter she was writing and was well into another when she heard the door into the hall open again. She glanced upward, expecting to see Simon again but beheld Adrian instead. Instantly she felt an increase of her heartbeat. She willed herself to remain calm and in control of herself, and felt that she did indeed regain much of her composure.

There was a look of surprise on his countenance. "You're still here," he said, sounding pleased. "I thought you might have left with my aunt."

"I thought of it," Isobel admitted, putting down her pen. She rose, feeling at a disadvantage with him looking down on her. Then she wished she had not, for in the space of a moment she was enclosed in a swift embrace.

But to her surprise, he didn't even try to kiss her again; he merely held her tightly against him for a long moment and then released her. She took a step back from him, symbolizing to herself the need to keep a distance between them.

He moved away from her also and indicated a sofa on the far wall. His features were grave, but the hint of a smile lurked there. "I have rather a long story to tell you. Too long for standing. We may sit at opposite ends if you like."

Isobel walked past him and took a chair adjacent to the sofa. Adrian's features spread into a brief grin, and he took the end of the sofa nearest her. It was obvious that though she was willing to listen, she would not be easily convinced. He launched into his tale without preamble, starting from the time he had received the letter from his grandfather suggesting that he come to England to take his rightful place as the heir to the earldom and continuing through to the afternoon in Grillon's when he had eavesdropped on her conversation with Simon and Quentin.

Isobel heard him mostly in silence, interrupting only once or twice to clarify something she did not quite understand. The story he told her was far from some of the dire imaginings that had occurred to her in her deepest doubt of him. If she could believe him, his motive for the pretense he had perpetrated was simple to absurdity. But could she believe him?

"I can understand that you would find our assumption that you would not be presentable galling, but what purpose did pretending to be as dreadful as we feared serve?" she said, her puzzlement genuine. "It was bound to make our acceptance of you even less likely."

"It seemed to me that acceptance was unattainable no matter how you found me," Adrian replied. "Frankly, by that point it didn't matter much to me. I realized I had made a mistake by accepting my grandfather's invitation, and if it wasn't for the damned war making passage back to America no easy thing, I might have returned without even coming to Audswyck."

"That still doesn't tell me why you affected such an absurd character," she persisted, determined to know every facet of his design.

Adrian sighed deeply. "I don't know. I've asked myself that same question. It amused me, I suppose. I don't know that there is any deeper answer."

Isobel had what she had wanted of him since she had first suspected that he was not as he appeared to be, and she found it far less satisfying than she had supposed. But there was another explanation, and to Isobel in some ways the more important, that he had not yet offered. "Did it also amuse you to dress up in a domino and mask and pretend to be Quentin to lure me away from my friends into the gardens at Vauxhall?"

"Yes," he replied boldly, and quickly added, "But

to be fair, you must admit that you knew I was not Quentin before you kissed me."

"I did not kiss you," Isobel said indignantly. "You kissed me."

"You kissed me back," he reminded her gently.

She bolted up from her chair, not, as he feared, to flee the room in anger, but to disguise her agitation. She walked back to the desk and stood, looking sightlessly out of the windows. She could not deny what he said; if he knew the extent of her feelings that night, he might have said far more.

Adrian stayed where he was and made no attempt to break the silence between them. The silence lengthened, making the ticking of the mantel clock inordinately loud.

"Was it to punish me for judging you so poorly before I had even met you?" Isobel said at length.

In part it had been precisely that, but also because he had wanted to know if her smooth alabaster skin was as soft and silky as it looked, if her lips would taste as sweet as he imagined. He had so far been completely frank with her, but he thought it prudent to keep this confidence to himself. "It was a stupid and ill-conceived idea, and I am truly sorry for it, Isobel," he replied. "I supposed that Quentin meant to disappoint you, and I thought only to make a brief appearance to see if you would mistake me for him and to leave again almost at once. I swear to you, I never meant you any harm in the least."

"But it has nearly come to that, hasn't it?" she said, her tone flat. "All this time you have known while I have been ignorant. Did you assume because of that night that I would be easy to seduce?"

He had thought something on that order, but again he chose discretion over honesty. His feelings for her had also undergone change. He still believed her response to him in the gardens of Vauxhall was proof of her passionate nature, but he no longer thought it equal evidence of her want of virtue. "I have made love to you since then not because I thought it would be easy to do so, but because I couldn't resist my desire for you."

Which was precisely the reason that Isobel had permitted him to kiss her and had responded with eagerness. She forced this thought away by saying angrily, "All that you had to do was bide your time and seek your advantage. You supposed that my virtue was not unassailable, and given time you had every cause to hope."

She finally succeeded in raising an answering spark of anger in him. "Perhaps I did in the beginning," he admitted finally. "But that is far from the truth now that I have come to know you." He got up from the sofa and crossed the room to stand behind her. He put his hands out to touch her and dropped them again, assuming her rejection. "I know I have hurt and disappointed you, Isobel, and I am sorry for it. God knows, I wish now that I had never embarked on such an absurd pretense."

"No more than I do," she said bitterly and turned to face him. But this was a mistake. It was not only the nearness of him that could affect her, even in anger, but she saw something in his eyes that amazed her and to which she responded without volition. In that moment she knew that her efforts to harden her heart against him came too late.

It must have been that he read her emotions as readily as she had read his. "I'm falling in love with you, Isobel," he said very softly.

"You can't do that," she said desperately.

"I can't prevent it," he said in fervid accents. "God knows, I never meant it to happen." He gave a wry laugh. "That makes me sound like a damned coxcomb, doesn't it?"

"I am betrothed to Quentin, you know that," she said,

thinking not at all of her promise to Quentin, but clinging to the safety of the familiar. She was frightened by the swelling of joy that rose in her at his declaration. She could not, would not be in love with this man. To love him would turn her entire life upside down and put at risk everything that mattered to her.

In response he gathered her into his arms, and his lips sought hers. Isobel did not try to resist him, but she let the waves of succeeding emotions—pleasure, desire, anxiety, and finally determination—sweep over her. When Adrian released her she calmly stepped away from him.

"You must never do that again," she said in a calm, level voice. "And you must never say such things to me again either. I am to be married to Quentin, and I will not be unfaithful to him."

"Damn Quentin," Adrian said with some force. "You know you are not indifferent to me."

"I know that," Isobel admitted with a surface composure that amazed her, for she was a churning sea of conflicting emotions inside. "But I won't destroy my future happiness with Quentin for a passing attraction."

Adrian's features set in a hard expression she had never seen before. "Is that what you imagine this is?" he demanded, his voice hardening as well.

"For me it is," she said, the tremor in her voice so slight that she had hope it did not betray her.

He recoiled from her as if she had struck him. "I see," he said without expression. Even his eyes told her nothing of his thoughts. Saying nothing more, he turned on his heel and walked away from her. As he reached the door, it opened and admitted Quentin with Simon following close behind. Adrian scarcely glanced at either man before he left the room without so much as a passing greeting.

Chapter 9

The week that unfolded after Lady Leyland, Carlton, and Kitty left Audswyck Chase was anything but satisfactory for those that remained behind. The threatened storm broke before noon on Monday and brought an end to the unusually warm weather. It rained for the remainder of the week, in torrents much of the time, and when it was not actually raining, cold, dank winds buffeted Audswyck and revealed every crack in the house's defense against the elements.

Simon's hope of spending long days fishing the river were dashed. He did not truly mind being forced to return to his studies for their own sake, but he was severely put out that he had not returned to London with his mother, for there, at least, he would have had some other diversions. The only thing he had at Audswyck that might qualify as such was his continuing study of Isobel and Adrian, and this bore little fruit. They were always polite to each other and even friendly at times, but it was no more than that. Simon, in his youth, supposed that Kitty must have been mistaken after all and that he himself had refined too much on what had appeared to be a growing intimacy between his sister and his cousin.

For Quentin the week began with an unexpected shock. When he and Simon had walked into the morning room on Monday, he had regarded Adrian's abrupt departure from the room with nothing more than mild curiosity. But looking at Isobel as she watched Adrian's retreating figure, he saw despair in her eyes. In the space of a moment she had recovered herself. The look was gone from her eyes, and only a slight distractedness betrayed her agitation.

Quentin was forced to own that Adrian was not as guileless as he had assumed. He had sensed the attraction Isobel exerted over Adrian, which was hardly surprising; she was very lovely and many men far more sophisticated than Adrian desired her. But he had never seriously supposed his cousin's captivation would be reciprocated or that he was in any serious risk of being cuckolded. He had finally learned his mistake.

It was not in Quentin's nature to suppose that Isobel's affections might be vulnerable to assault through any fault of his own. Nor did he particularly blame Isobel; in his philosophy women were weak creatures all too easily beguiled by a clever male. If he gave himself any blame, it was that he had judged that Isobel would be put off by Adrian's unprepossessing appearance and want of breeding and sophistication, and thus had seen no need for vigilance.

The culpability, to his mind, was entirely Adrian's. As a predatory male himself, he understood the delicate art of seducing a woman virtually under the nose of a husband or lover all too well. The usual redress for such villainy would have been to demand satisfaction for his honor, but Quentin had no intention of meeting Adrian with pistols at dawn. For one thing, the scandal that such an action within the family would create if word of the duel got out would be insurmountable. For another, he disdained Adrian as a gentleman and therefore more fit for a horsewhipping than an honorable meeting. Quentin set his thoughts to devising some form of administering the former that would sufficiently punish his cousin for his impertinence and leave him in no doubt that he had been chastised.

Isobel, Quentin supposed, had come to her senses, perhaps in the fear that she had given herself away, and was now keeping Adrian at a proper distance, while at the same time her manner toward Quentin was far more agreeable and conciliatory. Quentin noted this but did not react to it. Even if Isobel had merely been the victim of Adrian's attentions to her, her could not let her defection, however brief, go unpunished.

There was a charming and attractive widow in the neighborhood with whom Quentin enjoyed a mutually agreeable liaison whenever he was in residence at Audswyck who suddenly found him a frequent and most attentive lover. He proved that his imagination was quite fertile by the number and variety of excuses he managed to invent to explain his frequent absences from Audswyck in spite of the weather.

Isobel's erstwhile efforts to mend fences between them was of limited effect with Quentin so often gone from the house. When he was at Audswyck, his manner toward her had something of an edge to it that made it particularly difficult for Isobel to maintain her resolve not to quarrel with him again. She reproved herself whenever she felt the least annoyance or anger with Quentin, reminding herself that his coolness toward her was no more than she deserved for her infidelity.

Toward Adrian she behaved as circumspectly as was possible living under the same roof. This proved to be comparatively easy; Adrian seemed equally inclined to avoid her company as much as possible. She had no idea how he contrived to amuse himself during the long, bleak days, but she rarely had sight of him until they assembled for dinner.

On Tuesday afternoon, Sir George Cahill braved

the rain to pay a call with his American nephew in tow. Mr. Liddiard was a personable, well-bred young man with a charming drawl to his speech. Beal was sent to seek Adrian out, but he could not be found, and Mr. Liddiard was most disappointed, for he had looked forward to meeting a fellow countryman. Isobel did manage to discover in the course of her conversation with him that Mr. Liddiard had indeed attended the College of William and Mary.

It was some hours later, when the rain was falling with especial intensity, that Isobel happened to observe Adrian coming into the house by means of a seldom used side door. He was dressed for riding and was soaked to the skin. He did not appear to notice her but retreated toward the back stairs, leaving a small trail of puddled rainwater behind him. She had no wish to approach him or she would have asked him if he had gone out before the arrival of their guests or if he had made his escape after learning of it.

The only other diversion came the following day when a messenger arrived from London with a note from Carlton asking them to search for some papers he had inadvertently left behind. Quentin declared that his brother was becoming uncommonly careless and left the search to Isobel and Simon.

To Simon it was something of a game, and all the while they went through the desk in the library, he regaled his sister with possibilities of how the papers had come to be missing from Carlton's dispatch case, ranging from his favorite, in which Adrian figured as a master spy, to the ridiculous, which involved not only the new chambermaid, who had a curious lisp that might disguise a foreign accent, but also the bootboy, who tended to linger in the halls in the morning longer than Simon perceived as necessary. But the papers proved only to be mislaid, not missing, and the messenger was soon on his way again to London with them safely in hand.

Time would not only have hung heavy on Isobel's hands, but her tumultuous thoughts would undoubtedly have driven her to distraction if it had not been for Lady Adora and Lord Audwin. Isobel did not, in the normal way of things, court the company of either, but at this time she was grateful for it.

Lady Adora had recovered from her indisposition by Monday afternoon and was pleased to discover that Isobel had remained at Audswyck. She was a placid woman whose level of activity was rarely more arduous than a turn in the garden after luncheon on fine days, or a drive in her barouche to visit neighbors or attend some social function. The foul weather did not disturb her in the least, and she was very happily employed with her household duties, needlework, and extensive correspondence. She took it upon herself to instruct Isobel as she performed her duties, regaled her with long, boring family histories, or tales of Quentin's and Carlton's childhoods while she plied her needle, and found it most conducive to gathering her thoughts efficiently if Isobel played lightly on the pianoforte while she wrote her letters.

The earl was not so fortunate. His gout continued to pain him considerably, and he rarely left his own rooms even for dinner. Isobel was summoned virtually every afternoon to read to him, and since he permitted her to choose what she would read, she found the occupation agreeable enough. He quizzed her about Adrian's progress on a few occasions, and Isobel was able to reply with perfect truth that she did not think he would find anything to blush for in Adrian's manners when he was introduced to the *ton*.

"His progress has been most remarkable," the earl allowed. "Perhaps it was an excess of nerves that made him appear more gauche than he would have otherwise when he first arrived. I am pleased that my faith in both you and Quentin was not misplaced. You will be gratified as well, I think when the settlements are made. If I am not fit for the journey to London by the end of the month, I shall send for Horesy to come to me to draw up the necessary papers. You may have a Christmas wedding if you choose, or wait a bit longer and make it the event of the Season next spring."

These words should have filled her with happiness, but she was uncomfortable with the lie that she and Quentin were the cause of Adrian's improvement. "I think the real credit lies with Adrian himself, *Grand-père*," she replied. "I know some of us thought him stupid when he first arrived because of the way that he talked and the things that he said, but he is really quite clever and intelligent."

"He is a Renville," the earl stated simply.

Isobel glanced sharply at him to see if there were any layers of meaning in his words, and decided that the earl's prideful statement was no more than that. She had always regarded him as an exceptionally perceptive man, and she wondered that he could believe that the miracle of turning a sow's ear into a silk purse had really occurred. Adrian did not even bother to return to his provincial character any longer, and yet it seemed that only to her was this obvious. Perhaps it was because she knew the truth, or perhaps it was that the others did not want to give up their preconceived opinions of Adrian, the very misconceptions that Adrian claimed had caused him to hoax them in the first place.

By Sunday the sky was still overcast, but was a slightly brighter hue of gray and the rain had ceased completely. Simon would certainly have gone out immediately after breakfast, but neither Quentin nor Adrian were at hand, and Lady Adora threatened to succumb to the vapors at the very idea that Simon might go anywhere near the river alone, which she was certain must be a raging torrent from all of the rain they had had. She refused to even consider permitting him to leave the house, though he promised that he would merely cast a line from the banks to see if anything was biting.

Simon had shut himself into the library with his books, but he emerged by mid-afternoon and sought out his sister. He found Isobel reading in her sitting room. She smiled when he came into the room and put down her book.

Though his youth made him generally ignorant of insight into the feelings of others, it suddenly occurred to him that his sulks for the past sennight had made him a less than endearing companion for Isobel. He had intended to ask her to intercede with his aunt to let him go down to the river to fish, but instead he suggested that Isobel might like to go out for ride with him to exercise out their fidgets after being cooped up for so long. "I doubt Aunt Adora would object if we go out together."

Isobel gave him an indulgent smile from the reflection in the glass above her dressing table. "And just happened to take along some fishing tackle?"

Simon blushed, unaware that his hidden motive was so easily discernible. He smiled sheepishly. "I suppose we might, if you did not object. I mean, we must ride to *some* destination. I would just cast a line or two to get a feel for things, you know."

Isobel glanced toward the windows, which still showed a gloomy aspect. "The rain has stopped, but there is still a faint mist that I think will be more pronounced closer to the water. I should love to go out too, but I think Aunt Adora is in the right of it today."

Simon's countenance darkened for a moment, and

then he remembered that he did not wish to behave in a selfish fashion. With a long sigh he agreed but suggested, "Tomorrow, then? You could bring along a book and a blanket, and maybe we could even have Cook make up something for us to take along for refreshment if we get an early start."

Isobel would by far have preferred riding in earnest for the exercise, but she felt sympathy for her brother, caught between boyhood and manhood, who chafed under the restrictions of his elders. Lady Adora's protectiveness was excessive, but even his mother had been more restrictive since his riding accident, which had been the result of Simon's own recklessness. But though Simon often tried to emulate Quentin, in personality he was more like Carlton. He might resent the constraints placed on him, but it was not very likely that he would rebel against them.

"We could do that," Isobel agreed. "But only if it is warm and dry and with a bit of sun. I have no intentions of sitting shivering on the bank for hours while you cast your line."

Simon grinned broadly. "No, no, I promise. But you will see, it will be a glorious day tomorrow." With these words he kissed Isobel briefly and left to change for dinner.

Isobel received her summons to Lord Audwin shortly after Simon left her. The earl was in far better frame and had her continue until she had finished the book she had been reading to him. She went directly to the library to put it away before returning to her own rooms and was just leaving the library when once again she witnessed Adrian entering by the side door. As before he was dressed for riding; no amount of rain or mist appeared to deter him from his exercise.

She might have let him pass without bringing notice to herself as she had before, but she decided she would not resort to behaving like a frightened fieldmouse in the shadow of a hawk whenever she encountered him alone. "The pleasures of riding outweigh the discomfort of wet and damp for you, it would seem, cousin," she commented, continuing along the hall unchecked.

He turned when she addressed him, and as Isobel had already discovered during the past week, his eyes could conceal his feelings as effectively as they displayed them. "Since Audswyck is to be mine one day, I would do well to acquaint myself with the land," he replied in a tone that no longer held the special warmth that had been reserved for her alone.

She was mildly disconcerted that he fell into step beside her, but she did not permit this to constrict her manner toward him. "*Grand-père* told me yesterday that he is most pleased with your progress, Adrian," she said dryly. "You have not told him the truth yet, it would seem."

"No," Adrian replied, almost curt. "Did you tell him?"

"It is not my place to do so," she said with some chilliness. "You will have to make a full confession to *Grand-père* and the others eventually."

His response was delivered with an unsatisfactory indifference. "Shall I?"

"Of course," she said firmly. "You cannot mean to continue the lie now."

"What lie?" he said, meeting her eyes squarely for the first time.

They had reached the base of the stairs. She turned to him, her lips parted in astonishment. "That you are not gently bred."

"I never said that."

"You didn't have to," she said sharply, puzzled at his odd manner and not liking it much.

"No, I didn't," he said without argument. "My character was decided by all of you before I ever set foot in this house. You will forgive me, I know," he added, his tone formally civil, "but I must beg leave of you to go to my rooms to rid myself of my dirt before dinner." And so saying, he continued up the stairs without pause or looking back to see if she followed.

It was the first time they had spoken any words in private since he had left her so abruptly in the morning room on Monday. Isobel could not understand why his words and manner made her feel empty and forlorn when an end to the emotional attachment that had been growing between them was precisely what she had most wished for. It is just pride, she told herself. It was no more than pique that he could fall out of love with her so quickly. She was determined to be satisfied with this explanation.

Quentin had left the house after luncheon and did not return home until after dinner. He had not sent word that he would dine from home and offered no excuse for his absence when he joined the others in the drawing room, an omission that his grandfather swiftly brought to his attention. The apology given was perfunctory at best. "I only came in to bid you all a good night, in any event," he said, going to the sideboard and pouring himself a generous portion of brandy, though it was somewhat obvious that he had already been imbibing freely. "I spent the better part of the day with Tommy Beresford looking over some property he's thinking to purchase that marches to the west with his own. You know the land I mean," he said, addressing his grandfather. "That bit of the old Marchmont estate that was carved up some twenty years ago when Marchmont was done up in that gaming scandal."

The earl had finished his brandy and glanced toward Simon with a brief indication that he wished his glass refilled. Adrian rose before Simon could do so and took the earl's glass. As he poured out the brandy, he

Elizabeth Hewitt

said to Quentin in apparent innocence, "Didn't you say on Wednesday, cousin, that you took dinner with Mr. Beresford to wish him godspeed for a journey north to visit his grandparents?"

That he had used that excuse for his absence on Wednesday had quite slipped Quentin's mind. He cast Adrian a venomous glance but said smoothly, "Yes, but he had word the following morning that he might have the opportunity to purchase that property and decided to put off his journey."

Isobel heard the annoyance in Quentin's voice and looked up from her needlework. She saw Adrian's lips turn up in a slight, contemptuous smile, and saw the setting of Quentin's features that this evoked. Adrian poured a second glass of the dark amber liquid for himself, though Isobel could not recall that she had ever seen him drink spirits before.

"I should have thought he would have left it to his agent," said Simon artlessly, ignorant of the byplay between Adrian and Quentin. "It's not as if he's unfamiliar with the land."

"A thorough inspection is always a sensible action before purchase," Quentin said almost through his teeth.

It was at this point that Isobel finally realized that Quentin had been lying and then felt a fool that Adrian had recognized this on the instant while she had not. Even the earl was regarding his favorite grandson sharply.

"I imagine that it is the portion of the Marchmont land that contains Beaker's Hill," Audwin said and added reminiscently, "That bit of the old estate had a considerable reputation in my young days."

"It was a dueling ground, wasn't it, Grandfather?" asked Simon, his interest caught.

"You know I deplore such topics, Simon," Lady Adora put in. "They are not suitable for general discussion. It is very bad of you, Quentin," she said, rounding on her elder son, "to neglect us all day and then return to disrupt an otherwise pleasant evening." She rose and added imperiously, "You may escort me to my rooms."

The attack was unwarranted, since Quentin had not been the one to bring up the subject of dueling, and he was not Carlton to come meekly to heel. "When I have finished my brandy, Mama," he said in a voice that made it plain he would not alter this decision.

Though he was reluctant to leave the drawing room when, in his opinion, the conversation had just become interesting, Simon gallantly rose and offered his aunt his arm. But the dowager waved him back to his chair. "I grow increasingly concerned for you, Quentin," she said with severity. She bid the earl a good night and swept from the room with majesty.

"That was not well done of you, my boy," the earl said, but more as comment than censure.

"I hope I have only the greatest respect for my mother," Quentin said coldly, "but it doesn't do to encourage her to perpetually think of one as still in short coats."

"No doubt Simon's courtesy toward his aunt stems from his want of years," Adrian remarked and received yet another malignant glare from Quentin, which he parried with a signally sweet smile.

The earl noted this exchange without comment and turned the topic by addressing Simon as if there had been no interruption to their earlier discussion. "Beaker's Hill had been a meeting place for affairs of honor for over a century, though old Marchmont, the third viscount, that is, tried to put an end to it by closing in the field about it. His own son, my friend Cecil Marchmont, shed some blood from an impertinent fellow who jostled him in the courtyard of the Duck and Drake."

Isobel was now the only female present, and this conversation was certainly inappropriate in the circumstances, but she had chosen to sit away from the others, back from the fire, which the earl had built up to a degree that she personally found uncomfortable. It was likely that she was forgotten, and she did nothing to call attention to herself.

"Didn't you fight a duel once, Grandfather?" asked Simon, recalling vaguely a story told to him in his boyhood.

The earl's eyes glanced up at a portrait of himself as a young man, the pose insouciant. He stood, legs splayed, lightly resting his weight on a rapier he held point down in both hands before him. The rapier and its twin was mounted on the wall, crossed beneath the portrait. "More than once," the earl said. If he had been a sentimental man, which he certainly was not, Isobel might have thought his tone wistful. "But in my day we fought as gentlemen should, using our wits and swordsmanship. There was little of this putting holes into one's opponent nonsense that goes on today. Unless a matter was of the gravest importance, pinking your man was sufficient to satisfy honor."

Quentin removed one of the swords from its mounting while the earl spoke. He tested its weight and grip and the flexibility of the blade. "An excellent notion," said Quentin. "Don't you agree, Cousin Adrian? Ah, but then perhaps you have never had an opportunity to use a sword. We mustn't neglect swordsmanship in your education. It is an accomplishment as necessary in a gentleman as music or drawing is in a lady. Here, we'll start with the proper way to hold one."

With these words he tossed the rapier toward Adrian, hilt first. Isobel caught her breath on a gasp, Simon rose from his chair in alarm, and the earl barked out, "The devil!" But Adrian neither ducked nor flinched. To the amazement of them all he caught the hilt neatly and raised the point in a flawless salute.

For a moment there was silence in the room as a hard stare was exchanged between the two young men. Then Quentin smiled slowly and said, "Well, well, cousin, it would seem you spent your time doing more than swilling pigs on that farm of yours. Though, given my uncle's notorious reputation and the cause of his being driven from the family and, indeed, the country, I should not be surprised that he would pass that particular skill on to his sons."

"No, you should not be," Adrian said in a voice like granite.

In response Quentin took down the other sword. "On guard," he said, and after the briefest of salutes, their blades cut the air with a wicked hiss that sent a chill the length of Isobel's spine, and steel engaged steel.

"Quentin! Dear God, you must not," she said, springing up from her chair, the altar cloth she was embroidering falling unheeded to the floor.

"You will cease this moment," the earl said, raising his voice to a near shout.

But neither man paid either of them the least heed. All of their concentration was focused on each other, Quentin's fury fueled by brandy and the need to punish his presumptuous cousin, Adrian's by a deep-rooted dislike enhanced by the knowledge that Isobel had made her choice in Quentin's favor. There was not a great deal of space in the small area in front of the fireplace, and that made the encounter even more dangerous.

"Simon," the earl snapped, "get Beal and tell him what is going forward. And the need for discretion."

Simon hastily scampered from the room, and Isobel came to stand behind Lord Audwin's Bath chair. She pulled his chair, despite his protests, farther away from the combatants and the danger of their swordplay.

At first both men fought cautiously, feeling each other out rather than attempting to score on each other. But gradually the play intensified as Quentin became more bold in his desire to best Adrian, taking unnecessary risks to try to get past Adrian's guard and ultimately paying for his rashness. His expression was one of furious bafflement when Adrian lightly touched his shoulder with his sword point. Adrian withdrew before cloth or flesh was penetrated, but it demonstrated that his skill was superior, or at least that he was the more sober and in charge of his wits and reflexes. He stood back and lowered his point to indicate that he considered the fight at an end, but Quentin, his face a mask of rage, lunged at him and forced Adrian to engage again, the ring of the steel echoing through the silent room.

Beal, with two of the more brawny footmen on staff, came into the room calling to Adrian and Quentin that their foolishness must stop. He nodded to his henchmen, who bravely advanced one each toward the swordsmen, but Quentin stood back and turned his sword toward the servant approaching him. "You will stay back," he said in a hard voice that brooked no interference. "We will have this out."

Adrian's features spread into a brief humorless smile. "No need for concern. It will be over in a trice."

"We shall see," said Quentin through his teeth.

But Adrian's prediction, or his assessment of his skill, proved correct. Again he penetrated Quentin's guard, and this time disarmed him. The rapier went spinning into the hearth, and a thin line of blood showed on the back of Quentin's hand.

"Get their swords," the earl barked, and the footmen sprang forward, one to take the sword from Adrian, who handed it over without protest, and the other to gingerly retrieve its mate from where it had rolled nearly into the fire.

Beal stepped forward to take the swords from the footmen, and without comment he mounted each of them again in their place over the mantel. "Will that be all, my lord?" he said with admirable aplomb, and on receiving an affirmative from his employer, he nodded to his underlings and they left the room.

As soon as the door shut, Quentin, who was wrapping a handkerchief about his hand, suddenly laughed. "My compliments, Adrian, your father taught you well."

"He taught me never to fight when I had drunk more than was wise," Adrian replied caustically.

"No doubt that was the voice of experience," Quentin replied, his tone sardonic.

"No doubt."

Simon had returned to the room in the wake of Beal and the footmen, and he stood beside Isobel and his grandfather. He listened to this exchange with rapt interest. His curiosity overcoming both breeding and sense, he blurted out, "Did my uncle Francis fight a duel with someone and kill him? Is that why he had to leave England?"

The earl glared up at Simon, but Adrian answered him in a calm, unconcerned tone. "He chose to leave. The man didn't die, but he was badly wounded. It was a quarrel that was forced on him, but he was given the blame for all that occurred."

"So he would doubtless say," said Quentin, refilling his brandy glass. "Uncle Francis and the son of a royal duke both took a fancy to a fashionable demi-rep," he related to Simon, "or so my father told me. Francis appeared to win the day and set her up in a snug town house, but he visited her unexpectedly one afternoon and caught her, ah *en flagrant delit,* with the royal scion. What followed was much like what you have witnessed here."

"It was exactly like," countered Adrian. "My father had his sword forced on him also."

"But he should have had the good taste not to half kill the fellow," Quentin argued. "The king was bound to take a dim view of such behavior, especially after the meeting became *on dit.*"

"It is past history and best left in the past," Audwin said abruptly, bringing an end to their exchange. "Simon, you will see your sister to her room. She should not have been forced to witness such disgraceful behavior. I hold you both to account for this night's work," he added grimly, addressing Adrian and Quentin. "We shall discuss it further, I promise you." With these words he wheeled himself from the room, shouting for Beal as soon as he entered the hall.

There was a long moment of silence after the earl had left them, and then Simon offered his arm to Isobel. She looked from Quentin to Adrian, her expression openly displaying her disgust with them both, and then she turned without comment and left the room with her brother.

"*Touché,* coz," Quentin said, raising his glass slightly toward Adrian. "Deeply as it pains me, I shall acknowledge that you were right on one point. Next time I shall be in full control of both faculties and reflexes."

"You will need to be," Adrian replied solemnly. He picked up his glass from the table where he had set it down and drank off the contents, which was near to the full amount he had poured for himself. He turned and left the room.

Quentin finished off the remainder of his brandy and, after a brief pause, furiously smashed the glass into the hearth.

* * *

The following day was as gloriously sunny as Simon had predicted. Isobel awakened to a room filled with cheerful light, which lifted her spirits in spite of the melodramatic events of the previous night. It was not really surprising that the enmity between Quentin and Adrian should have been manifested in physical combat at last. The only reason there had been no open hostility exchanged between them before, she was certain, was because Adrian had maintained his equable temper in the face of Quentin's unrelenting vituperation. But Adrian had finally let his control on his temper slip, and Isobel was incongruously gratified that he had. She preferred not to analyze her emotions and was not displeased when Simon scratched at her door before she had even finished the cocoa her dresser had brought her when she awoke.

"Are you up, Bel?" he said, coming into the room without waiting for a reply. "I was hoping we might get an early start."

"Barely," she said, smiling at her brother's eagerness. "And I would like a bit of breakfast first, if you don't mind."

"Yes, but I would as lief be on our way before Aunt Adora comes down," he persisted. "You know what she is. Quentin has already had his breakfast and is gone out on his boat," he added conversationally. "I told him to look out for us somewhere along the banks."

"Then go away and let me get dressed," Isobel said, putting down her cup on the bed table and tossing back the sheets. "I never eat very much before riding, I promise you, and we shall be off within the hour."

That seemed a very long time to Simon, but he knew he could not expect more of his sister, so he left Isobel to await her in the breakfast room. He had not been there very long when Adrian entered the room.

"Are you going riding, cousin?" he asked when he

saw Adrian dressed in buckskins, a swallow-tailed coat, and top boots. "Bel and I are riding down to the river, and I thought I'd do a bit of fishing. Join us if you like," he offered hopefully. "We mean to have a picnic lunch, and Cook always imagines we have appetites for four each, so I daresay there will be more than enough food."

Adrian glanced up from pouring himself coffee. "Thank you, but I mean to ride out to the farms on the other side of Fanton Hollow this morning. Mr. Remy has told me that there is something of a drainage problem there, and I would like to see it firsthand. We were able to solve many similar problems at Blackoaks, and perhaps I may be able to offer some useful suggestions."

"Does Grandfather know that you are going out with Mr. Remy?" he asked diffidently, guessing that the earl would suffer no interference with the running of the estate even from his heir.

"It is at his suggestion," Adrian replied on a faintly dry note. His features eased into a slow smile. "I think he wished to test my mettle and thought I should be quite discouraged going out this past week in such abominable weather. But we are bred hardy in Pennsylvania."

"If you follow the river coming back, you may find us," Simon suggested, but received no promise from Adrian.

By the time that Isobel reached the breakfast room, Adrian had left the house. As promised, she had only coffee and toast to break her fast, and soon they were trotting through the park in the direction of the river. Simon would have led them considerably upstream from the house to the spot he most preferred for his sport, but Isobel insisted that they head in the opposite direction to the narrowest stretch of water, which was where the folly was located. Simon protested, but gave in at Isobel's insistence that she wanted a dry place to read if the ground proved to be still too damp for comfort.

But that was no more than a secondary purpose for her choice of a place along the banks. The river was bound to be higher and to flow more swiftly after a sennight of heavy rain, and she did not trust Simon not to attempt to wade into the water to cast his lines and put himself in danger of the current pulling his feet from under him, and it was likely in this spot the danger would be less. They could hear the sound of the river, set at the pitch of a muffled roar, when they were still some distance from their destination, confirming Isobel's fears. Simon was not deterred, however, and they pressed on.

The river was higher than even Isobel had expected it to be, and she saw that its roiling swiftness surprised Simon as well. The ground all about was soggy, and she gratefully spread the blankets they had brought on the wide stone bench along the inner circumference of the folly. It dismayed her a little to think of sitting the whole of the morning on the hard stone seat, however dry, and she made up her mind that they would have an early luncheon and she would persuade him to return to the house immediately afterward.

The folly was near enough to the water's edge for her to keep Simon in sight most of the time, and after glancing toward him numerous times during the first hour to assure herself that he meant to do nothing reckless, she gradually became engrossed in her book, a new novel by a favorite author. The only other thing that distracted her was the memory of what had occurred the last time she had visited the folly. Several times her eyes strayed to the steps leading into the folly, where she had sat beside Adrian and where he had first kissed her. But she would not let herself dwell on the recollection, and she soon was able to put it from her mind.

It was the soft whicker of a horse that eventually roused her from her concentration on the story she was reading. It was only the nearness of it that surprised her, and she looked up thinking that one of the horses had escaped its tether. She saw instead Adrian, still astride, regarding her in a disconcerting manner, his gaze on her fixed but entirely void of expression.

After a moment or so he smiled. "I have had an invitation to lunch," he said, his tone light, "and being nearby and peckish, I have decided to accept if the offer still stands."

Isobel returned his smile. Though she maintained her equanimity in his presence, she could do nothing to prevent the increase of her pulse. "Of course it does," she said, matching her tone to his. "And you are come in good time. Simon would never break from his casting for anything so unimportant to him as luncheon, and I was rapt in my book. We might have offended Cook grievously if we had returned to the house with not a morsel eaten." She rose as she spoke and walked to the center of the folly, where Simon had left the saddle baskets containing their luncheon and the extra blanket.

"Leave it a moment and I'll help you unpack," Adrian said and walked his horse to where the others were tethered. He dismounted and returned to the folly, pausing for a moment to regard Isobel, who was stooping to retrieve the blanket. Her profile was classical perfection. Thick, unexpectedly dark lashes brushed her milky cheek, and a golden tendril escaped its pin and gently caressed the hollow of her throat. The sight of her thus, so lovely, so dear to him, made his own throat constrict. If she was determined to choose Quentin over him, there was little he could do to prevent it.

When she had assured him that her feelings for him were mere physical attraction, she had handed him a leveler. His own feelings for her had been growing so apace that he had assumed his feelings as well as his desire was reciprocated. He had spent the whole of the week pondering his feelings for her, trying to understand them and hopefully convince himself that it was really no more for him either, but he had failed. He wanted to make love to her with an urgency that was near to desperation, but that would satisfy only his physical need; there was another that was equally urgent that only possessing her heart as well as her body could appease.

There was no table in the folly, and he helped her to spread out the blanket on the stone floor. "It would be much more comfortable if we could put out our luncheon on the grass," she said to make conversation that would avoid anything personal between them being mentioned, "but the ground is so damp, I fear it would seep through even if we used both blankets."

"We shall do well enough in here," Adrian replied. They continued to set out the luncheon, discussing nothing more than commonplaces, but in the thoughts of each was much more.

Adrian fetched Simon, and they sat down to a surprisingly comfortable and lively meal. Simon encouraged Adrian to talk of his own country, his curiosity on the subject apparently being insatiable. Adrian readily obliged him and Isobel contributed her might, glad of such a neutral topic and freed of the fear of any awkward silences between her and Adrian that might lead to things being said that she preferred not to discuss.

They were nearly done with their meal when Quentin unexpectedly joined them. "How very cozy," he said in his lazy drawl as he entered the folly.

Isobel was suddenly made aware of how close she

sat to Adrian, and she moved a little away from him. Simon's features broke into a surprised but welcoming smile, and Adrian regarded Quentin's arrival with neither dismay nor pleasure.

Simon scrambled to his feet saying, "You are just in time, Quentin. We haven't finished quite all the food yet."

"And there is still the better part of a bottle of claret," Adrian interposed. "How provident!" he added, ignoring Isobel's quelling frown. "We must have known you would be coming."

There were only two glasses, but Isobel had not drunk any of the wine. Simon offered to go down to the water to wash out his own glass for Quentin, and Isobel invited Quentin to sit beside her. As he crossed the folly to do so, Adrian rose and moved to sit on the stone bench. Quentin cast him a brief triumphant glance as he sat beside Isobel and kissed her briefly.

"I was up betimes this morning and decided it was a perfect day for sailing," Quentin said, accepting her offer of some of the remaining sweetmeats. "I didn't want to awaken you at that hour, but I wish I had. It was exhilarating to be on the water today with the river so high and the current so swift. I think you would have enjoyed it, my love. And we would have had a precious morning of solitude," he added, bending his head to kiss her lightly again.

Isobel would have been delighted by such attention if she hadn't feared that it was far more for Adrian's benefit than hers. She had sailed with Quentin only once some years before, and she had never even set foot on the new boat that the earl had bought him. It was Quentin's contention that on a small boat it was folly to take passengers who could not pull their weight if an unexpected storm or other emergency arose. With just a hint of wryness in her tone, she said, "We may do so tomorrow if you like. I had thought to ride in the morning, but I would by far prefer to sail with you."

Quentin gave her one of his brief smiles, but he made no pledge to act upon her suggestion. "We shall see if the weather is in our favor, love."

Simon returned with his washed glass and poured wine for Quentin. He was full of questions about Quentin's activities of the morning, and it was plain that he would have gladly given up his fishing expedition that morning if Quentin had invited him along.

Adrian took no part in this conversation, content to be an outsider while he observed them. Isobel was uncommonly attentive toward Quentin, intent on displaying her devotion, perhaps also because Adrian was there to observe it. He thought he could bring himself to accept her preference for Quentin if he really believed that she was in love with him, but he did not. They gave all the appearance of two people going through the motions of a past affection. He had seen similar behavior many times, though usually in married couples who had fallen out of love in time.

The conversation passed on to a discussion of Simon's successes that morning, which he acknowledged were meager. "You surprise me," remarked Quentin. "I have not fished much of late, but I seem to recall that the catch after we had a great deal of rain was always prolific. I seem to remember old Frimby, who was still head gamekeeper when Carl and I were boys, saying that after a heavy rain the fish would bite at anything."

"I daresay they might if one were in a place where the fish were to be found," Simon said with a bit of asperity. "But Bel is nearly as bad as Mama and Aunt Adora, thinking I would probably drown myself if I fished upriver where it is wider and deeper."

Quentin laughed. "You probably should, cawker," he admonished. "Carlton and I caught as many fish here as any other place. We often chose this spot because the treehouse was here to play in when we tired of fishing. We had all manner of sport and games to amuse us here."

"By the time I was old enough not to have my nurse following me about with leading strings," Simon complained, "the treehouse was in disrepair and the footbridge declared a hazard. I only vaguely remember playing in the folly under the eye of my nurse while you and Carlton and Bel made a deal of noise that hurt my tender ears."

"It was probably my piteous screams that you heard," said Isobel. "I seem to recall that Carlton's favorite pastime was to tie me up and hold me prisoner in the treehouse. He would convince me that it would be most romantic to be a damsel in distress, and it took me some time to realize that his real purpose was to prevent a tiresome schoolgirl from following him about like a puppy."

"But I remember that you rather liked it when I rescued you from your aerie," Quentin said, drawing Isobel against him. His glance strayed toward Adrian as if to be certain that this intimacy was noted.

"You are not alone, Simon," Adrian said, betraying no consternation. "My father often spoke of the treehouse where he and his brother played as boys, but I have never had the pleasure of seeing it firsthand either. It is just as well, I expect, for it looks pretty much a ruin from the distance and would no doubt disappoint."

"Oh, I don't think it is as bad as that yet," Quentin said, "though it is probably filled with old birds' nests, dead leaves, and spiders. By all means we must inspect it. You would not wish to neglect even this small portion of your inheritance, cousin," he added sardonically.

Adrian and Quentin were civil to each other, but

the hostility between them simmered dangerously just below the surface. There was in Quentin's manner the suggestion of a challenge, and Isobel feared another scene not dissimilar to the one the night before, though at least here there were no weapons available to them other than those nature might provide.

She rose to her knees and began to gather up the remains of their luncheon, attempting to disguise her anxiety in activity. "Don't be foolish, Quentin. You know the footbridge was in a sad state when we were children. It must be falling to pieces by now."

"There's only a missing plank or two, Bel," Simon assured her, unknowingly causing his sister to heap silent curses on his head.

"And why are they missing?" she queried tartly. "If the wood was not rotting, the bridge would be whole." She finished her task and stood to shake out the blankets and fold them. She had some hope that if she could be ready for them to leave before they actually attempted to cross the footbridge, she would succeed in preventing her forebodings from achieving fruition. "If you try to cross it you might well end in the river, and with the current as it is today, risking that would be idiocy."

"For God's sake, Bel," cried her aggrieved brother, "you sound exactly like Mama or Aunt Adora. You didn't used to be so bottomless."

"Silence, cub," Quentin said, holding up his hand. "Your sister is right that you shouldn't take the risk of breaking another bone when the last one you fractured is barely healed. In the spring or summer when you are in prime twig again, you may risk your silly neck all you like."

"I'm perfectly fine now," Simon said, his tone very near to sulking.

"Perhaps I ought not risk my silly neck either," Adrian suggested.

Quentin's smile was just shy of being a sneer. "I thought you were eager, cousin, to catalogue the whole of your inheritance. But if you agree with Bel that the risk is too great . . ."

Isobel prayed that Adrian would shrug off Quentin's taunt, as he had so often in the past, but this time he did not hesitate to pick up the gauntlet. "If you lead the way, Cousin Quentin, I've a fancy to see the place now."

They left the folly together, with Simon trailing behind them. Isobel felt compelled to follow. Though she had little hope of being heeded, she said, "It would be far safer to cross the river by the bridge at the home farm."

There were not steps leading to the footbridge, but only a wide-planked ladder nearly hidden by an aggressive vine and spreading tree branches that covered it. Quentin did not hesitate but immediately began to ascend the ladder. When he was nearly at the top, Adrian climbed up after him.

Isobel looked at the river and shivered at even the thought of either man falling into it. It was not only the swiftness of it that alarmed her, but the water looked cold and far deeper than usual. She knew that Quentin was a competent swimmer, and Adrian had spoken of swimming in the Delaware River, but in such a strong current even an accomplished swimmer would find his skill tested. She laid her hand on Adrian's arm, arresting him momentarily. "I wish you would not do this," she said urgently.

He seemed surprised by her concern, but he said, "The worst we may have of it is a wetting, Bel. There is no reason to fret."

He gently shrugged off her hand and continued up the ladder. Quentin had reached the top and stepped onto the bridge. Isobel more than half expected to hear the sound of rending wood, but the planks beneath him held firm. With her breath held, she waited for Adrian to add his weight to the bridge. When he did so without any unfortunate consequence, her tension eased, though only slightly.

Simon, watching them without Isobel's concern, said defiantly, "There's not a thing wrong with the old bridge, Bel. I'm going to have a look myself at the old treehouse."

He started toward the ladder, but at that moment, as Adrian and Quentin reached the center of the footbridge, it swayed slightly under their combined weight and began to creak alarmingly.

Isobel caught her brother's coat sleeve, her attention torn between preventing Simon from being foolish and fear for the safety of both Adrian and Quentin. "Simon, don't you dare go out on the footbridge. You may not only hurt yourself but Quentin and Adrian as well. It is barely holding under *their* weight."

"I'll wait until they have reached the other side before I step on it," he assured her, but he saw the apprehension in her eyes and added, "Adrian is right. The worst that can happen is that one or another of us might get a good dousing. We are all of us excellent swimmers.

"Simon," said Isobel in a voice of command, "don't you dare follow them. Even Quentin said you were not to do so."

"There isn't the least need for either of you to be anxious. If all you mean to do is spoil sport, you can leave us and go back to the house." With these words he began to climb the ladder. "Nothing at all is going to happen," he said, casting the words over his shoulder as he reached the top.

But then he looked at the footbridge, and an involuntary exclamation of alarm broke from him. Isobel glanced up and saw that Quentin was leaning dangerously over the side of the bridge, clutching frantically at the handrail. Adrian, immediately behind him, reached out his hand, but the handrail, rotted with age, gave way, and before her horrified eyes it snapped with a loud crack. Quentin fell into the water. Adrian attempted to regain his own balance but failed. He stood precariously on the edge for a moment longer and then plunged in after him.

Chapter 10

For a long, unsettling moment both men disappeared from sight in the churning water. Isobel was frozen with horror and helplessness, and then first Quentin and then Adrian reappeared and began to swim toward shore. She had only a moment of thankful relief that neither appeared to be injured from the fall before anxiety again overtook her. It was not just the swiftness of the current that hampered both men, but the weight of their sodden clothes and boots that pulled them downriver in spite of their valiant efforts to overcome the drag of the current.

It had been difficult to tell at a distance if Adrian had lost his balance and fallen into the river after Quentin or if he had deliberately leaped into the water, perhaps with the thought of aiding his cousin. But in Simon's mind it was unquestioned. "Good God," he said in much agitation, turning to retrace his steps down the ladder. "Adrian pushed Quentin into the river."

Isobel recoiled at these words. "Don't be absurd. The bridge was unsafe and they have fallen."

Simon began to struggle out of his coat, but Isobel caught his arm and held it firmly. "Don't be a fool, Simon. You can't help them with your injury, and you would make it worse if you had to be rescued too."

Simon tried to pull away from her. "I've got to help Quentin," he said frantically.

"They are both excellent swimmers," she said point-edly, nearly as upset by Simon's accusation. "Neither of them shall drown." She spoke with conviction, but it was to keep Simon from following them, not because she was certain of it herself.

The truth was that she wished with all her heart that she had the ability to leap into the water herself. It was maddening to stand on the bank of the river, watching both men struggle against the current, and be able to do nothing to help them. The river was not usually deep at this part, she knew, but the rain had added depth to all of the river, and as it traveled into Turvey land, it both widened and deepened naturally. If Adrian and Quentin did not manage to swim out of it before then, her very worst imaginings might well come true.

Adrian and Quentin were pulled inexorably toward this danger in spite of their exertions. Isobel and Simon ran along the bank, keeping pace with them and calling encouragement. It was the final bend in the river still on Renville property before Adrian, with Quentin close behind him, made it to the shallower water along the bank. He reached some protruding rocks and began to rise out of the water. Simon half ran, half slid down the bank to reach him.

Isobel's attention was naturally riveted on them, but for a moment she glanced away to assure herself that Quentin was also about to reach safety. There was no sign of him. She blinked, disbelieving her own eyes, but it was as if Quentin had vanished. Isobel turned back her brother and said urgently, "Where is Quentin? I don't see him at all."

Simon had his hand stretched out for Adrian to grasp, but Adrian turned away at Isobel's words and looked behind him. The sound of the river was too loud to hear his words, but Isobel saw his lips move in some uttered oath. His chest was rising and falling heavily from his labors, yet he abandoned his chance for immediate safety. He turned away from Simon and dived back into the water. In a few moments he too disappeared from sight.

Isobel had never given in to hysterics in her life, but for the first time she understood the wish to do so. It was the helpless frustration that was the hardest to bear, the sense of impending doom that was clearly observed but which she was powerless to prevent.

She followed Simon at a run along the bank. As they rounded the bend in the land, Simon suddenly cried out that he could see Quentin again and directed her attention by pointing farther downriver. Quentin was completely caught in the current, which was even stronger as the bend straightened again and the river began to widen. He no longer appeared to be swimming but merely struggling to stay above water. Adrian emerged as well and, swimming strongly, aided this time by going with the current instead of against it, he quickly reached Quentin. Quentin grasped frantically at Adrian, and they were both pulled under the water.

"They are going to die, they are going to die," Simon said, almost weeping.

"Be quiet, Simon," Isobel shouted in response, her patience snapping with fear and tension. "They are not going to die." She needed to say those words as if that would make it true, but her very heart was constricted with terror. Even if Adrian succeeded in helping Quentin, it was obvious that he was nearly as spent from fighting the river as Quentin was. As impossible, as horrible as it seemed, Isobel knew that both might perish in the churning water.

Suddenly there was the sound of other voices shouting and loud splashes as they dived into the water. Isobel and Simon ran in the direction of the noise, which came from Turvey land. Isobel badly rent the

skirt of her habit climbing the fence that separated
the properties, and nearly lost a boot when she caught
her foot in a tangle of bushes and fell headlong. She
caught up to Simon in a clearing along the river. There
were two other men in the water now, divested of
their coats and boots, which lay scattered on the
ground near the edge of the water. Glad to be of use
in even the most mundane fashion, Isobel went to
their horses, which the men had left untethered in
their haste. She drew them to the edge of the bank,
unable to take her eyes off the two men as they swam
to the rescue of Adrian and Quentin.

Adrian and Quentin had been separated again by
the strong flow of the water, though with the widening
of the river the power of the current was lessened.
Even as the first of the men reached Quentin, Isobel
realized that this time it was Adrian who had disappeared. She searched frantically downriver, hoping
that like Quentin he had only been caught by the current, but he was not to be seen. The two men reached
Quentin and began pulling him to shore. Simon at
once called out that there was another man to be rescued, but one of the men had already dived under the
water to search for Adrian. After what seemed an
agonizingly long time, he emerged and was seen to be
pulling something up with him. When Adrian's head
broke water, Isobel felt almost faint with relief.

It seemed an interminable time before they slowly
made their way out of the water, but finally the two
men pulled themselves and their charges onto land.
One of the rescuers proved to be Lord Turvey and
the other was Thomas Liddiard, the American nephew
of Lady Cahill's. Quentin managed to crawl on his
knees onto the bank where he half lay, half knelt on
the grass, coughing and gasping for air. It was plain,
though, that it was exhaustion that mostly afflicted
him. With Adrian it was quite another matter. He was

dragged onto the grass by Mr. Liddiard, and Lord Turvey, assured that Quentin was well, quickly hastened to them.

Adrian was very white and still, and seeing him so, Isobel felt as if she had been clutched inside by an icy hand. She rushed to him and knelt at his side. She turned terrified eyes to Mr. Liddiard, who was at Adrian's other side. "Please," she said, her voice a desperate whisper, "he can't be dead."

"He breathes," Liddiard said, bending his head to place it directly against Adrian's chest. "But I think he must have swallowed a deal of water, and there is a bruise on his head as if he had struck it on a rock or something."

He began to press on Adrian's stomach to force the water from him, and Simon, pushing Isobel gently out of the way, knelt to help him. Between them they succeeded finally in forcing Adrian to regurgitate a considerable amount of water. In another moment Adrian's eyes fluttered open, and he pushed himself up on one elbow coughing and choking and proving that he was still very much alive. At last he seemed to recover himself and looked up at the worried faces that surrounded him. He saw Isobel, her complexion wan with fright, and managed a slight vestige of his usual quizzical smile.

Quentin had slowly worked his way over to them and was the first to speak. He did so in a gruff tone quite different from the usual sardonic accents with which he usually addressed Adrian. "I thank you, cousin. In trying to save my life, you nearly lost your own."

All eyes turned to Adrian as he hoisted himself to a sitting position. Isobel thought there was an odd expression in his eyes as he looked to Quentin, but he only said in a level tone, "You would have done the same for me."

Isobel saw surprise flicker in Quentin's expression. "I hope I would have," he said in a flat voice and asked Simon to help him to his feet.

This Lord Turvey and Isobel would by no means allow. Both Adrian and Quentin were forced to remain where they sat while they were divested of their water-laden coats, waistcoats, and boots. Simon went to fetch the blankets and the remains of the claret from the folly.

Some of the shock of the ordeal began to wear off, and Adrian turned to his rescuers to give them proper thanks, but this was interrupted by the reappearance of Simon, who was then dispatched to return to the house as quickly as possible to have a conveyance sent to them to take Adrian and Quentin back to the house. Both of them appeared revolted by this prospect and insisted that they were quite capable of riding the distance, but Lord Turvey, who was near to an age that their own fathers would have been if still alive, refused to be swayed by their arguments and swiftly reduced both strong-willed young men to the level of the schoolroom.

Both he and Mr. Liddiard were also soaked, and there were no blankets for them in the chill autumn air. But his lordship refused to leave them until he had personally witnessed both Quentin and Adrian safely settled and on their way to the house. Mr. Liddiard seconded this and in speaking called attention to himself. It was plain that his accent, though subtly different from Adrian's, was also American. As Adrian looked directly at the young man for the first time, Isobel saw recognition flash into Mr. Liddiard's eyes.

Adrian saw it too and groaned inwardly. To him the young man's face was only vaguely familiar; it seemed probable that they had met at college at some time. Though he felt as if the muscles in his back and arms had been wrung in the grip of a giant, he stood up and held out his hand. He decided it was better to take the initiative if there was even a slim hope of salvaging the situation. "I am certain I know your face, but—I beg your pardon!—I cannot recall your name," he said. "Mine is Renville. Adrian Renville of Pennsylvania."

Tom Liddiard shook Adrian's hand with a vigor that made the latter wince involuntarily. He said he didn't wonder that Adrian did not recall him. "I was only a lowly underclassman at the time we met, and you were nearly a legend at college. I was so honored to be presented to you at the Richmond Hunt that I was too overcome to say more than how d'ye do. Lord, what a glorious hunt that was too. You gave us all the lead."

Adrian did not look at all pleased by these encomiums, and small wonder at it. He was properly dished and he knew it. He cast a swift glance toward Quentin and saw his cousin regarding him with puzzled speculation.

Lord Turvey, made aware that neither Adrian nor Quentin had actually been introduced to Mr. Liddiard, both having been absent when he had visited Audswyck with his uncle, repaired this omission.

"When my aunt told me that the Renvilles at Audswyck Chase had an American cousin visiting them," said Liddiard, "I did wonder if there was a connection, but I had no notion it would be you."

Quentin said, "I am no great hand at geography, Mr. Liddiard, but I rather thought that Virginia was a considerable distance from Pennsylvania."

"A two-day to a two-week journey at the least of it, depending on where in each state one wishes to travel and the state of the roads," agreed the affable Mr. Liddiard. "But Mr. Renville and I were at school together, though he left the year after I arrived."

"And what school was that?" Quentin persevered.

"Why, William and Mary, of course. The finest gentlemen's college in the United States, though," the young man admitted with a grin, "I daresay there are some northerners who would argue in favor of Harvard. No doubt Mr. Renville was too modest to mention that he enjoyed considerable repute in his college days. The sons of Virginia pride themselves on their horsemanship, but he, a Yankee, made us all look nohow. Sits a horse like a centaur, though you must know that."

"Yes," Quentin said after a moment of consideration. "He has given us an example of his skill. It comes from riding pigs to market in his youth, I imagine."

"Pigs?" Mr. Liddiard's face expressed his astonishment.

Quentin's eyes were fixed firmly on Adrian, and the latter did not flinch from his gaze. Adrian's expression was one of resignation tinged with a rueful amusement. "My brothers and I thought it a high treat when we were boys to go to market in Philadelphia with our father's herdsmen."

"What a very prosperous farm it sounds, cousin," said Quentin with a return of his usual sardonic inflection. "You are to be felicitated."

"I've never been to Blackoaks, of course," said the ever helpful Mr. Liddiard, "but I know it's considered one of the finest estates north of the Delaware even by Virginia standards."

"A singular encomium for a rude farm, cousin," Quentin said dulcetly.

"I don't recollect that I ever used quite that adjective," Adrian replied, neither put out nor repentant.

"No, I daresay we supplied it for you," Quentin agreed in much the same tone.

Of all present, perhaps Isobel was the only one not amused by this exchange. She wondered that she could ever have thought that this day would pass in tedium, and it was likely that further discomforts were yet to come. It was obvious that Quentin's changed manner toward Adrian, engendered by Adrian's efforts to save him from the river, had dissipated once he began to realize that Adrian had been hoaxing them since his arrival at Audswyck. In a way it could be argued that Adrian had made him look more the fool than anyone else, except perhaps for Lord Audwin himself, whose usual keen perception had for once failed to detect a sham.

There was no doubt now that Lord Audwin would be apprised of the change in his grandson's consequence before the day was out, but whether this would be by Adrian's own admission or Quentin's agency remained to be seen. Audwin's icy fury was far more annihilating than mere rage, and he was already in a temper from the scene between Quentin and Adrian the night before.

To the chagrin of both Adrian and Quentin, Simon returned with what appeared to be half the household in tow. Several footmen carrying blankets, dry clothes, brandy, and several nostrums sent by the hand of Lady Adora herself burst out of the overgrowth, and Beal himself was on hand to direct them. Four stout grooms arrived on their heels with litters in tow and the information that Lady Adora's well-sprung barouche awaited them on the nearest road navigable to them.

Both men kindly refused to be cosseted and insisted that their rescuers be attended to as well. Isobel tactfully began the walk toward the carriage while the gentlemen were helped into dry clothes. It was not very long before she was joined by Simon.

"What occurred while I was gone, Bel?" he demanded. "It might have been a bit grudging, but Quentin was grateful to Adrian for trying to save his life. Now he looks as if he would take the greatest pleasure in murdering Adrian with his own hands."

Isobel sighed. There was really no point in dissembling. Simon would know the truth soon enough, as would Lady Adora and eventually the entire family. As succinctly as she could, she told Simon that Adrian had admitted to her that his dreadful provincial manners and speech had been a sham, and that Mr. Liddiard, being known to Adrian, had inadvertently given him away to Quentin also.

Simon did not seem especially surprised. "I knew there was something havey-cavey about him. He is well served, then, for nearly drowning himself after he pushed Quentin off the bridge."

Isobel was startled by this reiteration of his earlier accusation, which she had assumed was made in the shock of the moment. "Adrian did no such thing," she said with conviction. "For heaven's sake, you admit yourself that he tried to save Quentin and was nearly lost himself in the effort." The return of this realization made her shiver inside. It was not a thought she could bear to dwell upon.

"He might not have meant to drown him precisely," Simon conceded, "but he would have little choice but to try to save Quentin with both of us looking on to say later that he let him drown. That would be murder and no doubt of it."

"Simon!"

"Well, it would," Simon insisted. "If he pushed Quentin off the bridge and Quentin drowned because of it—"

There were sounds heard of the others approaching. Isobel cut him off. "You *will not* say such things, Simon," she said in a furious undertone.

"I know what I saw," Simon said, his expression mulish.

"Very well," Isobel said, knowing that she had to

convince Simon that he was mistaken. "Tell me exactly what you did see."

Simon seemed a little surprised that Isobel meant to listen to him and hesitated. "It—it happened very quickly," he said stammering a little.

"But clearly enough for you to make such a dire accusation," Isobel said, having no intention of letting him hedge. "Surely you would not vilify a man unless you were certain of what you had seen."

Simon looked uncomfortable, but his chin rose in a determined manner. "I am. Adrian and Quentin were at the center of the bridge, and it seemed to sway. Quentin took a step and then Adrian's hands came out and pushed against his back. Quentin grabbed for the railing to keep from falling, but it broke beneath him as you know."

"And you have not the slightest doubt that when Adrian touched Quentin, he was pushing him?" Isobel asked leadingly. "The bridge was above you, after all, and they were at sufficient distance that you could not have seen them as clearly as . . ." She paused to seek out a suitable example, and her eyes settled on two of the footmen who were now seen approaching them from some distance ". . . say, Peter and John, is it not?"

Simon glanced over at the two young men and back to Isobel. "Yes, I did, quite as clearly."

Isobel said nothing for several moments, and as the footmen neared they proved to be two other than she had named. "Ah, I see I was mistaken," she said in a meaningful way. "It is Ralph and Jem coming toward us."

Simon said indignantly, "That is not fair, Bel. The distance was greater, and I am not well acquainted with all of Grandfather's servants."

"But you claimed you saw them as clearly as you did Adrian and Quentin on the footbridge. The point has nothing to do with identity, however, but only that you could not have possibly seen them so clearly to know that Adrian deliberately pushed Quentin into the water. Perhaps Quentin stumbled and Adrian was trying to steady him. Has it occurred to you, I wonder, that if what you say is true, it is hardly likely that Quentin would have said nothing when he was safe out of the water? I doubt it would have mattered to him that Lord Turvey and Mr. Liddiard were present. In fact, he probably would have relished accusing Adrian of pushing him off the bridge all the more."

"I can see that Quentin was right in one thing," Simon retorted, stung by her spirited defense. But what this was was to remain unknown, for these proved the last words in their discussion. The footmen reached the carriage and began loading their burden of blankets and wet clothes into the carriage, and a short while later Adrian and Quentin finally emerged onto the road with Beal hovering over them in spite of their protests.

They arrived at the house to learn that the earl, when the news of the accident had been conveyed to him by his daughter-in-law, had sent for Dr. Morrison to attend his grandsons. Neither Adrian nor Quentin were pleased by this, but it allayed Isobel's concerns that any unobvious injury in either man would go undetected.

After she had changed her soiled and torn dress for a primrose cotton day dress with a wide, charmingly piped and pleated hem, Isobel went immediately to allay the fears of Lady Adora as best she could. She also meant to prepare her aunt for the revelation that Adrian had been hoaxing them, but she proved craven in the face of Lady Adora's assurance that the accident had been entirely Adrian's fault, though she believed this was due to clumsiness rather than intent. In the course of her animadversion it would have appeared to anyone unacquainted with either Quentin or Adrian that the former was a pattern card of good sense and the latter a bumbling idiot.

At the end of this recital, Isobel was anything but heartened for the visit she meant to pay to Lord Audwin. She thought it unlikely that Quentin would emerge again from his rooms until he had enjoyed the relaxing bath she knew his valet had prepared for him and was fully dressed again. This gave her the chance to approach the earl first. She did not wish to tell the earl the truth about Adrian, but she doubted that Quentin would be so reticent, and his version was certain to be vituperative.

She found Lord Audwin not in his sitting room but in his study. This was a very good sign and meant that his gout was not troubling him as much, for he rarely descended to the ground floor when it was giving him pain. He looked up when he saw her and smiled in a fairly congenial fashion. "Have you come to give me the particulars of the scrape my grandsons have fallen into, Bel? I have spoken with Morrison, and he assures me that both Quentin and Adrian have remarkably healthy constitutions and have suffered no harm. Simon set the entire household on its ears when he came galloping up the drive hell for leather and had us all fearing that they were half killed."

With the appearance of unruffled composure, she took the chair confronting the earl's. "Simon does have a gift for telling story in a vivid manner," she agreed, returning his smile. "But what happened really was fantastical and dreadful. I still begin to quake when I think of what the outcome might have been if Lord Turvey had not happened to be out at that moment with Mr. Liddiard, who was trying the paces of a horse he is thinking of purchasing from Turvey." From this she launched into a fairly accurate accounting of what had occurred. The events lent themselves to melodrama, and she could not entirely disguise the emotions recalling these evoked.

Lord Audwin listened with his usual cool and impassive demeanor, but Isobel saw from the intensity of his gaze that he listened with grave concern. "How did this come to happen, Bel?" he asked at the end of her recital, his steady gaze on her demanding the truth.

She gave it to him as best she could. "I-I don't really know." She could not help feeling slightly uncomfortable with him watching her so, and knew it was because of Simon's ridiculous accusation. She did not believe it for a moment, but she felt absurdly that in keeping it from him she was somehow prevaricating. "Simon had decided to follow them and I was trying to dissuade him, so I was not watching precisely. One moment they seemed to be crossing the footbridge without difficulty, and the next the railing, which must have been rotted, gave way and Quentin went into the river and Adrian after him."

"It might have needed refurbishing, but the wood could not be rotted, or Remy would have had it repaired or taken down," the earl said with no doubt. "He knows I would not tolerate anything less. You will have Beal send Remy to me when you leave me."

Isobel had conveniently halted her story at the point where Adrian and Quentin had been brought safely to shore. There was nothing more for her to say other than to relate Mr. Liddiard's recognition of Adrian and to admit to the earl that she herself had known for certain that Adrian was not what he seemed almost from the day he arrived at Audswyck.

"*Grand-père,*" she said, coming to a decision, "there is something else that happened today that you should know, but I don't think it is my place to tell you. It concerns Adrian."

Audwin was silent for a moment and then said, "in what manner?"

"I would rather he told you himself," she said, unhappily aware of accomplishing nothing more than raising the earl's suspicions. "If you would send for him—"

The door opened as she was speaking, and Quentin came into the room. He was dressed with his usual elegance in a coat of Bath superfine fawn-colored breeches and boots with fashionably wide tops. He gave no appearance of a man who had very nearly stuck his spoon in the wall earlier that same afternoon.

"I supposed the tale of my adventures must have reached your ears by now, sir," he said as he advanced into the room, "and I wished to assure you in person that I am in fine fettle."

Lord Audwin subjected him to a sweeping search of his person and then nodded. "I can see that. What I can't see is what the devil made you do such a damned cork-brained thing as falling into the river. Don't try to gammon me that the railing was rotted and simply gave way."

Quentin pulled up a chair to sit beside Isobel. "Not rotted, precisely," he said easily, "but certainly dry and brittle. Of course, I believed the footbridge safe, or I shouldn't have suggested crossing it."

"And how was it you came to fall against the railing?" Audwin demanded.

Quentin gave a brief, self-deprecating laugh. "Pure clumsiness. I stumbled on a loose board." It was a very logical explanation, and it put an end to Simon's suspicions.

"Did Isobel tell you the whole of what occurred today?" Quentin asked, bending a quizzical glance on Isobel for a moment.

"If you mean that you were rescued by Turvey and Cahill's nephew, yes," replied the earl.

Quentin turned his eyes on Isobel, and to her disgust she felt her cheeks grow warm. "Not quite the whole, then," he said softly.

"I didn't think it my place to tell *Grand-père*," she said to Quentin, refusing to acknowledge the censure she read in his eyes. "Nor do I think it is yours. I asked him to send for Adrian so that he may speak for himself."

Audwin's brows knit. "What is it, then?"

Quentin hesitated. "Perhaps I should speak with you alone."

"Quentin, you could not be so mean-spirited," Isobel said sharply. "Adrian tried to save your life and nearly lost his own in the process."

"And I thanked him for his trouble very nicely," Quentin said with an infuriating smile. "That one noble action does not mitigate the fact that he has made fools of us all."

"And how precisely has he done that?" demanded the earl, his voice not raised but the command in it plain.

Isobel turned an imploring look on Lord Audwin. "Please send for Adrian, *Grand-père*. It would be much better if you heard this from his own lips."

"I shall certainly hear it from someone's before many more minutes have passed," the old man said grimly. "Ring for Beal and tell him to have Adrian sent to me."

The wait for Adrian was not a long one, but it was certainly uncomfortable, at least for Isobel. The five minutes seemed to be trebled, and she feared at every moment that Lord Audwin's patience would wane.

Adrian must have known the purpose of his summons, yet when he entered the study, he showed no sign of trepidation. He raised his brows slightly when he saw both Isobel and Quentin there before him, but his acknowledgment of them showed neither suspicion nor discomfort. He also showed no sign of his earlier ordeal, and he responded to the earl's inquiries that he was well enough to pass.

"Quentin and Isobel seem to think you have something of import to tell me," Audwin said, his piercing gaze designed to make prevarication impossible.

"Do I?" he asked as if with genuine surprise, though he had guessed the reason he had been called to his grandfather's study. "It can't be to tell you about our adventure at the river, for I am sure that Cousin Quentin and Cousin Isobel have already told you of that."

"Most of it, coz," said Quentin, a faint, satisfied smile on his lips. "But we thought to save the climax of the story for your own telling."

"Isobel seems to think it is something that you would prefer to tell me yourself, Adrian," said the earl, "but if you do not, I shall have the tale from Quentin."

Adrian bestowed a brief, sweet smile on Quentin. "I see that I have wronged you, cousin. I expected you to tell our grandfather everything as soon as we returned to the house."

"My mistake," Quentin admitted. "I had momentarily forgotten that my own dear Isobel has appointed herself your chief advocate."

"That is quite enough fencing, Quentin," Lord Audwin said sharply. "I don't know what nonsense this is, but I will have no more of it. It is time, Quentin, that you accepted that Adrian is my heir, however much you may dislike it. And you," he added, pointing an accusing finger at Adrian, "would do well to remember that you owe a considerable debt to Quentin for the transformation he has wrought in you. When you arrived, it was as if all my worst expectations had borne fruit, and under his tuition you have at least now the appearance of a gentleman. I don't give a

damn whether or not you like him, but you will respect the advice he gives you and seek to imitate him
in all things if you expect to continue to find favor
with me."

The prospect of doing any such thing was repugnant
to Adrian, but he held his tongue. This was not a
propitious beginning. It was useless to regret that he
had not followed Isobel's advice and admitted the
truth to them all once he had told her. A few short
weeks ago it would not have mattered to him overmuch to have been cast from the family, as his father
had been, for his duplicity, but as his eyes rested for
a moment on Isobel, he knew that it did matter to
him now.

He seated himself without invitation in the chair
beside Isobel's. "It is on the order of a confession
rather than a story, sir. I am afraid you give Quentin
undeserved credit. I was born and bred to be a gentleman's son, as you and my cousins might have expected
but apparently did not."

In this manner, Adrian began his relation of all that
had passed from the time he had received Lord Audwin's note in the common room of the Three Bells.
He spoke plainly as he had to Isobel, admitting that
he had perpetrated the hoax from a combination of
pique and self-amusement.

Quentin sat on the edge of the large desk where his
grandfather reviewed his bailiff's accounts. He witnessed the astonishment and growing anger in the earl
with a cat-in-the-creampot smile, certain that his actions that afternoon, which he had assumed failed, had
instead led by an unexpected encounter to the routing
of his rival, an unlooked-for but eminently desirable
consequence.

Though Audwin was justly feared for his temper,
his anger usually took the form of a cold, slashing
acrimony directed toward whoever had unwisely

roused his choler. But as Isobel watched him, his carefully neutral expression became a thunderous scowl. She began to fear that he might after all go off in an apoplexy of pure rage. His face took on a flush that gradually deepened to crimson, his jaw clenched, and his eyes, normally deep-set, seemed to protrude.

Adrian had almost come to an end of his confession when the earl interrupted him explosively. "Damn your impudence," he roared, half rising out of his chair with his cane to support him. "What you have done, sir, is insupportable. Your explanations palliate nothing. Were it in my power, I would at this moment set in train whatever was necessary to see to it that you did not inherit a ha'penny from me."

"I would it were in your power also, sir," Adrian said mildly. "I never looked to inherit anything from you other than the title, which cannot be prevented." The reaction of his grandfather was no more than he had expected. Adrian shrewdly guessed that this degree of rage was not only due to the hoax he had perpetrated, which had made a May game of the earl, but caused also by the realization that he had no need of the earl's fortune and thus was beyond his control.

"You have not only the look of your father," Audwin said savagely, "you inherited his degenerate character as well. Francis was cast off from the family for good cause. He would have brought nothing but disgrace on the name of Renville, and it is plain you mean to continue that legacy. I must be in my dotage to have sent for you. Well, you can take yourself back to the company of rebels and savages; it is clearly where you belong. I can't disinherit you, but I can refuse to acknowledge you."

Adrian bit back the defense of his father that sprung to his lips. He decided against giving his grandfather the satisfaction of knowing that he had succeeded in provoking him. "That would be regrettable, but you must do as you see fit," he said in a cool, detached manner.

This lack of both concern and contrition fed the earl's rage. "I want you out of this house by noon tomorrow, or I'll have Beal toss you out bag and baggage onto the front lawn," he said, almost sputtering.

Isobel glanced at Quentin and read satisfaction in his expression. Though she knew she was courting the earl's fire and would probably draw down upon her head Quentin's anger as well, she could not sit and say nothing in Adrian's defense. "What Adrian did may have been reprehensible, *Grand-père*, but was the behavior of the rest of us any more excusable? I think perhaps we deserved to be gammoned for judging Adrian before we had so much as met him, and for being so puffed up in our own conceit."

"I don't believe I was addressing you, Isobel," Audwin said, his brows snapping together ominously. "You may go and see if your aunt has need of you. This is not your affair."

But Isobel would not be so summarily dismissed. "It is the affair of all of the family, for we all had a hand in prejudging Adrian. I think you should be grateful rather than angry that he is not the dirty dish we all believed him to be. It is unjust to condemn him for being a gentleman instead."

"Now that you have edified us with your opinion, girl, you may go," the earl repeated, his cold and biting anger now directed at her.

Isobel did not want to leave, but neither did she wish to make matters worse for Adrian than they already were. She turned her head to look at him and saw that his features were as stony and set as Audwin's. As if he was aware of her scrutiny, he flicked a glance at her, and in his eyes, for the brief moment they met hers, she read just the hint of a smile and was reassured. She rose unhurriedly and without comment.

Quentin touched her arm as she passed, and she looked up at him, meeting his gaze levelly, though inside she felt a churning sensation. She knew he would see her defense of Adrian as a betrayal of himself. She had the foreboding that this would somehow bring matters to a head between them, and both her feelings and the outcome were far from certain.

Quentin's expression could only be described as forbidding. "Such devotion is quite touching, my love," he said, his tone heavily sardonic. "What a pity it is not for me."

"What a pity your gratitude is not for Adrian," she said, astonished at her own boldness. "I think if you had treated me with the scathing contempt you have heaped upon Adrian, I should have let you drown." She saw angry color flood Quentin's countenance, and she knew she had crossed a bridge. She held his icy stare for another moment and then turned and left the study.

After Isobel left them, silence reigned for several moments, broken finally by Quentin. "Piqued, repiqued, and capoted, coz," he said with no attempt to disguise his relish.

Adrian's smile was far from his usual pleasant expression. "But not by your agency, though God knows you gave it your best. My compliments for this afternoon, by the by. The railing was sawed partway through, I presume?"

Neither Quentin nor the earl paid the least attention to these remarks. "What astonishes me, sir," Quentin said to his grandfather as if Adrian were not even present, "is that the savage would dare to attempt to explain his duplicity with such obvious lies. He had some deep purpose for his masquerade, depend upon it."

The earl shrugged. "It doesn't matter in the least. I tolerated no impertinence from his father, nor shall I from his hell-born cub." Turning again to Adrian, he said, "You will find passage to return to America as soon as you may. I won't have you setting yourself up against me; even your father had more sense than to try that. If you attempt to defy me, I'll have you pressed onto the first man-of-war that comes into harbor, and the devil take you."

Adrian gave no appearance of being daunted by this threat. "I'm sorry to come to the same end with you as my father did," he said, rising from his chair, "but I doubt now that I could have done anything to prevent it, had I been a pattern card of gentility when I arrived. I don't excuse what I have done, but I think it is still my father that you wish to banish. I had hoped thirty years sufficient to heal old wounds."

The earl's flush took on a deeper hue, and he smashed his stick against the side of his chair with such force that the stick cracked audibly. "I'll have no more of your damned impudence."

Adrian remained unmoved by this display. "I shall certainly leave Audswyck in the morning, but it doesn't please me to leave England just yet, and the truth is, I've a fancy to please myself in most things."

He sketched the choleric earl a brief, mocking bow, shot a glance at Quentin that conveyed the promise of future confrontation, and left them.

Adrian had always known that the earl might react with violence to the knowledge that he had misrepresented himself, but he had hoped for a more auspicious circumstance in which to make his admission. He thought of Isobel, and a brief wave of despair afflicted him. When he had opened his eyes for the first time after being pulled unconscious from the river, the first thing he had seen was Isobel's lovely, dear face, her expression one of commingled fear and hope. He believed she had to feel something for him beyond mere attraction, even if she did not admit it to herself.

But surely now his hopes with her were dashed. She could never choose him over Quentin now without facing the severest disapprobation and risk cutting herself off from her family completely and perhaps forever. If she did truly love him, did she love him enough for that? Did he have the right to ask such sacrifice of her if she did? These thoughts had the effect of casting him down to a degree that nothing his grandfather or Quentin said to him could ever have done.

Chapter 11

Isobel found an old cloak in a cupboard near a door that opened onto the formal gardens near the rear of the house. The sun had disappeared behind darkening clouds, but the house felt oppressive to her and she wanted fresh air and exercise to clear the fog of conflicting emotions filling her head. She knew that Quentin would exact a reckoning for her defense of Adrian, but she did not regret it. Still, she was not anxious for the interview. She hardly knew what she would say to Quentin, for she certainly had no intention of apologizing for her words.

In the aftermath of all the violent emotions that had assailed her while she had helplessly watched Adrian and Quentin fight for their lives against the swift current, a truth had emerged and this time she did not push it aside or try to deny it to herself. If Quentin had been lost in the churning water, she would certainly have been horrified; if Adrian had died, she knew that her own heart would have died with him.

But the realization that she loved Adrian brought her no joy. She wanted to weep rather than rejoice. Perhaps the reality of her relationship with Quentin had not lived up to her fantasy of it, and perhaps she had not always been happy with him, but her future had been a settled thing; she knew the comfort of certainty. Now that was all dashed to splinters.

Isobel did not even have confidence that her feelings were returned by Adrian. He had said that he was *falling* in love with her, but she had rejected the love he offered her heartlessly, and this might well have destroyed the burgeoning feelings he had for her.

And if he did still love her, she wondered, would that dissipate all her dismay and uncertainty? She knew it would not. She was coming to realize that it was not only her vows to Quentin that had made her unwilling to recognize her growing feelings for Adrian. Jilting Quentin and accepting the love that Adrian offered her would have ramifications far beyond the distress of dealing with her own emotions. The scandal it would cause in the world was nothing to the upheaval such an action would cause within the family.

Isobel knew that neither her father and stepmother nor the earl particularly favored the match between her and Quentin, but they accepted it. The scandal that would be created if she left Quentin and went to Adrian would be significant, and she might well be cutting herself off from her family by making that choice. Very few people had the strength of will to stand up against Lord Audwin; none within the family ever had to her knowledge, with the exception of Adrian's father, who had suffered banishment as the penalty.

Isobel doubted that the earl had the power to drive Adrian, who was independent both of means and of spirit, away from England, but why should Adrian wish to stay in the midst of scandal, with a family that snubbed him and the rest of the world very likely taking their lead. She was not at all certain that she was ready to abandon everything and everyone that mattered to her for the sake of love. She had made one mistake in love that had cost her dearly. She was terrified of making another.

She walked for far longer than she had intended, going well beyond the park into the fields. The bright

sun that had favored her morning ride to the river
with Simon had teased in and out of clouds since mid-
afternoon, and now it was hidden completely. A faint,
misty drizzle began, and Isobel reluctantly turned back
toward the house. If the rain was to fall harder, she
would be in for a soaking, she knew, but she did not
regret her long walk, for the solitude and the exercise
seemed to have cleared her muddled thoughts considerably. There were no easy choices for her, but she
knew now what those choices were and what the consequences were likely to be.

Instead of skirting the home wood on the way back,
she went through it, which was a shorter route and
passed within sight of the stables. She saw a saddled
horse led into the yard, and a man mount and ride
off in the direction of the main drive. She was too far
away to see clearly, but she was reasonably certain it
was Quentin. She felt relief that she could put off that
confrontation for at least a little while until she made
up her mind for certain what she would say to him.

When she returned to her rooms, she informed
Dolly that she wished only a tray in her sitting room
for dinner. She then tried for a time to interest herself
in the book she had begun the day before, but her
thoughts intruded until she was thoroughly weary of
them. She was almost glad when she received a summons to wait upon Lady Adora for the diversion it
would bring.

Isobel found her aunt languishing on the chaise
longue in her sitting room. A table next to the chaise
was filled with a number of small bottles containing
medicines and cordials, and Lady Adora held a handkerchief damp with violet water in one hand and a
lovely silver filigree vinaigrette in the other. It was
immediately apparent that Lady Adora had been told
by Quentin that Adrian had hoaxed them. It was also
evident that Adrian would find no more understanding

or sympathy from her than he had from her eldest son. Lady Adora was indignant and convinced that Adrian had perpetrated the sham to cheat Quentin of his inheritance in some unknown manner. "I always believed he was a Captain Sharp determined to cut Quentin out if he could."

"But Adrian has no need of *Grand-père*'s fortune," Isobel argued.

"So he claims," Lady Adora said, clearly disbelieving all that Adrian said.

"Then he has gone about it in a signally stupid manner," Isobel commented with a bit of asperity. "*Grand-père* is angrier than I have ever known him to be and has cast him off as he did his father."

"Audwin should have done that the moment he set foot through the door," Lady Adora averred.

Isobel's love of the absurd was engaged, and she was forced to hide a smile. "No, Aunt Adora, how could he when he had just invited Adrian to Audswyck?"

"He should have known what any son of Francis's would be like and not invited him at all," the older woman declared. "He might have killed Quentin today, and it would be the fault of us all for having let a rogue take us all in."

Isobel's amusement was banished. She wondered if Lady Adora's remark was the result of her own surmising or a parroting of something Quentin had said to her. "Adrian swam back into the current after he had reached safety to try to save Quentin's life, Aunt Adora," she said. "It was an accident that they fell into the water."

"You and Quentin may believe that it was an accident," Lady Adora said with an indignant snort, "but I have no doubt in my mind that it was engineered in some fashion by that devil's cub to gain the whole of Audwin's fortune for himself. Very likely Carlton would have been next in jeopardy and Simon after him."

This was so ludicrous that Isobel might have laughed, but with the acknowledgment of her feelings for Adrian, it touched an exposed nerve. "That is a horrid thing to say, Aunt Adora, and entirely without justification. Adrian has never done anything to hurt Quentin or anyone else, while he has been ridiculed and snubbed since the day he arrived at Audswyck. He is the one who would be justified for casting us off."

Lady Adora suffered this defense of Adrian in astonishment. "I think you forget yourself, Isobel," she said in a reprimanding tone. "You will soon be Quentin's wife—"

"No," Isobel said, surprising herself a little at the sharp denial.

The older woman's astonishment was again evident. "No? What do you mean, no?"

"No, I am not going to be Quentin's wife soon," Isobel said. It was almost as if some inner self had spoken, for she had had no idea that she had meant to say this, or even that she had made up her mind definitely to end her betrothal to Quentin. She was surprised to find her agitation decreased as she spoke the words. She felt as if a burden had been lifted from her.

"Have you taken leave of your senses, girl?" Lady Adora demanded.

"No, I think I have come to them," she said, speaking in a cool, modulated tone in contrast to her aunt's shrill amazement. "Quentin and I should not suit. I know I have taken an unaccountably long time to come to that realization. Years ago I used to dream that Quentin would love me so much he would move heaven and earth for us to be together; now I am grateful that he was not the eager lover of my fantasies. We should be in a wretched coil now if we were already married."

"I think you have gone mad, Isobel," Lady Adora said, but with more astringency than amazement, "with the help, I imagine of that man. He is an even greater villain than I had supposed."

"This is to do with Quentin and with me, not Adrian," Isobel responded, with imperfect truth. "Quentin has become selfish and self-centered. He may be charming and delightful when he has his way and everything pleases him, but he becomes arrogant and sarcastic the moment that he finds anything to vex him. He barely disguises the fact that he finds escorting me to *ton* parties and balls a dead bore and prefers the company of his friends; he has kept me on leading strings for five years because we could not afford to marry without the consent of Audwin, yet he has squandered a fortune on himself to live in the highest style, and I daresay he has kept high flyers as well, for I know he has not been faithful to me. And to top all of this, he drinks a great deal more brandy than he used to do. He is often a third-part drunk, even early in the day, and by evening he is usually cast away. If I have fallen out of love with Quentin and in love with someone else, the fault does not lie with that man."

At the end of this invective, Isobel felt purged. She had never put her feelings about the dissolution of her relationship with Quentin in such a concise manner before, and certainly she had never shared them with anyone else.

But everything she said was the truth, and in saying it, she realized that it was the way she had felt, not just since Adrian had come into her life, but for some time before. He had filled a void in her heart that had formed over the course of years. Quentin might say he loved her, but love wasn't what one said, it was what one did, and Quentin behaved like a man who loved only himself.

Lady Adora said nothing in immediate response to this. She sat upright and poured out a dose from one of her medicine bottles into a small glass. She drank it and lay back again against the pillows that propped her, her eyes closed. Finally, she addressed Isobel. "I don't think you have spoken of these things to Quentin, have you?"

"Not all together, but in pieces when we have quarreled," she admitted.

Lady Adora nodded. "I thought not. Quentin would have told me when he visited me earlier to assure me that he was completely recovered from his accident. I suppose Quentin has done something to vex you and you need to express your anger with him. It distresses me to know that you could harbor such animosity toward my son, but I know he can at times be thoughtless, and you are young and never married and still not intimate with the ways of men. Your description of Quentin is nothing extraordinary, you know; it is what most women must bear. You may depend on me to say nothing to him of this, nor shall we discuss it again."

Isobel had not expected this response. She did not want to be given the opportunity to retreat from her decision; the temptation to grasp it was not yet completely overcome. "I don't think I could bear it," she said quietly. "But I do hope you won't say anything to him of this, Aunt Adora. He should hear from me that I wish to end our betrothal."

The older opened her eyes, and her expression was one of severe disapproval. "You will regret this, Isobel. Do you imagine it will be very different with that savage creature? Far worse, more likely. What you wish to do will humiliate my son, and Quentin won't take you back when you realize the mistake you are making; and you will realize it very soon. Do you imagine that Caroline and your father will welcome this charlatan as their son-in-law? You will find yourself as much an outcast as he is himself."

This so nearly echoed her own fears that Isobel was disheartened, but she would not let it show. "I shan't regret it," she said staunchly.

"Quentin is an exceptionally handsome man, with great address and the style to lead rather than follow fashion," Lady Adora said coldly. "With these qualities and his excellent birth, he might look as high as he wishes for a wife, and there are any number of unexceptional young women who would be more than willing to toss their caps at him. I shall henceforth look upon this as an opportunity for my son to discover a woman who will appreciate the honor that he does her by requesting her hand." She closed her eyes again and said in suddenly failing accents, "Send my woman to me, Isobel. You have distressed me very much. My health is precarious, you know, and is certain to be affected by all of this. Let that be on your conscience as well, girl."

Isobel hastened to summon her aunt's dresser and then escaped to her own bedchamber. Lady Adora's reaction had been predictable, but Isobel still found it extremely upsetting. She sat at her dressing table and saw that her face was flushed. She put her hands to her cheeks as if to draw off some of the heat. Her stomach felt knotted, her heart was beating at an increased rate; she wondered if she did have the courage to go through with jilting Quentin.

What had most struck her was Lady Adora's prediction that she would find her lot no better with Adrian. She recalled her surprise when Adrian had drunk the brandy because it was the first time she had seen him do so. Did she really know what his drinking habits were, or if he would be faithful to her, or neglect her for his own pursuits as Quentin did? It was startling to her to realize that she had known Adrian barely a month. She had known Quentin since she was seven and now realized that she had been mistaken about loving him for all of her life. How on earth could she know that what she felt for Adrian was true love in the space of a month? But she did love him and somehow she knew it was the real thing whatever reasoning might argue against it.

It was no easy thing to keep her doubts at bay, especially when she had no certainty that Adrian felt as she did. She might well be putting the cart before the horse in agonizing over whether or not she could bring herself to share his exile. For all she knew for certain, it was something quite other than marriage that he wanted from her.

Isobel was not very hungry and only picked at her dinner. It was unlikely that either her aunt or the earl had gone down to dinner, and she wondered if Adrian and Simon had enjoyed an uncomfortable tête-à-tête. Afterward she was more successful at fixing her interest on her book.

The mantel clock said it was after ten when Isobel put the book aside and rose from the chaise longue to stretch muscles that were becoming cramped from inactivity. Earlier she had begun a letter to her stepmother to tell her about the accident at the river and the outcome that had exposed the truth about Adrian. Isobel had taken the time to write at once because she wanted Lady Leyland to hear it all from her first. She knew that Lady Adora would be only too eager to inform her sister-in-law of all that had occurred and would make Adrian out as nothing short of a villain.

Isobel had found the letter more difficult to write than she had supposed it would be, and had put it aside gratefully when Dolly brought her her dinner. She still felt the tug of reluctance, but she made herself sit at the small writing table again and take up the letter where she had left off. She was not entirely pleased with the result, but it would have to do until she could speak to her stepmother herself, and it would, she hoped, mitigate the invective that was certain to characterize Lady Adora's account.

She rummaged through the drawer under the table for wax and a seal, but could find neither. Giving vent to an oath under her breath, she realized she would have to go downstairs to the writing desk in the morning room to search for what she needed. She didn't wish to leave it until morning in fear that she would miss putting the letter out on the table in the hall before Beal had one of the footmen take it into the village to catch the morning mail coach.

Isobel had not yet undressed, and she paused only to drape a shawl over her shoulders against the cooler air in the long corridors of Audswyck. She lit a bed candle and made her way downstairs.

The house was nearly in darkness; only the wall sconces lining the stairs were lit. Isobel saw a faint light showing under the closed door of the library and was careful to make no noise as she passed it. She had no idea if it was Adrian, Simon, or Quentin in the room, but she had no wish to speak to any of them at this hour. She entered the morning room and placed the candle on the desk while she searched for the wax and seal. It took no more than a few moments to find them and place them in the pocket of her skirt, and she was once again in the hall. She saw at once that the light was no longer visible under the library door. She paused for a moment listening; she had heard no one come out of the room, which she must have done in the silent house. She heard the door opening and felt a craven desire to run back and hide in the morning room. She stood her ground, however, and waited as Quentin came into the hall.

He seemed mildly surprised to see her. "I thought it was Beal securing the house for the night," he said, walking toward her. "But I am glad it is you, Isobel. I returned early particularly to speak with you, and I thought I should have to awaken you if you had already gone to bed."

Isobel heard his words with chagrin. She was tired from the exertions, both physical and emotional, of a difficult day and in no humor to discuss matters of such import that they would affect the rest of their lives. As he came up to her she could smell spirits on his breath. He did not have the appearance of a man who was inebriated, but she knew from experience that he carried his liquor well, and even far gone in drunkenness, he could disguise his condition at least on the surface.

"It is very late, Quentin," she said, hoping to discourage him. "I know it is important that we talk about things that have happened recently and—and about the future, but I am tired and it will keep until tomorrow."

He said nothing, but he took the candle from her and took her hand in his, drawing her toward the library. Isobel had no wish for an undignified struggle, and she resigned herself to a difficult interview. Perhaps it was better to get it over with. He did not seem to her so disguised that he would fail to comprehend what she meant to tell him.

He used the candle to light a small branch of candles on the long reading table, then he approached Isobel. He took both her wrists in his hands and pulled her against him. "You were surprised to see me, my lovely," he said, his voice soft and husky. "I am not the man you were expecting, I take it?"

Though there was no slur to his words, his eyes glittered dangerously in the dim, flickering light. She wanted to pull away from him, but she did not want to make the scene between them any more unpleasant than it had to be. "I wasn't expecting anyone at all," she said in a voice of deliberate calm that belied the sudden rapid beating of her heart. "I came down to get wax and a seal for a letter I wrote to my stepmother."

"At this hour?" he said with mock astonishment. "Surely, weary as you claim to be, such a homely task would have kept until morning. You shall have to do better than that, my girl."

"I have no idea what you are implying," she said with truth. "I wanted to put the letter on the table in the entrance hall tonight so it would be taken to the village in the morning in time for the arrival of the mail."

His laughter was deliberately coarse. "The arrival of the male is what you are awaiting, is it not my love? But it is the wrong male, alas. Afraid to have him in your bed, are you? Clever girl. That would have taken some explaining if he were discovered in your bedchamber."

Isobel felt more disgusted than angry. "I never thought you would add vulgarity to your faults, Quentin," she said coldly.

He put his lips against her ear, flicking his tongue into the cavity, and then whispering, "Where is he, Bel? Can we expect him to join our little discussion, or has he had his pleasure of you already tonight?"

She made an attempt to free herself from his grasp, but he tightened his hold on her. "You are disgusting," she said, spitting the words at him.

He bent his head and kissed her, a hard, bruising kiss that crushed her lips against her teeth until she tasted blood. He thrush his tongue in her mouth, and the taste of brandy was strong. For a moment she felt as if she would gag, but with effort controlled the reflex. He pulled her tightly against him, and she felt that he was erect. A bubble of alarm rose within her and she fought it down.

"It would seem that my gravest fault was underestimating my bumptious cousin," he said, pulling back from her just enough to speak in a hard, bitter undertone. "But he is not a rustic after all, is he? Up to every rig and row is Cousin Adrian. He means not only to have the title and the fortune, but you as well. Is this the first of your assignations, or has he already had you? You would do better to tell me the truth, you know, for I shall beat it out of you or whip it out of him."

Isobel succeeded in freeing one arm from his embrace and dealt him a stinging slap to his cheek. Quentin smiled in response and pulled her roughly against him again and kissed her with an ardor that had little to do with desire. Isobel began to struggle against him in earnest and finally freed herself by the means of pulling back from him sufficiently to bite his lip at the same time that she brought up her knee into his groin. They were too tightly locked together for her to inflict any real damage, but he gasped and slackened his hold and she seized the opportunity to free herself. She immediately tried to flee the room and had crossed half of it before she was seized by the shoulders from behind.

Quentin dragged her, struggling every inch of the way, to the wide leather sofa in the center of the room. He tossed her onto it with sufficient force to knock the breath from her, and then he added his weight to hers. For several moments she could do nothing to prevent the savage kisses he forced on her face, throat, and breasts.

She felt a moment of pure terror and an overwhelming desire to scream, but she held this back also. She did not wish to bring the house down on them; it was far more likely that one of the servants still up would come to her aid rather than Adrian or Simon, and there would be no containing the gossip that would result. She did not want to believe that he would force himself on her completely. She tried to convince herself that he was just frightening her to punish her because she had taken Adrian's side against his that afternoon.

This was what she reasoned to herself to still her fright and reassure herself as she did her best to evade his kisses and the wandering of his hands as she tried to regather her strength to push him away. "Quentin, stop that this instant," she said, putting as much command as she could manage into her voice. "If you rape me, you will dishonor us both."

This at last seemed to have more effect than her struggles had. He had pushed down her bodice, and he now raised his head from her exposed breasts. "Too late, love," he said with an unpleasant laugh. "You already did that when you gave yourself to the savage. You like it that way, do you? Primitive? Uncivilized? You should have told me, I like nothing better myself."

As he spoke, Isobel could feel his hand between them, working to undo the buttons of his buckskin breeches. Whether it was fear or the overwhelming smell of brandy on Quentin's breath, Isobel felt suddenly nauseated. The very idea of Quentin continuing to touch her in this intimate way made her stomach turn. If he did as he had the first time and forced himself into her, she knew she would be sick. "I have never been with any man but you, Quentin," she said, breathless under his weight. It was her last hope that if she could convince him of this he would release her. "I like Adrian, I admit it, but he is not my lover, I swear it to you. I haven't seen him since I left *Grandpère*'s study."

Quentin gave no sign that he even heard her. He

had apparently undone the necessary buttons, but there was still the matter of her long skirts and petticoats. He had no choice but to raise his weight from her to lift these, and the moment he did so, Isobel, her body already gathered for flight, tried to roll away from him off the sofa and onto the floor. She failed.

Denial could no longer sway her. There was no doubt in her mind at all now that he meant to rape her. Not caring now if every servant in the house came running to the library, she cried out in earnest. He cursed and placed a hand over her mouth, which she promptly bit as hard as she could. Quentin sprung backward with a yell of his own, and Isobel finally managed to drag herself from beneath him. She fell to the floor in front of the sofa with a thump, and wasted no time in scrambling away from him toward the door on her knees until she could find leverage to get to her feet. If he tried to follow her, she knew she would have no compunction about screaming until her lungs burst if necessary.

She had only gone a few feet when he caught her from behind and covered her mouth again. Before she could bite him again, he removed his hand, but her scream was cut off almost as soon as it began as his handkerchief was stuffed into her mouth.

She expected him to drag her back to the sofa, but he pushed her facedown on the carpet and started to raise her skirts from behind. She kicked one foot backward and caught him from behind in the groin. She heard him gasp and again managed to twist away from him and at least into a sitting position. The legs of a small table pressed against her back. She reached a hand behind her, searching for any instrument on the table that might come to her aid. Her fingers clutched at a vase and she found the strength born of desperation to pick it up, heavy with water and flowers as it was, in one hand and to swing it at Quentin with all the might she possessed in her awkward position. It struck him squarely against the side of his head, not hard enough to smash the vase, but water and flowers came flying out of it as she lost her grip at impact and it fell to the floor.

Quentin released her abruptly, apparently too startled even for a curse this time. He was on his knees and then, rather like he'd been pushed, he toppled forward on top of her. At that precise moment the door to the library opened.

Isobel did not look up to see who her rescuer might be but pulled herself away from Quentin's weight. She tore the handkerchief from her mouth and freed her body from beneath him, but a portion of her skirt was wedged under him and she had to turn again to tug it out. She was finally free of him and got to her knees. She looked up and saw Adrian, holding a candle in such a way that it might be used more as a weapon than as a source of light.

Adrian held out his free hand and raised Isobel to her feet. Instantly, she clung to him and held him very tight, as if assuring herself of his reality and her safety. He raised the candle and took in the scene before him, which told its own tale. Isobel's hair was pulled from its pins, the bodice of her dress was torn down to her waist, leaving her breasts very much exposed. He saw the soaking stain on the carpet, the scattered flowers, and Quentin lying in the middle of it all, a trickle of blood tracing a path across his cheek from a small cut on his brow. The vase, miraculously, had landed upright and still held some water.

Adrian held Isobel tightly against him for a long moment and then gently eased her onto one of the leather chairs. He stooped and picked up the vase and dashed the water in it onto Quentin's head.

Quentin groaned, shook his head as if to clear away some inner mists, and propped himself upright on one elbow. When his eyes began to focus properly again, he saw Adrian standing above him. His expression, brought into relief by the light from the candle that Adrian still held, was sardonic rather than chagrined. "Still hopeful of your assignation, are you?" he sneered as he pushed himself into a sitting position. "You're a day late and a penny short if you imagine you've found a blushing maiden in the fair Isobel. She was mine and bore my stamp before you ever set foot on deck to come to England." He struggled to his feet and was offered no assistance by Adrian, who still had yet to speak. "But take her if you like. I've had what I wished of her, and I make you a present of my leavings."

Suddenly Quentin was again on the floor, but this time Adrian was on top of him. The candle dropped, but mercifully had not fallen on the wet part of the carpet and was still lit. Isobel scrambled after it and placed it safely on the table.

Isobel heard the contact of flesh on flesh as the men struggled on the floor, but she could not be certain who had the upper hand. She was afraid for Adrian, for she knew full well that Quentin was a noted follower of the fancy and had trained with the Great Jackson himself. Carlton had said once that if Quentin had not been born a gentleman, he might have made a career for himself in the ring.

But, as it had been with the swordplay the night before, either through an excess of alcohol in Quentin's system or Adrian's superior skill, it soon became obvious to Isobel that Quentin did not have the upper hand. The fight came to an abrupt end only a few minutes after it had begun. Both men had managed to regain their feet, and Adrian narrowly evaded a blow to his groin that would have been far more effective than the one that Isobel had aimed at Quentin. In retaliation Adrian brought his fist up into Quentin's stomach with considerable force. Quentin fell back to his hands and knees, gasping audibly, and a moment later began to vomit copiously onto the carpet.

Grimacing in distaste, Adrian went over to Isobel, picked up his candle, then led her out of the room and up the stairs. Isobel realized that her breasts were still bared and tried to pull her hand from Adrian's to amend this, but he shook his head and gave her a quick smile. "Wait until we reach your rooms. I promise not to look if you like."

She returned him a hesitant smile. "I suspect it is rather late for such a promise."

Adrian sighed elaborately. "Caught out in another lie, alas." They reached the door of her sitting room, and he went inside with her. Isobel immediately went into her bedchamber while Adrian lit a lamp near a small sofa. In a few minutes she returned wrapped in a dressing gown.

While Isobel was changing out of her dress, she wondered how Adrian would interpret what he had seen. Did he realize that she had nearly been ravished, or would think he had interrupted a lover's quarrel gotten out of hand? She was embarrassed not only by what he had witnessed between her and Quentin, but that he should have seen her so disheveled and half naked.

Though she had not been long in repairing the outward damage to her person, Adrian had somehow managed to find a decanter of brandy and two glasses from some other room. Both glasses held a small amount of the dark amber liquid. He handed one to her. She sipped the brandy and felt its smooth fire course down her throat and then miraculously warm her every extremity.

She let him lead her to the chaise longue, and he sat down facing her. His eyes on her were searching but concerned, and she felt compelled to speak. "Quentin was very drunk."

"He usually is," was Adrian's caustic reply.

She shook her head. "He wasn't this way before, in the beginning."

"I never doubted that," he assured her. "You have too much good sense than to fall in love with a drunkard."

"Quentin was only fifteen when I first thought I was in love with him," she said with a brief smile that quickly faded as she dissolved into tears. Adrian took her glass and placed it on the table next to the chaise. Then he took her in his arms and held her while she cried, deep, wrenching sobs that were not just the aftermath of her ordeal but of what it represented, the last dissolution of all her young girl's dreams.

Adrian held her close to him, feeling her anguish and frustrated by his own inability to heal her pain. He rested his head against hers and murmured soothingly to her, careful to avoid endearments that might upset her even more.

Finally, her sobs diminished to a gentle weeping, and she raised her head. He handed her his handkerchief. She tried to thank him, but her words broke on a hiccough. He smiled and she gave him a watery one in return. "I'm sorry," she said when she had blown her nose. "I am not usually such a watering pot."

"Sometimes we all need to be."

Isobel lowered her eyes from his. "I know what you must think—"

He hushed her. "You need not explain anything to me if it would cause you distress, Isobel. It is enough to know that I was able to serve you in some small way. Not," he added with a soft laugh, "that you really had need of me. You seemed quite capable of handling the matter on your own when I came into the room."

Isobel had dreaded giving him any sort of explanation, but she had forgotten how easy he was to talk to. "Quentin *was* very cast away and very angry with me because I defended you to *Grand-père* this afternoon. I should not have provoked him."

"Forgive me," Adrian said, his voice surprisingly hard, "but I cannot imagine anything you could do to provoke a man, particularly one who has pledged you his protection, to behave in such a fashion that you felt you needed to plant him a facer with vase full of flowers. It was no mere argument, Bel. I would be a fool to pretend I thought it no more. Did he hurt you in any way?"

"Not really," she said with forced lightness. "I expect I hurt him far more than he did me."

"He was trying to force himself on you, wasn't he?"

Perhaps it was because she knew now that she no longer loved Quentin that she felt obliged to be generous toward him. But a flat lie was impossible. "Not precisely."

"Is Quentin your lover, Bel? I mean the word as you would use it now."

Isobel shrank away from him. "I don't think . . ."

"I ask because I need to know what it was that I saw tonight," he said, forestalling her before she could rebuff him. "To speak plainly, I think Quentin attempted to rape you tonight. But if you are lovers, if it was something other . . ."

She wanted to deny what Quentin had done, but found she could not lie about it. "He is not my lover in the sense that you mean."

"In what sense, then?"

She found the words difficult to say. "We have . . ." She hesitated, discovering that she could not bring herself to say the words *made love*. ". . . been together before, but that was some time ago."

He was silent for a long moment after this, his expression unreadable. "Willingly or like tonight?"

Once again the words of denial would not come to her, and quite unexpectedly her eyes filled with tears again. "Not like that, not as bad," she managed to say.

Adrian did not want her distress to continue, and he let it pass, but he understood well enough. "I think you need a bit more brandy," he said, rising from the chaise. "You have had a rather trying day, to say the least of it."

"So have you," she reminded him. "In all that has happened since, I had almost forgotten that you and Quentin nearly drowned this afternoon. Perhaps that was why Quentin behaved so badly tonight. We all have different ways of reacting to shock."

"The only reason I acquit Quentin of being an out-and-out rogue," said Adrian baldly as he refilled their glasses, "is that he is not clever enough to sustain the character. A true rogue wouldn't have botched the job this afternoon, nor would he try to ravish you when *he* was cast away. The accepted practice," he said, handing her her glass with a distinctly roguish smile, "is to make your victim bosky."

The laughter in his eyes was as infectious as ever. She smiled, but wondered at what he had said. "What do you mean he botched it? What happened this afternoon? Quentin was foolish to suggest crossing the bridge, but he could not have known it was unsafe or he would not have tried to cross it himself."

"It was not unsafe."

"What do you mean?" she said again.

Adrian wished he had held his tongue. He had no need to blacken Quentin's character more than it already was, and at times an excess could have the reverse effect. "I don't know why I said that. I fear I am stupid with exhaustion," he said, his voice weary enough to give his words credence.

"That isn't fair," Isobel insisted. "You have bullied me into confiding in you things I did not at all wish to."

Adrian smiled and placed his hand against her cheek. "Did I bully you? I am sorry I was so unfeeling. You have been through enough for one day." He bent forward and kissed her in a brotherly fashion. "I shall leave you to your rest, Bel."

Isobel felt a sudden sense of impending loss. "Please, not yet." He sat down beside her again. He watched her, saying nothing, and the silence disturbed her. "How did you happen to come to the library when you did?" she asked, for she had wondered at it even at the time. It was too long afterward to be in response to her cries.

"I heard you leave your sitting room earlier and became concerned when you did not return for some time." She looked in astonishment and he laughed. "The door to your sitting room creaks a certain way."

"I might have returned by the door to my bedchamber," she suggested.

"I checked," he admitted, his expression self-mocking.

"Why?" she demanded, almost laughing.

"I knew Quentin had not come up yet either, though he had returned to the house a good hour earlier. I supposed he would be drunk and I knew he was angry with you."

Isobel marveled at the thoroughness of his knowledge. In part it was exceptional discernment, but she knew of his penchant for acquainting himself with his environment in most situations. "Thank you," she said very quietly.

He took one hand in his and, turning her palm upward, gently kissed it. "You're welcome," he replied as softly as she had spoken. Their eyes held for a long minute, and this time many things passed unspoken between them. Adrian leaned forward and kissed her, not a brotherly kiss but with passion restrained. He sat back and said, his voice thickened, "I think I had better leave now."

Isobel shook her head slowly. "I want you to stay with me. Please, Adrian."

The invitation was plain, or at least he thought it was. He did not want to be guilty of being labeled no better than Quentin. He kissed her again, and it was Isobel who slipped her tongue between his teeth and hungrily sought his, Isobel from whom a tiny soft moan of sheer longing broke. She moved to give him room to lay beside her and he did, taking her in his arms and drawing her close to him.

Isobel could not explain her behavior, nor did she try to. It was perhaps her reaction to the shocks this dreadful day had delivered to her. She wanted to make love with this man so desperately that it was a physical ache. She had never in her life known such strong desire, never guessed she could feel this way. The fire between them was a tangible thing, to be felt, tasted, seen, heard, and smelled, and nothing would quench it now until they rested spent and satisfied in each other's arms.

Adrian's exhaustion inexplicably vanished. His body responded to the heat of hers. He felt her longing as plainly as if she had told him of it. There was a fierceness in her desire that stirred a primitive response in him. He felt as savage as he had been called, and was appalled to realize that he wanted to take her instantly and swiftly. He would not use her as Quentin had; he meant to take his time, to slowly and deliciously elicit every response from her, to give her pleasure before he even considered his own. It did not happen that way at all.

It was as if, once they had acknowledged that all restraint was ended, some wild thing was set loose between them. His gentle but thorough kisses quickly became impassioned, his mouth and tongue not seeking her response but demanding it. And Isobel met him with a passion that matched his own. When his lips moved from hers and his mouth sought to kiss, taste, tease, and bite the soft flesh of her throat and breasts, she responded in mirror fashion, licking his ear, gently biting his shoulder, loving the taste and texture of his skin.

Their lower bodies were so tightly melded together that only the cloth that separated them prevented immediate consummation. She could feel the moistness between her legs spreading, and the flesh there felt inflamed. She reached down and grasped him, reveling in the hardness of him. Their lips met again in a burning, scouring kiss.

Adrian realized at once that he was far too excited for finesse and that the best he could hope for was that he did not frighten her and completely disgrace himself. When his fingers found the soft, moist triangle between her legs she moaned from the pleasure of it and pulled him on top of her, not willing to wait another moment for the final mystery between them to be unveiled. In another moment he was inside her, enveloped in her, and lost to all thought, all feeling that was not pure animal need.

It was as brief as he had feared it would be, but there was no disgrace. Her moans turned into cries, and her cries began to crescendo until her hips moved spasmodically and her legs gripped him like a vise. She was overwhelmed with a wash of pleasure so intense she felt almost as if she lost consciousness for a moment. Then he gave a choked cry deep in his throat and flooded her with the proof of his passion.

Still clothed, still coupled, they subsided into each other's arms, their fevered motion stilled but their chests heaving in rhythm while frantic pulses gradually

began to return to a less rapid pace. When he finally
had the breath to do so, he kissed her forehead, her
eyes in turn, the tip of her nose, and at last her lips,
gently, with a little teasing flick of his tongue.

Isobel opened her eyes, their expression soft and
dreamy as if she had just awakened from a deep sleep.
"It was nothing like that with Quentin," she said,
speaking her thought aloud.

She succeeded in both pleasing and annoying him
at the same time. "Damn Quentin to hell where he
surely belongs and just as surely shall end. Come to
bed, Isobel," he said as he rose and held out his hand
to her.

"I thought you were tired," she said, quizzing him.

"I find I am strangely rejuvenated," he said, laughing as he pulled her to her feet.

This time they made love as he had at first intended.
They removed each other's clothing, stripping away
layers with teasing words and punctuating kisses. In
this fashion it was inevitable that they would soon be
entwined again, but this time their urgency was held in
check, giving way to the need to explore all uncharted
territory. When they once again came together, their
pace was slower, but there was no lessening of heat
between them, and once again Isobel experienced a
pleasure more incredible than anything her wildest
imaginings had supposed.

All too soon there as a faint but perceptible light-
ening of the darkness at the edges of the drawn draperies covering the windows. Adrian stretched
sensuously and pulled Isobel closer to him, awakening
her from a light doze. "The servants will be up and
about soon, though Lords knows, I don't want to
leave you."

He spoke these words between gentle kisses and
nibbles, and there was one more long, loving kiss before she released him with a sigh. "I'll be leaving

Audswyck Chase in a few hours, Bel," he said softly into her ear. "Come with me."

She was barely awake, but she managed to say, on another sigh, "Yes," before she fell into sleep.

Chapter 12

The sun was high when Isobel awoke. At first she felt a wonderful, languorous peace, and smiled to herself as she recalled why she should feel this way. Then she realized the lateness of the hour and sprang into a sitting position, alarmed that she had overslept. She picked up the heap of her petticoats at the side of the bed and put on her dressing gown. She rang for Dolly and was brushing out her hair when the maid arrived.

"Why didn't you awaken me, Dolly?" she demanded as she brushed the tangles from her hair. "We are leaving Audswyck this morning and must begin packing at once. But first I must have a bath. Have the kettles put on for me, and I shall start packing until it is ready."

"We're leaving today, Miss Isobel?" said her astonished maid. "You never said."

"I know, but I have only just made up my mind. Mr. Renville," she paused and added to clarify her words, "Mr. Adrian Renville, will be escorting us."

The dresser blinked in surprise and, bobbing a curtsy, went off to do her mistress's bidding. Isobel knew that the young woman's astonishment would soon be echoed throughout the house. It was a response she would soon face from many quarters. Perhaps at the end of this time leaving England for America would come as a welcome relief.

She stood in front of her wardrobe, about to choose something for her journey when she brought herself up short. She was still assuming a great deal. Adrian had asked her to come with him, but she really had no idea if he wished her to be his wife or his mistress. She felt a momentary sensation as if her heart had been squeezed. But she had no one to blame but herself if she was mistaken; it was she who had seduced him last night. And yet, surprisingly, she felt no regret.

It was very late when Isobel came down to breakfast, so late that she thought she might find the sideboard cleared and have to send to the kitchen for something to break her fast. But there were still muffins and marmalade to be had, and the coffee was still warm enough to drink.

She was nearly finished with her solitary meal when Adrian came into the room. Her doubts must have been visible, for his smile to her was reassuring. He bent to kiss her lightly before he sat down at table, and there was something so homely in this action, as if they were a comfortable married couple already, that she felt her heart swell with unexpected happiness.

"I see you are dressed for traveling, my love," he said, a teasing glint in his eyes. "Ready to throw caution to the wind, but not without some trepidation, I think."

"Some," she admitted, trying to match her mood to his. She knew she had to discover his feelings for her, or she would know no peace. "It isn't surprising, is it? I don't really know whether you want me for your wife or your whore."

He was applying fresh butter generously to a muffin, and he looked up, his expression startled. "Good Lord, Isobel!"

She pressed on boldly. "I can't read your mind, after all. I know that you desired me."

"You can't have any doubts about that now, can you?" he said, amusement returning to his expression. He returned to his chore, adding, "I must say that if by all of this you are trying to tell me that you're not certain you wish to marry me after all, it is very shabby of you, not to say wicked. My father did warn me that there were women in this world who would have iniquitous designs upon me, but I had always thought myself too knowing to be seduced and abandoned. Set my mind at rest, my love. Tell me you wish to marry me and make an honest man of me."

She did not respond to this quizzing proposal, and he looked up at her. What he saw made him put down his knife and get up from his chair. He went to her and drew her to her feet and into his arms. He kissed her with a fervent longing that made her heart soar. "You are mine, Isobel," he said when he released her, "and I am yours, if you will have me."

The surge of love she felt for him was so strong that tears filled her eyes. She lay her head against his shoulder and said to tease him, "But still I am betrothed to Quentin."

She heard his breath catch in a short gasp of outrage. "You can't believe you are still bound to him after what he did last night," he said, drawing back from her to search her countenance.

"He was not himself," she said, barely able to maintain her grave expression. "Perhaps I should give him a chance to redeem himself."

"You can give him something far more useful."

"Such as?" Isobel wondered innocently.

"His life. If you forgive him and take him back, I shall have to challenge him to a duel and kill him," he said with chillingly matter-of-fact assurance. "Then, vixen, you should find yourself married to a murderer as well as an outcast."

He kissed her again until this time she pulled away

from him. "I want us to be together so very much, Adrian, but I am frightened," she said, not wanting to hide her doubts from him. "We scarcely know each other."

"What does that matter if we know we love each other? I think I knew you were the one woman for me that day at Grillon's, but I was too ignorant then to recognize what I felt as love." He hugged her close to him again. "I have been afraid too, Bel. What right have I to ask so much of you? If you choose to marry me instead of Quentin, you could find yourself alienated from your family if they feel as Grandfather does about me and refuse to accept me. We could stay in England if you like, but if we are cut in public by Audwin and my cousins, we may find ourselves snubbed by the world at large, as my father was. He felt the only sensible choice for him was exile, and it may be mine as well. If it comes to that, you will be giving up all that you have for my sake. That is a very great deal to ask."

"It may not come to that," she said hopefully. "But if we are certain that we love each other, all that should really matter is that we are together, wherever that might be."

"May, if, should, and might are all conditionals, my love," he said with a soft laugh, and then turned serious again. "And here is another such statement. If we are to be happy together, you must come to me certain that you love me, as I am certain that I love you."

This, at least, she had no doubt of. "I am certain."

He let out his breath as if he had been holding it and kissed her again, this time with growing heat. He was wondering if the start of their journey could be delayed by another hour or so when their delightful occupation was brought to an abrupt end by the slamming of a door behind them.

Isobel, startled, moved away from him, but Adrian

kept his arm about her waist, refusing to react in a guilty fashion. Simon stood confronting them, his expression thunderous. Isobel started to speak, but her brother cut her off abruptly.

"You are a goddamned fool, Isobel," he said furiously. "Do you realize what you are doing?"

Isobel knew that she would be denying the love she had just avowed if she apologized or defended her actions. "Yes, I do," she said without hesitation. "Adrian and I are in love with each other. We are going to be married."

Simon looked as if he had been struck. "My God," he said, nearly under his breath. His angry gaze sought Adrian, who regarded him with no betrayal of his thoughts. "That's that, then, isn't it?" Simon said finally. "Does Quentin know?"

"I would imagine he surmises it," Adrian said. "He shall know it for certain before we leave today."

"You're leaving Audswyck?" Simon began to look more confused than angry. "Where are you going?"

"London for now," Adrian said. "We have to tell your mother, of course. I regret that your father is out of the country, but under the circumstances we haven't the luxury of waiting for him to return to receive his formal consent. I hope when he returns to England, I shall have the pleasure of knowing him."

Simon looked as if he had received yet another leveler. "Bel, you can't do this. Have you gone mad? You're pledged to marry Quentin."

Isobel went to her brother. She took both his hands in hers. "Simon, I know it must look as if I am behaving foolishly, but I promise you it is no such thing. I have discovered that I have fallen out of love with Quentin, and I think it very likely that he feels the same, if he will but admit it. I have searched my heart and I know that I love Adrian. Please wish us happy, Simon. I'm not certain if anyone else will."

Simon looked somewhat dazed. He said, "Did you know that Quentin is ill? Dr. Morrison was called while we were all still abed this morning. One of the footmen found Quentin unconscious on the floor of the library. He went for Beal and they could not rouse him at first and the doctor was sent for. My aunt told me that Morrison said it was a delayed result of what happened yesterday at the river. She has gone into hysterics, convinced that Quentin was at death's door and had to be seen to as well."

Isobel and Adrian exchanged glances. "I am sorry Aunt Adora is unwell," she said, pointedly not commenting on Quentin's illness. "I shan't disturb her before I leave, but will send a note to her room to tell her that I am going."

"And Quentin?" Simon said, incredulous. He had been certain that the information that Quentin was unwell would at least delay her decision to leave with Adrian.

"I shall send him a note as well."

"To tell him that you are jilting him?" demanded Simon in angry amazement. "You would do such a thing to him when he is cast down with illness?"

Isobel was becoming angry as well. "It is no more than he deserves," she said without explanation. "It is not really your affair, Simon."

"No. I can't help you if you are determined to ruin your life," he replied bitterly, and turned away and left them alone again.

Isobel turned with a distressed countenance toward Adrian. He took her hand and brought it to his lips. "Simon is only the first of many who will say the same to you, Isobel. Be sure you can bear it, for if you choose to leave with me today, you may not be able to undo that choice."

Simon's opposition had the effect of strengthening rather than lessening her determination to follow her heart rather than the expectations of others. "I am certain," she said again.

It was already after eleven, and they agreed that Adrian would ride to the Duck and Drake to hire a post chaise and outriders to take them to London. Under the circumstances, it was unlikely that the earl would make his own carriage available to them, and neither of them wished to give him the satisfaction of denying it. When Adrian left Isobel, she went to the morning room to write the notes to Quentin, his mother, and the earl. The letter she had written to her stepmother the night before understandably had been forgotten, and Isobel had torn it up that morning. She wished there was some means of preparing her stepmother for the several shocks she would receive the following day when Isobel returned to Upper Mount Street, but any letter she wrote today would not be posted until tomorrow, and she herself would be in London by then, probably arriving before the letter.

Simon's jibes caused Isobel a brief concern that she was being craven writing to Quentin instead of facing him with the truth, but his "illness," she well knew, was the result of his drinking and the fight he had had with Adrian. In that condition he was almost more difficult to deal with than when he had been drinking, and she thought she was justified in not wishing to subject herself to more abuse from him.

Isobel did not, however, escape a final interview with the earl. She had been watching out for Adrian's return from a window in the saloon that overlooked the drive when the summons came to her from Audwin. She wanted to refuse it, but would not permit herself to be so fainthearted.

It was Beal himself who fetched her, and she followed the butler to the earl's sitting room. His gouty foot was wrapped again and propped up on an extension of his Bath chair. Isobel felt her courage sink for a moment, for this certainly meant his temper would be easily exacerbated.

Audwin wasted no time on amenities. "Beal tells me you're packing to leave," he said curtly. "Are you going alone or with that damned charlatan?"

"I am leaving with Adrian," Isobel confirmed calmly, refusing to be intimidated.

"And Quentin?"

"I am ending my betrothal to Quentin," she replied. "In fact, you might say I ended it last night."

His brows snapped together. She did not explain that cryptic statement, but his surmises were not far from the truth. "Has Quentin's illness anything to do with your decision?"

"Quentin was very drunk last night," she replied, her tone commenting rather than judging.

"I suppose there was a quarrel."

"Yes." There was no point in elaborating, and the experience of her near rape had been humiliating and not one she wished to discuss with anyone.

"And as a result of it you are jilting him." His eyes narrowed. "Are you whoring with that savage?"

Isobel could not prevent the flush of anger that the earl would likely read as a blush of shame. She said in measured accents, "Adrian and I are going to be married."

"It certainly explains the behavior of Quentin the night before last if he suspected this," the earl said caustically. "How long have you known that Adrian was deliberately deceiving us, Isobel?"

She decided against playing cat-and-mouse games she knew she had small chance of winning. "Almost from the beginning," she admitted.

"And you did not feel obliged to share this knowledge with me?"

"I thought it was obvious for anyone who wished to see it," she said boldly.

The earl accepted this impertinence without comment. His lips curled in a smile that was rather unpleasant. "I hope you find that he hasn't lied about his fortune, my girl. All he shall have of me when I die is the barest minimum I can legally manage to leave him with the entail. You would have been a wealthy woman as Quentin's wife and far sooner than waiting for me to go to grass."

It suddenly occurred to Isobel that she no longer had a need to keep her thoughts to herself in the earl's presence. As a child she had been frightened of him; as an adult she thought him a selfish, mean-spirited man who had been allowed to become a petty tyrant by those members of his family that he controlled through his purse strings. Now that she was not to marry Quentin, she was free to say what she pleased. "That never did matter to me other than that it mattered to Quentin. You said yourself that we might have married if we chose and been far from paupers without your approval, but that would not have done at all for Quentin, nor for you, my lord," she said with acid in her voice. "He must be a Corinthian among Corinthians, an out-and-outer, a nonesuch, an nonpareil. He must dress in the first kick of fashion, have the best horses, the finest carriages, live in the highest style."

The old man's eyes narrowed again. "Quentin lives as he chooses to live."

"As you encourage him to live" was her sharp rejoinder. "He could never have done so unless you paid his debts and made him a generous allowance. It is because of you that he developed a taste for high living. He could not have borne to be just a simple gentleman like thousands of others if you no longer supported him, and whatever you may say now, you led him to believe that he could lose that allowance if he married before you gave your consent to it." Her voice had gradually risen as she spoke, and now she consciously lowered it again. "If you have given that consent, I should certainly have been married to Quentin by now. At times I hated you for controlling my life through his, but now I thank you for preventing me from making a terrible mistake. You said you didn't think that Quentin and I should suit. You should be pleased to be proven accurate in your judgment once again. The only place it is off is in your assessment of Adrian, for he is worth ten of Quentin and you should be proud that he is your heir."

The earl listened to her with his features cold and set as if in stone, or rather ice. He snorted at this last. "I can see there is one talent besides a gift for subterfuge that I may assign him. He has seduced you with wonderful efficiency."

Isobel reminded herself that nothing this horrid old man said to her really mattered. "Yes, he has. And it was accomplished with gentleness, consideration, and respect—qualities you do not appear to have thought worth encouraging in Quentin."

To her surprise the earl laughed, and even more astonishing it appeared to be genuine. "In all my years in the petticoat line, I found that approach was only worth the trouble for a very few and a very special sort of female. I can see that Quentin is not as shrewd as I had supposed." Like quicksilver his humor changed again. "When you leave here today, you won't return in my lifetime. If you stay in England you shall both be outcasts. I shall come out of my retirement from the world to personally see to that."

Isobel was very near to losing complete control of her temper and saying things that would put her on a level no better than his. She stood and said, with rancor that was rare for her, "Good-bye, my lord. I shall

return to this house one day as its mistress, and neither your power nor your spite can prevent that."

When Isobel left the earl's sitting room, she felt
something very like elation. She felt triumphant and
powerful, vital and energetic, and, best of all, free, as
if she had been bound by invisible fetters. She had
had no idea how oppressed she had felt until falling
in love with Adrian had given her the courage to set
herself free.

Isobel returned to her rooms to assure herself that
the packing was complete, and when she had given
her letters to a footman to take to Quentin and Lady
Adora, she was ready to start on the journey that
would change her life. Dolly had gotten over her surprise and chatted happily about returning to London,
while Isobel waited for the post chaise to arrive. She
wished that she and Adrian could be alone for the
journey, but Dolly would have to share the carriage
with them, which would make private conversation
quite impossible.

In the end it didn't matter, for she learned when
she went downstairs that Simon had invited himself to
accompany them as well. Isobel, fearing that her
brother intended to make matters as uncomfortable
as possible between her and Adrian, did not try to
hide her displeasure. "I wish you would not, Simon,"
she said bluntly. "I have told you that Adrian and I
are going to be married, so I have no need of an
escort or chaperon."

"It's no such thing," Simon said and sounded as if
he meant it. "I just don't wish to stay here any longer,
and I suppose I should have to wait until Quentin is
ready to return to London before I could do that unless I go now. Aunt Adora would fall into hysteria if
I suggested going up on my own, and I daresay Mama
wouldn't like it overmuch either."

"If you do or say anything to discomfit us during

the journey, Simon," she warned him, "I promise I shall put you down at the first inn and let you make your own way as best you can, whatever Mama might say."

Simon gave her an uneasy sidelong glance. "What is the point? I know I have no influence to change your mind. I don't like this, Bel. I might if I thought you would be happy, but I think you are making a wretched mistake."

"Depend upon it," she said firmly. "More than anything, I wish to be Adrian's wife. As soon as we arrive in London, he is going to go to his friend Sir James Stokes, who hopefully will be able to tell him how we may procure a special license. I have every hope we shall be married within a fortnight."

Simon seemed somewhat flabbergasted by this, but he accepted it with fortitude and an uncertain smile. "Perhaps by the time it happens, I shall be able to wish you happy, but I can't do that just now. I promise, though, I shan't do anything to embarrass you on the drive to London."

Isobel was not certain she believed him, but she had little choice but to accept his assurances unless she was to forbid him to join them. Adrian did not seem in the least put out to learn that Simon would be with them. "Then, at least," he whispered provocatively into her ear as they were about to enter the carriage, "the second bedchamber hired at the inn we stop at tonight won't go to waste."

They stopped at the first coach inn they came to when the sunlight began to fail. The late start they had made made it impossible to reach London in a single day, and there was no question that they would have to put up at an inn for the night. Adrian very properly hired a room for Isobel, another for himself and Simon, and made appropriate accommodations for Isobel's dresser.

Dinner was as tedious as the traveling had been that day. Simon kept his promise, but the excessive degree of civility among them which masked all the thoughts that could not be expressed was wearing to maintain. Simon commented several times that he was tired, and Isobel had hopes that he would go up to bed after dinner. Though he could not prevent his yawns and once even seemed as if he would fall asleep where he sat, Simon remained with them in the private parlor they had hired for the evening, not only making private conversation between Isobel and Adrian impossible, but making it awkward for them to retire to her bedchamber for the night as well.

Finally, Isobel made her excuses to go up to bed in the hope that Simon would join her and then Adrian might follow after a decent interval, but her brother bade her good night with no sign that he had any intention of leaving the private parlor until Adrian went up to bed as well.

"I shan't be offended, Simon," Adrian said in a carefully casual manner, "if you go up with Isobel. You've been yawning all night. I'll just finish the last of the claret and then I'll join you."

Simon set his glass down on the table with a sharp click. "No, you won't," he said astringently. "You think I am too young or too foolish to realize what has been going on between you and my sister. You hope I'll fall asleep and never know that you've spent the night in her room."

Isobel could have gladly throttled her brother, but Adrian seemed quite unperturbed. "Yes, you're quite right, Simon, that is exactly my intention." He finished the wine in his glass without haste and stood. "Since you prefer the tree with no bark on it, then there is no need for polite pretenses." He crossed the room to stand beside Isobel and placed her hand on his arm.

"I mean for us to have an early start, Simon, so leave word to be awakened in good time for breakfast."

Simon rose so abruptly he knocked his chair over. "No!" he cried out explosively.

"Simon, you promised me," Isobel said furiously.

"But I didn't know then that you would do something like this," he said, confronting her. "You have not even sent a notice to the papers that you have ended your betrothal to Quentin. You could wait until then to take him for your lover," he said a desperate note in his voice.

"Adrian is already my lover," she said quietly.

Simon turned away from them with a short exclamation. Adrian touched his shoulder, but his hand was shrugged off violently and Simon returned to the table, picked up his toppled chair and, setting it so that he would sit with his back to them, cast himself into it.

Isobel met Adrian's eyes unhappily. She wanted to go to her brother, but there was nothing she could say to Simon that he would wish to hear. She supposed she might spend a solitary night and let Adrian share the other room with Simon, but she knew she could not retreat at the first engagement. There would be many to follow when her intention to marry Adrian was generally known.

It was a busy post inn, and no one paid them the least heed when they went upstairs together and no one challenged their right to share Isobel's room. They slipped into a hungry embrace as soon as Adrian had closed the door and lit the small candle branch on the chest across from the bed.

After several minutes, Adrian released her and said very quietly, "You are upset by what Simon said. It is only the beginning, you know."

"I know," she acknowledged, and told him briefly of her conversation with the earl. "It doesn't matter.

I admit it upsets me, but it truly doesn't matter. I love you, that is all that matters to me." Her words were brave, but in her heart she admitted to herself that she was still afraid her courage could flag.

He kissed her again, though more lightly than passionately. "It isn't too late yet, Isobel, to change your mind."

In response to this, she showed him the proper way to kiss, to make their pulses race with dizzying speed. They undressed where they stood, and if there had been more on the hardwood floor than a thin scatter rug, they might have made love on the same spot. As it had been the night before, their first coupling was hot and urgent, the second more deliberate and, for Isobel, instructive. He seemed to know every sensitive place on her body, as if he had a map to study, and he caressed and teased each one until the tension became unbearable and pleasure flooded her once again.

Isobel expected to awake in the morning to find Adrian gone from her, but he was still beside her, still asleep when she awoke not long after the sun had come up. The room was not especially warm, but it was stuffy and he had thrown off most of the sheet and blanket that covered him. She sat up carefully, not wishing to awaken him. She had seen and explored his naked body before by candlelight, but that had been in the heat of passion. She wanted to look her fill at him in the pale morning light seeping through cracks in the shutters, to trace with her eyes the defined muscles in his shoulders and arms, the powerful curve of his hip and thigh. But it was impossible for her to look for very long without wanting to touch him.

The impulse proved irresistible and she began to caress him, feeling the firmness of his flesh, reveling in the latent strength of his muscles at rest. It was inevitable that she would eventually draw away the small bit of sheet that did cover him. She was mildly surprised and quite pleased to find him aroused. By this time she had succeeded in arousing herself considerably.

Blushing a little at her own wantonness, she admitted to herself that she wanted him now, and she had no hesitation about turning him gently onto his back. His eyes opened slightly and he gave her a sleepy smile. He made no objection when she straddled him and began to shower kisses on his closed eyes, his nose, and cheeks until finally his arms encircled her and they kissed properly.

But Isobel broke away from him. She wanted to make love to him, and she pushed his hands away when they sought to caress her. She kissed his chest and teased his nipples with her teeth. Her tongue traced the line of his breastbone down to his navel. When the now familiar ache between her legs intensified until it was nearly unbearable, she gently lowered herself onto him. She had no idea consciously what was required of her in this position, but instinctively she knew exactly how to maximize pleasure for them both. She moved very slowly at first, almost teasingly, then gradually intensified the pace until it was fevered. When she felt nearly certain that consummation was imminent for them both, she stopped abruptly and after a few moments' rest moved with tantalizing slowness again. She repeated this until he begged her for release and she herself found the deliberate frustration excruciating. Incredible pleasure at last overwhelmed them both, and they lay panting and coated with sweat from their exertions.

"What a very good thing you were born to be a lady," he said when his breathing had slowed sufficiently to make speech comfortable. "In any other estate you should have become the queen of courtesans,

I have no doubt of it. What a damn fool Quentin is not to realize what he has lost."

"How could he?" Isobel said reasonably. "I wouldn't sleep with him, and when I did that one time, it was dreadful."

"It needn't have been, even though it was your first time with a man," Adrian said, kissing one white shoulder. "Was he drinking that time too?"

"Yes." She pulled away from him and sat up. "But I don't want to talk of Quentin. I would rather worry about the future than the past, and I rather think we shall have quite enough anxiety there to occupy us."

Adrian stretched and sighed deeply. "That's all very well, but if you ignore the past, it can emerge and haunt you when you least expect it."

"I shall chase it away again, I promise," she said, laughing. "As I mean to chase you. Your clothes are in the room where Simon is, and it is your penance for being so gloomy that you shall have to wash and dress with his black looks for company."

Adrian groaned in protest, but Isobel pushed him until he got out of bed and put on his clothes to go to the other room.

Isobel waited for Simon to treat them to the sulks, if not worse, at breakfast. He was somewhat subdued and didn't speak unless spoken to, but he was civil when he did, and nothing was again mentioned about Isobel and Adrian spending the night together.

They arrived in town by the middle of the afternoon. Their careful plan received a leveler when they reached Sir James Stokes's house and saw that the knocker had been taken off the door. This should not have been surprising perhaps, given the lateness of the season, but Sir James had indicated to Adrian that he had intended to remain in town at least until the end of November. Isobel suggested that Adrian come with them to Leyland House, but Adrian refused to be thrust upon Lady Leyland before Isobel had a chance to speak to her stepmother. He suggested that a hotel would do very well, but Simon surprised them by protesting this.

"I think you should go to Carlton first and see if he will take you in for a few days," Simon recommended. "If it becomes known that you are in a hotel instead of staying with one of the family, it'll cause a great deal of talk."

"My dear Simon," Adrian said, smiling, "there shall be a great deal of talk no matter where I am once it is known that Isobel is ending her betrothal to Quentin to marry me."

"If Carlton, who has a great deal of credit in the world, is seen to accept you, it could make things less difficult, not only for you but for all of us."

"Why should Carlton wish to help us?" Isobel wondered. "He was not deliberately cutting to Adrian in the way that Quentin was, but he did not seem to accept him any more readily."

"Carlton might be willing to cut Adrian if he thought it might drive him back to America, but that isn't likely now that you are to be married. With his position in the government, he won't want scandal on his own doorstep if he can do anything to prevent it. Besides, Carlton envies Quentin, and despises himself for doing so," Simon said, displaying insight into his cousin's character. "He might not dislike to hear that Quentin has botched it and lost you to Adrian."

"But he doesn't know yet that Adrian hoaxed us about being provincial," Isobel said. "If he is as outraged as Quentin and *Grand-père* were, Adrian might find staying with him uncomfortable even if Carlton does not refuse to take him in."

Adrian was thoughtful for a few minutes. Finally he said, "Simon does have a point, Isobel. I don't care a great deal for myself if I am the victim of whispered malice, but I don't want you to be punished for my sins. I shan't need to accept Carlton's hospitality for very long, after all. I think we shall go to Stokes Hall as soon as we are married. It is likely that that is where Jamie has gone, and I know he will welcome us, for he has already asked me to come to him for the holidays if I preferred not to remain with the Renvilles. Perhaps we could spend some time at one of the resorts after that and return to town in spring when the Season is well underway. By that time it will be old news that you jilted Quentin and married me, and there will be all the usual *on dits* and Crim. Con. stories of the Season, which shall cause us to fade into obscurity."

This made a great deal of sense, but Isobel had grave doubts that Carlton would be acquiescent. He rarely rebelled against his mother's rule, and would be reluctant to challenge the wishes of the earl once he knew that his grandfather had disowned Adrian. It was true that Carlton harbored jealousies against his more favored brother, but she thought it questionable that he would take Adrian's part against Quentin's even if doing so paid off some old scores between them.

But Simon proved to know his cousin better than she did. Carlton was at home when they called at his lodgings, a large and comfortable set of rooms in a private house situated just off Bond Street. Adrian suggested, and Simon concurred, that it would be best if he remained in the carriage so that Carlton did not feel constrained by his presence to agree against his will to take Adrian in.

As it was, Carlton was plainly surprised and perhaps not best pleased when his servant showed Isobel and Simon into the large drawing room that he had converted partially into a study. Bookcases flanked two walls, and a mahogany desk dominated one end of the room. The desk was encircled by several satellite tables, and the surfaces of these were obliterated under a weight of parchment documents, some appearing official and portentous and others innocuous. Carlton's dispatch case was open on the desk, and papers spilled out of this onto the surface. There were several pens in various need of mending on the desk, as well as two standishes and a wide silver bowl holding sand for blotting. The remainder of the room was scrupulously clean and tidy, and it was obvious that they had interrupted him at his work.

Carlton's excellent breeding would not permit him to betray his annoyance, however, and he requested his servant to bring them refreshment and led his guests to chairs at the opposite end of the large room. "I had no idea you had arrived in town," he said, "or I should have called at once. I had the impression that you intended to remain at Audswyck for another fortnight yet at the least. Has Grandfather come with you, or my mother?"

Simon, having brought them there, abandoned Isobel to make explanations while he restlessly roamed the room. "No, Simon, Adrian, and I have come alone," she began, and as concisely as she could she told him about the accident at the river, the rescue of Quentin and Adrian by Lord Turvey and Mr. Liddiard, and the aftermath of this.

Carlton did not seem unduly surprised by these events and said as much. "I always knew matters would come to a head between my brother and my cousin. I suppose Quentin pushed Adrian off the footbridge and then was gudgeon enough to fall in himself."

Isobel glanced quickly toward Simon, but he had pulled a book out of one of the cases and did not appear to be listening. "They both claim it was an accident," she replied.

Carlton gave a derisive snort of laughter. "Much I believe that. So Adrian has been hoaxing us," he said, sounding amused rather than angry. "Why? And if Grandfather disowned him, why have you and Simon left Audswyck with him? I'll wager the old man forbade you to acknowledge the poor fellow's existence."

Not certain whether this remark boded well or ill, Isobel took it as her opening. "I have come to town with Adrian because we are to be married as soon as I have Mama publish the notice that I have ended my betrothal to Quentin and we can obtain a special license. Simon has come to bear us company," she added, which was at least near to the truth, though his efforts to chaperon his sister had failed.

Carlton's eyes opened wide when he heard this. "Hell and damnation!" he uttered, his tone betokening more awe than censure. Suddenly he began to laugh, convulsions of mirth that incapacitated him for several minutes. "Tipped my brother a regular settler, didn't you, Bel?" he said in a broken way when he began to catch his breath again. "Cut out by the Savage. Dear Lord, but I wish now I'd stayed to see it with my own eyes. That's not to say," he added when he had wiped his tearing eyes with his handkerchief and blown his nose, "that I'm not concerned for you, my dear. I can understand that you might wish to give my self-centered brother his *conge,* but you may do so without entangling yourself with Adrian. What do you, or any of us, for that matter, really know of him other than what he has told us, and now you say most of that was lies?"

"I am in love with him, Carl." She saw a skeptical look come into his eyes and hastened to add, "I know it seems very soon to everyone—it does even to me at times—but I know what I feel for him, and I have never felt this way before, not even with Quentin."

"Have you any idea what manner of bumblebroth

you shall cast us all into, Bel?" Carlton demanded. "If the old man is set on ruining Adrian, he will do so, depend upon it. If you are his wife, you will find yourself ostracized as well."

Put into words by the most sensible of her cousins, she felt rather daunted, and some of her shining hope for the future seemed tarnished. She said bravely, "If that happens, we shall leave England and go to America as soon as we can find passage."

This seemed to upset Carlton even more. "Dear Lord, Bel, you know there's a war going on with the United States. Even if you can find direct passage, which will take some doing, the dangers are far greater now than when Adrian made his crossing. Ships suspected of harboring Americans are stopped at midsea now by our frigates, who fire upon them if they refuse to obey and deliver up any passengers on board. The men are pressed into service or cast into the brig, and I shudder to think what would become of a woman found traveling with such a man."

Isobel could not help catching some of his alarm. "Then we shall live retired somewhere until it is safe to cross," she said, refusing to be intimidated by these dire predictions. "*Grand-père* can't hurt us if we do not go into society."

"Are you certain you have thought this through, Bel?" he asked in a milder manner. "You might take a few quiet days to give it a proper amount of thought before you make a decision that will affect the whole of your life."

Carlton had not condemned Adrian, but his attempt to persuade her against marrying him made her doubt that he would be willing to help them. But she had agreed to ask for his assistance, and she said, "I know you don't approve, Carl, but I hope that doesn't mean that you will refuse to be my friend in this. We need to have a special license to be married, and neither Adrian nor I have any idea how we may obtain one."

"Through the archbishop of Canterbury," Carlton said without hesitation. "But it is not always a simple matter, and since Adrian is not even an Englishman, it may be even more difficult than usual."

"But will you help us get it?" She saw him regard her speculatively and said in a determined way, "If we are to be ruined anyway, I shall live with him as his mistress rather than give him up, Carl."

"I'll do what I can for you, Bel," he said reluctantly. Then he smiled. "I've seen before how unmovable you can be if you are determined on a course."

"Then I wish you would do something else to assist me," she said, deciding to capitalize on her success. "Adrian had hoped to stay with Sir James Stokes, who is a friend of his, but Sir James has left town. Adrian doesn't think it proper that he should come to Leyland House until Mama has been apprised of all that has happened. Do you think he might stay with you until we are married, Carl? That would only be for as long as it takes to get the license, for we mean to leave London immediately afterward."

Carlton looked nothing less than stunned for a moment. "But, Isobel, I barely know the fellow."

"He is your cousin."

"So he says," Carlton returned. "But if he has told so many lies, that may be one too."

"He is the image of Uncle Francis," Simon interjected.

Carlton's eyes held a hunted look, and Isobel feared he was about to refuse them. "What will Audwin say when he discovers that I have had Adrian here? I'm not hanging out for a fortune like Quentin, but the old man can make things dashed unpleasant for me in the Foreign Office if he has a word with the right people."

"You may plead ignorance," Isobel advised. "Adrian never told you that he had been disowned. He shall be here so short a time it will be entirely plausible."

"I think Carlton's right, Bel," Simon said, walking over to her and seating himself on the arm of the chair. "He is taking a bit of a risk. And even more to the point, what will Quentin say when he learns that Carlton helped Adrian? You know how he despises Adrian. Quentin is bound to give Carl the devil of a rake-down for harboring the man who cut him out with you."

"I should like to see him try," Carlton said in belli-cose accents. "I hope I may have who I please to stay here."

"I'll fetch Adrian, shall I?" said Simon, and was up and out of the room almost before Carlton could draw breath to object.

"Do you think Quentin will call Adrian out for cutting him out with you?" Carlton asked a few moments later as a new anxiety beset him. "I can't imagine he will accept being jilted without demanding some sort of satisfaction—or revenge. This is a devil of a coil, Isobel. In my profession I can't find myself embroiled in a scandal."

"You need only do what American politicians and bureaucrats do when they are caught out, cousin," Adrian suggested as he came into the room. "Assume an air of astonished innocence and declare that you were completely taken in by the dastardly fellow."

Carlton rose to take his hand. "I suppose there is no point in pretending that I am entirely comfortable with the turn of events, but if Isobel is convinced that she loves you, I can only hope you value the prize you have won."

"I am not a trophy in a tournament, Carl," Isobel said, bristling.

"Nothing so trumpery, my love," Adrian said with

a quizzing grin. "You are more like an exquisite thoroughbred claimed at the end of a forfeit race."

Carlton listened to this raillery with mild surprise. Gone entirely was the blank look and dull expression that Adrian had often assumed in his company. The man before him was self-possessed, with a distinctly authoritative air that declared he was not to be lightly reckoned with.

"I vow I shall do my best to give you no trouble, Carlton," Adrian said. "I am grateful that you are willing to receive me under the circumstances. I wish matters were different between us, and I know I am much to blame for it. I have cursed myself for my damn-fool notion that made me come to Audswyck under false pretenses far more thoroughly than our grandfather could ever do, I promise you."

Carlton smiled a bit reluctantly. "Then you are certainly your father's son. My father told me once that his brother was the only man on earth who could match the old man oath for oath."

This was a propitious beginning, and Isobel had to admit that Simon's notion was a happy one after all. It was decided that Adrian would set down Isobel and Simon at Leyland House and then return to Sir James's house to see if he might, by means of the service entrance, achieve admittance to the house to retrieve his own clothes. He and Isobel decided that she would tell her stepmother only about Adrian's pretense and the earl's violent reaction to learning the truth. They agreed that he would call after breakfast, and together they would tell her that she was ending her betrothal to Quentin and that they intended to be married within a few days' time.

With Simon and her dresser looking on, Isobel could receive reassurance from her lover with nothing more intimate than a smile. At the entrance to the house, she turned to watch the post chaise as it pulled away. She felt momentarily bereft of the courage that had carried her through so much in the past two days, but it was a fleeting apprehension. She had faced the earl alone, and she had all but vanquished Quentin even before Adrian had come to her rescue. It was a new thing to think of herself as capable and strong and in charge of her own existence. In spite of the occasional moments of fear, she reveled in her new self-assurance, and she knew nothing would ever dishearten her enough to relinquish it again.

Chapter 13

Lady Leyland was at home when Simon and Isobel arrived at Leyland House, and quite surprised to see her children return so much sooner than she had expected them. Isobel did not wish Simon or Kitty to be present when she spoke to her stepmother about Adrian, so that lady's curiosity about their unexpected arrival was satisfied in only the most perfunctory manner until Isobel was able to draw her stepmother into the privacy of her own apartments.

Caroline Leyland exclaimed in amazement and dismay upon learning that Quentin and Adrian had both nearly drowned, and expressed a mother's gratitude that Isobel had prevented Simon from casting himself into the river to attempt to rescue them, which his injury would have made impossible. When Isobel introduced Mr. Liddiard to the narrative and described his recognition of Adrian, Lady Leyland said, "Oh, my! Isobel! You did try to tell us that Adrian was hoaxing us, and we thought you were imagining things. I feel so very stupid. Now that I think of that night we celebrated Papa's birthday and how we all commented on what pretty manners Adrian had learned in just a fortnight, I wonder that I can have been so blind. Papa must have been astounded, if he had not already guessed, for he is usually so very perceptive."

"Yes," Isobel averred, "and quite angry also."

Lady Leyland gave a silvery laugh. "I'll wager that

is a considerable understatement, my love. If I know Papa, he flew into a rage, or rather he probably froze poor Adrian to crystal in the way that he has."

Isobel sighed, "No, you were right the first time, Mama. *Grand-père* was so furious that he raved at Adrian in a way I have never seen before."

"I have," Caroline said with a small shiver of remembrance. "The worst time was when he sent my brother Francis from Audswyck and told him he would never be welcome there again." Her fingers flew to her lips in dread as a thought occurred to her. "He didn't do the same to Adrian, did he?"

Isobel admitted that the earl had repudiated his heir and sent him from Audswyck. "But you always said that you thought *Grand-père* ultimately regretted what he did to Adrian's father, so perhaps he will come to accept Adrian when his anger cools. After all, he should be very pleased that Adrian is really a gentleman with excellent manners instead of the gapeseed he supposed him to be."

Lady Leyland allowed that this was possible, but it was plain she did not place any reliance on it. "Papa's temper has always been irascible, you know," she said, "and as he grows older, I have found he takes offense at the most ludicrous things. But we shall see." It suddenly dawned on her that it was odd that Isobel should have left Audswyck in Adrian's company, particularly in light of the circumstances. "You have not quarreled with Papa as well, have you, my dear?" she asked with some trepidation. If her father had been in a towering rage, she supposed it was possible that he had denounced anyone who had been foolish enough to come into his sights.

Isobel saw the difficulty of keeping from her stepmother until tomorrow her own part in the events that had occurred. "Yes, Mama, I'm afraid I have. He said dreadful things about Adrian, and I could not hold my tongue."

Lady Leyland took Isobel's hands in her own. "You *have* fallen into a scrape, haven't you, love," she said to Isobel, but the kindness in her voice robbed her words of any offense. "You should have ignored him. You know how he is."

"That doesn't excuse him or preclude him from being challenged," Isobel said in combative accents.

"And what of Quentin? Have you quarreled with him also?" Lady Leyland asked with dread. "He cannot be pleased that you have left Audswyck with Adrian."

Isobel, hoping that Adrian would forgive her for not waiting for him to be present, gave in to the inevitable and told her stepmother an expurgated account of her final quarrel with Quentin, which had led to her decision to end their betrothal. But Lady Leyland was not deceived by the evasion, and her wits were quicker than they were generally credited to be. Isobel appended to her recital a brief history of her growing unhappiness during her betrothal, and when she was done, her stepmother astounded her by saying, "Has Adrian anything to do with your decision?"

Isobel was a bit startled by her stepmother's unexpected insight. But she saw neither the point nor the need for lying and admitted that she had fallen in love with Adrian, adding, "I have come to love him for his kindness and consideration. We think alike in so many ways, and we laugh together at the same things. There is already between us a closeness, as if we had been the dearest of friends for all of our lives."

"Perhaps it is just that with Adrian you have recaptured some of the romance and excitement that has faded from your relationship with Quentin," Lady Leyland suggested gently. "It might be best to wait a little before we send a notice to the papers that you are ending your betrothal, to be certain it is what you truly wish to do."

"No," Isobel said firmly. She was becoming weary of defending her decision to marry Adrian. "Adrian and I intend to be married as soon as possible. I am sorry Papa is not here to give his formal consent, but I am of age and may please myself."

Lady Leyland did not respond to this bellicose statement but said quietly, "Is it necessary that you marry him so quickly?"

Isobel colored rosily. "No," she said sharply, and then surprised herself by saying, "At least not that I am yet aware of."

"Oh, dear," the older woman said with some agitation. "Your papa will not be pleased. He is certain to think that this is my fault in some fashion, or at the least that I could have prevented it from happening, though I don't at all see how. I hadn't the least idea that Adrian was making love to you or I should never have left you alone at Audswyck while he was there." Tears stung her eyes, and she rose to find a handkerchief. "But I am being very selfish," she said, dabbing her eyes when she had unearthed a pretty bit of white lace from a drawer, "to think of such things when it is you I should be concerned for."

Isobel went to her, saying, "There is not the least need for concern. I promise you I truly love Adrian, and he loves me."

It took the better part of the next half hour for Isobel to completely convince her stepmother that her feelings for Adrian were entirely genuine and not the result of anger, hurt, lust, or mere infatuation.

In the end, Lady Leyland was wise enough to realize that Isobel had made up her mind to have Adrian. When he called the next day, she treated him with kindness, though she playfully admonished him for perpetrating his hoax on them. She did not speak to

Isobel of her fears for their future if the earl was determined to ruin his grandson as he had his own son,
but she knew the only hope of mitigating the ostracism
of them both was for the remainder of the family to
show the world that they did not share the earl's harsh
judgment of his heir. Thirty years had passed since
her brother Francis had preferred exile to being
snubbed by the world, and the legendary fourth earl
of Audwin, though his name was still revered in political and court circles, was no longer the power in the
world he once had been.

With luck, she informed them both when Adrian
came to Upper Mount Street the following morning,
they would not fare as badly as she had originally
feared. She agreed to place an official notice in the
Morning Post to inform the world at large that Isobel
had ended her betrothal to Quentin, and she advised
them against going at all into the world until they
returned in the spring as a married couple.

It was also Caroline Leyland who spoke both to her
son and her ward to convince them that however
much they might think Isobel's decision to marry
Adrian capricious, they had to respect it and accept
Adrian unless they wished to be alienated from her.

Kitty was the more difficult to convince. She wept
with considerable emotion, but both Isobel and her
stepmother knew this had much to do with the loss of
the romantic fantasy of the perfect union the young
girl had built around Isobel and Quentin. Kitty was
persuaded, cajoled, and threatened into behaving at
least with civility toward Adrian, but it was plain that
she was determined to see him as an evil seducer and
Quentin as the noble hero betrayed.

Isobel was so outraged by this that at first she was
almost tempted to impart some of the grimmer truths
about Quentin and his behavior toward her to Kitty,
but Adrian, with his love of the absurd, was plainly

amused rather than offended, and she was persuaded to see the diverting aspect of it instead.

Simon seemed to be more resigned to his sister's decision, if still not ready to dance at her wedding. When Adrian and Carlton came to dinner the following night, it was plain that some degree of understanding had been worked out between them as well, and both Carlton and Simon were very civil to Adrian, if not precisely cordial. This and her stepmother's determined efforts on her behalf made Isobel begin to feel that her anxiety that Adrian would never find acceptance within the family was grossly exaggerated.

This good feeling continued with her until the afternoon following the next. She was completely unprepared for the turmoil and distress that would darken her coming days. The summons brought up to her dressing room, where she was happily sorting through the clothes in her wardrobe, informing her that Mr. Renville had called, did not seem to her in any way foreboding.

She was not expecting Adrian. He seemed to have much to occupy him in the city, visiting the solicitor he had retained to represent his interests when the time came that he would inherit the earldom, and seeing also the earl's man of business, which as heir was within his right to do. Then there was also the matter of procuring the special license, though Carlton had obligingly offered to undertake that task himself.

She went down to the rose saloon, where he awaited her, hoping that perhaps this unexpected visit meant that progress had been made in this latter effort. Now that the die was cast for her, she was anxious to make her decision permanent and irrevocable. The notice that she had ended her betrothal to Quentin had appeared in the *Morning Post* the previous day, and now only her marriage to Adrian remained to be accomplished.

She entered the saloon, and the welcoming smile died on her lips. Quentin rose and faced her. There was a copy of the *Post* on the table beside the chair in which he had been sitting, and she felt ready to sink at the prospect of this confrontation, which she was unprepared for but which she could not now avoid. Lady Leyland had taken Kitty to pay a visit to an elderly relative, and Simon was spending the day with some friends, so she could hope for no one to interrupt them and bring an end to the unwelcome tête-à-tête. As with her final interview with the earl, she had to draw on her new reserves of self-confidence to face Quentin on her own.

He did not waste his efforts on niceties. He rose when she entered the room, picked up the paper from the table, and thrust it at her when she approached him. "What the devil is this, Isobel?" he demanded in accusing accents.

Isobel did not even look at the paper; she had no need to. "It is the announcement Mama placed in the paper to make it officially known that our betrothal is ended," she said.

"Didn't you think I would have some interest in hearing that you were about to do so before I suffered the humiliation of reading it in a newspaper?" he said, nearly speaking through his teeth.

There was no question that Quentin was entirely sober, and Isobel had no fear that his anger would become physical as it had the night before she had left Audswyck Chase. But even so she felt her stomach knot, knowing that the next quarter hour or so would be extremely unpleasant. "I told you that I was crying off in the letter that I left you, and I returned your ring to you. Surely that was sufficient to prepare you for this. But I should have thought it would be obvious to you that it was ended between us even if I had not done those things," she said, keeping her voice as level as she could.

"Oh, I knew you were upset with me," he said, his manner dismissive. "But I thought you just meant to punish me for our quarrel. I never supposed that you meant what you said in that letter."

Isobel felt as if she were regarding him for the first time. He was unquestionably an exceptionally handsome and elegant man, though his features at that moment were marred by his cross expression. She could scarcely credit it now, but she knew that in the past just looking at him and marveling that he had chosen her above all others was sufficient to melt any anger or hurt he had caused her.

It was very different this time. She felt no pleasure in beholding him. She was not angry, nor did she feel bitterness or resentment at this moment for the years she had wasted for his sake. She felt nothing at all. For the first time she was well and truly certain that she had fallen out of love with him. His words evoked only amazement in her that he could be so self-deluding.

"I meant it, or I wouldn't have written it. You know that what passed between us was something more than a quarrel, Quentin." Her lips curled in a slight, contemptuous smile. "But perhaps you were too drunk to remember it."

"Of course I was drunk," he said with no apology. "What better reason for it than to celebrate the vanquishing of the Savage? Good Lord, Isobel! You aren't going to tell me that you jilted me because I was cast away?"

"You tried to rape me," she said in a cold, flat tone.

Quentin's eyes slid from hers, and he turned and threw the paper onto the table. "Don't be absurd, Isobel. There is no need to make high melodrama out of an attempt to make love to you. Do you blame me if I became a bit precipitate? We are betrothed, and yet you behave as if I were trying to give you a slip on the shoulder. I think I have been more than patient."

She knew that he remembered well enough what he had done but that he had already found justification to excuse himself. Not only wouldn't he admit his offense to her, he would not admit it to himself. She wasted no further effort attempting to extract an apology from him. "I have come to believe that we should not suit after all, Quentin. I am sorry if I distress you in any way, but I am persuaded that this is the best course for us both."

He listened to her formal words in patent disbelief. "Distress me! Hell and damnation, Isobel! You can't be serious."

She saw that he was genuinely discomposed, which softened her toward him slightly. "I am quite serious. I have known it for some time, but I couldn't easily accept that my feelings had changed."

"Mine have not, I assure you," he said, plainly agitated. "Why? You owe me that surely?" His visage suddenly darkened. "It is the Savage, isn't it?" he demanded, grasping her wrist. "You're sleeping with him, aren't you?"

Isobel's indifference finally resolved into anger. "It isn't Adrian. If he left me tomorrow, I still would never wish to be your wife."

His sneer was prurient. "And do you really believe that you will be his wife now that he has had you?" He jerked her arm to pull her nearer to him. "You will find you have made a poor trade when he abandons you with your belly growing."

"You are odious," she said her eyes flashing fire. "You have said that you love me, but you are more considerate of your horses than you are of me. You care for nothing and nobody but yourself. You wonder why I do not wish to marry you, Quentin? What I wonder is that I ever wanted to be your wife in the first place."

The color drained from his countenance as she spoke but was then replaced by an angry flush. He released her and said in a voice that was plainly in tight control, "If that is your reading of my character, then I am the one who has had a fortunate deliverance. I suppose I owe you my thanks, but I doubt you deserve even that." With these words he turned on his heel and left her, closing the door behind him with such force that every picture on the walls and every ornament on every surface trembled and danced.

For a few moments Isobel was beside herself in a rage that Quentin did not even acknowledge his sins, let alone regret them. But as her swift, angry breath began to become more regular, she realized that his selfish nature was incapable of admitting that he could be responsible for causing her to jilt him. Her anger faded, but she was left with restlessness in its place.

She had no fear that Adrian was anything but sincere. But Quentin's aspersions affected her even while she told herself he had made them out of his spitefulness toward Adrian. She could not help longing for the reassurance that Adrian loved her as completely as she loved him. They had not been alone for even the shortest time since he had left her bed at the post inn. Nor had they managed any private conversation since then. She ached to feel his arms about her, to taste his lips again. She was certain that even just to hear him say he loved her again would make her feel secure against any doubts.

She went to her dressing room to change for the street and had Dolly have a footman send for her stepmother's barouche, since Lady Leyland had taken the closed town carriage for her visiting. She directed the coachman to Carlton's lodgings in the hope that she would find Adrian there and Carlton still at the

Foreign Office. But her luck was out; both young men were from home.

Rather than return to Upper Mount Street at once, she told the coachman to proceed to Hyde Park. During the Season this would have been foolhardy, but with London so thin of fashionable company, it was not likely that Isobel would meet anyone well known to her. She had scarcely left the house since her return from Audswyck and not at all since the notice that she would not marry Quentin had appeared.

The park proved to be nearly empty, and the fresh air and change of scenery greatly improved her spirits. They were headed back to Leyland House, and were not far from the gates of the park, when Isobel saw three horsemen drawn up in conversation at the side of the path. She gave them little notice until the carriage drew nearer and she realized that one of them was Adrian. She had the coachman pull up when she reached them, and Adrian's warm, welcoming smile made any risk of gossip worthwhile.

One of the gentlemen with Adrian was Mr. Liddiard, and the other was unknown to Isobel. Adrian introduced the latter to Isobel as Mr. Ames-Harding. Mr. Liddiard, who had been so friendly and amiable the times that Isobel had met him at Audswyck, was somewhat perfunctory in his greeting to her, and after exchanging the barest pleasantries, he excused himself and he and Mr. Ames-Harding rode off toward the gates.

"Throwing caution to the wind for the sake of a bit of air?" Adrian said, smiling as he bent down from the saddle to take her hand.

"I doubted I would meet anyone who would quiz me, but I see I was mistaken," Isobel said dryly. "I called at Carlton's hoping to see you. Mama and I would like you to join us for tea, if you are free."

Adrian saw that she issued this invitation while regarding him in a very speaking manner and correctly assumed that it was unlikely that Lady Leyland was aware that she had requested his company. "I should be delighted. I'll escort you to the house, since the house is so advanced, but then I beg you will permit me to return my job horse to the livery stable and change from my dirt."

Isobel had to curb her impatience at least in front of the coachman, but once again her eyes conveyed her true thoughts to Adrian, who quickly assured her that he would not be above a half hour delayed.

Since she could not discuss the true direction of her thoughts until they were alone, she said, "I didn't know Mr. Liddiard had come to town, did you?"

"Yes, I did actually," Adrian admitted. "I met him at the Duck and Drake when I went there to hire the post chaise, and he told me he was leaving for town the following morning. He is anxious to see London and didn't care to wait until his aunt and uncle came to town themselves for the Season."

"You weren't quarreling with him just now, were you?" Isobel said, thinking of Liddiard's odd abruptness.

This brought a surprising burst of laughter from Adrian. "No, of course not, though I admit I was thinking myself just now that he must be a rather moody fellow. He didn't seem at all pleased when I caught them up. It wasn't him that I first recognized and spoke to, but Mr. Ames-Harding, who dined with Carlton and me only last evening. He is also employed by the Foreign Office, and I gather he is a protégé of Carlton's."

"Yes, it is something of a habit with Carlton to take young men who are just entering the service under his wing," Isobel said. "*Grand-père* has said it is very clever of him to build a rank of underlings who have reason to be grateful to him. Trust him to put the most selfish connotation on any charitable act."

The carriage finally drew up at Leyland House, and as soon as Isobel was seen safely from the carriage, Adrian left her and reiterated his promise to return to her within the half hour. It was rather longer than that before he arrived, though, and Isobel was chafing for fear that her stepmother would return first; she desperately wanted at least a few minutes alone with him. The invitation to tea had been only a polite excuse for him to come to the house, but Adrian had changed his clothes and was elegantly attired in a coat of dark blue superfine and fawn-colored pantaloons that clung to his muscular legs like a second skin. Meritt, the Leyland butler, showed Adrian into the saloon where Isobel had settled herself to wait for him, and Adrian very properly bowed over her hand as if this was indeed only a social call.

"Thank you, Meritt," Isobel said to the servitor, "that will be all. As soon as Lady Leyland returns, inform her that we are awaiting her, and then you may have the tea tray made ready and brought up to us." It was most improper of her to be left alone with Adrian for what might be an extended period, but her longing to be with him made her have little patience for propriety. In a few days the servants and the remainder of the world would know her as Mrs. Adrian Renville.

The butler bowed himself out of the room, and as soon as the door was shut behind him, Isobel turned back to Adrian and cast herself into his arms. He kissed and embraced her with as much fervor as she could wish for, reassuring her that nothing had changed between them. She had wanted to tell him of Quentin's visit and to discover how soon they might hope to leave London, but he drew her to the sofa and all thought of such things was erased temporarily from her mind.

They kissed and caressed each other for several minutes, murmuring soft endearments, until Adrian said daringly, "How soon do you expect Lady Leyland to return? Is it likely that we shall be interrupted before then?"

Isobel understood the direction of his thoughts and was shocked and aroused at the same time at the prospect of making love in her stepmother's gold saloon in the middle of the afternoon with all the attendant risks of discovery. But she wanted him no less than he wanted her, and she abandoned discretion to give him the answers he hoped for.

It was a little more than thirty minutes later that Lady Leyland came into the room, still dressed for the street. Isobel was seated at one corner of the sofa, and Adrian was at his ease in a facing chair. There was nothing disheveled in the appearance of either, nor were they guilty in their demeanor. Isobel was a trifle flushed, but that was not remarkable given her very fair complexion.

"Meritt told me you had called, Adrian," Caroline Leyland said, smiling as he rose and took her hand. "I hope Isobel has asked you to stay to tea?"

"She has been so kind, yes," Adrian said very properly.

"I'll have Meritt order it to be prepared at once, and I'll join you as soon as I may. Kitty developed one of her migraines, and we had to stop several times on the way home for her to be sick, which is why I am so delayed. I just wish to see her settled as comfortably as she may be." She cast a small conspiratorial smile toward Isobel, obviously thinking that she was conferring a kindness upon them by allowing them a few more minutes alone.

Adrian sat again and gave Isobel a lazy, satisfied

smile. "If she was to look in on us again in another minute or so, she would be quite disappointed, I think, not to find us locked in a desperate embrace. Will it take her long to change, do you imagine?"

Isobel's flush deepened. "I had no idea I had accepted an offer of marriage from such a shameless libertine," she said with apparent dismay.

"I, shameless?" he said in outraged accents. "That is an unfair accusation coming from an abandoned wench who has twice now seduced me when my own intentions were most proper."

"Your intentions were quite improper from the day that we met," she retorted.

"Oh, even before that," he said, daringly recalling the night he had first kissed her at Vauxhall.

"Quentin thinks you haven't any proper intentions now either," she informed him. "He called today and was very upset by the notice in the *Post.* He thinks you have no cause to marry me now that I have abandoned my virtue to you without benefit of a proper ceremony."

Adrian appeared much struck by this. "Do you know, I hadn't thought of it before, but I do believe my cousin has an excellent notion. I suppose that means that I can return this to Rundell and Bridges and have my money returned to me." As he spoke he pulled a small box from an inner pocket. He went over to the sofa and sat beside Isobel, proffering the box to her. "I didn't think it appropriate to give you this until the notice that you were ending your betrothal to Quentin had appeared in the newspaper."

Inside the box was an exquisite diamond-flanked sapphire just exactly the color of Isobel's eyes. He slipped it onto her finger and kissed her in a sweet, lingering fashion. After several delightful minutes of this activity, he asked her to tell him more of her interview with Quentin.

Isobel gave him a fair accounting of her conversation and saw as she spoke that Adrian's eyes took on the shuttered look that she had come to recognize that he assumed to disguise strong emotion.

"Damn him to hell for eternity," Adrian swore roundly when she had finished. "Attempting to put the blame for his attempt to ravish you in your dish puts him beyond redemption. I think we may place no reliance on him to maintain a dignified silence in this matter. If he feels as you say, he may wish to do us harm if he can, and with the added incentive that he will be pleasing Audwin, he is certain to spread his venom against us as soon as may be. This makes it all the more important for us to be married as quickly as possible so we may leave London and be out of reach of his acid."

Lady Leyland came into the room at this point, and Isobel hastened to show the betrothal ring Adrian had given her. Lady Leyland assured her that it was indeed the loveliest ring she had ever set eyes on and said, "Now it wants only the special license for it all to be quite proper." She gave Isobel a brief hug. "I so want you and Adrian to be happy and together as soon as you may."

Isobel returned the hug. "So do we, Mama. We were just saying that we hope it will be very soon."

"Carlton seems to be encountering more difficulty than he supposed getting the license," Adrian commented. "I don't know very much about it other than it is necessary to have one in order to be married without calling the banns, but I suppose I may trust Carlton to know better than I how to go on."

Isobel had never supposed that Carlton would deliberately attempt to prevent her marriage to Adrian by not doing as he had promised, but for the first time she wondered if that might be the case. There was something in his tone that told Isobel that Adrian had had a similar thought.

Lady Leyland proved she was in tune with them by saying with more doubt than assurance, "Surely Carlton may be trusted to know exactly how to go about getting the license. He always seems to know exactly how one should go on about most everything."

"I wish I could be certain, Mama," Isobel said, a small troubled crease between her brows. "I don't like to think he would deliberately deceive us in such an important matter, but he did say to me when I told him I wished to marry Adrian that he thought I should take some time to think things through. He may think he is doing this for my own good."

"I suppose I could ask the solicitor I have retained about it," Adrian suggested, but Lady Leyland said he must on no account do so.

"I know that solicitors are not ever supposed to break the confidence of a client," she said, "but it is well known that there are many in the profession who employ clerks in their offices who are not above supplementing a meager income by selling gossip to the papers."

Adrian saw her dread that news of her stepdaughter's marriage so soon after the end of her betrothal would be broadcast precipitately and didn't press his suggestion. "I suppose I might go to Dorset myself to enlist the aid of Sir James. He has a brother who is a barrister, I think, and he may be able to discover from him how I should go on."

The tea tray was brought at this point, and conversation passed on to become more general until Adrian rose to take his leave of them. Isobel sent her stepmother an imploring glance, and Lady Leyland dutifully remembered that she had an urgent need to speak with her housekeeper before another minute had passed.

When they were alone, Adrian took her in his arms, and their kiss continued several tantalizing minutes to last them until the next time they could be together. This was to be longer than she had supposed.

"I think I shall go to Stokes Hall tomorrow, Bel," he said. "I really think I should settle the matter of the license myself. I'll ride rather than hire a carriage, and the journey won't take me above a day and a half. If Jamie is willing to return with me to London, or if he can tell me how to go about getting the license myself, I should be back with you inside of a sennight."

It was absurd, but Isobel was suddenly fearful of letting him go, as if something dreadful might happen while he was gone and she would never see him again if he went away without her. "Take me with you, Adrian," she implored him.

He caught the note of anxiety in her voice and said reassuringly, "I do wish we could be together from this moment on, Isobel, but you know I couldn't take you to Stokes Hall under the circumstances, and I won't leave you at an inn like my doxy to be visited as the fancy takes me. Although," he added thoughtfully, "there is a disused gamekeeper's cottage on the estate. It looked sound enough when I saw it on my earlier visit, and it is deep enough in the home wood that it is virtually hidden and no one need know you are even there. It would be ideal if you wouldn't mind sharing it with the squirrels and field mice for a few days."

"At least I shouldn't go hungry," she said wryly.

He cupped her head between his hands. "Doubt whatever you will about me, Isobel, but never doubt that I love you and want us to be together for the rest of our lives." He kissed her and then held her close to him. "When I return, nothing will part us again, I promise you."

This assurance was rather high-flown but so wonderfully romantic that Isobel was captivated and finally allowed him to leave her with her misgivings dispeled, at least for the moment.

Chapter 14

Isobel felt that she could not simply wait quietly to have her fate decided for her, and the morning that Adrian left for Dorset, she sent a note to Carlton asking him to call on her at Leyland House, intending to discover if he was being deliberately obstructive in the matter of the special license. She received in reply his regrets that he was tied up in meetings with the prime minister and the foreign secretary and would call as soon as he was able. Though she chafed at the delay and even wondered if it was not just a further evasion on his part, there was little she could do but compose herself to wait.

Already lonely at the thought of being deprived of Adrian's company for several days and thwarted in her attempt to take her own positive action, she was further bedeviled by Kitty, who decided that in Adrian's absence it was the perfect time to convince Isobel that Quentin was the epitome of masculine perfection. It mattered not at all to Kitty that Isobel assured her that it was unlikely that Quentin would take her back if she even wished it. She regarded this as further proof that Isobel was unjustly cruel in her opinion of the "handsomest, kindest, most noble man on earth."

Isobel hardly knew whether to laugh or be vexed by the young girl's absurdities. But she did not at all laugh when Simon took up the litany against Adrian two days later during Carlton's visit to Leyland House.

She was with her stepmother and Kitty in the morning room mending linens when a footman came to inform her that Carlton had called. Lady Leyland was about to rise with her, but Isobel asked if she might speak with Carlton alone for a few minutes. Her stepmother readily agreed, but this wish was thwarted when she went to the gold saloon and found Simon already with Carlton, discussing a horse that Carlton was contemplating buying from an acquaintance. Isobel asked Simon to leave them, but he took offense and Carlton took his part. She gave it up as a waste of effort and confronted Carlton directly about her suspicions.

Carlton infuriated Isobel by admitting quite without apology that he had made no real effort to procure the special license for her to be married to Adrian. "I think it's a dashed bad idea, Bel," he said in his sure way, which for the first time Isobel thought of as pompous and self-important. "If I am mistaken, time will prove that and no harm done. If I am right, I am saving you from more trouble and strife than you can know of right now."

Isobel demanded to know what he meant by this, and she received a rather cryptic answer by means of another question.

"Does Adrian know Mr. Liddiard, Lady Cahill's nephew, well in your opinion?"

She did could not make a connection between his question and her own, and she frowned, puzzled. "No, not at all," she replied without hesitation. "I don't even think he recognized Mr. Liddiard that day at the river until Liddiard had recognized him. Why do you ask?"

"I had a different impression," Simon interjected. "When I first saw them together, I saw them exchange the most peculiar look, as if conveying some warning or something. I even wondered at the time if Liddiard had been out looking for Adrian and that was why he was so handy on the scene."

"Simon, you are making this up," said his sister, indignant. "If you had seen or thought any such thing, you would have said so at once when you were all too ready to accuse Adrian of being responsible for the accident."

To Isobel's surprise, Carlton, who had been ready enough to blame his brother for the mishap only the other day, seemed to find this accusation suddenly credible. "Do you think it could be possible that Adrian was responsible?" he asked Simon.

Simon had not really expected to be heeded, but had merely repeated his earlier slanders of Adrian. "I-I thought so at the time," he admitted, avoiding Isobel's eyes. "Bel tried to convince me I was mistaken, but I still think it could be possible." His fertile imagination obviously fired, Simon dared to add, "After all, Adrian did lie to us from the very beginning, and the reason he gives for doing so is rather lame. He must have had some better motive than he claims, and if it wasn't to try to cut Quentin out of his inheritance, it may be he is a spy or some such thing after all."

"Simon! No one but you with your absurd imagination would ever think such a thing," she reproved him.

Simon was not so easily unseated from his hobbyhorse. "Adrian may have counted on that, and he may have supposed that if we all thought him ignorant and vulgar, we would think him harmless and be unguarded."

"And how many state secrets are you privy to, Simon?" Isobel said caustically.

"I didn't mean myself, of course. But there is Carlton," he said, plainly pleased with himself for his quick thinking. "What if those papers of Carlton's weren't mislaid, but Adrian had stolen them to read and for some reason couldn't put them back before Carl left Audswyck? He may even have given them to Liddiard in a secret meeting that we know nothing about. Carlton told us plainly at Audswyck that his work he had brought with him concerned the war with the United States."

Isobel would have reacted to her brother much as she had to Kitty, caught between a desire to laugh and to shake him. But she saw that Carlton was listening intently to Simon instead of laughing himself, as he was usually wont to do at one of the young man's flights of fancy. "You are totally ridiculous, Simon," she said with considerable sharpness. "Adrian would have had to have been very well informed indeed before ever coming to our shores to have planned all this beforehand."

"He might have learned what he needed to know from his friend Sir James Stokes," Simon retorted, proving that his mind was as quick as it was imaginative. "He met him in the United States, after all, and Stokes has property there and might be a sympathizer with the Americans."

Isobel sent an imploring look toward Carlton, for it was obvious that Simon, well warmed to his theme, would not be silenced by her admonitions. Carlton caught her glance and read it accurately. He said to Simon, "Enough, gudgeon. It is one thing to malign our American cousin, who is not likely to bring an action against you for slander, but Sir James, if he could hear you, would probably not be so reluctant."

"Don't *you* think there is anything havey-cavey about Adrian, Carl?" Simon demanded.

"I think that you are upsetting your sister with your wild imaginings," Carlton returned with more severity. "I can't say I'm devilish pleased that Isobel has promised herself to a fellow we know so little about, but she's of age and has a right to make her own choice."

Simon was rather crestfallen by this reproof and in a very little while left them to return to his studies. When he was gone, Isobel remonstrated with Carlton for failing to help them, and Carlton pointed out that though they had asked him to get the special license for them, he had never promised to do so.

Isobel saw clearly that he would not be brought to realize that no amount of delay would change her mind about marrying Adrian and did not waste breath any longer on the subject. "That is the reason that Adrian has gone to his friend Sir James in any case," she told him and saw that he was not pleased that his efforts were being circumvented.

Carlton finally rose from his chair, saying that he had to return home to change for a meeting with the prime minister and the foreign secretary before dinner. As he took up his hat, gloves, and walking stick, Isobel placed both hands on his arm and said, "You don't pay any heed to Simon's nonsense, do you, Carl?"

Carlton put his hand over hers and smiled. "I have been the victim of his inventiveness myself from time to time. I think that it is entirely likely he will put us all to the blush one day by writing tales for publication even more lurid than those of Monk Lewis." He took one of her hands, raised it to his lips, and bade her farewell. It was quite a quarter hour later that Isobel realized he had never truly answered her question or explained why it was that he had wondered about Adrian's acquaintance with Mr. Liddiard in the first place.

Isobel had not looked to see Adrian for several more days, but it was later that same night that he returned to London. The hour was nearly eleven when he arrived at Leyland House and requested not Isobel, but Lady Leyland. Simon and Kitty had both retired for the evening, but Isobel and her stepmother were still awake, and he was shown into the drawing room by a plainly disapproving Meritt.

"I most humbly beg your pardon, my lady," Adrian said, raising her hand to his lips and actually bestowing a soft kiss on it. "Even a savage like me knows it is shockingly rag-mannered to call at this hour, but I have come to throw myself on your kindness." He then turned to Isobel and kissed her lightly on the lips.

"But why are you back so soon?" Isobel demanded. "You can scarcely have had time to do more than reach Stokes Hall and return again."

"Well, this is a pretty welcome, beloved," Adrian said, his expression wounded. "I thought you would be overjoyed to have me restored to you so quickly."

His beloved ignored this sally. She led him to a sofa to sit beside her. "I should be more overjoyed to learn that it is because you were able to convince Sir James to return to London with you in the space of an hour, but I think rather that something must be amiss."

Adrian sighed. "Sir James is not at Stokes. There is only the housekeeper and a small staff there, and they had no idea at all where Jamie might be found. They thought it likely he is visiting with friends, but his staff here in town assumed that he had gone to Stokes, so I really have no idea at all where he may be found and only the assurance of his housekeeper at Stokes that he is expected there within a fortnight. With a fine regard for your feelings, my love, I thought it better to return rather than wait for him and keep you on tenterhooks."

The vague sense of foreboding that had assailed Isobel when she had last parted from Adrian, rather than being assuaged by his return, was revitalized by what she heard from him. It was as if there were some malevolent spirit that wished them ill and made hash of all their plans. She told him that Carlton had admitted to her that he had not made any effort to procure the license for them to be married.

"We shall attempt to manage on our own," he said, displaying no concern. "In the meantime, though, I have come to beg a bed for the night."

Lady Leyland did not seem precisely dismayed by this request, but she was certainly taken aback. "Has Carlton gone out of town also?" she asked.

"No," Adrian said, and added with careful neutrality, "but he was entertaining a guest, and I thought it would be best if I did not intrude for the evening."

"But why should he mind if you joined them?" Lady Leyland said, not comprehending the more subtle meaning Adrian attempted to convey. "Most likely it is one of his stuffy friends from the Foreign Office, and he would probably be glad of the diversion."

"If it was, they probably had private matters to discuss, Mama," said Isobel, who had realized at once that Adrian had surprised Carlton while he was entertaining a lover.

Lady Leyland caught Adrian's faint, amused smile and the speaking look that Isobel directed at her, and finally she understood also. She blushed a little and said, "Oh! Very likely. I didn't think." She then recalled Adrian's request and assured him that she would be very happy to have a room made up for him. Privately she was concerned that Isobel and Adrian might be indiscreet and spend the night together in Isobel's room, but she needn't have worried; Adrian paid no visit to Isobel in the early hours of the morning.

The next Isobel saw him again was at breakfast. She was more than a little disappointed, but pride and the concern that perhaps she was a bit too eager for his embrace prevented her from going to him. She assured herself it could not mean that he was tiring of her already, but only that he was weary from making the journey to and from Stokes Hall on horseback in the space of only three days.

Immediately after breakfast Adrian was closeted with Lady Leyland in her sitting room, but he sought out Isobel a short while later, practicing on the pianoforte in the drawing room. This time Isobel, determined not to be the first to make advances, did not rush headlong into his arms. His smile was as warm and intimate as ever, but *he* did not make any effort to lift her from her seat to take her into his arms either. "I have spoken with lady Leyland, and we have come to an agreement that it might be best if I remained here at Leyland House until we are married," he said, explaining the purpose of his interview with her stepmother. "There is no enmity between Carlton and me, but neither of us were comfortable with the arrangement we had made, so I think he shall be as relieved as I am that I shan't be returning to stay with him again."

"I thought that you and Carlton had come to an understanding of sorts," she said, looking up at him.

Adrian shrugged and then sat at the edge of the seat with his back to the keyboard. They were almost but not quite touching, and Isobel looked down at her hands, still poised over the keys, to avoid his eyes, which she was certain would be able to read the longing in her own.

"He doesn't trust me," Adrian said bluntly. "It is in part my own fault for having lied to all of you when I came to Audswyck, and in part it may be that Simon's nonsense has had some effect on him after all. He guards his damned boxes like he expects me to pounce on them the moment his back is turned."

Isobel remembered her surprise that Carlton had seemed to listen to Simon's imaginings the day before. "Simon has been making up his stories against you again," she said.

"You sound concerned, my beauty," Adrian said, quick to hear a slightly doubtful note in her voice. "Has that young scamp convinced you as well as Carlton that I am really a desperate fellow?"

"Of course not," she said tartly, "but I wish we could be married and leave here." She turned a little to be able to see his face clearly. "I know I am foolish, but it seems as if all of our plans are going awry, and I am beginning to think that something may prevent us from being together."

Adrian stood and held out his hand to draw her from the seat as well. She went to him and finally was enfolded in his strong embrace. They kissed and murmured love to each other for several minutes until Adrian drew away from her and, with smiling mischief in his expression, put her firmly at arm's length. "There will be none of these improper goings-on, Miss Leyland," he said severely. "I have given your step-mama my promise that we would not court scandal by living in sin under her roof as a condition of my remaining here, and it is very wicked of you to tempt me so grievously."

Isobel laughed and blushed. "Mama never said such a thing to you!"

"Well, implied is more accurate, I suppose," he admitted, "but her politely couched 'suggestions' were really quite transparent." Seeing that Isobel's amusement was about to turn to indignation, he added quickly, "It will not be for very long, my dearest Bel, I promise you." He kissed her again and then put her aside with determination. "I think it would be wise if we are properly chaperoned from now on, or I shall never be able to keep my promise."

Isobel had mixed feelings about the bargain Adrian had struck with her stepmother. On the one hand, she had more of his company than when he had stayed with Carlton, but on the other she was a bit piqued that he seemed to be able to accept their physical separation quite easily while she was in torment to be so near to him and yet unable to hold him or kiss him or share with him the overwhelming pleasure he had taught her to expect whenever they made love.

Adrian told her privately that he intended to speak with the solicitor despite her stepmother's objections. But when he called the following day on Friday, he discovered that gentleman had been called away from town until the middle of the following week. "I think I am beginning to believe in your malevolent spirit," he told Isobel when he returned from the city. By this time she had no doubt of it.

Perhaps it was knowing that he would have to wait even longer to claim Isobel as his wife, but in the early hours of Tuesday morning, Adrian proved that his stoic control over his desire for her was not invincible.

Isobel had slept fitfully since going to bed, and she awoke with a start some time before two and nearly gasped when she perceived a shadowy figure just barely silhouetted in the faint moonlight coming through cracks in the draperies. In another moment she realized it was Adrian. He came over to the bed and sat beside her. "I have found out a sad truth about myself," he said in a rueful way. "My intentions are good, but my flesh is weak."

Isobel was awake but languorous, and she felt the first delicious tendrils of desire entwine about her. "Then you may find yourself on the road to hell," she countered. "If for no other reason than punishment for your wretched metaphors."

"Ultimately, I have no doubt of it," he said agreeably. "For now, though, I mean to enjoy heaven." He bent and kissed her with a barely constrained passion that made it obvious that his arousal was already full-blown.

He was still fully dressed, and she could just faintly

taste brandy in his mouth. She had the impression that he had been out and was just returning to the house, though she had no idea where he might go without friends. She could not prevent the comparison to Quentin, who was always at his most amorous when disguised. She wanted Adrian very much, but not like that. "You've been drinking," she said, unable to keep the accusation from her tone.

"I am not Quentin, Bel," he said quietly. "If I am drunk it is only with desire. Do you wish me to leave you to sleep?"

Isobel felt a little ashamed of her insinuation. She sat up and put her arms about his neck, drawing him near. "I wish to sleep, but with you."

Adrian needed no greater encouragement, and in a very short while they both lay naked between the sheets, entwined in each other's arms, whispering softly of their love and desire until sweet satisfaction left them at peace and finally to sleep.

Isobel did not expect to find Adrian still in her bed in the morning, and he was not. The morning was bright and gloriously sunny, and her mood was sunny to match. She was far too full of good feeling and energy to spend a quiet day in needlework or household chores with her stepmother and Kitty, and she dressed in her habit determined to ride that morning and to persuade Adrian to go with her, whatever risk there might be of encountering quizzes in the park.

Adrian was more than agreeable, and shortly they were trotting though the gates of Hyde Park. It was not cold, but there was a brisk autumn breeze, and they were in agreement that a good warming gallop would do them and their mounts a great deal of good. There were only a few other riders out at an early hour at this time of year, and there was no one to censure this unseemly behavior. Isobel doubted that anyone who observed Adrian on horseback would ever find anything to criticize about him. They came to a hedged area separating a more wooded portion of the park, and she held back to watch him take the hedge in perfect form. She was no mean horsewoman herself, and she followed his lead, but not, she knew, with his skill.

They returned to the promenade by more conventional means along the bridle path. There were more riders in the park now and several people on foot, and they decided it was time to return to Upper Mount Street.

It was on the street that they met up with Carlton. He hailed them and they trotted over to the side of the road to speak with him. Isobel thought he looked even more tired than the last time she had seen him. Worse, he looked haggard, as if he had some deep concern.

"I'm afraid I have grave news for you," Carlton said, addressing them both equally. "It is a matter of the utmost discretion and should not at all be discussed. But I think perhaps under the circumstances I should share it with you, trusting to your own discretion. I should not do so at all if it did not closely concern Adrian himself."

Isobel had difficulty curbing her impatience, but it was Adrian who said with unusual ruthlessness, "Cut line, Carl. We understand that no word of this is to pass our lips, but if you did not mean for us to know what this is all about, you would not have mentioned it in the first place."

Carlton regarded Adrian with cool dislike for a moment and said, "There is a small tavern on a side street about a quarter mile down this road. It's called the King's Horse. Ride on ahead of me and engage a private parlor for us. This is not a thing I care to discuss in the open street."

Adrian was plainly amused at such cloak-and-dagger

behavior, but he agreed, and Isobel, because she was curious and afraid Carlton might change his mind about telling them his news if she put his back up, went along without uttering the scathing comment that came to her lips. They were settled in the parlor and Adrian had ordered home brewed for himself and Carlton and lemonade for Isobel by the time that Carlton was shown into the room by a servant at the inn.

As soon as their refreshment had been brought and the door shut again, he finally came to the point. "Thomas Liddiard was taken into custody last night as an agent of espionage for the United States of America. He was arrested at the Clarendon."

"My God," Isobel said with an indrawn breath, her eyes flying to Adrian's.

Adrian was watching Carlton with a steady, unreadable expression. "I assume there is good evidence of his guilt?"

"Good enough," Carlton said repressively. "You knew him, I think, in the United States."

"We went to the same school," Adrian replied easily. "But perhaps you knew him also, Carl. I met him in company twice recently with your good friend Mr. Ames-Harding."

Isobel had no idea why this comment should make Carlton's color deepen and cause him to poker up and say with cold neutrality that he doubted he was acquainted with all the acquaintances of his friends.

"Just so," Adrian said with a brief smile over the rim of his tankard.

Isobel finally understood the insinuation in Carlton's query. "You can't for a moment think, Carl, that Adrian would have anything to do with spying for the United States? I can't believe you have permitted Simon with his absurd nonsensical stories to cause you to suspect Adrian of such a terrible thing."

"There was a second man, perhaps also an American agent, who slipped past the guard and escaped through a window off a corridor," he said with a flat inflection. "Liddiard has been persuaded to admit that much at least."

"And because of that you think it may have been Adrian?" she demanded with angry incredulity.

Carlton, looking directly at Adrian, said, "I think you were not at Leyland House last night."

Isobel was about to exclaim that this was false, but she recalled her impression that Adrian had been out of the house when he came to her. She had retired before both Adrian and Simon, who were playing billiards for imaginary pound points after they had taken tea with the ladies.

It was a long moment before Adrian replied, and Carlton said quietly, "You were seen last night near midnight at the Clarendon, cousin. It was going on one this morning when Liddiard was arrested."

Adrian raised his brows and his smile was sardonic. "Is this an official questioning, Carlton? Who saw me? No one knows me in London except ourselves."

"Were you there?"

"You believe I was."

"Don't fence with me, Adrian," Carlton said with sudden vehemence. "I am trying to do you a service. I would be ruined if it came to light that I had warned you. It is good fortune that I came across you in the street so soon, for I dare not call at Leyland House until this is settled, and I thought I should have to arrange a meeting in some other way. If you can manage to get out of the country before inquiries can go any further, I think I can promise, with the assistance of Castlereagh, who will do what he can for Grandfather's sake, to see to it that your activities aren't questioned further."

Isobel felt as if all her internal organs had turned

to ice. She was reasonably certain that if Carlton's information had been false, Adrian would have laughed at him the way that he had at Simon's attempts to turn him into the villain of his imaginings. In the worst of her forebodings, she had never imagined anything as horrible as this occurring. She was not certain how she managed to find her voice, but she heard herself saying, "It had to be Quentin who told you that he saw Adrian last night, for who else could it be? How could you listen to him when you know he has every reason to harm Adrian if he can? That is worse than believing Simon, Carl, for at least his stories can do no real harm."

Carlton looked genuinely shocked at this. "Quentin would not lie about such a matter as this, even to revenge himself on Adrian. He is not that base, Isobel."

"He is and he did lie," she said vehemently. "Adrian was with me last night, and he did not leave me until first light."

"Isobel, don't involve yourself in this mess," Carlton said urgently. "There is more than what Quentin has said that leads me to such a dire conclusion."

"What more?" This sharp demand came from Adrian.

But Carlton ignored Adrian now and addressed himself to convincing Isobel that this was not just the spite of a jilted lover but a real and very serious charge. "There were documents found in Liddiard's possession," he said reluctantly. "Haven't you wondered how it is I came to be involved in this at all? They were papers that directed certain classified information to me alone for dissemination. It wasn't a matter I needed to deal with immediately, but rather a detailing of political strategy for the coming months in the war with the United States, so I cannot say when exactly they went missing, though I know I had them the day before Adrian left my lodgings for Dorset. I keep my dispatch cases locked when I am not engaged in work, but a clever man—which I credit you as being, cousin—would make easy work of finding a means of overcoming such a minor obstacle."

"Then you are in the suds too, cousin," Adrian said dryly. "If I was arrested and tried, it is not just a matter of scandal tarnishing the name of Renville, it is the end of your promising career. And, in fact, you are astonishingly careless of your papers, Carl. I think I was not the only one who might have walked off with whatever information one pleased."

"I shall come out of it," Carlton insisted, "you shall not. Your father was an Englishman, and you would be hung as a traitor without much hope of being returned to America in a trade of agents. The most that will be said of me is that I was not careful enough, and I shall receive no more than a reprimand from my superiors."

"Carlton, stop this, at once," Isobel said, her fright growing with each word spoken. She was so upset she could not remain in her chair. "You are terrifying me. You are despicable and so is Quentin to do this to Adrian."

"The truth is the truth, Isobel," Carlton said implacably.

"It is your truth, Carlton," she said. "I have no idea what the truth is for me." She fled the room on these words and did not even send for her horse to be brought round, but went directly to the mews behind the small inn, heedless of the heavy skirts of her habit trailing in the mud and dirt of the yard.

An ostler had gone to fetch her horse by the time that Adrian caught up to her. When he found her, she was taking short, deep breaths as a means of concentrating a fragile control on her desire to sob unrestrainedly. When he put his hand on her shoulder to turn her to face him, he felt that she was shaking inside.

"Isobel, there is no need to be so upset," he said softly behind her. "I would never become involved in anything like spying. Carlton, or perhaps he and Quentin between them, have hit on a way to be rid of me for good, if they can frighten me into leaving the country. We were together when Liddiard was taken."

Isobel said nothing, and he said in a voice of absolute astonishment, "Isobel? You can't tell me you doubt me in this?"

"It was after one-thirty when you came to my room," she said in a very small voice that even his excellent hearing nearly failed to distinguish. "I had awakened before you came into the room, and I heard the clock at the end of the hall strike the half hour."

"Isobel, what is this? I startled you awake when I came into the room."

The ostler brought her horse, and she stepped up on the mounting block without replying. Tears bathed her cheeks when she raised her head to look at him, and her lower lip was held between her teeth to keep it from quivering. He made to put his hand on her bridle, but she jerked her horse's head away from him, causing the startled animal to shy. She held her seat and applied her heel to its flank, leaving the mews at a perilous speed.

But if Isobel had hope that she would escape Adrian, she underestimated his tenacity. She went directly to her room and rang for Dolly to help her out of her habit, telling her to inform the staff that she had the migraine and was not to be disturbed by anyone, not even her stepmother or any of the others in the house.

Dolly exclaimed over the mud clinging to the hem of the amber velvet habit and put it aside to be taken to the kitchen to be brushed after the dirt had dried. Isobel's petticoats had also been removed and she stood in her shift, about to put on her dressing gown, when Adrian came into the room without warning.

Dolly saw the dismay in her mistress's expression, and she said bravely, "Miss Isobel has the headache, Mr. Renville, and is about to lie down."

Adrian made no comment, but he took the startled dresser by the arm and led her out of the room, protesting but not daring to struggle, and firmly shut the door against her.

"How dare you abuse my servant?" Isobel said, finding refuge in outrage. "Leave me, Adrian, I don't want to see you now."

"Do you think I was working with Liddiard as a spy, Isobel? Answer that and I promise you I shall give you all the peace you desire."

The only other time she had witnessed his anger had been against Quentin. Now it was directed at her, and she felt it as a palpable force and knew it was dangerous to court. But she would not back away from what she knew to be the truth. She had found strength and self-esteem in facing the disapproval of her family for the choices she made; she would never return to accepting the unacceptable for fear of the consequences. It was ironic that falling in love with Adrian had made her strong and now that courage would be used to condemn him, though she wished with all her heart that it needn't be so.

"I don't know what I think," she said. "But I know you left the house last night after I had gone to bed. Where were you?"

"At the Clarendon, though I never set eyes on Thomas Liddiard. I had no idea he was there. Isobel, I barely knew the man."

Isobel was nearly floored by his admission and heard little else. "And then you escaped capture and came back here. You came to me so that I could say exactly as I did to Carlton, that you were with me last night and provide you with an unassailable alibi. It wasn't longing for me that made you break your promise to Mama, it was expediency."

"No. It wasn't that way at all."

"It was precisely that way," she said, unmoved by his denial. "Not even Quentin would have used me so cruelly to serve his own base purpose."

This was more than Adrian could swallow. "I have no need to hide behind a woman. If I was engaged in espionage, the last thing I would do would be to involve or endanger the woman I love."

"Do you love me?" Isobel said bitterly. "Or is that just another pretense? How can you expect me to believe anything you say when you do nothing but lie?"

"Dear God," he said explosively as anger overtook him again. "I have not lied to you or to anyone, Isobel. What I did was nothing more than a harmless hoax, and even then I told the truth but led you to the interpretation that you already wished to believe. You question my love for you? How strong is your faith in me if you believe the worst of me at the word of my cousins, who you know wish me no good? What is it really, Isobel? Have you come to realize that if they drive me from England, you will have to leave your family and everything you value behind if you stay with me? It is easier to convince yourself that I am unworthy of your love than to admit that you are unworthy of mine."

Isobel's overwrought emotions were near the breaking point. She did not want to cry in front of him, but she could not completely choke back her tears. "Damn you," she said on a sob. "Leave me. Please, God, I may never have to see you again."

In spite of his hard words to her, he looked stunned

by this. "You don't mean that, Isobel," he said, his voice becoming quiet and devoid of emotion.

"I do," she shouted, heedless of whether or not anyone might now hear their argument. "Get out! You are more base than Quentin could ever be."

Even while she vented her anger and feelings of betrayal against him, some small voice inside her cried out that she was going too far. Their eyes held for a long moment, and then he turned and left her without another word. Isobel stood where she was until she shut the door quietly behind him.

The tears that she had been unable to control when Adrian was with her now deserted her. She felt utterly wretched, and assurance that she had done the right thing failed her as well. Was he a spy? She wasn't even certain that mattered to her, but that he had used her for his purpose was more than she could bear.

Quentin had said that he loved her, but his actions had said otherwise. Adrian told her that nothing in life mattered to him more than she did, but he would make love to her for the sake of an alibi. The self-confidence and strong spirit that had carried her through so much in the past few weeks seemed to desert her, and for the first time since she had met him, Isobel wished that Adrian had never come into her life to make her see a vista of happiness that was as much an illusion as the fantasy she had had of Quentin, as a man he never was.

Chapter 15

As little as Isobel wished for solitude, even less did she want to have to pretend that she was anything other than wretched in front of her stepmother or Simon or Kitty. She continued the pretense of her headache, and Kitty, a migraine sufferer herself, tried to offer her some of her own favorite remedies, only to find herself quite brusquely rebuffed by Dolly, who had reason to know that no physical remedy was likely to ease the pain her mistress felt.

That first day was one of unremittent anguish for Isobel, but gradually her misery evolved into numbness, and the next day she woke, dressed, ate, conversed with the others in the house, and went to bed again like a mechanical device rather than a flesh-and-blood woman. Finally, on Friday, some feeling began to return to her, and like a limb numbed in sleep, the first pangs were painful.

Neither her dresser nor anyone else in the house brought Isobel the news, but she knew, even before she left her room for the first time, that Adrian was gone. Now that she had rejected him, he had no cause to remain in England, whatever became of Carlton's suspicions. Without her safety to concern him, it was likely that he would not wait to make connections to find direct passage, but would go to Portugal and perhaps from there to South America.

She had sent him away, and yet her eyes filled with

tears at the thought of Adrian continuing on with his life without her. It was distasteful to her to think that he might have used his connections with his father's family to garner information to send to the United States, but for all that his father was an Englishman, he had been raised as an American, and it was not wonderful that his loyalties would be to the country of his birth.

She could forgive him that, even if Carlton thought him a traitor. She would even have lied for him willingly to save him if he had not been with her that night. But it was unbearable to know that he had deliberately and cold-bloodedly professed that he had come to her bed because he needed her so desperately when in fact he had been moved by a far baser motive: saving his own skin. If all the subterfuge he had engaged in since his arrival in England were to that same purpose, then she could not trust even one time when he had sworn that he loved her.

But was that reality, or what Carlton, and no doubt Quentin as well, wished her to believe? What had really happened that night? Adrian had admitted being at the Clarendon but not why, and she had been too upset even to listen to any logical explanation, let alone think to ask him if he had one.

More than anything, she had to set her own mind at rest. So tumultuous were her thoughts as her belief in Adrian ebbed and returned that she feared she would drive herself to madness in time wondering if Adrian had betrayed her love or if she had betrayed his by refusing to believe him.

Isobel had to speak to her stepmother the day after Adrian left them, apparently with little explanation of his own, about what had happened, but she said nothing of Mr. Liddiard or Carlton's accusations at the King's Horse, only that she and Adrian had quarreled in a manner that made reconciliation impossible and that she believed he had returned to America. She left it to her stepmother to say what she would to Kitty and Simon, but it was apparent that Lady Leyland made them realize that Isobel was suffering for her loss, for they left her in peace and made no comment at all to her about Adrian or his abrupt departure from Leyland House.

It was on that same Friday afternoon that Quentin called to see her again. She had hoped that after she and Adrian were married, Quentin would come to accept her decision and they could resume at least their relationship as cousins, and perhaps eventually as friends. But if he had been the instrument of the destruction of her happiness, she thought she would never forgive him.

Quentin was glancing through a copy of the *Sporting News,* which Simon had left in the room, when she entered the gold saloon. He closed the paper and folded it with care as he turned to face her. He met her halfway into the room, taking her hand and bowing over it in a formal way he never did in private. "Thank you for seeing me, Isobel. You must wish me at Jericho."

Isobel gave him a small smile. "I shall if you mean to say the same sort of things to me that you did when we last met," she said with frankness. He still held her hand, and though his manner was not loverlike, she thought it prudent to gently pull away from him.

He resisted for a moment and then let her go. "I beg your pardon, Bel, for any distress I may have caused you." He paused, seeing in her expression that there was to be no easy pardon for the mistakes he had made. "If this is a poor apology, I cannot help it, Bel. I know there are no adequate words to ask your forgiveness."

She saw contrition in his eyes, but she was not certain it was sincere. He made the picture of a man who wished to be thought contrite, though she acknowledged that her suspicions of him might unfavorably color her observations. "You must be more specific, Quentin," she said plainly but not combatively. "I am not certain which offense it is that you regret."

He was surprised and not pleased by this. A flash of annoyance crossed his features. "I had no idea you had counted so many," he replied, his smile rueful but with a hint of asperity in his voice. "I beg your pardon, Isobel, for the things that I said to you when last we met and for what happened between us at Audswyck. I truly never meant to ravish you, and I'm sorry if I became impatient and rough and you believed yourself in danger from me. I would never do anything to hurt you, Isobel, believe that of me, please."

Even determined to apologize, he could not quite bring himself to admit his culpability. "I can't believe it, Quentin. Not because you tried to rape me at Audswyck; I wish only to forget that horrible night. But you have hurt me in another, far more painful way by doing your utmost to destroy Adrian. I think you have finally succeeded, and for that I can never forgive you."

"What the devil is that supposed to mean?" Quentin said, his brows snapping together. "Whatever has become of Adrian, he has only himself to blame." He took her hand before she could prevent it and held it in a strong clasp. "I haven't come to quarrel with you, Isobel, but to mend our fences. I know I may be precipitate, but I hope that in time I can convince you that the devotion you gave me for so many years was not misplaced."

Isobel regarded him incredulously. She supposed she misunderstood him. "Are you suggesting that we might after all be married, Quentin?"

His smile was crooked, and in the past it would have tugged woefully at her heart. "I have not dared to hope to that extent yet. I know I need to rehabilitate myself in your eyes."

"You know that I am in love with Adrian," she said baldly. "That I have been his mistress since before we left Audswyck."

Though his lips still smiled, the expression in his eyes hardened. "I know that you have been seduced by a very clever man. My mistake was that I allowed myself to be fooled along with everyone else by his absurd exterior. I only wish I had recognized him for the devil he is. But now that the truth is out, Bel, you must see that he is unworthy of your love."

His damning of Adrian had the effect of making Isobel even more inclined to believe that she had been foolishly hasty to condemn Adrian herself on the words of men who had every cause to see him ruined. "Why are you doing this, Quentin?" she said harshly. "I find it hard to believe that a man like you would still want me knowing that I have given myself willingly to Adrian."

"You belong to me, Isobel," he said, this time attempting to draw her into his arms. "I'll be damned myself if I let him have you."

Isobel successfully eluded his grasp, though his fingers pinched her arm in trying to take hold of her. She moved away to put a distance between them and also to come closer to the bell pull in case she needed assistance, which she now began to fear she might. "I belong to myself," she said. "Is that why you told Carlton that you saw Adrian at the Clarendon the night that Mr. Liddiard was arrested?"

"It was the truth. I was at the Clarendon myself at a private party for a friend of mine, and I saw Adrian going into one of the public rooms. I thought it odd until I heard from a friend at the Horse Guards that an agent from the United States had been taken into custody at the hotel that same night."

"And from such paltry evidence you and Carlton have concluded that he must be a confederate of Mr. Liddiard?"

"No sensible person could believe in such an astonishing number of coincidences, Isobel. Just think of it," he entreated her. "Adrian and Thomas Liddiard are both Americans with connections to the English aristocracy, they admit they were at school together, they came to England only weeks apart, each one just happens to have family in the same neighborhood, each returned to London on the same day, and Adrian was at the Clarendon, where Liddiard was staying on the very night that he was arrested and a second man escaped."

Put so plainly into words, the evidence, though still circumstantial at best, did appear damning. Isobel felt her heart sink, but the desire to defend Adrian that Quentin's animosity provoked was still strong. "Just because it seems impossible doesn't mean it isn't the simple truth that it is nothing more than a remarkable series of coincidences. You know such things sometimes happen."

Quentin's responding smile was condescending, but before he could respond to this, Meritt knocked discreetly at the door and entered the room. "I beg your pardon, Miss Leyland. Mr. Carlton is here and insists that he speak with you at once. I have told him you—"

Carlton, who had no intention of being denied, pushed past the butler and came into the room. Isobel saw his face and quickly dismissed the servant. Carlton walked past her and confronted his brother. "Have you taken complete leave of your senses, Quentin?" he demanded angrily. "You may hate Adrian as much as you like with my blessing, but you go too far when you are willing to drag the name of Renville into the mud to crush him."

Giving Quentin no opportunity for explanation or

defense, he turned to Isobel and said, "Where is Adrian? We have to get him out of here as quickly as we can."

Isobel regarded him, bemused and alarmed. "He isn't here, Carlton. What has happened?"

"Do you know where he has gone?" Carlton said, his urgency almost manic in comparison to his usual calm demeanor. "We may have only minutes before they come to arrest him. Once that happens, I can't help him any longer without ruining myself in the effort."

"Arrest him!" Isobel felt as if she had received a blow. "Why would they arrest him? Based on coincidence and innuendo? Surely a Renville would not be treated like a common criminal."

Carlton gave a short laugh. "Why don't you tell her, brother? Or shall I?" Quentin said nothing, though he glowered at Carlton as though he wished he might horsewhip him on the spot. Carlton for once was not at all intimidated by his elder brother. He turned to Isobel and said, "Quentin told his friend Freddy Gilbraith about seeing Adrian at the Clarendon, and very likely he found other means of raising suspicions. I think you know who Gilbraith's uncle is, the position he holds at the Horse Guard, and how deep and violent was the rivalry that once existed between him and our grandfather. There is little Lord Bertram wouldn't do to smash the house of Renville and see our name expunged from all political power and influence."

"You greatly exaggerate the matter, Carl," Quentin said stringently. "I suppose I may have let something slip to Freddy when I was in my cups, but I never supposed he would have a damned loose tongue."

"You counted on it," Isobel said, her eyes filling with furious tears. "For you it wasn't enough for Adrian to be driven away, you wanted him disgraced and hung as a traitor."

"No," said a voice from the doorway. "Quentin wouldn't do that." Simon, who had obviously been eavesdropping for some minutes, came into the room. He was visibly upset. "They can't hang Adrian simply because he was at the Clarendon that night, can they?" he said imploringly to the room at large. "Even if he stole some papers from Carlton, it isn't as if he would be able to get them to the United States very readily. If all the missing papers could be returned, they'd let him go and just banish him from England, wouldn't they?"

"Adrian is Uncle Francis's son and Grandfather's heir," Carlton informed him. "He'll be tried as an Englishman and hung as a traitor."

Simon looked as if he might be sick. "But he really hasn't done anything. I-I took those papers from your dispatch case, Carl."

His words produced a stunned silence that was finally broken by Quentin. "You did what?"

"I stole them. I can prove it because I still have the papers. I did it the day that Bel and I went to Carlton's lodgings to ask him to put Adrian up for a few nights. I got the idea because of all the fuss that was made when Carlton accidentally misplaced his papers at Audswyck. I thought that if Carlton suspected Adrian was a spy, he could get him deported back to the United States and then Isobel would see she'd made a terrible mistake and would go back to Quentin and we could all be comfortable again."

Tears filled the young man's eyes by the end of this recital, and, embarrassed, he rubbed them away with his coat sleeve like the boy he had not yet outgrown. Isobel sat on the nearest chair as if her legs would no longer hold her.

It was then Carlton's turn to amaze them. "I know you did, Simon, I missed the documents almost as soon as you had left that day. But you took only copies, and the information they contained was neither classified nor very important. I thought I might as well let you enjoy your game. The documents found with Liddiard were of a later date and far more serious in nature."

"I still don't think Adrian is responsible," Simon blurted out. "He came here and hoaxed us, made fools of us. I thought he meant to cut Quentin out of his inheritance, and he did cut him out with Isobel. I thought I should hate him, but I couldn't. He's a very decent fellow, Carl, if you bother to get to know him. You never would have thought this of him if it hadn't been for the stupid stories I made up about him."

"Well," said Quentin with a short laugh, "it would seem the Savage's seduction of the Leylands is now complete. What I have done, Isobel, I have done for your own good. When the Savage is tried, convicted, and hung for the traitor he is, perhaps you will recognize your folly. It is even possible that I shall still be of a mind to forgive you and take you back, though as a betting man I warn you the odds will shorten the longer you delay." With these audacious words he made them a perfunctory bow and left them.

Simon was the only one who seemed surprised or upset by Quentin's arrogance. Carlton simply addressed Isobel, saying quietly, "Where is Adrian, Isobel?"

"I have no idea," she admitted miserably. "We quarreled after we spoke with you, and he left the house soon after that. I presume he intends to leave England. He would be foolish to stay with so much effort being made toward his ruin."

"I think you know what he plans, Isobel," Carlton persisted. "I wish you would tell me where you think he is. I could warn him of his imminent arrest and keep him out of sight until he can get away from England."

Isobel didn't deny that she had guessed where he might have gone. "I'll go to him myself," she said.

"Don't be absurd, Isobel," Carlton said crossly. "You can't go after a man who is wanted for crimes against the government on your own. Suppose you are mistaken about him and he proves to be dangerous. I see you mean to be stubborn," he said with a sigh when she did not respond. "I hope you don't end being the instrument of his destruction for your lack of trust in me."

Isobel recognized that she would waste precious time trying to convince Carlton that she had to go after Adrian herself. If there was any chance at all that Adrian was still in England, she knew that she had to find him and speak with him. Simon's confession had been the last thing in convincing her that she had dreadfully wronged him, and he had to know that she realized this. If he would listen to her, she would beg his forgiveness and do all in her power never to doubt him again.

Then there was the matter of their future together. She refused to believe that matters were as dire as Carlton and Quentin believed them to be. It was true Lord Bertram would relish seeing the earl's heir, the son of Audwin's own black sheep son, bringing down the proud nobleman, and irreparably tarnishing the name of Renville, but he would only succeed if a crime was proved against Adrian. Even though the earl had disowned his grandson in a fit of rage, she could not believe that he would not do what he could to save Adrian and prove his innocence rather than allow his old enemy to wreak such a terrible revenge on the name of Renville.

Carlton stayed only a few minutes longer to try to convince his distraught younger cousin that nothing he said or did had resulted in Adrian's being suspected or charged with espionage. It was enough time for

Isobel to formulate at least the outline of a plan of action.

Carlton took both her hands in leavetaking. "I know you must be in anguish, my dear, and I truly wish there was something I could say or do to ease your unhappiness. You won't believe me now, but in time you will heal."

As soon as he was out of the room, Isobel hastened to shut the door and addressed Simon. "Do you believe Carlton and Quentin that Adrian is a spy?"

Simon shook his head, his expression one of painful uncertainty. "I wish I knew. Whatever Carlton says, I know I put the idea in their heads in the first place. When I saw what a first-rate horseman he was, I knew he had made game of me at the Duck and Drake, and I only thought to pay him back a little at first. And then when you"—Simon broke off, blushed, and turned to look out the window—"when you went with him that night at the inn coming to London, I did mean to make trouble for him. I didn't think it through, I know. I thought he would just be sent away or become frightened and leave on his own."

"Do you have enough doubt that he is guilty to wish to help him?"

Simon looked doubtful. "What could I do, Bel?"

"You can go to Audswyck and see *Grand-père*," she said, hoping she had the power to convince Simon of the necessity of his intervention to save Adrian, over what would undoubtedly be his trepidation about facing and confessing his own sins to the earl. "Tell him everything that has occurred, your part and Quentin's part in this, and what Carlton believes is going to be the outcome. Let him think what he will about Adrian's guilt or innocence; the important thing is that he knows it is Lord Bertram who wishes to hurt him by seeing that Adrian is tried and hung as a traitor if the charges against him are proven."

"Grandfather would never listen to me, Isobel," Simon said miserably. "He thinks I'm little more than a scrubby schoolboy, and he might even think I am just making up stories again."

"Then prove that you are not, Simon," she said firmly. "Make him listen and above all things, be sure that he knows that Lord Bertram is behind this. I know he has had some means in the past of preventing Bertram from venting his malice against any of us. Perhaps he may still be able to hold Bertram in check. It may prove that even if *Grand-père* doesn't wish to help Adrian for his sake or even the sake of the name of Renville, he will do so rather than let his old enemy do this terrible thing."

Simon only vaguely understood Lord Bertram's part in what was happening and said so. "You must come with me and talk to *Grandfather* even if you did quarrel with him before you left. He'll listen to you better than to me, and you know so much more about it all than I do."

"I shall be in Dorset," Isobel replied. "No, don't argue with me. I mean to go to Stokes, and that is the end of it. Adrian must be there, Simon. Where else would he go? Come, we can't waste any time. We must leave as quickly as we may before Mama and Kitty return home from their visit to Great-aunt Martha. I feel like a wretch leaving Mama only a note to tell her not to worry about us, but I dare not commit more to paper, and I don't want to have to explain what we are doing to her in person, for I know she will try to prevent me from going to Adrian."

"What if Adrian isn't there, Isobel?"

"He must be," she insisted and then left him to do what was needed.

Simon, though with considerable trepidation and misgiving, set out as his sister requested, on horseback, to cut the time of his journey to Audswyck. He was instructed to come to her in Bournemouth to the Three Bells, which she recalled was the name of the inn that Adrian told her he had gone to when he first arrived in England, the moment he had finished with the earl so that she might know the outcome of his efforts. By the time Simon was mounted and trotting along the road that would lead him out of London, his ever active imagination, resigned to the task at hand, was conjuring an ending to this story that cast himself as the hero of the piece.

Isobel also made her escape before Lady Leyland returned to Upper Mount Street, but not before there were other callers to Leyland House. She had ordered her mother's traveling carriage made ready and had packed two bandboxes with the barest necessities for her journey. She was tying the ribbons of her bonnet under her chin when Meritt came into her dressing room himself to inform her that there were military gentlemen downstairs who wished a word with Mr. Renville and appeared disinclined to believe the butler's claim that he had left the house with no indication that he meant to return two days previously.

Isobel, her heart in her mouth, went down to the front hall, a footman trailing behind her with her bandboxes. There were three soldiers in the hall, and the senior of these came forward, made Isobel an elegant bow and introduced himself as Lieutenant Bennet.

"My superiors wish to have a few words with Mr. Adrian Renville, Miss Leyland," he said when he came to the point, "and we have been given to understand that he has been staying in this house since his arrival in London."

This was not precisely correct, but Isobel did not care to come to points. "Yes, but he has gone. He left Wednesday afternoon."

"And where has he gone, if I may ask, Miss Leyland?"

"To Yorkshire, I believe," she said, choosing it for its great distance from Bournemouth. "He has friends there, Americans like himself who have chosen exile because of their strong royalist beliefs. The name is Hopewell, or something very like it."

She caught him exchanging an uncertain glance with one of his underlings and thought that he must be very inexperienced as a soldier to give himself away so readily. She knew that she had routed him and needed only take a strong hand to avoid being detained herself.

"You are certain Mr. Renville is not in the house?" the lieutenant said, his insistence an attempt perhaps to redeem himself.

Isobel sighed, rolled her eyes heavenward, and then laughed. "Meritt told me you seemed to think he was lying. Search all you like if you think we are hiding him somewhere. But why should we? He hasn't committed any crime, has he?" she added innocently.

"I-I couldn't say, Miss Leyland," the lieutenant said, uncomfortable facing this poised and coolly elegant young woman. He was not born to a life of privilege like so many of his fellow officers, but had advanced on his own merit. He had no instructions from his superiors about searching a grand house like Leyland House, and he would not dare to do it on his own authority. "You were about to leave?" he asked, trying a different tactic. "May I ask where you are going and if you travel alone?"

"I am going to visit my aunt who is sick," Isobel replied dutifully. "She lives near Bristol, and yes, I am traveling alone. My maid has come down with a putrid sore throat." She hoped he would not be sufficiently conversant with the customs of her class to know that in that case another female servant would have taken the maid's place.

"Would you mind if we just have a look in the carriage, miss?" he said in a last effort to be as thorough as he dared. Her lack of concern and complete self-confidence had all but convinced him that she spoke the truth.

"Not at all," Isobel said with her most captivating smile.

Of course, the chagrined young officer found nothing in the carriage and was forced into retreat to await further instructions. Isobel devoutly hoped it would not include another visit to Leyland House to alarm her stepmother. Several minutes later she was herself underway. She instructed the coachman to head north out of the city in case the soldiers had watched to see her direction, but once they neared the Great North Road, she changed her instructions and bade him to take her southwest to Bournemouth.

Adrian had little expectation of finding his friend Sir James at Stokes Hall when he returned to Dorset. The housekeeper at the hall had been certain he was not expected for at least another fortnight and that was only a few days ago. There was no point in going to the hall without Sir James in residence, and it was a rather obvious place to look if any wished to find him.

He did not seriously expect that he would be hunted as a spy after he had left Leyland House, but neither was he careless of the trail that he left on his journey from London. He believed that Carlton was deliberately trying to link him to Thomas Liddiard in the hope of driving him from England, and he didn't know to what lengths his cousin would go to accomplish this. The motive for this had at first eluded him, but Carlton himself had inadvertently supplied his reason, or rather, he had given Adrian the clue he needed and Adrian's quick mind had supplied the rest.

Adrian scarcely knew Thomas Liddiard, but he realized himself that there was a remarkable concurrence between his own recent activities and circumstance and those of Mr. Liddiard, which, if it were detailed to him concerning someone other than himself, he undoubtedly would have had trouble believing it to be no more than happenstance. It was a particular bit of ill luck that had taken him to the Clarendon that night, the only night he had ventured out on his own since returning to London from Audswyck, and Madam Fate was quite plainly toying with him to have seen to it that Quentin should be there as well to observe him.

He could understand completely that Carlton might choose to believe the worst of him and that Quentin would do what he could to paint him as black as possible. It was expected under the circumstance and, to some degree, accepted. The only word to describe the emotion he felt about Isobel's refusal to believe him was heartsick. But this was now, two days later. In the beginning he had felt only a cold, biting anger and a feeling that the love he had offered her had been betrayed. This was what had moved him to leave Leyland House so impetuously and had decided him not to fight his cousins but to leave England for good instead. It had not even mattered to him if he was not able to return directly to the United States. To remove himself from the source of his pain required only distance.

It was only logical that he would return to Dorset. He wanted to see his friend again before he left, and this was the only port with which he had familiarity. Once again he chose to ride rather than hire a carriage, and he went by a circuitous route, using his superb sense of direction to guide him along some less used roads and asking directions when the opportunity arose to be certain he was on a steady course. He spent Wednesday and Thursday night in small, out-of-the-way inns that normally catered only to local trade, and it was late Friday morning, at about the same time as Quentin was announced at Leyland House, that he reached the turnoff for Stokes Hall.

His intention had been to go on to Bournemouth and to put up at one of the lesser-known inns such as the Green Man, where he had stayed until Sir James had taken him away to Stokes Hall as his guest. But he paused at the entrance of the long drive to Stokes. The gates were open, and the road and surrounding area were completely deserted. On impulse he turned his job horse onto the drive, but a little beyond it he found a path through the wood surrounding the walls and took this rather than continuing on toward the house.

Isobel wished that she could ride to Bournemouth as well. But for an unescorted female, over such a distance, it would have been foolhardy even though she was an excellent horsewoman. Instead she rattled along the roads in her stepmother's well-sprung carriage, with a guard and two outriders, traveling at a pace the coachman considered safest for his charge, and chafing at the distance still left to her with every long mile covered.

It was early Sunday morning when she reached Stokes Hall and quickly learned both that Sir James had not returned and that Adrian had not come to the hall again to look for him. She then went on to Bournemouth and the Three Bells. The landlady might have looked askance at a young and lovely woman traveling with only the protection of servants, but the landlord was nearby when she gave her name and asked if Mr. Renville might be staying at the inn.

"Which Mr. Renville might that be, miss?" he asked, his curiosity piqued.

"Mr. Adrian Renville. He is my cousin and has been staying with the family at Audswyck Chase, the principal seat of the earl of Audwin, who is our grandfather. I know he had business in Bournemouth, and I believe he took a room here before when he first arrived from America a number of weeks ago."

"Ah, that Mr. Renville," said the landlord. "No, miss, I've not seen him. You're mistaken about him being one of my guests back then, though I know well who the young gentlemen is that you ask for. I was full up and he went along to the Green Man, a mile or so beyond the town. Happen he might have gone back there again."

Isobel ordered a room for herself, a private parlor, and accommodations for her mother's servants. She received directions from the landlord and thanked him and then went on to the Green Man, but Adrian had not been seen there either. She decided then to return to the Three Bells, from which base she could send one of the outriders to try the other inns and boardinghouses. She did not suppose that finding Adrian would present any great difficulty, for where else would he be if not in another of the inns?

It was near the end of the afternoon when the young groom that she had sent to seek Adrian returned to the private parlor she had hired with the unhappy information that he had not been able to discover any evidence that Mr. Renville was in Bournemouth.

"But he must be," Isobel cried out in frustration. She knew her stepmother's servants must think very peculiar things about her for this unescorted journey and her search for Adrian, but with so much at stake she didn't care for such things. The only thing that mattered at all to her was finding Adrian before Lieutenant Bennet, or whoever might be deputized in his stead in Dorset, should do so. "Are you certain that you have gone to every inn, hotel, and boarding-house?"

"Begging your pardon, miss," ventured the groom. "But Bournemouth isn't no village, and people don't know who Mr. Renville might be by sight. If he was wishful not to let people know he was here, he could just give another name and no one the wiser."

Isobel had thought this too, and with more cause to believe it possible. "Very well," she said, concluding the interview with a sigh. "I shall manage on my own from here."

Isobel had little to occupy her but her thoughts, and since she could not escape these or the constant recrimination with which she teased herself, she thought she might at least enjoy what was a fine day in the invigorating salt air. There was also the thought in the back of her mind that luck might be on her side and she would come across Adrian on her own.

This she failed to do, but Adrian was with her in her thoughts the entire hour that she walked through the streets and along the shore. She recalled again and again every significant thing that had passed between them in the time since they had met, fallen in love, and parted so abruptly. And it was in recalling their conversations that she remembered something he had said to her only days before, and suddenly she knew precisely where she would find him.

She did not bother to return to the Three Bells to change, for she had brought no habit with her and her traveling dress would do as well as any other she had brought for riding. It took her only minutes to find a livery stable, and only a few more after that to conclude her business there. Conscious of leaving a trail herself, she did not ask for directions cross-country to Stokes Hall until she was well away from the center of the town. Less than an hour's ride later, she halted her horse at the edge of a break in the dense wood on the Stokes property. Directly ahead of her, looking deserted but not in disrepair, stood the squat, stone gamekeeper's cottage.

Chapter 16

Adrian watched Isobel approach the cottage with mixed feelings. One part of him wanted to rejoice, for he could only suppose that she had taken the trouble to come after him and find him because she realized that she loved him and needed to be with him no matter who or what tried to come between them. Another part was still bitter that she had been so ready to reject him and believe the lies and innuendos against him. It gave him no satisfaction to know that she loved him unconditionally if she believed him capable of the base design she had accused him of when they had quarreled. He didn't want to believe it, but he even wondered if Isobel was a decoy, sent to find him and take him off guard so that he could be captured.

He came out of the cottage when she was only a few yards away. Isobel pulled up her horse when she saw him. She saw his cool, steady, unsmiling regard and felt dismay. She touched her horse's flanks with her heel and continued toward him. "I hoped I would find you here," she said, smiling in spite of his cool welcome. "I didn't think you would mind the company of a few squirrels and field mice."

The grave look in his eyes was slowly replaced by the laughter she knew so well and which was so dear to her. "They were delicious," he responded. "Are you alone?"

Isobel supposed she deserved his suspicion and did not take offense. "Yes. I've come to warn you."

He took hold of her horse's bridle. "Have you? Come inside, then. If I am to be hunted, I would as soon not make an easy target here in the clearing." When she dismounted, he sent her inside and led her horse to a shed behind the cottage where his own horse was housed.

Isobel was surprised by what she found inside. It was a simple one-room cottage with a sleeping loft above the rear half of the room. It was neither dirty nor unfurnished, though what furniture there was looked homemade and ancient. On the well-scrubbed table was a corked half-full bottle of red wine, a half-loaf of dark bread, a heel of cheese, and some fruit. There was no fire in the hearth and the air was chill in the cottage, but wool carriage robe, which she imagined he used for warmth at night, lay folded on a wooden settle near the back wall. If there was a bed and if it was usable, it was in the loft, she supposed.

Adrian soon joined her. He offered her some wine and apologized that they had to share the same glass. "I wasn't expecting company, you know," he said with his quick smile. "I gather I may expect more of it if I remain in the neighborhood? It would seem I have mistaken Carlton; I thought he was just trying to rid himself and the family of an embarrassment and did not wish me any real harm."

"It was Quentin who saw to that," Isobel said bitterly. "He wanted his revenge on you, and he has had it in full." She told him of Quentin's visit, of Carlton's belief that Adrian would be arrested, and finally of Lieutenant Bennet's coming to Leyland House.

When she was done, Adrian let out his breath slowly. "There is nothing for it, then," he said. "I must leave England as soon as I can. I haven't even the luxury of waiting for Jamie to return to Stokes Hall.

There isn't much hope of direct passage to the United States, but I might make it to South America." He laughed shortly. "Who knows, I might make the acquaintance of your father after all, if I end up in Brazil."

"It isn't that desperate yet," she hastened to assure him, and then told him that she had sent Simon to Audswyck to try to obtain the earl's assistance. "If you can stay here without detection for just a few more days, all may yet be well. I told Simon that he must come here directly after he had spoken to *Grand-père*. He may even be here tomorrow, since Audswyck is much closer to Bournemouth than to London."

Adrian listened to this without showing much of what he was thinking in his expression. He finished the wine in his glass, placed it on the table, and then went to sit beside Isobel on the settle. He took both her hands in his and kissed first one and then the other.

"The last time we were together, you thought I had used you to save my own skin," he said, looking at her hands in his. "Does all this effort on my behalf signify that you would prefer not to see me hang and turn the name of Renville into a malediction or a change of heart?"

This was the moment she had most dreaded. "If you say that you are not involved with Mr. Liddiard in any way, I must believe you," she said.

He smiled wryly. "Yet I detect the hint of a question, the barest rising inflection. Where was I that night? You want to ask me, Isobel. Don't be afraid of your doubts, you're entitled to them."

"It isn't doubt," she said, knowing that her vehemence only made the truth suspect. "You told me you were at the Clarendon but that you never met Mr.

Liddiard." She took great care to keep her tone entirely level.

"But why was I there? Ask me, Bel. Get it out before it festers into poison."

"Why did you go out that night after we had all gone to bed and why to the Clarendon?"

"Odd as it may seem, I had an errand to take care of that hour. There was a man I wished very much to see, but he was out of town. But I learned that he was expected that evening to attend a gathering of colleagues at the Clarendon and that the dinner—punctuated by a number of long-winded speeches, I understand—was expected to go on until after midnight. I went to the public rooms and waited until my business could be concluded, and then I returned to Leyland House.

"It may not be the best answer to your question, but it is the truth. And there is one more point to clarify. While waiting, I was foolish enough to imagine that I could drink a bit of brandy with no effect. I was mistaken. It destroyed my fragile control on my baser instincts. The moment I let myself back into the house, I knew I had no intention of going to my own room to sleep that night."

Hating herself for it, she asked a final question. "Who was the man you met at the Clarendon?"

In answer Adrian opened his coat and drew a folded paper from an inner pocket. He handed it to her, and she unfolded it and began to read. It took only a few words for her to realize that she held a special license granting the bearer the right to be married without the calling of banns.

She refolded the license and looked up to find him watching her. She found she could not meet his gaze for the shame she felt for doubting him. Ten minutes in his company and she knew she had been a fool not to believe in him, even if he had never explained himself for that night. She squeezed tightly the hands that held hers. "I'm so sorry," she said in a very small voice, nearly weeping. "So very sorry. I loved you, I didn't want to doubt you. I don't know why I did. I'm sorry, Adrian." After this disjointed speech tears overtook her, and she was gathered against him to weep tears of mixed shame and gratitude that she was here with him now and that he was not lost to her as she had feared.

When her sobs diminished, she moved away from him and saw that his eyes and cheeks were wet also. He took his handkerchief and gently dried her eyes. "This is catharsis, I believe. We should jog along very well now that we have had our first major misunderstanding and have come through it with our love intact. I didn't like to alarm you, but I was a bit concerned about being married before it occurred and tested our mettle."

"You are ridiculous," she said with a watery laugh.

"A fool for love." Then he kissed her and it was as sweet, as hungry, as the very first time. He stood and held out his hand to lead her to the ladder going up to the loft. "My humble bed is only covered straw, but I promise we'll share it only with each other. I had the last of the field mice for dinner last night."

As he settled beside her on the straw and took her lips with his, Isobel reflected that to be with him again she would have even borne with the field mice. When they kissed, she could feel it throughout her body, sensations of flowing warmth that flowed to every extremity. The chill air of the unheated loft seemed to dissipate in the glowing heat rising between them.

He began to kiss her all over. He kissed her throat and her shoulders, his lips sending hot trails along the inside of her arm, and he took each finger one by one into his mouth. He raised her skirt and petticoats and kissed the faint roundness of her belly, letting his tongue trace the line to the sweet, moist warmth between her legs. He kissed the triangle of soft gold hair and continued his progress along her inner thighs, untying her garters and removing one stocking after the other with delicious slowness, kissing the path to her furthest extremities. He used tongue, lips, teeth, to make every nerve come alive, and when he had aroused her to restlessness, she moaned softly and her legs opened of their own volition. There his tongue flicked teasingly, sending flashes of sensation through her loins and into her thighs.

It was wonderful, but gradually it became maddening. She raised her hips and gently rotated them to make the contact of his mouth against her flesh more exact. Still he eluded and teased her until she cried out for release. "Adrian, please," she said, the plea moaned rather than spoken. In response his tongue began a circular motion that made her so acutely sensitive she wanted to beg him to stop almost as much as she was desperate for him to continue. The deep sensations of pleasure began low in her thighs and coursed with aching slowness along her flesh until it settled between her legs and a white-hot explosion fragmented her awareness.

He was inside her then, and incredibly, she could feel the pressure building again almost immediately. Her legs were wrapped tightly about him, the motion of her hips synchronized to his, making her feel as if they were somehow melded together into one being. She heard him cry out, but she was already lost in his pleasure, feeling it flow into her and become her own.

Consciousness seemed to slip away from her again, for she opened her eyes and discovered that they were now side by side, covered against the cold air by the carriage robe. He opened his eyes as if becoming aware of her regard. He kissed her with exquisite gentleness and whispered, "Never leave me, Isobel. I'll never let you go again." The light had gone while they made love, and a cozy darkness settled about them. They slept.

The first light was illuminating the darker corners of the loft when Isobel awoke again. She was curled against Adrian for warmth as much as to be near to him. She moved away and shivered as part of the blanket slipped from her shoulder. She also discovered how stiff her muscles had become. It was one thing to make love in a bed of soft straw, but quite another to have nothing more separating her body from the hard wood floor for the entire night.

Adrian stirred, stretched, and then drew her against him again and kissed her. Isobel returned his kiss willingly, but afterward she gently pushed him away. "I think not," she said with mock indignation. "Another ten minutes on this wretched bed and I am certain I shall be crippled for life." She gingerly raised herself to a sitting position and, casting back the robe, sadly surveyed her wrinkled traveling dress. "Dear heavens! My reputation shall be destroyed when I enter the Three Bells again. No one could doubt this dress had been slept in."

Adrian had removed his coat and neckcloth and had fared a little better. He too was stiff and sore from sleeping in the crude straw bed, which had been considerably flattened from their earlier activity. "Then I'll have to see if I can fetch you something else to wear," he said, sitting up as well.

"How could you?" she wondered. "I think the landlord might recognize you, and if anyone is looking for you—"

She was silenced by his lips. "No one will see me, I promise you," he said when he could. "I'll get some fresh bread and butter for us if I can as well."

"Please don't take unnecessary risks," she implored. "My dress isn't important. I would rather not risk anyone knowing you are here until I can speak with Simon and learn what *Grand-père* has said to him."

Adrian said nothing. He sat with his knees drawn up and his arms resting on his knees. He lowered his head to his hands and said, "Isobel, we can't rely on help from Audwin. Even if Simon could convince him to help me, which I very much doubt, I don't know what he can do now that it has gone this far. Perhaps he can save me from being hung, but I don't count on that either. Our countries are at war, and if they are determined to have my neck, it would be easy to stir sentiment against me. No matter what the outcome, it is likely I shall spend weeks or months in a prison, and I've no fancy for that either. I intend to leave England as soon as I can, perhaps even today if I can find a ship trading with Lisbon that soon."

"No, Adrian, you can't leave," she said urgently. "*Grand-père* has got to help you."

Adrian drew her into his arms. "Come with me, Isobel, if you love me enough to leave everything behind. It will be with little more than the clothes on your back, and not even as my wife, for we daren't take the time or the risk to use that license. I don't want to leave you again or be parted from you for even a day, but I can't stay here and wait to see which of us is right. The peril is too great. In Lisbon we shall find a ship to take us to America in good time, and when the war is over, we'll return and try to mend our fences within the family."

Isobel wanted to argue with him, but how could she insist that he stay and risk his freedom and even his life for her? She knew she did not wish to be parted from him again either, but the reality of leaving everyone and everything behind was more wrenching than she had imagined it would be. It could be years before she saw her stepmother, father, or Simon again. "I left only a short note for Mama to tell her that I had to go away for a few days with no explanation or even a direction."

"And you can't send her further word at least until we are out of the country," Adrian said, his eyes regarding her with unnerving steadiness.

The moment of decision was upon her and was unescapable. She had to choose between the man she loved and her family, an empty, loveless life or exile with Adrian. If she chose wrong, there was no turning back to erase her mistake. But in spite of all these thoughts tumbling chaotically through her head, she knew there was only one answer she would make him. She lay her hand along his cheek and kissed him softly. "I shall go anywhere you go, even in just the dreadfully creased clothes on my back, and as your mistress rather than your wife if need be," she said, her voice choking on the strong swell of love for him that came over her.

He hugged her so tightly that she thought her lungs would burst. "That shan't be for long, Isobel. As soon as we arrive wherever we are going, I'll find out what is required for us to be married, and then we shall make our union legal as soon as it is possible. You may be breeding, you know," he added with a teasing grin. He let her go and got to his feet. "This time I shall trust my own instincts instead of allowing anyone else to do my reconnoitering. We would be married now if I had."

"Simon and Carlton thought they were doing the right thing to obstruct our plans," she said sadly.

"Well, they won't have the opportunity to do so again," he said as he eased his foot into one of his boots. "There is a pump in the back of the house where you may wash. The water is icy though, and we daren't light a fire for cooking or warmth. I want no one guessing this cottage is no longer empty."

Isobel drew on her stockings and scrambled to her

feet as Adrian shrugged himself into his coat. "What if Simon does come to Bournemouth with good news? We might not have to leave at all."

Adrian regarded his ruined cravat with a sigh and lay it over his arm. He looked up at Isobel not with anger or sternness but with a cool, unmovable set to his features that put her strongly in mind of the earl. "It is all or nothing, Isobel," he reminded her. "Either you remain with me, or you return to the Three Bells and the protection of the family. Half measures could jeopardize my safety, or even my life."

Isobel privately thought his caution excessive, though the thought of even the most unlikely risk to his safety was sufficient for her not to press her point. She might not be the only one to guess that Adrian had come to either Stokes Hall or Bournemouth, but anyone searching for him would have no better luck than she had had, and without her knowledge of the gamekeeper's cottage, it was not likely that they would know to look for it or even stumble upon it easily, hidden in the deepest part of the wood as it was. She herself had nearly despaired of finding it, and she knew it was only because she had seen the peak of the thatched roof through the barren trees that she had found it; in spring and summer it would have been virtually invisible until one found the small clearing.

She remarked to him as he helped her down the ladder that it was just as well that she had chosen his protection rather than returning to Bournemouth on her own, for she doubted very seriously that she would have found her way again out of the wood.

"Good," he replied, kissing the tip of her nose. "Then I know you won't be up to mischief while I am gone. I shan't be above two or three hours. It is less than a half-hour ride if one knows the best way to go, but I have already learned of an inn at the far west of town where I might find what I seek. Brandy and

French lace are not the only goods they smuggle, apparently."

He removed his shirt and went outside to wash, returning with his skin pink from the cold. When he had dressed again, he bade Isobel farewell and went to the shed to saddle his horse. She washed herself while he did this, shivering in the cold. The day before had been considerably warmer, and now her dress, in addition to being creased and soiled, was inadequate for the temperature. He saw her shivering when he led his horse from the shed, and he drew her close to him for warmth. "Stay inside until I return. I'll fetch your cloak if I can get into the inn undetected. In the meantime, wrap yourself in the carriage robe and try not to think about how hungry you are until I return."

"If you are gone too long, I shall be hungry for more than food when you return," she said boldly.

"Then I shall attempt to satisfy that appetite as well, beloved," he replied, grinning, and he released her and swung himself into the saddle with his usual grace. "Go inside, Bel. I want to know you are safe."

She laughed. "There is no one here but us, the squirrels, and the field mice. But I promise," she added hastily as she saw his brows begin to come together.

He waited until the door was shut behind her, and then she heard him trot out of the small yard. It was only a minute or so later that she heard another sound, that of a gun being fired very near the cottage. For a moment it didn't register as anything alarming; she had lived enough in the country to be used to such sounds. Then another shot was fired, and horror began to dawn for her. In this lonely portion of Stokes wood with the owner of the estate not even in residence, no one would be hunting even rabbit or squirrels, and poachers didn't generally ply their trade in broad daylight.

But if it were soldiers miraculously discovering Adrian's whereabouts and come to take Adrian back to London for trial, why didn't she hear their horses or cries from the soldiers for Adrian to halt? She strained her ears and heard only the distant sound of one horse galloping. That must be Adrian, she knew, and she felt a wash of relief. It had to be poachers, however unlikely.

She succeeded in convincing herself of this for all of five minutes. In this quiet place a poacher would have heard Adrian's horse, and would surely have hidden himself rather than shoot at prey. If it was someone from the estate, he would probably have challenged Adrian to ask who he was and why he was at the cottage. Cold tendrils of fear began to make their way throughout her body, starting in her legs, making them feel liquid, and working through her until she felt a swell of pure panic. She wanted to go outside to assure herself that Adrian had ridden safely away, but self-preservation held her frozen for fear that she would be shot at as well if she left the safety of the cottage. But her love for Adrian was the stronger drive, and after several more minutes of straining her ears to hear nothing more than the usual carolling of the birds, she felt that she had to assure herself that he was not outside lying dead or injured in the wood.

She opened the door cautiously and looked about her. The sun was strengthening and, without the heavy canopy of leaves, illuminated the scene with bright rays and slanting shadows from the tall, bare trees. She saw no one and nothing out of the ordinary. The only sound was still that of the birds. She ventured away from the house toward the path, just wide enough for a single horseman, cleared through the thick wood. She walked along it for a way and felt a rush of self-congratulation for her powers of observation when she noted the spot where the mulch of moldering leaves and dirt had been ripped and shredded and flung about, indicating that this is where Adrian had urged his horse into a canter or gallop. He must have been just here when the first shot was fired.

She drew in her breath for courage and made herself search for possible bloodstains on the fallen leaves, but she found nothing but residue moisture from the early morning dew. For a few minutes she was able to convince herself that she was being fanciful, but her mind was too sharp to be blinded by mere hope. Someone other than Adrian had been out there. Someone twice had fired a gun, which meant that whoever it was had had more than one weapon or had not been alone. That someone had disappeared immediately after shooting at Adrian or was at that moment in hiding and perhaps watching her every move.

She fought her panic again and retraced her steps to the cottage. Her fear caught her up when she reached the clearing, and she raced inside the cottage and hastily bolted the door behind her. Her next action was to hasten up the ladder to assure herself that no miscreant had hidden himself in the loft while she was outside. When she reached the loft, she sat on the straw bed and laughed at herself in relief. What would she have done if someone had been lying in wait for her?

She sat pondering what had happened and why, but no logical conclusion presented itself. She had eliminated every possibility in her mind that it was anyone trying to arrest Adrian for being an American spy. Such an action would have taken place openly, and surely there would have been no reason to shoot at Adrian unless he resisted arrest and that too, she was certain, would have been aboveboard with an appropriate warning for him to halt. The same held true if it had been some employee of the estate who might have taken him for a trespasser. No sane person without wicked intent would shoot first and ask questions later unless there was a per-ceived threat.

But who was there that would wish Adrian harm who also knew were to find him? As far as she knew there was no one but herself who knew he was at the cottage. Though she doubted it was possible that he could know anything about what was happening to his friend, Sir James might have guessed where Adrian would choose to hide, but why would he shoot at Adrian?

Inevitably her thoughts turned to Quentin and his undisguised hatred for Adrian. However much Quen-tin had changed for the worse in recent years, she did not want to believe that he could be capable of true evil. Yet there was the incident at the footbridge when they had fallen into the river. It had not seemed to her that Quentin could have engineered what happened to look like an accident, but that had been Carlton's first assumption and no one had better acquaintance with his brother's character than he did. For some time now he had endeavored to convince her that Quentin had changed from the man she had fallen in love with so many years ago, and she had not wanted to believe him until Adrian had come into her life and forced her to face the truth. Adrian also had hinted that Quentin was at fault for the accident, though he had stopped short of telling her why and she had never pressed him, not really wanting to know the worst of Quentin at the time.

But if Quentin was capable of trying to injure or kill Adrian, how could he have known where Adrian was to be found? She remembered Adrian's brief sus-picion that she might have led others to find him, and she wondered if she had done just that inadvertently.

For a short while she was able to convince herself that, however mysterious, the shots she had heard weren't cause for further alarm, and she need do nothing but remain in the cottage and wait for Adrian to return to her. In the end she recognized it as self-delusion, and she knew that however afraid she might be, she had to try to assure herself that Adrian was well.

She had cause to be grateful that her father had insisted that she learn as a child how to tack a horse herself, and when she had saddle and bridle in place, she led her mount to a rock high enough to give her leverage into the saddle. She took the reins into her hands and gathered up her courage as well and left the small clearing to once again go down the path that Adrian had taken.

This diverged several times and gave her pause, for she could not remember the way she had come through the wood herself, and she had no idea if any one of the other paths was not the one that Adrian had spoken of as being a more direct route out. She could do little but trust her instincts, which told her not to be diverted, or at least not yet, and to continue along the main path instead.

She kept her horse to a slow walk, searching for signs of Adrian's passage or, with greater dread, for an indication that he had suffered an injury. When she thought she must be as far from the cottage as it would be likely that she would still have heard the sound of his horse, which she had, she finally gave up her futile search. She felt she should be reassured, but she was not. Impulsively she chose the next diverging path, praying that she would not lose herself in the woods and force Adrian to rescue her when he returned if he was well and still on his way to Bournemouth.

She found nothing there either, realized the futility

of guessing which branching path he might have taken, if any, and turned her horse around. She had ridden for a few minutes before she realized that she should have returned to the main path again by then. She murmured an oath beneath her breath and pulled up her horse. She looked about her and behind her and saw no sign that she had passed the turnoff. She sat for a full minute, irresolute and annoyed with herself for doing precisely what she had determined not to do, lose her way.

She was startled when her horse suddenly raised his head and whickered softly, and even more amazed when she heard the response of a second horse. Though she looked in every direction, she saw no other animal. But in this portion of the wood the trees were not quite as tall or as dense, perhaps as the result of fire years before, and the number of bushes and shrubs, many of them evergreen and still containing foliage, was greater than in other parts she had passed where sunlight rarely managed to provide sufficient light in spring and summer for anything beyond mere brush to grow beneath the trees. There were three or four small copses to be seen in the near distance, though it would mean leaving the path and possibly losing herself even more. There was no choice at all, though, and she selected a copse and rode toward it.

It was at the third of these that she found the horse, and there was no doubt at all that it was the same one she had seen Adrian mount that morning. But there was no sign at all of him. She called out his name as loudly as she could several times and received no response. Once again, with her heart in her throat, she searched the fallen leaves for splatters of blood. She found nothing. She dismounted and searched among the bushes and small scrub trees that made up the little thicket and still found nothing. There could be no doubt at all now that Adrian had been shot or perhaps injured in a fall from his horse, but the horrible truth was he might be anywhere in the wood, lying dead or injured. Because she had found his horse here, it was not a guarantee that he would have fallen nearby. There was a bit of exposed grass in the thicket between some of the bushes, and that was what had probably attracted the hungry animal.

She shut her eyes tightly to try to keep back tears of fright and frustration. She had to go on, she had to keep looking. If Adrian wasn't dead—and she could not even bring herself to think that he could be—then he might be injured and desperately need help. When she had her courage in hand again she continued her search. She continued on in this way for some time, searching through piles of fallen leaves and even under bushes that were really too small to conceal him.

By the end of a quarter hour of this she was weeping openly, her futile search not aided by the tears that blinded her. But this was just an outpouring of her overwrought emotions; she had no intention of giving up until she found Adrian. There had never been any other choice for her. Finally, nearly an hour later she literally stumbled across him. He had fallen by the side of another copse into thick leaves that his fall had disturbed and that had come to settle again on top of him, partially covering him. To add to his concealment, the upper part of his body was camouflaged by the spreading branches of an evergreen bush under which he had by design or accident rolled.

Isobel was about to enter the copse to search it when she tripped on something, looked down, and to her horror saw that it was an arm encased in a dark blue sleeve, with a thin line of white linen showing at the edge. Gasping, she fell to her knees and began to brush away the leaves that half covered him. He was lying on his right side, nearly on his stomach, and finally she uncovered his face. His face, his dear, beautiful face, was streaked with drying blood that had also soaked into his neckcloth. Again she caught her breath, and then a cry of pure anguish broke from her.

Chapter 17

The courtyard of the Three Bells was never a quiet place. Bournemouth was a busy port even in wartime, when goods from most of Europe, the Near East, and North America no longer flowed steadily to England in the normal exchange of trade. There were now ships of the line and privateers in the slots along the dock that had once held merchantmen, but intranational trade flourished as well in this island nation, and travel of goods by water was still the cheapest and most efficient means whenever practical.

Waterfront inns like the Three Bells that catered to the carriage trade always enjoyed good custom, not only from merchants and ship owners, but from naval officers and their visiting families and other members of the quality who had business to conduct in Bournemouth and need of lodging. The sleek, well-sprung traveling carriage, pulled by a sweating team of four barrel-chested bays that were certainly not job horses, received little more notice than Adrian had when he had entered the same courtyard about three months earlier.

A handsome, fair young man opened the door and leaped down from the carriage the moment it halted. Before an ostler could reach the carriage to perform the task, he himself drew down the stair tucked under the body of the carriage. He stood on this and leaned into the carriage again and this time emerged with an elderly man clutching his arm.

One of the ostlers, impressed by the crest emblazoned on the panels of the doors, hastened to assist him, and in a moment more the earl of Audwin stood on the cobbles. Simon reached inside the carriage again and came out with two canes, which he gave to his grandfather. Declaring himself now quite capable of entering the inn on his own power, the earl refused all further assistance.

The inside of the inn was, also as usual, even more bustling than the outside. Simon held the door for his grandfather's entrance, and the old man made his way to the nearest table with an empty seat. Two young bucks were also seated there, but one glare from beneath the aged nobleman's heavy parchment lids was sufficient for them to think it wise to find another table to enjoy their libations. Satisfied that his grandfather was settled, Simon grasped the arm of a servant hurrying past him and asked for the landlord. The man nodded in the direction of the tap, and Simon went over there. He heard voices raised in altercation coming from an adjoining room, and after a moment or so, he realized that he recognized one of them. He entered the room without announcing himself and saw Carlton, his face red and his voice raised and higher than usual in pitch, evincing his distress.

Simon was astonished to see his cousin at the inn. "Carl, how do you come to be here?"

Barely casting Simon a glance in acknowledgment, he continued to reproach the landlord. "I don't care how busy you are, man. How the devil could it not be noticed that a guest in the inn, and a woman traveling unprotected at that, had disappeared and has now gone missing for better than a full day? If nothing else, didn't you wonder if she had skipped out on you during the night, leaving her shot unpaid?"

"It were paid in advance, sir," the landlord said, his matter-of-fact voice making it plain that he did not mean to be drawn into a full-blown argument. "My guests are entitled to their privacy, sir. If they choose to hire a bedchamber and a private parlor and then not use these apartments, that's their right to determine." As if this concluded the discussion, he turned an inquiring countenance toward Simon. "Do you be needing assistance, sir?"

Simon ignored him and said to Carlton, "What do you mean, missing? Are you speaking of Isobel? Why are you here, Carl, and how did you know that she would be in Bournemouth and at this inn?"

"Of course I'm speaking of Isobel," Carlton said tersely. "Only a damned flat would have failed to guess that Adrian would return to Dorset and Isobel would not heed my warning that she should not go after him. It was just a matter of inquiring at as many inns as necessary until I found her. But she's gone. Her clothes are here and in the bedchamber she hired for the night, but the bed hasn't been slept in and she never used the private parlor or ordered any meals."

"Then where is she?" said Simon, nonplussed by this information.

"I don't know, but if she isn't safe and well, I swear I shall have this fellow pay for his neglect," he said, turning back to glower again at the landlord.

The landlord, unmoved as always by the takings of the quality, addressed Simon. "As I would have informed this gentleman if he had let me have a word in edgewise, Miss Leyland came in her own carriage and driven by her own coachman, attended by a pair of outriders and a guard. I'll have them fetched to you if you would like, and maybe one of them will be able to tell you where Miss Leyland's gone off to."

Carlton's color deepened angrily, but before he could hurl any further invective at the landlord's head for keeping this information to himself until now, Simon said with gratitude, "Thank you! Do you think you might send them to the private parlor Miss Leyland hired? I've left my grandfather, the earl of Audwin, in the common room, and I know he'll want to speak with the men himself in private."

This information had a startling effect on both the men facing Simon. "Is your name Renville, then?" the landlord demanded, getting his speech in first.

"Why, no, it's Leyland. Miss Leyland is my sister."

"Mine is Renville," Carlton said with icy fury. "You deliberately withheld that information from me, man."

"Why, no, sir," said the landlord with a show of surprise, "and if you'd said your name was Renville, I'd have had a bit more to tell you. Miss Leyland was most anxious to find another Mr. Renville, Mr. Adrian Renville, and in my opinion it is most likely that that is where she's gotten herself to. Either she's found him and hasn't returned from wherever that is, or she's still out there looking."

Simon and Carlton exchanged looks at this, and the landlord, taking advantage of this welcome lull in the altercation, quickly called for an underling to show them to the parlor in question and himself went out to attend to the earl.

Simon, the first into the parlor, had thought his amazement complete when he beheld Carlton, but he received a further shock when he walked through the door and found Isobel sitting in a chair by the fire, staring straight ahead of her at the door as if she had been expecting them.

She stood when they entered the room. "I knew you wouldn't fail me, Simon," she said and embraced him when he crossed the room to her.

To his dismay she began to cry. Simon did what he could to comfort his sister and quieted her tears so that she could tell them what it was upsetting her while Carlton dispensed with the services of the land-lord and the other servant and himself made his grandfather comfortable in an armchair near the fire. Finally, Isobel's sobs began to diminish, and she let Simon return her to her chair. Carlton had drawn two other chairs from the table to the fire so that the gentlemen all faced Isobel in a semicircle, rather like a tribunal sitting in judgment.

But it was Isobel, her expression uncommonly grave, who had the demeanor of a judge. "I didn't think I would see you, Carl," she said enigmatically. "I was expecting Quentin."

"Where the devil have you been, Isobel?" Carlton demanded querulously. "You've given us the devil of a fright. The landlord said you'd gone out before dinner yesterday and hadn't returned. I told you not to go jauntering about by yourself, that I'd do what I could to find Adrian and warn him. There was no need for you to put yourself in needless danger, or for you to do anything at all."

"It's a damned good thing Isobel was clever enough to ignore such foolish advice," the earl said, his cold gaze settling on his elder grandson. "You've made a proper hash of things, haven't you? Isobel at least had the sense to send Simon to me. If you couldn't see the sense of nipping this matter of Adrian being linked to Liddiard in the bud from the beginning, then you aren't worthy of the position you hold in the government. What the devil did you think would happen if he was captured and tried? You might have found yourself ruined along with him, and you might have taken the entire government with you if suspicions and innuendo became rife."

Carlton went pale and then deep color returned to him. "Sir, I did try my best. The moment I had even a hint that there might be unpleasantness concerning Adrian, I spoke to those I felt would be most likely to be of assistance. Once Bertram learned of it, though, there was nothing I could do. You know that if we tried to cover the matter up once Bertram had wind of it, he would scream conspiracy, and that might have been worse than if we had a full-blown trial."

The earl regarded him without expression during this speech and at its finish said scathingly, "My God, you are a fool. I may be old, but I'm not dead yet. Do you imagine Bertram would take me on through the means of my heir unless he believed me incapable of retaliation? I have the means, and well he knows it, of destroying him in turn. Only if he was led to believe that I couldn't or wouldn't use it would he dare do this. Someone has been whispering lies about me to my old enemy, it would seem."

"Perhaps he was led to believe that you wished Adrian destroyed," Simon suggested. "You had cast him off as you had his father, after all."

Carlton appeared chastened, but his voice still held anger. "Then we need look no further than my brother, who had every cause to wish Adrian permanently disposed of. It was he, after all, who saw Adrian at the Clarendon and made certain that word of it, along with some carefully planted suspicions, would reach Bertram's ears."

The earl raised one brow. "Bertram is no greater fool than I am. It would take more than secondhand information to make him confident that he could proceed with impunity." Without explaining himself further, he addressed Isobel for the first time. "Where is my grandson?"

"He's been shot," she said with such harsh bleakness that Simon gasped aloud.

"My God! He's not dead, is he?" demanded Carlton, his expression horrified.

Isobel paid no heed to this outburst but continued, "I remembered yesterday that he told me once about a disused cottage buried deep in the woods of Stokes. I hired a horse and found the cottage, and Adrian was there. We had decided to leave England, and he was going into Bournemouth to a place he knew where we might be able to buy passage." Her voice became frailer with each word she spoke, and she broke off to choke back a sob.

Simon came to stand beside her, holding her hand tightly in his own, trembling with a fear and wretchedness of his own. "Don't, Bel, if it hurts too much to tell us now."

She shook her head both in the negative and to clear the memory of the sound of the shots that still could clutch her heart in a grip of ice. "No, I must. Adrian left the cottage, and a few minutes later there were shots. I found his body in a pile of leaves where he'd fallen from his horse."

Simon gave a sob and dropped to his knees beside Isobel's chair. She put her arms around him and her head next to his, and in a few moments he had control of himself again. "But why would he be shot?" he asked Isobel. "Was it the soldiers, had they come for him? Why would they shoot him, even if he tried to escape, and then leave him in the wood for you to find his body?"

"There were no soldiers," Isobel said absolutely. "There was no one at all when I went outside only five minutes or so later."

"Poachers!" said Carlton with deep disgust. "Dear Lord, to think of all that has happened and all the dangers Adrian has faced and he ends shot by poachers."

"I saw no sign of poachers, Carl," Isobel said, turning her disturbing, unblinking gaze on him.

"Well, you probably wouldn't," he answered. "No poacher successful at his trade leaves evidence of his presence, and if he realized that what he had shot at was a man on a horse and not a deer, it is very likely that he made himself invisible as quickly as possible."

Lord Audwin spoke again. "I don't believe that you mentioned that Adrian was on horseback at the time he was shot."

"I didn't," Isobel replied.

"It is interesting that you expected to see Quentin here rather than Carlton."

"Yes."

"What has that to say to anything? Of course he was on horseback. He wouldn't be walking to Bournemouth from that distance," Carlton said, rising in an agitated way as if he could no longer sit comfortably. He came to rest again in front of the hearth, his back to the others. "It is a good thing that Quentin isn't here, or he might find himself bearing the blame for it."

"That would be unjust," said the earl, "though not undeserved. He has done his poor best in the past to do as much harm as possible to my heir, but this is one crime of which I think he may stand exonerated. You are worse than a fool, Carlton, you are a disgrace to the name of Renville. No clear planning went into your actions. If you could have found some reason to have brought Quentin to Bournemouth, the blame would undoubtedly have fallen to him. You need never have feared detection."

Carlton had one hand on the high mantel, leaning his weight into it as he stared into the fire. He straightened slowly and said without turning, "Detection of what?"

"Attempted murder, cousin" said a soft voice with a distinctive accent.

Carlton spun about as if he were a top and its cord pulled. He seemed incapable of speech as Adrian approached him. Adrian did not have the look of a man who had been shot and left for dead only hours before. He had bathed and changed his clothes, and only a bandage holding sticking plaster in place against the graze along the left side of his head gave evidence that he had been wounded.

"I really have come to believe," Adrian said easily, "that a benevolent God has future designs for me, for he has blessed me with the longevity of a cat these past months." He turned his head to display better the area that was bandaged. "Twice I have been shot at and once nearly drowned, and yet I survive against the odds, cousin." There was mocking challenge in his eyes. "Not a very good shot considering I must have presented a very clear target. Only a graze and a concussion. I'm afraid I live to tell another day."

Carlton opened his mouth as if to protest and then brought his hands to his face and began to weep uncontrollably. Simon, at a glance from his grandfather, left Isobel and put his hand on Carlton's shoulder, leading him back to his chair. Carlton began to cough and gulp air and finally gained control of himself again. "I know you won't believe me, Adrian, but I'm glad I missed you," he said at last. "I'm a damn good shot, actually, anyone will tell you that. It's the one sporting skill in which I can best my brother. I was shaking so badly when I pulled the trigger of the first gun that I think the shot went into the ground. It was the second that hit you. I never saw you go down, but when I followed you I saw your horse riderless, and I knew you must have come off somewhere in the leaves or bushes." He buried his head in his hands again but this time without weeping. He said at length, "It is easier to say you will kill a man than to do it."

"But why, Carl?" Isobel said, unable to reason his action to her satisfaction. "Why would you wish to harm Adrian? He's never done anything to make you hate him the way he has with Quentin."

It was Adrian who answered her. "I didn't see you,

you know, Carl. When Isobel brought me around again, I was certain it had to have been Quentin. As soon as I was able to sit a horse again without threatening to swoon off it, Isobel brought me here, and we planned with the help of the landlord to surprise Quentin into a confession. But as soon as I came through the door and saw you here, Carl, I knew. And I knew why."

"Then tell us why," commanded the earl, "for it is as much a mystery to me as it is that I am cursed to discover that you are the only one of my grandsons with wits that haven't gone begging."

Adrian looked at the old man seated before him and said, "With respect, sir, I think I won't tell you." He then addressed Carlton. "And I wouldn't have told anyone else either. Your life is your own, Carl, to lead as you choose."

"Thank you, Adrian," Carlton said, speaking barely audibly. "I'm as great a fool as Grandfather believes me to be. I beg your pardon for what I have done, though I know you can't forgive such a heinous offense."

"Oh, I can," Adrian said, his voice light again for the first time. "It is my bloodthirsty consort that would like to see you on the gibbet," he said, smiling down at Isobel, "but she will be far too busy acquainting herself with her new duties as a wife to be wasting time on exacting revenge."

Carlton stood again. "And I beg your pardon too, sir. You are quite right, I didn't think ahead at all." He started to leave the room but turned back. "For what it's worth, I never spoke to Bertram, or anyone that could have carried information to him. That was Quentin's doing, however it was he managed it. In fact, it was learning that he meant to have Adrian taken in to charge that made me do this. I only wanted him to leave England until I learned there would be a trial for espionage." With these cryptic words he left them.

"I don't understand," Simon said after a minute or so of silence. "Why would Carl rather shoot Adrian than have him be arrested?"

"You don't need to understand," the earl said witheringly. "Go find that landlord again and see to it that we have rooms for the night. You may return to help me to bed when you have seen everything settled."

Simon's expression was mulish. "You wish to talk with me out of the room," he said indignantly, inspired by the success of Adrian's defiance. "I am not a child to be banished. I've played my part in all of this too."

"Which will fit you for a career as messenger and little else," the earl informed him plainly. "Do as you are bid, boy. I dare say you will tease the details out of your softhearted sister in good time."

"You aren't easy to cow or to kill, are you?" Audwin said to Adrian when Simon left them.

"No, not very," Adrian admitted.

"You're a Renville, no doubt of that. You're not only the image of your father, but you have his quick mind as well and his strength of character."

"If that was your opinion of my father, sir," Adrian said coolly, "why did you denounce him and drive him away from the family?"

The old man's lips spread into what he probably meant as a smile but which appeared as more of a grimace. "He had too damn much of both, as do you. While I live I won't be challenged, do you hear, boy? I haven't forgotten that you tried to make a fool of me when you first came here, pretending to be a ridiculous savage, but you've bought yourself another chance." He paused and said, as if the words were difficult to voice, "Remy found that the railing of the footbridge had been sawed nearly through where you and Quentin fell." He got himself to his feet with the aid of his two canes. "Mind yourself for the future, for I intend to live to a hundred, by means of sheer bloody-mindedness if necessary."

The door opened and Simon returned, his indignation obviously dissipated. "There was only a single room left for hire, Grandfather," he said. "I hope you don't mind that I've taken it for us both."

"Of course I don't," the old man snapped as he accepted Simon's arm to lean upon. "Since I came without my man to keep the servants out of this mess, who the devil else is there to valet me?"

Finally, Isobel and Adrian were alone again. She made him sit in the comfortable chair the earl had vacated, and she knelt on the hearth rug beside him, regarding him with love and concern.

"If you keep staring at me like that," he said after several moments, "you shall make me think I have not washed all the blood out of my ears."

She shivered at these words, but smiled too. "I am almost afraid to blink for fear that you'll disappear and it will only be a dream that you are still alive and well." Once again her voice caught as the memory flashed through her head. "You were so still and there was so much blood. I was certain you were dead."

He drew her onto his lap and kissed her despite her protests that he needed rest and must not think of such things at least for this one night. "When that happens, I promise you, you had better check my pulse for signs of life."

After some time had passed in soft words and gentle kisses, Isobel said it was time that he went to bed. "The doctor said you have had a concussion and must sleep if you wish to heal."

"I can see that I have promised myself to a fish-wife," he lamented and stood up as she got up from his lap. His head was throbbing with pain, but having

Isobel in his arms was better than any medicine a doctor could prescribe.

"There is one thing I wish you would tell me," she said when they reached her room. "Why did Carlton try to shoot you? What possible motive could he have? Does he really believe you took those papers from his dispatch cases?"

"That is not one question, my love," he reproved her as he sat on the bed. "I think your governess must have been deficient when she taught you arithmetic."

"No, I always escaped outside when I knew we would have those lessons," she corrected and added tenaciously, "Why did he do it, Adrian?"

He hesitated before answering. "I told Carlton I would not have said anything to anyone, but perhaps under the circumstances he deserves that I betray him at least to you. You suffered more than I did, my love, for I never knew I was supposed to be lying there dead. Carlton shot me because he knew I didn't take his papers."

Isobel exclaimed at this. "That's absurd! I wish you wouldn't quiz me about everything all the time."

"Careful, my love," he admonished her. "We haven't actually tied the knot yet, and I may still cry off if you show me too plainly how you mean to keep me under the cat's paw. He shot me because he knew I knew who did steal those documents. It is ironic that I might not have guessed if I hadn't run into Liddiard and Ames-Harding that afternoon at Hyde Park, or if I hadn't returned from Dorset rather sooner than I was expected."

It was only concern for his injury that kept his love from shaking him. "If you don't stop this at once, Adrian, I swear that the next time I find you lying unconscious in a pile of leaves, I shall leave you there to fend for yourself."

Adrian was the picture of outraged innocent. "My

love, you wound me grievously. I thought the truth was self-evident. I told you that day in the park that Mr. Ames-Harding was Carlton's protégé. It was he who Carlton was, ah, entertaining the night I returned from Dorset. Very likely he wished me at the devil just for that bit of knowledge alone, but it was the fact that I knew that Ames-Harding was the only other person besides Carlton's valet, who has been with him since childhood, I gather, who might have filched those documents, that no doubt made him determine to be rid of me. I don't know if Ames-Harding was the man that escaped capture that night that Liddiard was taken, but it is probable. How large an acquaintance could Liddiard have amassed in such a short stay? Ames-Harding must have been a prearranged contact himself for him to have made the connection so quickly."

Isobel frowned as she mulled these things over in her head and finally enlightenment struck her. "Oh! You mean Carlton's protégés are ... are particular friends of his. I had no idea. Yes, I think I understand now, though how he could have behaved so cruelly and so desperately even under the fear of exposure, I shall never comprehend, or forgive either."

"I think he meant what he said about not really wishing to hurt me," Adrian said, and laughed at Isobel's outraged refusal to believe this. "If he could have just scared me into leaving England, he would have been satisfied, but when Quentin spitefully tried to involve me in Liddiard's disgrace by trying to make Lord Bertram believe that I was the other man who got away, he knew that the truth would have to come out if there was a trial."

Adrian held out his hand to her, and she took it and sat beside him. "There is something that just occurred to me," he said musingly. "If Simon took the last available room for Grandfather and himself, that means we must share this one for the night."

"There is always the Green Man," Isobel suggested. "I understand they sometimes have rooms free when the other inns are full."

"Yes, my love," he replied meekly, "but would you care for a mile's drive in a gig on a chill night like this?"

Isobel did not dignify this absurdity with a response, but silenced her love with a kiss that quite dissipated his headache on the spot.